The Spare Wizard

William Wilkin

Bell Street Publishing, LLC

Published by Bell Street Publishing, LLC,
7360 Middlebrook Cir
Nashville, TN 37221-6545

ISBN: 978-0-9903164-4-2

First Published in the United States, 2019

Contents

Acknowledgements

I owe an immense debt of gratitude to several people who have contributed substantially to this book's artistic integrity.

There are my two sons, James Wilkin and Matthew Stone.

James and Matthew contributed a number of graphic design suggestions that are incorporated in the cover design and interior of the book.

He exhibited attention to detail and artistic consistency far beyond my capabilities.

My wife, Lou, contributed in both obvious and subtle ways to the completion of the book. She is a Spanish teacher and has extensive experience editing and correcting texts – both student and professional. Any remaining grammatical and spelling errors must not be accounted to her. They proceed from my eccentric ideas about the value of deviating from standards occasionally to accurately portray a state of mind or emotional content. A subtle way that she supported the completion of this book was her endless patience with those eccentric ideas.

In addition, she was willing to endure the many, many times that I worked into the early morning hours pursued by my characters who insisted on telling their stories at the most inconvenient hours.

She has always been emotionally constant in the shifting winds of our lives throughout the long thankless years of the struggle to bring these stories to print. Bravo Lou!

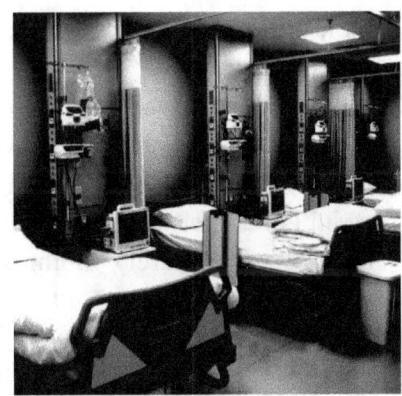

Professor Dumbledore

The entry of Dumbledore caught everyone's attention. The Healer was properly impressed. He extended his hand and introduced himself. He started to introduce the rest of us, but Dumbledore admitted that he knew the rest of us.

Dumbledore strode over to me and asked, "What kind of a mess have you gotten yourself into this time?"

I shrugged and admitted that I had no idea how it happened. Dumbledore shooed the Healer away and then sat down next to me on the exam table. Minerva was on a chair. He stared at me intently and asked, "Tell me what happened after we parted."

I went through all the events of the night before, including a good deal of the concert. Minerva was surprised, "You went to a concert and didn't invite me?"

I was surprised at her reaction, and it showed on my face, because she added, "I thought we enjoyed being together."

"Well, I've tried dragging you to serious music concerts, and I couldn't do it with wild festrals."

She was taken back a bit and her features softened. "Well, how was I to know that Correlli was 'serious music'?" I admitted to myself that it was a bit out of character for her to recognize the composer. I was still struggling for something to say that would be apologetic without being. . uh . . too apologetic.

Dumbledore brought us back on track, "You didn't recognize the wizard and witch. Would you recognize a photo of either?"

"I don't know. The lighting was not good until the end when we were in Diagon Alley, and even then, they were in shade. I was backing away from them and rather distracted by the idea of just getting away safely."

"Well, the Aurors will be back at you to look at photos. If you recognize them, ask who they are. I want to know what Deatheaters are still active."

"Sure. But what did I do to get such attention?"

Minerva offered, "It was surely nothing you did. Those Deatheaters don't need anything beyond you're being a Muggle to want to torture you."

Dumbledore grimaced slightly and said, "I'm not so sure. It's been almost thirteen years since Deatheaters did anything so blatant AND there was another case recently."

Both Minerva and I stared at Dumbledore. He went on, "You needn't ogle me. Yes, there was a Muggle death recently that I'm almost certain was Deatheater related."

I didn't stop ogling, "Really? Where did it happen?"

"It was near a small town in the southwest—Little Hangleton."

Minerva commented, "Never heard of it. How do you know that it was not a 'normal' death?"

I shook my head in agreement. Dumbledore went on, "It was investigated carefully by the Muggle CID."

Minerva asked, "What?"

Dumbledore explained, "Criminal Investigation Division. They are really quite good at investigating ordinary crimes, but there was no explanation that they could find for the death. And they tried very hard. It made *The Times* each day for a couple of weeks running. They were pretty sure that it was a simple case—probably a prank of a gang of youth that had gone too far. But they have given up that theory—and every other that they ever had."

I nodded, "I remember reading about that case, but I didn't follow it closely. Why did you?"

Dumbledore gazed at us a moment before going on, "I was expecting something of the sort. I was looking for it."

Minerva asked, "May I ask why?"

He gazed from the one to the other of us and said, "I have an informant who tells me to expect more Deatheater activity this summer."

"Is your informant a Deatheater?"

Dumbledore said, "You know that I can't tell you."

"I suppose it would put him—or her—in more danger. Have you shared this with the Auror office?" I asked.

"Now, now, Mr. Wendt. You know perfectly well that they wouldn't take it seriously without attribution. They would just become a nuisance pestering me to learn my source. Besides that, in the current political climate, no one wants to hear that Deatheaters are becoming active again."

I asked, "Not even if it's true?"

"Especially if it's true. You have no idea how frightening the era of Deatheaters and Valdemort was."

I had to admit that I was beginning to understand. Dumbledore insisted that we not keep me up any longer and took Minerva with him. That left me defenseless against the Healer when he returned. He insisted that I lay back and get some rest while my injuries healed. He'd release me the next day unless some complications arose.

Dinner proved that hospital food was the same regardless whether it was a Muggle or Wizarding hospital—bland, boring and nutritious. A female nurse, woke me up every 2 hours during the night checking my aura—or so she said. I was actually convinced by the end of the night that the nurse was attracted to the healing profession by the love of sadism. In the early hours of the morning, I decided to have a little fun and declared that we needed to stop meeting like this. Everyone would think that we were having an affair.

She had no sense of humor and thought I was propositioning her. She virtuously declared that she had no interest whatsoever in patients—that we bored her to tears. I decided to push it to the limit, so I declared that she protested too much—she must have an ulterior motive. She turned beet red and I began to wonder if I were right.

She asked me if I were really a Muggle. I asked her where she'd heard such a scurrilous rumor. She said that she'd heard it from the nurse on the previous shift who'd heard it from the admissions triage nurse, who'd over-heard it from an older woman who'd brought me into the hospital, who'd been talking to the head of Hogwarts.

"With such an impeccable pedigree, I suppose that rumor must be the truth." When I said that, she turned a brighter red. I crooked a finger at her to get her to lean close to me. I whispered in her ear, "I AM a Muggle."

Now she turned a ghostly white, 'That's not true! I've got such an awful fascination with Muggles. Are you really one?"

3

I shrugged and said, "Yes."

She took me by the forearm and whispered, "You could ask me out some time. Just wait a couple of weeks after you're released. I wouldn't want to get in trouble for dating a patient."

I simply said, "I'll see."

She again turned a deep crimson and giggled her way out of the room.

◁

The next morning, the healer from before took a good look at me and declared me fit to get in trouble again, so I was released. I was wheeled to the entrance of the hospital. The nurse from the night shift casually walked past and gave me a surreptitious wink as I walked from Saint Mongo's. I winked back and turned my attention to the street where I found two wizards walking rapidly toward me. I thought about running back into Saint Mongo's, but I decided that if I stood my ground at the entrance, I should be safe.

They stopped at a comfortable distance away, and one said, "Are you Professor Wendt?"

I admitted that I was with a little squeak in my voice as I tried to maintain control.

"I'm Frank Vendredi. This is my partner, Joseph Cannon. We work the magical assault division of the Auror office."

They both were average height with brown hair, brown eyes and average build. A closer inspection of their cloaks revealed a symbol at the right collar. It was a highly stylized symbol that seemed to consist of the number 1 inscribed inside a zero inscribed inside a triangle. Frank noticed my attention to the symbol and asked, "Haven't you ever seen the shield of the Auror Office?"

I had to admit that I hadn't. I asked if they had any other form of identification. The man who called himself Frank pulled out of an inner pocket of his cloak what appeared to be a blank card and held it up toward me.

"Is that supposed to be a magic card?"

He looked at me with a look of exasperation. "Just use a revellio spell and you'll see my ID."

4

"I'm sorry. I'm a Squibb. I don't even have a wand." I tried to look apologetic although I wasn't feeling very apologetic. They couldn't expect everyone to be wizards. His partner pulled out a different card that had a photo (moving, of course) and his name and rank in the Auror office. It too had the Auror symbol on it as a sort of watermark.

He said, "Sorry." He looked like he was truly sorry that I didn't have magic. "We also have these for the Squibbs. They're not as secure, but . . . " He trailed off, not quite sure how to end his point.

I looked at it carefully and his photo was not great, but it was clearly him. "I suppose that's OK. What can I do for you?"

"We'd like you to go down to the Auror office so that you can file a criminal report on your abduction and torture yesterday. Do you feel up to it now?"

I decided that I did, but I remembered filing a report the previous night. I said so.

Joe said, "That was just a preliminary report. We need a formal one witnessed by a notary."

Frank said, "Well, since you're a Squibb, we'll have to help you disapparate there. Take Joe's hand and we'll disapparate to the Ministry."

I sighed and put out my hand. Joe took it and we disappeared in a whirling cloud of dust. We were standing inside a large chimney. I couldn't help asking, "How did we end up in a floo if we were disapparating?"

Joe was nonchalant, "Oh, lots of people disapparate into the floos rather than go by floo powder. It's not a big deal."

We walked out into the atrium. I'd been there a few times before, so I was not surprised by the general appearance—the fountain with the degrading statuary of the other magical creatures at the feet of the more than life-size wizards, the huge banner with Minister Fudge's visage, and the paper-airplane memos flurrying around. We walked to an elevator and took it up to the Auror office. The office itself was one that could be found in any modern office building—with the exception of the presence in most cubicles of some sort of flying ornament. One had a poster of the Holyhead Harpies flying in formation—apparently after a win.

We reached a cubicle that had lots of little things flying around —a model of a Quidditch player on a broom and a photo of a middle-aged witch with a boy about 8 years old and a girl who was probably 5.

Frank invited me to sit. Then his voice changed subtly. It had a touch more authority in it and the diction became clearer.

Joe said, "I'm going to use a quick quotes quill to record this interview. We'll have you review it and sign it when you've finished."

Then Frank resumed, "This interview began at 9:13 AM on June 23rd, 1995. It concerns an alleged attack by two or more unidentified wizards on one James Wendt of . . ."

I supplied, "Hogwarts School of Wizardry."

Frank resumed, "Now, Professor, would you please tell us—in your own words—what happened on the night of June 21st and the morning of June 22nd. Please take as much time as you need and don't leave out any detail that you can remember—regardless how insignificant it may seem to you."

I worked through the events of the evening. They had very few questions. However, they were interested in the Glock. I explained that it was a Muggle weapon that I carried because I couldn't use a wand. That rather perplexed them because they'd never encountered one. I'd not gone into the nature of the threat that it posed to my captors lest they think it was too dangerous for me to have.

Frank asked, "Just one more thing, Professor Wendt—do you have any idea for the motivation of the attack?"

That was a difficult question for me. If I admitted what I believed—that it was Deatheaters on the rampage, it might be that they would discount my entire story. So, I stuck with the simpler, more believable, partial truth that they wanted the galleons that I was carrying in the moke-skin purse that I had. They seemed to accept that, and everyone was happy. They had me review the Quick Quotes Quill transcript of the interview. I agreed that it was accurate, and I signed it in the presence of a notary who duly notarized it.

I was getting up to go when Frank said, "Wait a minute. We're not quite done."

I thought to myself, "Great, now what?" But I just smiled.

"We need you to try to identify your assailants. We've got photos of criminals that have been arrested. Joe, go get the Face Book."

He got up resignedly as he'd undoubtedly done a number of times and was back quickly with a large photo album. It had four photos per page. The background had a ruled scale of heights. Each person in the book seemed to be fidgeting—each in his own way. I turned page after page.

Eventually, I saw a face that seemed familiar but I wasn't sure. Frank noticed my hesitation and asked, "You see someone you recognize?"

I looked at the photo—it seemed to be positively manic, going through a cycle of looking off camera and returning to the front its maniacal gaze at the camera. I said, "This man seems familiar. He wasn't one of my kidnappers, but I know I've seen him recently."

Joe gave a laugh quickly suppressed when he saw the expression on Frank's face. Frank said, "You probably have. It's a rather famous face. It's Sirius Black's. His photo was somewhere in most newspapers —even Muggle newspapers—for months and months. Keep going."

I went on and on through the many pages. I saw one or two faces that might conceivably be one of the ones who kidnapped me, but none were close enough. "I'm sorry. I don't see anyone who fits."

Joe patted me on the back and said, "Well, it was always a long shot. What with Polyjuice potion, criminals can always disguise themselves as Muggles or just about anyone."

Frank handed me a card and said, "If you think of anything else, drop a line by owl, and we'll talk with you again. My name and office address is on the card." I recognized that the card was what Joe had showed me to prove his identity. I put it in a pocket and thanked them. Then I started to leave. I'd almost reached the outer door when I realized something. I immediately turned around and went back to their cube.

"I just realized. I don't know how to get out of here."

Joe said, "No problem. I'll drop you off wherever you like, so long as it's in London."

I gave him a street intersection near my lodgings. We went to the hearths and shortly I was standing at the intersection that I knew best in London.

I had taken only a few steps when Minerva showed up and asked, "Do you want a lift, Mister?"

I was astonished. "How did you know that I'd show up here about this time?"

She smiled a sly smile, "It's above your pay grade."

I grumbled, "Everything's above my pay grade. But that hasn't stopped you from telling me or me from finding out." But she remained silent, and I took her hand as we walked, "I think I will. Where are we going?"

She drawled, "Well, from your story, I'd say that the Deatheaters probably don't know where you live, but I wouldn't take any chances if I were you."

"And just what would I do if I didn't want to take chances?"

"You'd come along to a clever witch's lair, if I were you and lay low for a couple of days—until you had a chance to see if the Deatheaters were watching your place."

"Sounds good to me."

"You mean that you're not going to take an opportunity to go out with a buxom, young nurse."

"How do you know these things! I was thinking that I'd spent enough time in the hospital for a while, thank you."

She nodded and said, "Durn tooting, you're right."

The next couple of days at Minerva's sister's home were relaxing and good for recovery.

I returned home and started to prepare for the finals of the World Cup.

Cup Mondiale

The finals of the World Cup of Quidditch were fast approaching. A letter came by owl about a week in advance. It was from Minerva and asked me to be ready to go to Diagon Alley the next day. It said that I should be prepared to spend real money—whatever that meant.

Minerva dropped by on schedule. She disapparated directly into my room—which was not unusual for her.

I asked why I should be prepared to spend real money. Her answer was that her sister had thrown out the family tent.

"OK. What has that got to do with anything?"

She has this exasperating way of expecting that everything she says not only makes perfect sense but should to anyone who hears her statements—even if they don't know the context. On this one, I really didn't know the context. She gave me one of her patented, "You're either a complete moron or just trying to irritate me or both" looks.

I could only ask, "What??!!"

"Oh, come on, you've got to know that I'm thinking of the World Cup!"

No one could deny knowing something that she insisted that you did know. So, I simply asked, " Yeh, but what do we have to spend money on for the World Cup." I quickly supplied a couple of possibilities. "You mean things like binoculars or new casual clothes or . . ."

"No, no, no. We've got to get a tent. My family's tent is gone."

At the risk of incurring her wrath again, I asked the forbidden question, "And, again, why is it that we need a tent? Are we pitching it in the stadium?"

She just stared at me for a moment and said, "Think, Wendt. There are lots of reasons. You know that Quidditch games often go on for a long time. At the championship level, it's not unusual for games to go on for days."

I admitted that I knew that in theory a Quidditch game, like a baseball game, could go on indefinitely. "So, we have to be prepared to take a break from Quidditch and catch a little shut-eye in a tent?"

"Well, yes. But also, do you think that you're going to show up the day of and get a good camping spot, just like that?"

I admitted that I'd not really thought about it.

Minerva nodded her head wisely and said, "Just so. You've not really thought. Why, the year that we hired you, the Quidditch Cup final went on for more than 60 hours, and people started camping two weeks in advance."

"Those were people without jobs."

She snorted and said that the Minister of Magic of France was one of them who camped at the Jura Mountains Regional Natural Park.

I nodded sagely and said, "I rest my case."

She just snorted again.

She disapparated us to the Leaky Cauldron. We entered just before the lunch crowd normally came. Tom, the barman, saw us and motioned us over, saying, "Join me for a pint?"

Minerva and I declined with thanks, and we went on through to Diagon Alley. It turned out that the only reason we were there was to collect some galleons from our accounts to buy a tent and other supplies for the World Cup.

We entered the wizarding bank of Gringotts and went to an available teller. He verified our identities, mainly by examining the keys that we'd brought to open our vaults. We were assigned a bank employee to take us down to our vaults. We each pulled out a couple of hundred galleons. I stowed mine in my infinitely expandable purse. Minerva had a handbag that she used. On our way back up from the vaults, I noted how unpleasant the ride down and up had been on the little car that the three of us sat in.

"You know, I think there must be something about wizards—you just like to be uncomfortable when you travel."

"Oh, don't be ridiculous. We don't like to suffer any more than Muggles do." Minerva retorted.

"Then I defy you to name a single Magic means of conveyance that isn't a royal pain to use."

She thought a minute and said, "You know perfectly well of one."

It occurred to me which one she was thinking of, but I wasn't going to make it easy for her. I just shook my head.

Her lips hardened into a frown. "Don't give me that. You know about the Hogwarts Express."

Meanwhile our conductor who was driving the shuttle was rolling his eyes. He said, "You don't have to take this."

Surprised, I asked, "I don't have to?"

"No, you can leave your gold in your vault."

"Thanks."

When we got to the surface, we had no further business and started for the main exit. However, a goblin in a pin-striped suit approached us and said, "Excuse me, Mr. Wendt. One of the bank officers would like to speak with you for a few minutes. Can you come with me?"

I looked over at Minerva with a question in my eyes, "Would she excuse me?" She answered verbally, "Yes." I turned back to the goblin and said, "Yes, can my companion accompany me?"

The goblin seemed surprised by the question but said, "I think the business is confidential."

Minerva took me by the arm and said, "Just go ahead with him. I'll wait for you at Madame Malkin's. I'll be looking over the latest fashions."

"You sure?"

"Yes, I'll be fine."

So, I accompanied the goblin into the back offices of the bank. I marveled at the artwork on the walls and commented on it to my guide. He stayed mostly silent, and I asked again if he didn't enjoy working among such fine art.

"I can't comment on such matters."

"Really? Why not?"

"The bank has a policy against discussing art acquisitions of the bank."

"Hmmmm."

11

We arrived at an office that was on a corner of the building and had windows that faced out on Diagon Alley. I was introduced to the same executive who had helped me get a credit card several months before. I asked, "What can I do for you?"

He stayed seated and motioned me to a chair. Then he began, "Actually, it's something that we can do for each other.

"You remember the financial deal that we made to obtain a credit card for you?"

"Of course."

"Well, a strange thing has happened. Several of our clients have asked us to help them do business on a regular basis with Muggle institutions. The problem, of course, is that Muggle businesses don't accept payment in galleons. So, they have to exchange galleons for pounds sterling when they want to do business. It's a serious nuisance for them and is even threatening to become more than a nuisance.

"The solution to that problem that you came up with has come to the attention of my superiors and they would like to offer it to our clients."

I asked, "Well, that seems reasonable, but how do I fit into the picture?"

He leaned in toward me across his desk, "My superiors feel that you have invented the process. They feel that you deserve to profit from your invention. My superiors want to license the process from you so that they can use it with our clients."

That was a surprise. It seemed inconsistent with the general greediness of the goblins, but maybe it was consistent with their view of art. Maybe in some bizarre way they regarded this "process" as a work of art that they had to license to enjoy. In any case, I had to think carefully about this offer of theirs. "What do you offer me for the use of this process?"

The goblin narrowed his eyes as he stared at me, seeming to evaluate me in some way. After a moment, he said, "We think that you should propose a fair re-imbursement."

I began to see that the goblin was not as disinterested as he seemed. If I suggested something, and it was more generous than they were prepared to be, then they could always bargain me down. If they were prepared to be more generous, but I suggested a lower number, they could argue a bit but accept. As I was thinking, another idea occurred to me.

"I think that you've already done some preliminary negotiations with these people and have come up with a tentative agreement, so you just want to get a number from me to finalize it."

The goblin maintained a poker face, not even replying.

I went on, "Well, I'm pretty sure that's what you've done." Then an inspiration occurred to me, "Soooo, I'll offer you this, "I'll take 50% of whatever you charge them IN EXCESS of the rate that I'm paying you for the service."

That caused the goblin's face to make an expression. I think it was a genuine expression of surprise. I'd never seen a human face contort like that. I think it required unique muscles. Quickly his face returned to the imperturbable mask that it had been, and he said, "I need to talk with my superiors about this. Please wait."

He left his office, and I wondered if someone could see my face while he was gone. I decided that I needed to keep a poker face myself— even when he was out of the room. After about fifteen minutes and just before I'd decided to leave, he returned with another older goblin. The older goblin introduced himself as Gaeber.

He did the talking from there on. "That's a rather greedy offer Mr. Wendt. Surely you see that we do most of the work and you only reap profits."

I answered, "I really don't think that it's meaningful to talk about greed or not. With or without my process, you'll make a lot of money. I have the right to price my license at whatever price I choose. That's what I've decided on, and frankly, I think it's elegantly fair. You have only to decide whether you'll accept it or not.

"If you decide not to accept, you can always return with a new offer, which I'll either accept or not."

Gaeber stared at me for a while, probably trying to decide if it would be possible to change my mind. He eventually decided that I wasn't convincible, so he simply said, "We accept your proposal. We'll have it drafted and send you a copy by owl to review. If you have changes to propose, return it by owl, and we'll send you the revised version. When you're satisfied, you can come back to sign the final version."

I nodded absently as he spoke and replied, "That sounds very acceptable. It would be easier for me if we could conclude this business before Hogwarts School resumes for teachers in late August."

Gaeber said that it shouldn't be a problem to finish during July.

"Then I'll be back later this month."

Gaeber asked his associate to see me back to the bank lobby, and as we were about to leave the office, I turned back and added, "Oh, one more thing. I'm planning to attend the final round of the Quidditch World Cup. I hope that doesn't interfere with our business."

Gaeber said, "Quidditch. I've never been able to understand the fascination that you wizards have with that sport."

I simply made a noncommittal grunt and left. We quickly found our way back to the lobby, and I left the bank, heading for Madame Malkin's.

I found that Minerva was still there, trying on dress robes. When she saw me, she asked, "Do you think this is too dressy for the Quidditch Cup."

I recognized that the question didn't have anything to do with Quidditch but everything to do with how I thought she looked, so I said, "I think that it would be impossible for anyone to criticize you if you wore those robes to the Quidditch Cup or anywhere."

Her wide-eyed, wide-mouthed expression turned slightly arch as she said, "Quite charming, but I know that you are not being honest in that flattery."

"Oh, but I'm being perfectly honest when I say that you look fantastic in those robes."

She sniffed, but the smile broadened. Then she insisted that we had to get going to buy our tent. We left Diagon Alley. When back on the London streets, Minerva took my hand, and we appeared in a small rural town. I learned later it was Greater Stoney Littleton. We landed ouside a store called the Whole World Camping Store. It looked pretty much like any camping store I'd been in.

However, Minerva asked, "These are all nice Muggle tents, do you . . . " But she couldn't finish her question because the clerk just nodded vigorously and motioned her toward the back of the store. He preceded us and tapped the apparently blank wall, which dissolved and we walked through the archway that was revealed to see a showroom with a number of rather unusual tents. There were tents that had two and three stories. There were tents that had verandas on the front; there were tents that looked like they were castles with moats.

The salesperson apologized and said, "We've not got much variety at the moment. There's been a real run on tents what with the World Cup coming up so soon, but we have a few nice models left. The

14

more interesting ones that we have are sold-out except for the display models here. For example, there's the Big Moat model. That's very popular. We sold that out first and have refused to sell the display model, buuut we might just be persuaded to let that one go."

I looked over at Minerva and rolled my eyes. I spoke to her, "I just want something simple." She took me by the arm and pulled me aside.

"I agree. I think that a simple three room tent would be good. I know you can't argue against that."

"How is it that you know that?"

"Because one of them is the bedroom."

I couldn't help laughing and said, 'You really know how to take unfair advantage. But seriously, we could do with two rooms—bedroom and combined dining/kitchen, right?"

She shook her head but turned back to the sales person and said, "Do you have a nice simple two room model?"

The salesman's face took on a mournful look as he said, "You're really not going to do that to yourselves are you?"

I said, "Do you have one or not?"

"Well, yes. It's something that I'd hesitate to be seen in if I were going to the World Cup."

I forced him to cut to the quick, "How much?"

His face assumed an even more pained expression, "It's two hundred and fifty galleons."

Minerva's jaw dropped and she said, "You have the audacity to sell a two room tent for over two hundred galleons!"

"Well, the World Cup is coming up, and the demand for tents has gone through the roof." He said apologetically.

I decided that we needed to get the pain over with, so I simply said, "We'll take it." He went back into a back room and came out with a small package. I pulled out all of the galleons that I had and found that I only had a dozen or so left after I counted out the two hundred fifty. Minerva put the package in her handbag and we left the store.

After we were outside, I said, "You're going to have to treat me to supper, I'm pretty near broke."

We went back to London, and she let me choose the restaurant. I suggested that we go to Leicester Square and just walk until we saw something that we liked. We landed in the square behind a large tree. No one seemed to notice us. We then went toward Gamick street. We reached it and turned to the right

As we reached a corner, Minerva asked, "Oh, Oh, look there." She was pointing at a Burger King. "A Burger King! You surely want to exercise your American taste for a Burger."

I sniffed and said, "Don't kid with me. You know that I don't have any interest in Burger King." We turned down the short street called Bear street to the right of that corner.

As we walked, I saw a restaurant that did look interesting—Bear and Staff. I suggested that to Minerva.

She only rolled her eyes and said, "You only like it because of the strange name."

"No. No. It's got outside seating. It was established in 1873."

"Oh, so you're being a typical American—always going for the new fads."

I sniffed at that and said, "You're being what we call in America an Indian giver."

"And what would an Indian giver be? Perhaps a New Dehli blood donor?"

"No. An Indian giver is someone who promises something and then Welshes on the promise."

"I thought you said it was an Indian giver, not a Welsh giver."

"You know what I mean. For example, a certain lady promises to let you chose what restaurant and then doesn't honor her agreement."

"Oh, all right. Then you can eat at your old Bear and Staff."

We were seated and decided on the three course meal. Minerva selected the Creamy Tomato Soup (it was fairly creamy) for the appetizer. I chose the deep fried Brie (Minerva commented that it was an American dish if she'd ever heard of one). And we shared.

For the main course, she chose the Fish & Chips, and I chose the Sausage and Mash.

For desert, I had the warm chocolate brownie (with ice cream). She had the toffee and date pudding.

After ordering, she asked what had happened at Gringott's. I explained the situation. "I invented a new sort of financial transaction, and they decided that they wanted to use it with other clients. They also decided that they needed to license it from me. So we dickered over the royalties that I'd get."

Minerva's mouth tightened, "Oh, it's bad uh. uh. "

I supplied the word Karma.

"Yes, it's bad Karma to go into financial dealings with goblins. They nearly always find a way to make you regret it.

"And what kind of financial transaction is it anyway?"

I tried explaining my problems with buying Christmas presents for friends and relatives in the States. She understood that fine. BUT she didn't get at all how my solution helped me. She asked the same question about a half-dozen times in slightly different forms and asked again, "I still don't quite get it. Even if you use this tele-thing to place your order, they still have to wait to be paid to send it, don't they? How does that save you much time?"

"That's it. They get paid almost instantly. Just as soon as I give them my credit number, the computer checks that my credit is good and . . ."

"But how can this compooter thing possibly check that? It can't make a tele-call thing to Gringotts because Gringotts doesn't have these tele-things and even if they did, they'd have to go into your vault to know if you had the galleons to pay for the presents you buy."

I was trying to figure out how to answer that when she went on, "I know all about these mail order catalog things. The Weasley twins have this catalog where you can order all these fancy practical joke things of theirs.

"The way it works is that they send a paper catalog to their customers. The customers that want to buy a tongue ton toffee send an owl to them with the money, and when they get the order and the money, they send their customer the tongue ton toffee. And then their customers play practical jokes on all their friends and enemies. I don't see how your invention speeds up that process."

I was forced to just shrug and assure her that it had worked for me last Christmas. Besides that, it must work or the goblins wouldn't want to pay me to let them use it. I finished with, "Look, I'm all the time having to accept on faith all these magical spells that don't make sense to me. You could do that once or twice."

She shook her head exasperatedly and asked, "Are you sure that you don't have to pay them some money to start this process thingee going?"

"No, they were a bit disgusted by it, but they agreed to pay me half of their profits above the profit that they make from me."

"And you trust them?"

17

"Sure. If they wanted to cheat me. . . "

She broke in on my argument and said, "I know, I know. If they wanted to cheat you, they didn't need to offer you any kind of deal. Still, it just seems completely against goblin nature."

"Well, I agree that they're a bunch of money-grubbing ingrates but they do seem to have some kind of sense of fairness and justice. And, besides that, what's the worst that can happen. Say they completely cheat me and never send me a brass knut. I wouldn't be worse off than I would have been had I never been offered the deal."

Minerva wouldn't let it go completely. She was determined to have the last word. "Wellll."

That was all right with me too. How was I worse off if she had the last word on this discussion?

So, we finished the meal (which she liked), and she dropped me off at home.

◻

Over the next couple of days, I scanned both the *Daily Prophet* and *The Times* for signs of more unusual events that might be attributed to the activity of Deatheaters. Of course, there are lots of unusual things that happen every day. It's hard to see any of them being the work of Deatheaters—unless a Monk found wandering aimlessly in Notting Forest after eating psychedelic fruit is the work of Deatheaters.

But there was a strange story about a former Auror attacking a trash bin. The combination of Auror, attack, the name of the Auror— Mad-eye Moody—got my attention. The *Prophet* was treating it as another goofy story about a potty retired civil servant. I wasn't so sure that that was what was going on at all. I called Minerva on her cell phone. I did that periodically to keep her in practice.

She answered after the third time that I'd rung her up. She was fit to be tied. After she calmed down and realized that it hadn't been some sort of emergency, I asked her about Mad-Eye Moody.

'I see that you've seen the article in the *Prophet* about him."

"Yes, so what's the word—is he potty?"

Minerva sneered (she had a way of doing that over the phone that left no doubt that she was sneering), "Of course not. He was one of the greats. He brought in more Deatheaters than any other two Aurors combined."

"How did he get the nickname?"

She laughed, "Oh, the reason that he brought in more than anyone else was that he would take crazy risks. One time he lost an eye. Afterwards, he crafted a replacement eye. It was absolutely unique. It let him see behind him. It is slightly telescopic. I've even heard rumors that he can see through disillusionment charms with it."

I interrupted to ask about disillusionment. Minerva answered, "Disillusionment is the process of becoming invisible. It works mostly on the brain of the viewer, making them not notice someone or perhaps forgetting that they've noticed him. If the "mad eye" can let its wearer see a disillusioned person, perhaps it's due to the fact that the "mad eye" is mechanical rather than human."

Minerva went on, "Anyway, the eye is also much more easily directed than a human eye. Moody can look in two completely different directions at the same time with it. The independent motion and the odd angles that he sometimes looks with it brought about the "Mad Eye" nickname. It is quite disconcerting watching him when he gets interested in looking at something with that eye."

"So, you don't put much store in this story?"

Minerva smiled whimsically, "Are you kidding? Put much store in a story in the *Prophet*? Of course, not."

"So, do you think that this was an attack thwarted?"

"Possibly. When you put away as many Deatheaters as he did, you're going to have lots of enemies. and not all of them are in Azkaban. Consequently, he lives on a perpetual short fuse. Every now and then it goes off for no good reason.

"But it might have been a real attack." She went on.

I thought a moment and said, "If I had to bet, I'd bet it was an attack."

Minerva nodded.

"So, he's on Valdemort's short list of enemies to get if he ever returns?"

"Sure." She hesitated and then went on, "You'll know this shortly anyway, so I'm going to tell you now. You'll have a good chance to form your own opinions. Dumbledore has recruited him to teach the Defense Against the Dark Arts classes at Hogwarts."

"Hmmm. Sounds a bit chancy, but if he works out, the kids would get a first rate education in D.A.D.A."

"Yeh, if they survive it, it would be first rate."

"Well, we're getting together tomorrow to travel to the Cup?"

"Right. I'll drop by at 9AM."

The next day at nine, I was ready. I had a duffel bag, packed with clothes for several days and a couple of books because we'd be there for two days before the final game occurred. Spot on 9AM, she showed up and rang the doorbell. I was sitting in the entryway waiting for her, and I greeted her warmly. She was wearing a jeans skirt and a light blouse.

"Well, you look good today. I'm glad that you decided on jeans. If we're camping, denim makes life so much easier."

She rolled her eyes and said, "You just like to see leg."

"Well, that's true too," I had to admit.

I took her hand, and we started to walk toward a nearby alley. I hoped that she'd just surprise me when she decided to disapparate so that I wouldn't have to worry about it.

My stomach lurched, and I felt the world spinning. We arrived in an auto junk yard beside a stack of Ford Anglia bodies. I looked around and said, "Somehow I expected the World Cup to be a little newer and with more people."

"Oh, don't be facetious. We're just here looking for the Port Key."

"We're looking for the porky what?"

"No. No. Port Key. P. . O. .. R. T. . K . . E. . Y. It's supposed to be a tire iron, whatever that is."

"Oh, good, I was afraid we'd have a hard time finding it, but this certainly makes it easier."

"Oh, youuu can be soooo exasperating," she said crossly.

I was confused about what we were looking for. Was it a tire iron or a port key? "I thought you said it was a port key, whatever that is."

"It is a port key. A port key can be anything—a mop, an old Wellington boot, a scroll of parchment. The idea is that it shouldn't attract attention to itself from Muggles."

I had been looking around, now that I knew what I was looking for and I noticed a tire iron partly stuck into the ground nearby. "I wonder if this could be it."

Minerva swung around and asked what I was talking about. I pointed at the tire iron.

"So, that's a tire iron. Why do they call it that?"

I was more interested in why we were looking for it, so I had my own questions, "Why are we looking for a port key? Why aren't we at the World Cup—assuming that this isn't the World Cup?"

"Of course, it isn't. And we're looking for a port key because it's our way of getting to the World Cup."

I looked at the tire iron. I looked at Minerva. "Oh. Oh. Don't tell me. I know what this is. You wizards have invented another crazy means of travel that involves me throwing up—right?"

"Don't be silly. It wasn't invented to make you throw up."

"I see, it was invented to make everyone who uses it throw up."

"Just give it a rest." As she was saying this, a couple of strangers rounded a pile of Rolls Royce undercarriages and waved.

The older said, "Oh, I say. We didn't miss the port key, did we?"

Minerva said, "No. It's that tire iron there."

The younger, who looked to be about eight or nine, ohhed and ahhed and said, "So that's a tired iron. What do Muggles use them for? And why are they tired?"

Since I was the only one present who knew the answer to that question, I introduced Minerva, and I and explained, "First, the word is tire—T I R E.- not tired. Well, tire irons are called that because they are tools that are used with tires, and they're made with iron, usually." The youth opened his mouth and was about to ask a question when I interrupted, "I know that you want to know what a tire iron is used for.

"Tires are a kind of wheel that are used on Muggle automobiles. Tires hold air. If the tire gets a hole in it, the air goes out and it isn't any good as a wheel any more. So, the tire iron is used to unbolt it from the car. Then a good tire can be bolted to the car using the same tire iron."

That seemed to satisfy the son, but the dad asked, "But why do you want air in a Muggle tire?"

I took a deep breath and tried to answer that question, "I know it sounds crazy, but if a tire is full of air, it keeps its shape and can hold up a car."

With that the dad interrupted, "Oh, I see that you're a joker. You don't have any idea what Muggles use tired irons for. You're just trying to see how long you can keep making up this drivel before we'll catch on."

I glanced at Minerva who shook her head. I was trying to come up with an answer when the tire iron started to glow. Minerva burst in and said, "The port key is about to leave, we've got to take hold of it right away." We did—I with trepidation, wondering what awful thing would happen when it transported us to the World Cup.

When it did go off, we suddenly found ourselves spinning through the air. I felt like I would loose my grip at any moment. Suddenly, the kid did and then his dad. Minerva slipped away. I tried to take a deep breath and released my grip. I seemed to be flying through the air for a moment and then landed with a thud. I picked myself up and found the other three nearby. We were on the top of a hill that overlooked a vast field of tents. I turned around slowly and eventually an immense stadium came into view. Minerva surprised me when she took my arm and said, "There's the World Cup Stadium."

I admitted that I was impressed. A wizard came up the small hill and spoke to the man and his son, briefly. They waved back at us and shouted, "See you at the game!"

Then the wizard approached us and asked, "Do you have a reservation?"

I shook my head but Minerva nodded and said, "BYZ123".

The wizard consulted a list and said, "Yes. That's over that way," pointing, "and you'll find that the spot is marked with your reservation number. Hope you enjoy the game."

We walked off down the hill and followed the slightly winding trail down through tents. There were signs pointing off the main route that were labeled with three letter combinations. Eventually we saw BYZ and turned down that aisle.

The tents had an amazing variety that exceeded what we'd seen at the wizard camping store. Some had clear signs of nationality. There were national flags of all sorts and the architecture of the tents was interesting. I could swear that some had been inspired by Frank Lloyd Wright. There was even one tent that had an unusual design with round wings and three small towers in the middle. When I saw it at a distance I thought of the old riddle, "What state is round on the ends and high in the middle?". As we got closer, I saw an Ohio pennant flying at the top of the "I".

We found our site, BYZ123, and Minerva pulled out of her large handbag the small package. She took out her wand and said, "Engorgio." With that the package split along several seams and seemed to inflate like a rubber balloon. When it finished, it looked like a nondescript bungalow made of canvas.

We entered and discovered a main room with sofa, table and several chairs. There was a door leading off to the right. I looked to the left and discovered the kitchen area. Minerva had taken the one to the right and said, "Well, we'll put this to good use later."

The rest of the day we settled in, stowed food in the kitchen area, and prepared meals. In the early evening we went for a walk in our neighborhood. We seemed to be in an international community that had few English. There were the Ohioans and a few other Americans, but mostly, we were among Asians—Japanese, Chinese and a few other related nationalities—like Vietnamese. As we went, we spoke to many. Most understood English and those who didn't understood other European languages that we had at least a passing familiarity with— French, German, Spanish. We got back to our immediate neighborhood and enjoyed reading for the rest of the evening until bedtime.

The next day, we were up early and decided to walk more widely. We discovered that the neighborhood to the East of us had mainly the Irish contingent that had come to root for their team in the finals. Further to the west were the Polish who had come to root for their team. We saw many posters of their seeker—Victor Krum. He could be seen perpetually performing acts of devil-may-care acrobatics on his broom. The Irish had some posters of their seeker—Moran, but it seemed like there were a lot more posters of their team as a whole. Learning that we were English and therefore, perhaps not having a favorite, both sides tried to woo our favor. I said that I was rooting for the American team. That usually got stares of disbelief that I could think that one of the teams in the final was American.

We spent a lot of the day wandering to see if we could find someone whom we knew, but we didn't have any luck. I was sure that the Weasleys were attending the game but I saw no sign of them. We kept wandering around and accepted an offer to join a group for lunch. They were a group of Irish who were having Polish sausage and mash washed down with Harp Ale. There were a lot of jokes about how the Irish would feast on the Polish the next night.

That night Minerva had an awful time getting to sleep and she kept waking me up. She'd toss and turn and eventually, the movement would wake me. I'd spoon her, but I'd fall asleep. She'd be close to falling asleep, but as soon as I fell asleep, it would disturb her. It began to get light at 5:00 AM, and we finally gave up and just got up and she made some tea.

As we sat and drank hot tea, she admitted to being excited about the game. I asked her, "Surely you've been to an important Quidditch match before?"

She admitted that she hadn't and asked me how I kept calm. My answer was, "Oh, I've been to a lot of big games—NCAA basketball tournament games, football bowl games. I even attended a World Series game."

"What in the world is a basketball game? I know about football. Every Muggle kid in England plays football."

I thought, "You think you know football", but I didn't say anything. It would be hard enough explaining basketball. What I did say was, "Basketball is a strange game that has weird similarities to Quidditch. You score points by throwing a large ball, somewhat like a Quaffle through a hoop at one end of the field. The ideal way to do it is for a player to fly through the air and push it through the hoop. You get two points for every score. More if you do it from farther away."

"Is there something like the Snitch?"

"No, there's nothing in all Muggle sport like the Snitch."

"What about this World Serious game? That doesn't sound like a lot of fun."

"It is a pretty serious game, but it's actually "series"—as in a series of games. You have to win four games out of a series of seven games. The sport is baseball. It's so bizarre that even Quidditch doesn't seem very strange beside it. So, don't ask me to explain it."

We walked around the campgrounds hoping to see someone from Hogwarts but it wasn't looking very hopeful. So, we packed ourselves a little bag of goodies for what might turn into a long night and headed for the stadium. We reached the stadium long before sunset, but there were long lines. Apparently, they'd just opened the gates, and people were slowly working their way through to their seats. Our seats turned out to be fairly low. There was a squad of Quidditch players working out in the Pitch. They zoomed overhead on brooms. They were wearing green uniforms. To see them, we had to crane our heads skyward most of the time. I commented, "Makes you long for the Pitch at Hogwarts where we're on a level with most of the game."

Minerva pulled out a pair of binoculars from her handbag and looked up at them. She asked, "They must be the Irish?"

I asked for the binoculars. She corrected me. They were omni-occulars. They were sort of instant-replay binoculars. They even provided commentary on what was going on. She handed them to me, and I used them to follow a couple of the players for a minute. "No, those must be the second team. They aren't the players that are on the posters of the Irish that I've seen."

We passed the time waiting for the game to start by speculating on how long the game would last. I'd bought a *Prophet* and looked in the sports section. Their analysis was that the strength of the whole Irish team would overcome the one-man play of the fantastic Seeker, Victor Krum. None-the-less, since Krum was, after all, Krum, the game couldn't go really long because he would catch the snitch sooner or later. Most likely it would be sooner rather than later.

Minerva asked, "So, who are they predicting will win?"

"Funny. They don't give a prediction. My own feeling is that it will depend on how long the game goes. The longer it goes, the more likely that it will be won by the Irish. If they can keep Krum off the snitch long enough, they'll wear down the Polish chasers and goalie."

"OK. Then how long do they have to keep the game going?"

"Oh, I don't know. Maybe a couple of hours."

"So, you think it'll only go at most a few hours?"

"I didn't say that. You know Quidditch. One team could get ahead a thousand to nil, and the game has to go on until someone gets the Snitch. I don't think it'll be that bad here, but you never know. I am convinced of this, the Polish had better hold off Krum if they want to win."

Just then, the public address system made an announcement. The teams were about to be introduced. The first out were the Irish. They had a scintillating light show. Minerva told me that the green lights zooming around and making patterns in the night sky were Lepricorns. The show climaxed with the Lepricorns showering what appeared to be galleons down on the crowd. I commented, "That can't be real money. It would be a large fortune."

Minerva caught one and examined it. She agreed, "It's Lepricorn gold."

I smiled, "Fool's gold."

"I've never heard it called that, but it's a good name for it. In a few hours, it will return to the base metal that it's made from."

Then the Polish arrived. Whereas the Irish had flown in a simple wing formation with the Seeker Moran leading it, the Polish had put their top man well in front with the rest of the team being a sort of honor guard. He was a barely visible blur as he swung around the stadium at blinding speed all the time doing acrobatics on his broom.

Minerva said that she heard that he was virtually a secret weapon. They kept the press away from him that effectively. She bent her soft lips close enough to my ear for me to feel the warm breath, "I hear that he's not even legally an adult yet."

"Interesting. In the States, you've got to be legally an adult to play in major league sports. The last minor that I have ever heard of playing in the Big Show was a sixteen-year-old fifty years ago. It's astounding. He'd probably not have been playing then if there hadn't been a war going, and every profession would take just about anyone who could pretend to work."

"Who was he?"

"His name is Joe Knuxall."

Minerva thought a second and asked, "Sixteen is awfully young to be starting a career. What did he end up doing after he retired from his sport?"

"Oh, the same as your Mr. Bagman. He's a sports broadcaster."

The Polish had a secret weapon that didn't even get onto the field of play. Their team mascots came out on the field and started singing and dancing. As they did, I thought, "What the hell is this?" I had an insane desire to jump up on my seat and rip my shirt off. As it was, I had already stood when a pair of gentle hands covered my ears— effectively enough that I didn't hear their song. I almost immediately sat down and would have thanked Minerva if I could have heard myself speak. The mascots whatever they were finally stopped singing, and I asked Minerva what the hell they were.

26

She laughed and said, "I do think that you would have done something really crazy if I hadn't covered your ears. They are Veela. Quite possibly they are the Sirens that Homer wrote about in the Odyssey, who lured sailors to their deaths on the rocks. They are still up to their old tricks even after three thousand years."

"Sirens. Yes, they certainly are. How is it that they go un-noticed by Muggles?"

"Well, they don't entirely. Remember Homer. But they are attracted only to wizards, because wizards have powers. After all, Muggles don't have. They don't sing their seductive song in the presence of mere Muggles—except when they want to influence them. I sometimes wonder if some of the fashion models aren't Veela."

"Yes, you may be right."

Bagman announced the beginning of the match and we watched, with sore necks, the aerial acrobatics of both teams, but especially of Krum, who seemed unequalled in his skills on a broom. The play, though, went almost like clockwork. The rest of the Polish team was clearly outclassed by the Irish. They slowly, consistently built a lead that seemed would inevitably carry the day (or night, as the case may be) if it were given only a little more time.

The Irish reached a 150 point lead and the Polish were so desperate that they turned routinely to fouling the Irish. That only sped the approaching end. But just at that point, Krum seemed to catch sight of the Snitch and took off in a power dive that I could barely stand to watch. I was convinced that he was going to end up crumpled on the ground. He didn't. He pulled up miraculously at the last instant. But Moran was not quick enough. He couldn't pull up completely and landed in a partial crash. The game was halted as he was attended to by healers.

I don't know how it was possible, but somehow he got to his feet, remounted his broom and was in the air. Shortly after that, Ireland scored the winning goal—or what would be even if the Snitch were caught. I began to wonder if the Irish would totally skunk the Polish by capturing even the Snitch, but it was not to be. Krum seemed to catch sight of the Snitch again. This time, it was for real, and he easily captured it without serious opposition from the still-stunned Moran. But the Irish had won. The score would look close, but it had really been a runaway from the start.

I looked at my watch and saw that it was 11:39 PM local time. I smiled and said, "Well, we can sleep in tomorrow."

27

She said, "I'm way ahead of you."

We were in bed and were in the middle of a very happy embrace when there was the sound of an explosion that sounded distant. Between kisses, I commented, "Sounds like the Irish are enjoying their victory". A moment later I wished that they weren't doing such a good job of celebrating. An explosion rocked our tent. I was suddenly startled out of my romantic intensity, and I immediately rolled over Minerva to shield her from any incoming shrapnel. She whispered in my ear, "What's going on?"

"I don't know, but I think that we'd better find out quickly. I'm going to put on my shoes and you'd better too."

She added, "And your trousers—right?"

I nodded heedless of the fact that she couldn't see my non-verbal assent. I quickly slipped my jeans on and reached into the pocket to retrieve my purse. I reached in and found the Glock. I quickly retrieved it, removed the magazine, checked it for live rounds and replaced it in the Glock. I flipped the safety off and took a deep breath. I said to myself, "Stay frosty." Then I looked to Minerva and asked, "Do you think that you're up to going out with me?"

"Of course."

We stuck our heads out through the entrance and found that there were fires breaking out over an area only a couple of hundred yards away. There were a lot of people running generally away from the heart of the commotion. It was hard to see what was causing the disturbance. As the fires grew larger, it became clear that there was a group of wizards that was at the center of it, and suspended in the air above them were several figures. It was hard to see what they were.

Minerva said, "It looks like they're headed this way. If we stay here, we're going to find out what's going on from close range."

"Yeh, let's head off to the right, where we can observe from a safe distance." We went that way as quickly as we could in the dark, tripping over tent pegs and wires, picking up bruises and cuts. We reached a spot that seemed like it would be a safe distance.

As the fires got brighter and the group got closer, we realized what was suspended in the air because we could hear their screams. Minerva gasped, "Those are people!"

28

"Right. What can we do?"

"If we attack them, there's a good chance that they'll fall. And I think they're Muggles."

I gasped and realized that she was right. They were Muggles. We seemed helpless to do anything for them. I sat down and dragged Minerva down next to me behind a partly deflated tent. "There's no point in our being seen. Think! What can we do?"

"Oh, we can do lots. We can stun the Deatheaters."

"You think they're Deatheaters?"

"Oh, yes. They're hooded and they're torturing Muggles. And . . ." She gasped, "And there's the Dark Mark."

"The what?"

She pointed up in the air, and I followed the direction of her finger. It pointed to a bizarre green image in the air. It was hard to describe in the confusion and difficult lighting, but without doubt, it was gruesome. I unsurely said, "So?"

"That is the mark of the Deatheaters. When they killed someone, they set that mark in the sky over the place."

"Well, we've got to do something. Think!" And then an idea occurred to me. "Look, there's a war story, too long to go into. The point of the story is that you can attack a larger force by getting behind them and picking them off one at a time—the last one first. You hit the last one. If one of the Muggles starts to fall, you take over and you keep it up. We slowly work our way forward and . . "

"And what happens when we're down to two or three?"

"We improvise." She looked at me in the dark with an expression that I couldn't read, and that I chose to ignore. I hoped that she would be resourceful if it came to that. I went on, "Let's go as soon as they're past."

"OK. What makes you think they won't notice?"

"They're too fascinated with terrorizing everyone else. They couldn't imagine that someone would try to terrorize them."

Minerva shook her head, but she got up and said, "Let's go. They've past. We don't want them to get too far away."

I got up and we followed them. Minerva decided that she'd use the petrificus totalis spell. We took a few minutes to get close enough that she wouldn't miss and hit someone further along. She held her wand steadily with both hands, and the closest Deatheater just dropped. The

Muggles continued their bouncing journey under the remaining Deatheaters.

She waited a few more minutes and then took down the next Deatheater—still no change in the Muggles. There must have been about a dozen Deatheaters left. I began to worry about them noticing something unusual, but so far they hadn't.

She put down a couple more, and on the next one, one of the Muggles started to fall. She managed to keep the Muggle from falling very far. She took down another, and the Muggles bounced along unchanged. I was beginning to think that it might just work when a bunch of Aurors ran over a little hill and ordered the Deatheaters to let the Muggles down.

The remaining ones disapparated, and the Aurors had their hands full letting the Muggles down gently. Some Aurors got sight of us and shot stunning spells at us. That was the last that I was conscious of for an hour or so.

When I awoke, Minerva and I were in some sort of cell. Minerva had come to first. When I started to show signs of life she said, "Don't ask where you are. You're in a holding cell at the main Auror office in the Ministry.

"I've managed to convince them that we're innocent bystanders."

"How did you do that?"

"Oh, it was a pretty good help that you're a Muggle. A Deatheater would hardly be walking around with a Muggle when they could always use the Levicorpus spell on them."

"You must have found a brilliant Auror."

Just then an Auror opened the door and said, "You're free to go. Oh, and your boss is out there. Oh, one more thing. I heard the comment about brilliant Aurors."

I winced. It wasn't a great thing to have your boss show up when you're released from the holding tank. Dumbledore was waiting for us. When we emerged from the cell, he shook his head and said, "I trust you two had a good time at the World Cup."

"Oh, it was peachy keen," I commented. "There's nothing like running into some Deatheaters on the way home."

"You do seem to be a sort of Deatheater magnet."

"It's my charming personality."

'Minerva, you really must keep him under better management. I didn't make you his mentor so that you would end up in jail."

She frowned and said, "It just seemed the right thing to do—everything considered."

"Well, let's get the two of you home. I presume that you've been staying with your sister, Minerva?"

"Yes, but I don't think that I need help getting there."

"Do you need a ride, Mr. Wendt?"

"Well, I was sort of supposing that Minerva would give me one."

"Oh, I think that she's had a busy enough night as it is without escorting you home."

Minerva turned her head at an angle and focused one gimlet eye on Dumbledore, but he was imperturbable. He just smiled an innocent smile and shrugged. Minerva backed down and said, "I guess it would be nice to just disapparate home and not have to worry about anything else."

Dumbledore nodded and said, "You see, Wendt, I'll give you a —what do the Muggles call it—a lift, and you can be in bed in a few minutes."

I was happy at the thought of sleeping in most of the day and agreed. We all walked to the elevator that took us to the atrium and the fireplaces. Dumbledore commented, "It's not normal, but I don't think that anyone would object to our disapparating directly from the atrium."

Minerva disappeared, Dumbledore held out his hand, I gritted my teeth and took his hand. We arrived on the street outside my rooming house. I was tired, but I wasn't too tired to wonder how Dumbledore had known where I live. He simply said, "I wouldn't be much of a Headmaster if I didn't keep track of my teachers' homes away from Hogwarts, would I?"

I agreed and wearily rummaged around in my purse looking for my key. Dumbledore simply tapped me on the shoulder and shook his head when I looked up. He twiddled his wand and I heard the snap of the lock unlocking. I thanked Dumbledore and fumbled into the rooming house and up the stairs to my attic room. I fell into bed without locking my door (not that I did that very often).

I did sleep in the next couple of days and took my time getting onto my normal routine once I was up. There was still a week until teachers had to report to Hogwarts for in-service before the beginning of the term. I was still healing from the two adventures that I'd had this summer, and I was not anxious for the new term to start. So I rested as much as I could.

Defense Against The Dark Arts

The day came when Minerva stopped by my flat to give me a lift to King's Cross where we'd take the Hogwarts Express to Hogwarts. She berated me for not agreeing for us to disapparate there.

"Now, you know perfectly well that I take the Express—not to avoid disapparating. After all I had to disapparate to get here with you. But because I need the full day trip on the Express to get me into the right state of mind for Hogwarts.

"There's nothing harder than transitioning from Muggle society to magical society. This trip helps me make that transition."

She rolled her eyes, but I'd been practicing mimicking that little trick of hers. This time I rolled my eyes back at her, "More than one can play at that little trick."

That surprised her so much that she broke out giggling,and that turned into a full laugh. It took on a life of its own. At times she seemed to get control of it and be finished. Then it would re-assert itself and she'd be laughing uncontrollably. She did eventually get control and simply said, "Let's go."

There were always a few teachers who preferred the train to disapparating or taking the floo network to Hogwarts. Minerva assures me that those who do take the train only do so because they aren't confident of their Disapparation skills and don't like traveling by floo—too sooty.

"I fully agree. My reasons precisely."

Minerva sniffed, and we boarded the Express. We started off quickly because there are very few cars on the train for this trip—really only the teacher's car and a dining car. When the students ride the express, there is a trolley that is rolled down the aisles by a witch, selling candy and sandwiches. For the teachers, there is a dining car that has a few house elves from Hogwarts who provide lunch. Since they are Hogwarts house elves, the lunches are superb. They are more like brunches with a buffet line that includes crepes, omlets, bacon, sausages, various pastries and fruits. They will even make you a waffle.

Minerva commented that it wasn't very long ago that the house elves would act as waiters and take orders from the passengers.

"Ah well, *The Times*, they are a-changing." I commented.

"You sound like you're quoting someone?"

"Yes, a Muggle singer named Dillon."

"Not very original, was he?"

"It seemed original when he composed it." Then, I quickly added, "And no cracks about Muggles not being original."

Minerva just raised an eyebrow in a "who me?" expression. I chose a bagel and some fruit. Minerva had a house elf make an omelet with cheese and sausage.

We sat observing the countryside roll by as we lunched. Minerva stroked my leg with her knee. I knew that she enjoyed this trip by train at least as much as I did. And there were several other professors on the train. The dining car was very popular. I looked around. I found that there was a table with Professor Flitwick, Trelawney, Babbling and Hooch. Sitting at another table was Professor Vector.

I commented, "Professor Flitwick surely doesn't have trouble with disapparation."

"Well, I suppose this pre-term run of the Express does have a little reputation as a party train."

We arrived at the Hogsmeade station and hiked to the school. The in-service period was not quite the normal school in-service. There were few meetings. The main purpose was to encourage professors to do lesson planning. But the truth was that you could lead a professor to school but you couldn't make her plan—that is, unless she were going to plan anyway. So what was the point? No one could answer that question. Minerva and I had argued about it. She is a traditionalist. If it had been done for the last five centuries, it must be worth doing. Professor Dumbledore's answer when I'd asked him about it was that it was uniformly popular with the staff, so he wasn't going to interfere with the tradition.

And he was right. Everyone that I'd talked to had defended it staunchly. Everyone, that is, except for Snape. He regarded it as a crutch for those who didn't have sufficient will-power to force themselves to do pre-term planning. I asked him, "When do you do your planning?"

"Oh, I'm finished. I do planning for the next term immediately the current term ends."

That raised a question for me. Where did he go for the long holidays? I asked him that in as inoffensive way as I could. He was a bit evasive and I decided to press him. He finally said, "Well, if you must know, I borrow homes."

I'd never heard the concept before. "What do you mean, 'borrow'?"

"Hasn't Minerva told you about that wizardly custom?"

"Why would I be asking?"

"Of course. I suppose Minerva never engages in this sport. Well, you see, it's possible to live in a house for a week or two and return it to precisely the state that it was in before your visit." Snape had assumed his supercilious professorial attitude.

"And what about the residents of the houses?"

"Oh, we never occupy a house where the Muggles are present," He hesitated and then added, "Although we could." He stopped for a moment again, seeming to look to his interior, and went on, "Anyway, we find a house whose owners have taken a vacation or are selling their house.

"We enter it and live there until the owners are about to return. Then we return it to its original state."

"And that's what you do when you're on Holiday?"

He nodded. I asked, "And you don't see that as morally questionable?"

Snape seemed a bit embarrassed. He looked down at his feet and mumbled something like, "Well, we do return the house to exactly how it was."

I simply said, "Hmmmmm."

Immediately he looked up and said, "Don't be so holier than thou. Some of the best wizards do it!" Then he whirled around and strode off.

The first week of in-service began at the first meal the evening that we arrived. It was rather like the banquet at the beginning of the term with students. But there were differences. We sat at a student table. The table rotated each term. This term it was the Huffelpuff table.

Dumbledore gave a speech as he did at the beginning of term Banquet. He gave us a forecast of the current year. "This year, something is going to happen that hasn't in more than two centuries—the Tri-Wizard Tournament." There were a few gasps around the table, but since I didn't have the slightest idea what it was, I didn't know how to react.

He went on, seeming to speak directly to me, "For those of you who aren't aware of the history of the Tri-Wizard Tournament, let me give you a little history. It goes back 700 years. It was always a tournament between the three great European schools of wizardy—Hogwarts, Beaux Batons, and Durmstrang. It happened once every four years,and it occurred at each of the great schools in turn. It was a competition based on a race to complete a magical task. Each school submitted a small number of contestants. A magical object, the Goblet of Fire, selected the best contest from each school to compete.

"Generally speaking, the tasks were intrinsically dangerous and occasionally, a contestant died. The awful competition of 1792 resulted in all three contestants dying. A review board ended in recommending that the competition be terminated.

"That happened. For over two centuries, there were no TriWizard Tournaments—until this year. The last couple of years there has been a desire on the part of some of the schools to revive the competition. The idea is that the rules will be modified to make the competition safer. The most important rule change was the exclusion of contestants under the age of 16. This, in effect, limits the competition to 6th and 7th year students. Also, as a result, most contestants are legally adult wizards and witches.

"Now, where do you fit in the picture? We need competition tasks that are challenging but not significantly dangerous. Each of the schools must submit tasks, and a committee of the school heads will select the three that are used. We'll expect every teacher to come up with practical proposals. We'll be having meetings to choose a few good ideas and flesh out all details.

"What questions do you have?"

There was a shocked silence that was broken by one laconical question: "Will there be a reward for successful submissions?" It was Snape.

Dumbledore nodded and said, "Ah, yes, Severus. I think that I will offer a prize for any proposals that are ultimately accepted by the committee."

A female voice that turned out to belong to Professor Sinistra asked, "What about tasks that depend on knowledge rather than skill?"

Dumbledore said, "Aurora, I think that you could come up with a good task that depended on intelligence and knowledge."

Somebody said, "Do we have to?" in a sort of whiney voice.

Dumbledore said, "No one has to try to come up with a task. No one will be reprimanded for not doing so, but everyone must attend planning meetings. Remember, the sooner you come up with a good task, the sooner your group will be done."

Minerva stood and asked, "Apparently, we'll be having some guests for a while. Just how long will we be hosts?"

"A good question. Our guests will be with us for the rest of the year. Which brings up the point of hospitality. I expect everyone to be good hosts to our visitors and make them feel welcome. That is something that you 'Have to' do."

The questions tapered off to the trivial.

Afterwards, Minerva and I discussed what could be magical tasks that would be good. Since she was an expert in transfiguration, she suggested several possibilities based on transfiguration. I had to interrupt and suggest that what she was talking about was more a transfiguration final exam than a task for the Tournament. She harrumphed and said that she'd come up with a good idea yet.

Dumbledore organized the staff into three teams. There were to be three events and we would have a team for each event to try to come up with one good proposal. Minerva, Sinistra, Flitwick, Sybil, the arithmancy professor, Vector, and I were on one team.

We brainstormed for an entire morning. First we came up with a list of magical skills that we wanted to force the candidates to exercise. We didn't limit ourselves to our own specialties. There were arguments about what constituted a magical skill. Was astronomy a magical skill? If it wasn't, why had it been on the curriculum for centuries? Well, maybe it wasn't. What about logic? There wasn't even a course in logic, but when I suggested it, no one stood up to defend it's being on the list but nobody opposed it either.

Then there was the skill of reading runes. That was raised by the arithmancy professor. Everyone was sure that it should be included but everyone was apologetic about it. The list was beginning to look like a list of skills that a smart Muggle could do pretty well on.

Someone, glancing at their watch, announced that if we didn't get a move on, we'd miss lunch. It was already 12:30. We dropped everything and headed for the Great Hall. We arrived and were dismayed that nobody was there. We wondered if we'd completely missed lunch, but we discovered that there was still food on the tables. As a matter of fact, all the tureens and platters and goblets were still full. We shrugged at one another and dug in. Shortly after, the other groups dragged in.

Professor Dumbledore asked the room in general, "How is everyone doing?"

No one said anything. As a matter of fact, nearly everyone looked pretty surly. He went on, "That well, eh?"

Minerva spoke for our group. "We've broken down the task into deciding what magical skills we want the Tri-Wizard Champions to have to use successfully. Then, we will try to come up with challenges to force them to use those.

"So far, we've been having a pretty hard time coming up with magical skills that we can agree on."

There were noises of agreement around the room. Snape reported next, "We've just been trying to come up with challenges and then we'll evaluate them according to how much magical knowledge they reveal.

"But frankly, we're not having much better luck than Minerva's group."

Professor Pomfrey's group had tried a different approach but didn't seem to be having much better luck.

After listening carefully, Dumbledore said, "Well, I'm declaring a holiday from this. But you must use the afternoon to work on your lesson plans."

Everyone groaned.

We finished lunch and gradually talk began to re-start.

The next day was a similar cycle. We briefly discussed taking a different tack from what we were doing the previous day but eventually decided that our best bet was just to keep on our original plan. It went better than the day before, and we came to a comprehensive list of skills before lunchtime—which we were not late for.

The following day, we started trying to come up with tasks to satisfy those skills. The easiest turned out to be one that had caused the most controversy before. Someone suggested that maybe we could test the logical abilities of champions by giving them a clue at the end of one task that would, if solved successfully, help with the next task. It seemed like a good idea but you had to know what the next task was to know what clue to provide. I suggested that the clue should have multiple layers like an onion. You solve the first and then you're faced with a puzzle at the next level and maybe a level below that.

We had a couple of ideas about the main challenges but none that we were happy with. So, we went back and decided to brainstorm about the resources that we had that we could turn into challenges. The ones that we came up with were the Forbidden Forest, the Loch with its monster, the castle itself with its hidden passages and rooms.

I said, "You know, the Forest has a herd of Centaurs. Maybe, we could involve them somehow in the task."

Sinistra sneered, "Good luck with that! They are fiercely jealous of their freedom. Any suggestion that they 'serve' humans by helping with a human competition would get you a couple of arrows shot your way."

"Ok. Ok. It was just an idea."

Then Flitwick reminded us that the Loch also had a colony of mer-people. That sparked a discussion about how to include them in the fun. I suggested that the mer-people could hide something of value that the Champions would have to find. The winner would be the one to find it.

Minerva's eyes lit up. She stood and began walking up and down. I reflected that the old adage that lovers begin to take on each other's characteristics might have something to it. Finally, she said, "What if each of the champions had a prize of their own that they had to find." More silence and walking followed by, "What if the prize wasn't a thing but a person—a close friend or relative that would be in apparent danger."

That received mixed reviews, but it had really sparked Minerva's enthusiasm, "No, no, we wouldn't put them in any real danger but there'd be a time limit and you get points for how much you beat the time limit."

That excited everyone's interest and we began to write up the detailed specifications for the challenge. We even included the puzzle clue idea. The champions would be given a clue that, when solved would tell them the essential nature of the next challenge.

Flitwick shouted, "A song!"

"What," a half-dozen voices asked.

"The clue will be a poem delivered in the form of a song."

The arithmancy professor whispered to me, "I knew he'd figure out a way for his choir to get involved."

Flitwick turned sharply and said, "I heard that. And I wasn't thinking of the school choir. I was thinking of . . of . . of the mer-people who would sing in Merish."

I asked, "Do any students anywhere study Merish?"

Flitwick frowned and then his face cleared, "We can provide a way to translate it into English—if you figure out what it is."

No one could find an objection to the idea. We finished composing the first draft of the proposal. Since it was close to lunch, I suggested that we sleep on it and re-look at it the next morning before submitting it.

We arrived at the Great Hall early and were pretty smug when the other teams dragged their way in. They were apparently still struggling with the assignment. We all were bursting with the desire to announce our success.

When Dumbledore arrived, he noticed our team's good spirits and asked, "Well, it looks like Team-McGonagall has some success that they might like to report."

She looked around at the table and seemed to make a decision about how to proceed. She said, "We've got a brain-storm that we need to do a little more work on before submitting."

Dumbledore nodded contemplatively. "Well, good luck. I hope it pans out."

That night I had a hard time getting to sleep. I was anxious to put the final polish on the proposal and submit it to Dumbledore. I think most of the team had the same problem sleeping because we all skipped breakfast and went directly to the room where we'd been meeting and attacked the plan.

It took a good bit longer than any of us thought. Every time we read a paragraph, someone thought of an objection to the way that it read. Most of the objections were legitimate, and we labored until noon.

Everyone was really anxious to submit it to Dumbledore at lunch, but we still had a couple of paragraphs to review. We all agreed to work straight through until we were finished whether we missed lunch (in addition to breakfast) or not.

The last couple of paragraphs turned out to be pretty easy and we arrived at the Great Hall about a quarter after noon. We probably looked pretty be-draggled having not gotten much sleep and missing breakfast. However, we were all beaming as Minerva took our final parchment up to Dumbledore and announced that we had finished our proposal.

He accepted it and unrolled a couple of inches of the scroll and read the abstract of the proposal. He nodded and smiled at one point. Then he rolled it up and said, "We'll see what the committee has to say about it. You've completed your assignment."

Meanwhile the rest of the teams were giving us the evil eye.

Then Dumbledore turned back to us and said, "Oh, one more thing. You know of course, that if this is accepted, you'll have to actually set up everything for this challenge."

Our faces fell, and the rest of the teams initially had smiles until it occurred to them that Dumbledore would be telling them the same when they finished their proposals.

After lunch as we headed back to our offices, Minerva smirked and told me, "There's another fine mess you've gotten us into."

I harrumphed and replied that I was no more responsible for the proposal than anyone else and probably less responsible than she was.

For us, the rest of the in-service period was more like the standard. I slept in late and had no trouble finishing my lesson plans before the students arrived.

The night before the students arrived, Dumbledore gave a little speech in which he usually announced last minute changes to plan for the term. He also made little announcements such as that the hall monitor schedule had been posted in the Teacher's Lounge.

But this time, after all those things he seemed ready to sit down when he announced, "Oh, yes. One more thing." Everyone groaned.

"You may have noticed that the post of Defense Against the Dark Arts has not been announced." He gazed around the table and said,

"We are greatly honored to announce that the post has been filled by the former Auror, Alastor Moody. I expect that everyone will go out of their way to make him welcome and help him learn the 'ropes' here at Hogwarts."

There was absolute silence for at least a minute. Then, I heard Sinistra whispering to Professor Vector, "Do you know what his nickname is?"

I didn't hear the rest of the conversation, but I didn't have to. I knew what his nickname was and why he had it.

The night that the Hogwarts Express arrived, I was with Minerva at the main entrance to Hogwarts where she greeted the first-years. She gave her standard speech, and we accompanied the first-years into the Great Hall. I was just thankful that I hadn't been with Haggrid when he was ferrying them across the lake. There was a storm brewing, and it hadn't broken yet, but it would soon.

The sorting went as usual, and Dumbledore was giving his normal speech of beginning of term announcements. He hadn't mentioned the new Defense Against the Dark Arts Teacher. What was going on? Well we found out quickly. The new DADA Teacher walked in dramatically. Mad-eye Moody swaggered in. Amazingly, he was carrying a flask and took a swig from it just before he sat.

After the banquet and the first-years had settled in, Minerva came down to my office. I offered her a drink, which she gladly accepted. She shook her head convulsively after taking a sip of Dewars, "At least I waited until the first-years were safely in bed."

"Yeah, I wonder if that is Moody's normal procedure or was he just doing it for effect."

"Effect?"

"Yeah, reinforcing the tough Auror reputation."

"The way to do that is in the class-room by teaching his students well. By the way, have you talked with Cedric recently?"

"No, why?"

She seemed to slither forward resting her elbows on my desk and gazing longingly into my eyes, "Just wondering if there were a chess tournament coming up that you might need some help with?"

"Well, you know, we don't have to be accompanying a player to go to a chess tournament."

She smiled wickedly and said, "I hadn't thought of that." She lifted herself slightly off the table, stretching her arms out, "Wonderful idea." She brought her arms down around my shoulders and pulled me into her embrace.

The next day, classes started. The beginning of term proceeded as normal, but I began to hear some strange reports. At first, they were merely overheard snippets of conversation. Then one day in class, a couple of fifth-year students were whispering at the back of the classroom. Without turning from the blackboard I announced, "Mr. George and Mr. Peters, please remain after class for detention assignment, and you may cease gossiping."

After class they showed up at my desk and I took out the pad of detention forms. I asked them, "Do you have a class right now?"

"No, sir."

"I don't either. Then you'll serve right now, here. What were the two of you discussing?"

They looked at each other trying to decide how much to reveal. They seemed to come to a silent decision. Peters was the spokesman. "Well, sir, it was just the Defense Against the Dark Arts class. Yesterday, Professor Moody, uh. . . " He hesitated, apparently afraid that he was snitching, but George poked him and he continued, "Well, Professor Moody demonstrated the Unforgivable Curses—IN CLASS."

I'd not heard of these before. "What do you mean, unforgivable curses?"

"Well, you know sir, the BIG THREE. Cruciatus, Imperious and . . ." He stopped, and neither George or he would name the last. I watched them for a few minutes.

Then I decided that I had to give them something to do, so I told them to write Hamlet's famous Soliloquy on the blackboard until they could recite it. George groaned, and Peters said, "Oh, Professor, do we have to?"

I assured them that they did. They spent a half hour trying to learn it and begged me to let the lines they were writing be enough. I relented slightly and let them recite it together, correcting each other's errors. On the second try they got it and I let them go.

That night, after dinner, Minerva and I were walking in the courtyard. I asked her what the BIG THREE were.

43

She stared at me a minute and then gasped, "You're talking about the Unforgivable Curses, right?"

I agreed.

"And you've not heard of them before?"

"No."

"Well, then, let's see. There's the Imperious Curse. It conquers the will of the victim and is used to make the victim a slave to the wishes of the curser.

"Then there's the Cruciatis curse. It simply inflicts terrible pain on the victim. Every nerve burns with pain. It seems like every square inch of .. ."

"Yes, yes, you know that I'm intimately familiar with that one. Go on. What's the last?" My skin was crawling at the memory of that curse.

"The Avra Kadavra curse—the killing curse. There is no counter jinx for that one."

I nodded. She asked where I'd heard of those terrible curses.

"Oh, a couple of my students were whispering during class. It turned out that they were gossiping about how Professor Moody was demonstrating them."

"Yes, I've heard that too. I think it must be true."

"Is Professor Dumbledore aware of this?"

"He must be. There are very few things that go on at Hogwarts that he isn't aware of."

"Why are they called 'Unforgiveable'?"

Minerva shook her head at me, 'I would have thought that that would have been obvious. You get sent straight to Azkaban for those. Don't pass 'Go'. Don't collect two hundred galleons."

"You know about Monopoly?"

Minerva stared at me, "What's Monopoly? Haven't we played Trip to Gringott's?"

"Not that I can remember."

"Well, the next time we're visiting Maggie, we need to get that board game out and play it with her and Beryl.

I wondered how closely they'd copied the Muggle Monopoly, so I asked, "Each player gets a token that represents a means of getting around. I'd guess a broom, a port key, uh.."

"Yes, you've got the idea. There's a Fireplace, a flying carpet, a Disapparating wizard. I forget. There's a couple of others."

"Maybe a train, like the Hogwarts Express?"

"Yes. That's one of them. You have played it before."

"No. I'm just really good at guessing."

She stared at me doubtfully, but didn't say anything.

The next day after lunch, I caught up with Moody, which wasn't too hard. One of his legs was artificial. As we walked—apparently to his office—I asked him if he'd been using the Unforgivable Curses lately.

He stopped and stared at me searchingly for a moment. "Why laddy, do you fancy a private demonstration?"

"Well, no. I was just wondering if that's on the syllabus for your course." We'd resumed walking. He considered the question and when we reached the door to his office, he asked me to come in and take the weight off.

We entered the office, and he literally took the weight off. He removed his artificial limb and asked me if I'd fancy a drink. I didn't.

Since he didn't seem about to open the conversation, I did. "If you don't mind a personal question, I've been wondering about the prostheses. You don't see them much in the wizarding world. Usually the healers can re-grow what people loose."

He stretched and said, "No, I don't mind the question. Those are old war wounds. You see ordinary injuries can be healed but these are loses that are all occupational injuries. When a powerful dark wizard sets out to injure you, you stay injured. In both the cases, I had to have the part amputated. It was that or die."

"Hmmm, I said.

"Yes, hmmm. I have that in common with Potter."

That comment threw me. I started to ask what he had in common with Potte, but then I realized what he meant, "You're talking about Potter's scar. It will never heal, right?"

"Right. It's a little bit more difficult dealing with a lost leg than with a scar that makes you famous—or maybe even sexy."

I was surprised at the show of, well, bitterness? But I tried to keep the reaction off my face. "So, who gave you those wounds?"

"Oh, this one," patting where his leg used to be, "came from Belatrix LeStrange. She can be nasty when she puts her mind to it. And she does like putting her mind to it.

"And the eye. Yes, the eye. I was a young Auror when that happened. You've heard, no doubt, of the wizard, Grindelwald?"

I had to admit that I hadn't.

"Oh, that's a story worth hearing. It goes back before I went to Hogwarts as a student. I suppose even before I was born, when you come to it.

"Grindelwald started out, as all dark wizards do, as a promising young student. He went to Durmstrang Academy."

My puzzled look took him by surprise, "You mean to say that you don't even know about Durmstrang?"

I had to admit that I hadn't.

"Well, where have you been? Never mind. That's your story, not mine. Grindelwald attended that institution of higher learning. It's always been more, shall we say, tolerant of the Dark Arts. They used to have a class that taught the Dark Arts. They also had a class that taught how to resist them. They were equal opportunity teachers.

"Anyway, Grindelwald went to Durmstrang. He was a spectacular student. He formed a 'club', consisting of the best and brightest people who later became dark wizards. This club had a motto —'The Greater Good.' The idea was that they would become the great wizards and would do good for everyone—even, ultimately, the Muggles.

"Well, he was graduated and discovered his greatest ally. For a short while he and his buddy plotted the overthrow of the world wizarding order. Many believe that the dynamic duo together were the two most powerful wizards of this age—possibly the two most powerful of any age.

He hesitated, watching me carefully, seeming to size me up and then he proceeded, "And do you realize that you are acquainted with his ally?"

I instinctively replied, "No." How was that possible? I quickly searched my list of acquaintances.

He winked his "mad eye". That was really disconcerting. "That ally is here in this castle, this very moment."

My eyes widened and I concentrated and came up with a name, "You can't mean Snape?"

Moody laughed a sort of choked wheezy laugh. "No. He was in diapers when this happened."

And the answer occurred to me, "You mean Dumbledore, don't you?"

"Of course, I mean Dumbledore." he spit it out contemptuously. "He had just graduated from Hogwarts himself. He ate up all that 'Greater Good' stuff."

"But what happened?"

"Oh, you can't fool Dumbledore for very long. He quickly began to realize that this Greater Good stuff was for the masses of wizards and that Grindelwald just wanted to rule the world. The two split up after a little battle." I must have been staring because he quickly added, "Oh, nothing titanic, just a little scrap to convince the both of them that they'd never work together again. Certainly, it wasn't anything like the final battle."

"You saw that fight?"

Moody laughed and it seemed to be full of bitterness. He said, "Saw it? I was part of it, in a funny way."

"Well?"

"I'm coming to that. Anyway, Grindelwald took his lesser followers and went to play with them. He was more honest than the Dark Lord. He drew a circle of powerful dark wizards to himself. He offered them power in the new regime.

"When he'd gotten enough followers, they assaulted the magical governments of the European countries. He started in the east and worked his way west. He destroyed the seats of government and carried his assault ever westward.

"When he reached Durmstrang, there was a pitched battle. The governments of Europe had sent their Aurors there and they lost. The casualties on both sides were grievous. We didn't send Aurors, but we wished that we had.

"Then an amazing thing happened. Dumbledore, then a professor here at Hogwarts, issued a challenge to Grindelwald for one on one battle. It was to happen on 'neutral' ground at the other great school of wizarding of Europe—Beaux Batons. It was to be wizard to wizard. Winner would take all.

"It was to be a lonely duel with no one else present. But I was a little bit of a rebel myself and I was determined to be there—just in case Dumbledore lost. I disobeyed orders and snuck into the grounds on foot. I had to slip past Dumbledore's hastily erected barriers.

"What I saw was astounding. The two faced each other. Dumbledore counted to three. On the stroke after three, the two began a duel that I think has never been equaled. The two started by testing each other's defenses. I would have used an instantaneous frontal assault with everything I had, hoping to take Grindelwald by surprise. Had I done that it would have been disaster.

"Instead, each tested the defenses of the other in little ways. Dumbledore flung a single petal of a single flower at him. It came to within an inch of Grindelwald's nose and remained there, unmoving. But I knew that there was a powerful struggle going on over that petal. Neither could move it closer to Grindelwald or further away. In a few seconds it simply dis-integrated under the forces being used on it.

"Then Grindelwald lifted a small stone from the ground in front of Dumbledore and spun it around and around. A vortex of wind formed and approached Dumbledore. In this case the vortex became larger and larger and faster and faster, but stood motionless at Dumbledore's feet until it too dissolved into nothing.

"The two began circling each other ever watchful for a sign of a slip of attention. First one and then the other thought they detected it. Then titanic forces struck the other's defenses. The very space between them rippled and distorted from the forces invoked by both. But neither yielded.

"Grindelwald launched an attack that I thought would end the fight. The forces had started a thunderstorm above. Drops of rain began to fall. Grindelwald seemed to seize one and suspended it before him. It began to glow, brighter and brighter. It became an intense, searing, burning blue light that flung itself at Dumbledore. It flew like a thunderbolt but shattered about a foot from Dumbledore's face. Fragments rebounded every direction. One of them struck my left eye. I had been prepared for something like that and had a shield up, which I strengthened as much as I could just before the fragment struck it, but it went through my shield as though it didn't exist. It hit my eye, and my senses were overwhelmed by pain and light and the sound of thunder, as though I were in the heart of a lightning stoke.

"I didn't see what happened next, but somehow Dumbledore had overcome Grindelwald. He was kneeling before Dumbledore and asked for a quick death. Instead, Dumbledore took the proffered wand and told him to stand. Then the two disapparated. I fainted.

"When I awoke, Dumbledore was standing over me as I lay in a hospital bed in Paris. I realized that I had only one eye. Dumbledore was saying something about how foolish and lucky I was. After I had recovered further, Dumbledore offered to help me fashion a replacement eye. I thanked him profusely, but insisted that I would like to try my hand at that myself.

"I did succeed in creating an artificial eye that is in some ways better than my original, but I would happily trade it for my real eye in a second."

I asked about his leg.

He smiled for the first time since he started telling his story. "That is a story that I never tell."

I left his office feeling that I had no standing to critique his teaching style.

The Tournament

Shortly after that, events happened that took my mind off Mad-Eye for a while. The next Sunday evening, at supper, there was an unusual announcement. Dumbledore told all students and teachers about the TriWizard Tournament. During the announcement, in walked the Headmaster of Durmstrang—Victor Karkaroff along with a couple of dozen students and Madame Maxime of the Beaux Baton Academie along with a group of her students.

Dumbledore explained about the revised rules and the fact that any student over the age of seventeen could apply to be school champion. The application simply consisted of a piece of parchment with your name and school on it placed into the Goblet of Fire. Dumbledore had devised a way of preventing those under seventeen from being able to submit their name. It seemed foolproof.

Afterwards, there was a reception of all the guests and all the students and staff of Hogwarts. I was fascinated by Madame Maxime who was clearly and easily the tallest woman, indeed the tallest person I had ever seen or heard of. It was difficult judging her height—it was so much greater than mine. But I roughed it out to be between ten and eleven feet. Yes, I think she could actually look down into a regulation height basketball hoop standing flat-footed.

There seemed to be a general reaction to her that consisted of wanting to get a better look at her, but also not wanting to actually get too close to her. Consequently, the only people actually talking to her seemed to be Dumbledore and the other Headmaster and a couple of high ranking teachers, including Minerva.

I decided that I would break the ice and walked up to the group that consisted of Maxime, Snape and Karkaroff. I stepped up and decided

I'd make an impression by using a little French, "Bon Soir, Madame Maxime. Je m'appelle Jacque Wendt."

She replied, "Il est bon de rencontrer ici l'autre qui parle français."

"Je ne parle pas tres forte, mais je voudrais vous faire bienvenue."

"Merci, peutetre, nous pouvons parler en Anglais?"

"Merci. Yes. Thank you."

Snape immediately helped by saying, "When Wendt here is finished showing off his French, perhaps we could go back to our discussion of the Tournament."

"I'd like to know how you'll continue to run your schools in your absence."

"I have my deputy who I am confident can run Beaux Batons in my absence, as I am sure Professor Karkaroff has his own, Of course, Dumbledore has Madame McGonagall.." Karkaroff nodded brusquely.

Another question occurred to me, "Madame, is that form of address purely honorary or is there a Monsieur in your life."

Snape interjected, "Be careful how you answer, Wendt here may have a new conquest in mind."

"Mais, non. I don't have the husband or the—how would you say it—seche-coeur in my life."

"Is that because you can't find," And there I stopped because I was about to ask if she couldn't find someone who rose to her stature of accomplishment.

She was ready to finish the sentence for me. "Perhaps, the word that you were thinking of is height?" Her face and voice had turned definitely unfriendly.

"Actually, the phrase that I was going to say, was 'Professional Stature'."

Snape intervened to help, "As I say, Mr. Wendt is perhaps looking for a new conquest."

She seemed somewhat softened and asked, "Do you have a romantic conquest?"

I was happy to change subject, "Actually, I'd like to make a minor correction. It's Mademoiselle McGonagall. It would be more accurate to say that she has a conquest rather than I have a conquest."

She stared at me somewhat incredulously, but quickly recovered, "I see. Then, the English sometimes share the French appreciation for the mature woman complait?"

"Well, I'm not actually English. I'm American and I, at least, have an appreciation for one particular mature woman."

I turned to Karkaroff, "Headmaster, I'm not familiar with any of the schools outside of England. Where is yours located?"

Immediately, Karkaroff turned away and started a conversation with Snape. At that moment Minerva came up and joined us. She whispered in my ear, "I see that you've gotten off on good footing making our guests welcome." With that she started to drag me off by my arm, but Madame Maxime interrupted.

"Ah, Mademoiselle McGonagall," she emphasized the title as she spoke it, "I did not understand that you have the 'boy friend'?"

McGonagall turned back with a large fake smile and said, "Well, some might wonder whether I have him or he has me. I hope you will excuse us as I need to have a little discussion about hospitality with him."

After we were out of earshot she hissed, "What in the world did you say to upset Karkaroff?"

"I'm not sure. I was just starting to talk to him and I admitted to ignorance about other magical schools and I asked him where his was."

She rolled her eyes and said, "Aren't you aware that magical schools are hidden most carefully?"

"Well, I'm aware that Hogwarts is and that's about it."

She kept walking me further away and went on, "ALL magical schools are hidden from Muggles AND other wizards as a safety feature and to keep their secrets, uh, Secret!"

"OK, I get it. It's impolite to ask where a teacher's school is."

"Impolite! To say the least!"

"Hey, Maxime is the tallest person I've ever heard of. What is it with her? There must be a story behind that."

'You are a regular faux pas magnet, you know? How is it that you can't pick a topic of conversation without finding something to be impolite about."

I was beginning to feel a bit defensive, "Well, you know it's kind of hard to ignore. But seriously, what gives?"

Minerva looked around to see if we were out of earshot of everyone. Then she said, "Look, this is something to be kept strictly _sub rosa._ She has to be descended from Giants."

I wasn't sure that I'd heard right. Had she actually said "Giants". So, I asked.

"Yes, I said Giants. There have been Giants around for a long time. Possibly they were descended from what you call Neanderthals. I have no idea. But yes, there are Giants. They can mate with humans. And you know someone else who is descended from Giants."

I had a sinking feeling that I knew whom she was talking about. "Haggrid, right?"

"Yes, Haggrid. We have no doubt about him. He went to Hogwarts and we have records of who his parents were."

I thought about that for a moment. "Since she was touchy about her height, I suppose that she doesn't want it officially known that she's a descendant of Giants?"

"Right. They are pretty nasty people."

"And no one really wants to admit that they have Giants in their family tree?"

"No."

By this time the reception was breaking up and I asked Minerva where everyone was staying.

"Oh, either in the ship from Durmstrang or the great carriage from Beaux Batons."

"OK. Let's go to my office to continue this discussion."

When we arrived, I offered liquid refreshment and Minerva accepted. Then I asked the question that even I wouldn't have at the reception, "OK. Everybody seems to have a past—sometimes a really distant past. Does Karkaroff have something to hide?"

She pursed her lips for a couple of moments and took a good swallow of Dewars and finally said, "I suppose it's not really a secret, but he'd rather it wasn't a subject of conversation." But she still hesitated.

"Well?" I prodded.

"Karkaroff was a Deatheater."

That was jaw-dropping. "A real live Deatheater?"

"Yes."

"Why isn't he in Azkaban? Or at least, why is he the Headmaster of a school?"

Minerva swirled her drink for a moment and gazed into it. Then she began, "You have to understand how it was in the bad old days. No one knew whom to trust. Lots of people were under the Imperious Curse, and lots of people claimed to be under the Imperious Curse.

"It was all very murky, and no one knew whom to trust. Anyone who would step forward to reveal names that were verifiably Deatheaters were treated specially."

"You mean anyone who slunk forward."

"Sometimes it was that. Sometimes it was an act of great courage. Anyone who double crossed the Dark Lord had much to fear."

"Go ahead."

"Well, there was this deal that was made with many Deatheaters. If they would reveal fellow Deatheaters that lead to arrests and if they would promise to no longer act as Deatheaters, they would get a conditional pardon."

"Yes, conditional—on the condition that the terms of the agreement were all kept.

"Anyway, Karkaroff was one of those. He spent a little time in Azkaban and then was anxious to deal. He was crafty though. He tried to use old names—ones that were either dead or had already been discovered. That wasn't good enough.

"He finally released a big name—a fresh name—Bartaemius Crouch."

I thought about that. "I've heard that name and recently, haven't I?"

"Oh, yes, you have. He's the Minister for International Wizarding Cooperation."

"HE was a Deatheater?"

"No, he wasn't. But his son was. You may remember the name because of the work he did on the Quidditch World Cup or maybe his involvement with the TriWizard Tournament."

"Wow! Then these two guys have a lot of reasons to hate or fear each other's guts." I chewed on that in silence for a few minutes.

Minerva added, "Oh, one more thing. It wasn't a big headline in the *Prophet*, probably because of Bartaemius asking the *Prophet* to keep it low-key. But his son died in Azkaban this summer, and his wife died about the same time as well. The rumor is that she was quite sick anyway, but the death of her only child surely had something to do with it."

"I'm surprised the *Prophet* was willing to soft-pedal that story. There are so many connections. They must be seething."

Minerva looked at me quizzically, "I didn't think about it, but you're right. They will be looking for some kind of juicy story out of the Tri-Wizard Tournament to make up for their lost opportunity with the Crouch's."

"Great! That means that they will be snooping around here all term."

Minerva corrected me to "all year".

I went back to the original question, "So, you let Deatheaters off?"

"Well, I didn't, but the Ministry let them off. And I suppose I would have let off some of the ones they let off."

"God! I hope we never get in that place again." On that somber note, we finished our drinks and said "Good Night."

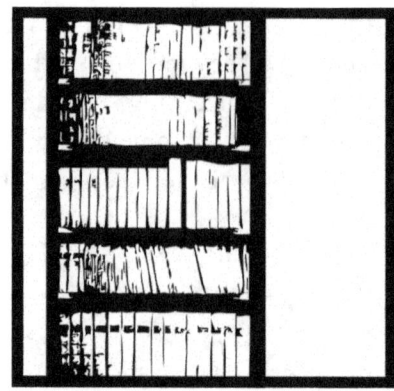

The First Task

Minerva and I met a few days afterwards. She said that she had a bad feeling about the Goblet of Fire. I objected that with Dumbledore's protection, it was foolproof.

Minerva stopped dead in her tracks and looked at me, "You know, if you make something fool-proof, they'll just invent a better fool."

I had to add, "I suppose you're thinking of the Weasley twins." She nodded and we continued our walk.

"Well," I asked, "do you think that we should set up a watch to prevent at least that pair of fools from making a monumental act of foolishness?"

She walked a few more steps and shook her head.

I pressed further, 'If you were trying to fool the spell, how would you do it?"

She said, "Come to my office."

"OK. Sounds good."

We got there, and she said that she didn't want to be overheard. I asked her how she would do it. "I would probably use Polyjuice potion."

I had an immediate objection. "But let's say that you were, oh , Fred Weasley."

"Heaven Forbid"

"Yeh, yeh. Anyway, you're Fred, and you use PolyJuice Potion to impersonate, oh, let's say, his brother Percy."

"But Percy's graduated."

"Sure, sure, but Percy's clearly old enough to compete. Anyway, Percy's card gets pulled out of the proverbial hat. Now what happens?"

Minerva ran a hand through her hair and said, "I guess Percy would have to compete."

"Which Percy, the real one or the fake one?"

"I suppose it would be the real one, unless the false showed up, still using PolyJuice potion, and the real one didn't."

"I agree. Pretty big risk to take."

"But big risks have never deterred the twins before."

Actually, the twins did try to confound the Goblet, but it didn't work out so well. I was talking to Snape at lunch the next day and asked him if he'd heard about the twins. Snape cracked one of his very rare smiles and said, "Not only did I hear about them, I saw them. They're down at the Gryffindor table right now. They're mostly recovered, but you can still catch the remains of their attempt to beat Dumbledore."

"Just what did they try?"

"Oh, a simple aging spell."

I finished lunch quickly and walked out via the Gryffindor table. There were the twins with some remaining streaks of silver in their red hair. I smiled at them, and they just stuck out their tongues.

Things had been going well. Right up to the big banquet when the champions were to be announced. Minerva and I had been having a little friendly bet about who would be the Hogwarts champion. I was betting on a Ravenclaw whose name was Daniel LeBeau. He was just about the 2nd smartest student that I'd taught at Hogwarts. Minerva was betting on a Slytherin—Michelle Corbin. She was the most skilled at transfiguration that Minerva had ever taught.

I kept telling Minerva not to trust people who are good at your specialty. Anyway, we were in the Great Hall sitting together when the champions were announced. First out of the Goblet of Fire was the Beaux Batons student, Fleur Delacort. Then came the Durmstrang champion, the Seeker for the Polish team in the World Cup, Victor Krum. So far, so good. The last was Cedric Diggery, of HufflePuff. We all gave him a good round of applause. And then something totally unexpected happened. A FOURTH scrap of Parchment came out of the Goblet.

Minerva and I stared, unbelieving, but there it was. Dumbledore caught it, opened it, and read—Harry Potter. Dumbledore called all the Champions back to the Teacher's Lounge and invited the sponsors and the heads of houses to join them.

Afterwards, he called me in. I arrived at the Teacher's Lounge. Dumbledore gazed around at all of us in the room, the Heads of House and me, and demanded, "What do you have to say about this?"

We looked as innocent as we felt and I said, "What are you talking about? Why would we want to put a fourth Champion out?"

He looked from one to the other of us and just said, "How did it happen then?"

I asked—quite reasonably, I thought—"There was to be one champion from each school? Was there a second from Hoggswart OR was there a fourth school?"

He opened up the scrap of parchment that was all that was left of Potter's submission. He read aloud, "Harry Potter, VMI."

I responded, "The only VMI that I know of is a boys school in Virginia, in the States. It stands for the Virginia Military Institute."

Minerva added, "There is a school of wizarding in the United States called VMI. It stands for Victoria Magical Institute."

I frowned, "Is there any other wizarding school that could have initials VMI?"

No one else seemed to know of any.

Dumbledore said, "That was what Professor Moody thought. Someone confunded the Goblet into thinking that there was a fourth school and that Potter was the only student submitted from that school."

I asked, "OK. Who could have pulled this off and had access to the Goblet?"

Snape said, "I could have done it. Probably all the heads of house could have. Professor Moody surely could have. As a matter of fact, the only person in this room who couldn't have done it asked the question."

"Convenient, eh?

Moody asked, "So, you think that someone here, in this room, is responsible?"

I pointed out, "Not necessarily. We have Karkaroff and Madame Maxime as well."

Dumbledore asked, "What would their motivation be to add additional competition?"

I thought it was obvious, but I answered, "I think they wouldn't picture Potter as significant competition for the likes of Krum or even Delacourt. BUT, his addition would cause lots of consternation for the legitimate Hogwarts champion. But, I don't think they would do it."

Snape shook his head as though trying to clear it, "So, let's see. You've just argued in favor of Karkaroff and Maxime as guilty parties, and NOW you say that you don't think that they did it?"

"Yes, they're possibles but I don't think they'd do something like that because I don't get the impression that they have the ingenuity to think of it.

"But that leaves us with the people in this room." I could see an objection forming on Dumbledore's lips, so I quickly went ahead, "I don't say that people outside the room are absolutely incapable of it, but they have even less reason to do it than the people in this room do."

Minerva asked, "But you think some in this room have reason to?

"I do. Think. Lately, Gryffindor has been dominating the other houses. What better way to have some revenge than to embarrass Gryffindor just as it has been embarrassing the other houses. This is a scandal,l and it looks bad for Gryffindor no matter how you slice it."

Snape strode up to me and said, "Are you accusing me of doing this?"

I held my ground and stared back at him, "No. But there are several things that I think we can all agree about:

- Potter didn't do this himself. He's not got the wizarding chops.
- No Gryffindor would do it. If a Gryffindor were to add another Gryffindor to the list of champions, they'd select the best person available, which I think you'll agree isn't Potter.
- Just about the only people capable of this are in this room.

Dumbledore stroked his beard and said, "I'm afraid that Mr. Wendt is correct. Someone here now wants to embarrass Gryffindor and wants Potter to do it."

Snape sat and stared at the floor. Moody seemed speechless. Madame Sprout said, "Well, that leaves Hufflepuff out."

Dumbledore said, "I'm afraid not. You didn't know who would be selected. You might still want to embarrass Gryffindor." Her mouth dropped open for a moment and closed.

Snape then said, "OK. Then how do you propose to find out who did it?"

I had to admit that I didn't have an idea.

He taunted me, "What? The great Wendt without an idea?"

I thought a moment. In the meantime Dumbledore asked, "Is anyone out by your calculations?"

"Well, I think you're out, because despite any preferences you might have of one house over another, this reflects badly on the school. And if you wanted to improve the chances of some Hogwart champion to win, you'd certainly not choose Potter."

Snape said dryly, "Point taken."

I went on, "Minerva's out because she wouldn't want to embarrass Gryffindor."

Snape sniped, "And, of course, because she's your sweetie."

I frowned at Snape, "And because she wouldn't want to embarrass the school.

"And, of course, I'm out because I haven't the slightest capability of pulling it off."

Moody said, "I suppose that lets me out as well. I don't have a horse in this race."

"Oh, not so hasty. Did you attend Hogwarts?"

"Well, yes."

"And what was your house?"

Minerva volunteered, "Weren't you in Ravenclaw?"

Moody said, "Yes."

"Well, that might be motivation, but I doubt it. Very few people would hold a school grudge through an entire career and into retirement. But you may have other motivations."

Moody was, well, moody and just muttered under his breath.

Snape, sat again, and asked, "Well, what do you propose?"

"Well, I suggest that everyone keep an eye on everyone else. Someone who would put a name in a hat and endanger the person for the sake of a grudge would go further. We need to be watchful for evidence of helping or hindering Potter.

Snape asked, "I get it about hindering Potter, but why do we need to watch out for signs of helping Potter?"

"Well, for one thing, it's hard to tell helping and hindering apart until after you've observed something. Besides that, the guilty party may feel some of that guilt and want to minimize the likelihood of seriously hurting him."

Dumbledore said, "I don't like this. Living under suspicion introduces real problems for running a school well. Don't you have another idea for how we can find out the responsible person?"

"I'm afraid not. I wish I did. But the problems this causes have been introduced, and we've got to live with the consequences, like it or not."

Nobody else had anything to add, so we went our separate ways.

Minerva said, "Well, here's another fine mess that we've gotten into, eh Olly?"

"I didn't want to admit it to the rest of them, but I really don't think this house jealousy thing is the real reason for what's happened to Potter. Anyway, we have to have some sort of working hypothesis and even if it isn't the real reason, I think nobody else could have done the deed. Do you agree?"

"I suppose."

I was hesitant to ask the question that I was about to put to her, but I had to, "Do you suppose that Potter himself could have done it. I really hardly know him. Snape would probably say that it's just the sort of thing that his father would have done had he had the opportunity."

"No. I sometimes wonder how well I know him myself, despite the fact that he's in my house. If you saw the look on his face just after his name came out, you'd hardly believe that he could have done it."

"Well, I like to believe that people act out of self-interest, and it's hard to see how being in the tournament is in his self-interest. But you never know how people are going to regard these things."

Neither of us felt like frivolity on this night, so we went our separate ways when we came to the stairs to the Gryffindor tower.

⌒⌒

A couple of days later, I was sitting in the Teacher's Lounge, grading papers. Snape had entered the room with Moody and was arguing with him. It didn't surprise me, but I was curious nonetheless and listened carefully. Snape appeared to be complaining about how Moody had cursed one of his students. I couldn't believe that Snape wouldn't have taken the matter directly to Dumbledore if there weren't some extenuating circumstance. I hunched down in my armchair and strained my ears to hear more, but that was all that I could make out.

Finally, Snape left the lounge apparently without having gotten satisfaction. Moody seemed to be fairly happy with himself though. I decided that I'd look up Moody later in the day, pretending to have heard a rumor rather than overhearing a conversation.

That evening after dinner, I approached Moody and asked him about a rumor that I'd heard concerning him cursing a student. He was gruff as usual, but I pressed him about it. He agreed to tell me the story in my office.

After we arrived, he did a short walking tour of my room, examining the bookshelves, the desk, and the fireplace, of all things, before taking the proffered red leather chair, "An interesting office. I always wondered what a Squibb's office would be like. Especially what books he'd have."

"Well, are you intrigued or bored?"

"A little of both. Lots of novels, plays, some poetry, as I'd expect—boring. But you seem to be interested in what the Muggles call Science as well. That is interesting. How does a Squibb become interested in a Muggle study?"

I shrugged. "Sorry to give you a boring answer, but I was an orphan. I was raised by an aunt and uncle who were Muggles. As a matter of fact, all my close relatives were Muggles. I didn't have an idea that I might have magical roots until a distant relative suggested to my 'parents' that I go to an American school of magic.

"It never went anywhere on either side. My aunt and uncle were opposed to it, and the American magic school was not really interested in having a student who couldn't learn any of the magic arts. They might have relented had my aunt and uncle been big donors but they weren't. Consequently, I had a traditional Muggle education including college and graduate school."

"Interesting. So, you're somewhat like Potter. How did your parents die—if I'm not being too nosy?"

"No, you're not. My parents and I were visiting family who lived in Los Angeles. The family was non-magical, and we were going to a park called Disneyland. Because my relatives were non-magical, we were all in a car. We were driving on the main Los Angeles freeway. A truck driver, who had been driving for twenty hours straight tried to pull into our lane. It hit the car and pretty much destroyed it. My parents and my cousin who was driving were all killed instantly. The rest of us were injured.

"I came out of the hospital a couple of weeks later, but never really had much memory of the accident." I stopped and then finished, "My parents had died in the car crash."

Moody stared at me a minute and said, "Sorry to hear it. Well, I see that your floo connection has been used a few times."

"Oh, yes. Some of the other teachers are kind enough to take me to town via floo when I have an errand or two to do—you know, Christmas shopping, banking, that sort of thing."

"Kind of them."

"Yes, but you were going to tell me about the incident with Snape's student."

He barked a short little laugh, "Yes. I was, wasn't I?

"Well, there's not much to tell. Mr. Malfoy was about to curse Mr. Potter when Potter's back was turned. It was both despicable and against school regs. I just transfigured Malfoy into a ferret. I thought he might be more comfortable as the animal that he most resembles."

I couldn't help laughing out loud! It took me a moment to regain my breath. "Did you say a ferret?"

"Yes. So."

"Oh, I have to admit that I've had temptation once in a while to do something drastic like that with Malfoy and the Weasley twins, but I never imagined that someone would do it." I was on the verge of returning to a laughing jag. "Oh, let's see. Would you like something to drink?"

He shrugged and lifted his flask, which he seemed always to have with him. "OK, I'll take that as a 'no', but I'm going to pour myself a shot of whiskey." I did and returned to him, "But really, you could have done other things—maybe used the petrificus totalis spell or something else?"

"Oh, that was what came to mind. I didn't have time to think it out. Besides, that seemed perfectly appropriate. I wanted to convince him that he should never do that again. I think I made an impression."

"I'd say so. At least that would have made an impression on me."

I grimaced as I turned to a subject that would not be pleasant. "You know, Dumbledore has really given you a lot of slack. I don't mean to offend, but I can't think of another teacher that he would let drink. Uh. whatever it is that you drink in front of the kids. Now, you've transfigured a student—even a moron like Malfoy—to a ferret is really pushing the envelope."

Moody, got up and seemed to be stretching his wooden leg, "Well, laddie, Dumbledore was lucky to get me to teach Defense. There probably wasn't anybody else in the world who would've taken that job. He was lucky to get me." Here, he looked directly at me and finished, "And he knows it."

A question that just popped into my mind surprised me so much that I just blurted it out, "Who do you think put Potter's name into the Goblet?"

It seemed to take him by surprise. He sat again and looked around, as though an answer would come out of a wall or the floor. His mad eye was still roving around, seemingly looking for an answer, but he said, "I don't know. I don't think that a student could have, but what teacher would have, I can't say."

I just shook my head and said, "I've just got a bad feeling about it. Something bad is going to happen, but I don't know how to attack the problem. And I think someone should."

He just opened his hands, palm up, as if to say that he had nothing to offer. That seemed to sum it up.

The *Prophet* Strikes Again

For the next couple of weeks, things were quiet. That is, except for the *Daily Prophet* and other newspapers and magazines sending people to interview the champions, the heads of the schools and just about everyone else. Most publications put these on the sports page, but the *Prophet* had a feature story every week that was on the front page.

Their main correspondent was Rita Skeeter. She even interviewed me one time. She found me on the way to class. I put her off until I had a break in classes. She tried to convince me to cancel class that one day, but I refused.

"Oh, come on. The kids will love you for canceling class."

"It's a good thing they don't pay my salary. I'm not going to let this commotion keep them from getting the education they deserve."

She pouted at that and took my arm, wanting to pull me aside. I looked down at the hand on my forearm in disbelief. She was persistent, but I simply said, "Hands." Then she released me,and I went on to class, but I promised that she could see me after my 3 PM class, in my office. She smiled at that and let me go.

When I got back to my office, I was surprised to see that she had broken in. I normally keep my office locked because I keep exams and current student papers there. She was sitting in my chair. She seemed to be perusing my current copy of *Scientific american*. I harrumphed, and she looked up but was not the least apologetic about having broken into my office.

"Are you considering taking up a new career as a cat burglar?" I asked her.

"Oh, don't be a party-pooper. The public has a right to know."

"They don't have a right to know what I had for lunch." She had been rummaging around in my waste basket and had pulled out my brown bag that had had my lunch in it.

"Oh, you'd be surprised what they have a right to know. Now, what is this Scienterrific American magazine that you read?"

I walked around the desk and pushed her feet off my desk and said, "If you want to interview me, sit in the red leather chair and I'll sit at MY desk in MY chair."

She pouted, got up and walked around. As she did, she asked, "Do you mind if I use a Quick-Quotes™ pen?"

"Yes, I do mind if you use a Quick-Quotes™ pen. Please use one of my quills."

She stared at me and then frowned, "But, I always use a . . . "

"Yes, I know, I know, but if you want to interview me, you'll have to humor me."

She didn't seem particularly excited about that, but she took one of my quills and started to scratch on her parchment. "Well, this is just background and none of it may get into the paper. I don't care how interesting you think it sounds."

"That's just fine with me. I rather hope it doesn't.

"By the way, would you like something to drink? I have some bottled water."

She sighed, "I suppose it's too early in the day for something stronger?"

"Yes, during school, I never drink anything harder until after dinner."

She accepted water with thanks and marveled at the idea of water in bottles. Then she reflected, "I suppose Squibbs can't just conjure a glass of water?"

"Right."

She stared at me again for a minute before going on, "How well do you know the contestants?"

"Practically not at all. I'd never seen LaFleur or Krum before the day they arrived and their Headmasters keep them pretty well isolated from everyone else." As I said that, I realized that it wasn't strictly true. "Oh, one correction, I did see Krum in the World Cup final game."

"What do you think of him?"

"Well, he's a great flyer and Seeker, but outside of that I don't know anything."

She laughed and said, "No kidding, he's as hard as nails. I couldn't get him to say anything except 'Yes', 'No' and the occasional 'Maybe'. Are you sure you don't know anything more?"

"Yep".

"What about Potter? You must have had him in a class or two?"

"Well, actually, no."

"No! Isn't your class required? AND what is it that you teach anyway?"

"My class is required, but not in any particular year. Eventually, Dumbledore is thinking of making two years of it required, but at the moment, it's just required one year and is optional an additional year. And it's English Literature."

She stared again. It was beginning to seem like she'd never had an interview that went more differently than she expected. She eventually asked, "English Literature! What has that to do with Magic?"

"Nothing and Everything."

"Do you enjoy being irritating?" She crossed her legs and her attitude.

"Look. Obviously, English Literature won't give students any new spells or charms or whatever. But, Dumbledore thinks that English Literature has a lot to do with forming character and character has a lot to do with whether his students use magic well or poorly."

Rita's patience seemed to be reaching an end. Her next question was sharp. "Is it true that you're a Squibb?" Before I could answer her, she went on, "You know if this interview keeps going this way, you might find yourself in a front page *Prophet* story about the Squibb at Hogwarts."

I hesitated a moment. I didn't want to get Filch in trouble, but then, I decided that I'd keep the focus on me. "Go ahead. All the students know I'm a Squibb. AND, more to the point, all the parents know that. I don't care if the rest of the wizarding world knows that I'm a Squibb. This may be my Andy Warhol moment."

She stared again, "Andy Asshole!"

I corrected, "Andy Warhol was an artist who once said that everyone would have fifteen minutes of fame sometime in their lives. I'm just saying that that might be my fifteen minutes."

"Why don't I know about this artist?"

I shrugged, "Maybe because you don't have an art column."

She nodded and muttered, "Probably it."

I found myself wrapping up the interview, "Well, if there's nothing else?"

"You haven't told me anything about Cedric."

I stopped for a quick 5 count to regain my composure. Then, I started carefully, "I do know a good bit about him. I'm his. . ." I hesitated as I tried to figure out what our relationship was and finally said, "his chess mentor. He's an amazing chess prodigy."

"Are you a chess expert yourself?"

I had to think how I'd answer this. I decided it would be better to give a brief history of our chess experiences together. "Not really. As a matter of fact, I discovered his chess ability by watching him play another student on the Hogwarts Express. At that point he was probably a better chess player than I've ever been or ever will be.

"It was almost the first time he'd played a game, but he was clearly better than his opponent, one of the Weasley twins. I didn't know which, but chess ability seems to run in their family. The strongest of them was their brother Ron. Anyway, it was clear that he had a natural talent for chess, and he could become a very good player. So I suggested that he spend some time and effort trying to develop that talent. He agreed and I became his chess mentor."

Rita was hastily scribbling away and eventually caught up. She breathed a sigh and asked, "Just how good is he?"

I hadn't seen his latest ranking, but I decided to give her an educated guess, "There's a rough ranking system. In it, you start at novice and proceed up. At the top are Master, Grand Master, International Grand Master and, of course, World Champion. On this scale, he is currently at or near the low end of Grand Master."

She took that in and her eyes narrowed, "Just how do you get rated in chess? Is there a committee that reviews games or something?"

I chuckled, "No. No. Nothing subjective like that. You play in officially sponsored tournaments. There is a mathematical formula that calculates your current rating based on your rating before the tournament, the ratings of players that you play against, whether you won, lost or drew with them. The ratings range from 1300 points up through 2700 or 2800. The top end can vary."

"What's Cedric's current point rating?"

I had to admit that I didn't know but guessed, "It's somewhere around 2400 points."

She whistled, thought a moment and went on, "This is wizard chess we're talking about, right?"

"Well, not exactly. The wizard chess rules are exactly the same as normal chess. But there aren't any wizard chess tournaments that I'm aware of. Cedric has been competing in Muggle chess tournaments."

Her body seemed to deflate, "Hmmmm. Well, has he won any tournaments?"

"Yes, last year he won the annual British Junior Chess tournament, and this spring, he won a major tournament that was played in Paris."

She brightened again, "Paris, France?"

I rolled my eyes, "No, Paris, Texas. Of course, Paris, France."

Her eyes lost some of their sheen, "Of course, it was a Muggle chess tournament?"

"Right."

"Is he going to attend any tournaments this year?"

"There's a tournament in London every year around Christmas. It's very good and has lots of international attendees. I hope he'll compete in that. A win there or even a very good showing would put him solidly in the front ranks of international chess."

Her eyes brightened again, "What tournament is that? Will you be in town for it?"

'It's called the Trafalgar Tradewise Tournament. In the past when we've competed in it, we've disapparated in each day."

She looked puzzled and sounded suspicious, "You don't disapparate and Cedric's too young yet. Is it his parents who do the Disapparating?

"Usually not. A fellow teacher, Professor McGonagall usually takes us."

She nodded and smiled.

She asked for a refill of her glass of water and then went on, "I know that he plays Quidditch. He's on the HufflePuff house team."

"Yes, he's their seeker. He's quite good athletically. I can tell you that he's the only seeker that Potter has ever lost to in inter-house play." I paused for effect and added, "Of course, that was a game when Potter was unseated by an encounter with a Dementor."

"Ohhh, that's right. The Dementors were here last year, looking for Sirius Black."

"Yes. Also, he's quite strong academically. I am trying to decide whether to recommend that he try to attend a Muggle university after graduating."

She made a face, "Why in the world would he ever want to do that?"

"I think it's a waste not to use talents that you've got. And I think he's got quite a lot of talent for studies." I thought to myself that I wish I knew what Rita's talent was. It certainly wasn't being a good writer or reporter, as far as I could tell.

"Still, a Muggle school!" She seemed to remember that I'd attended several Muggle schools. "But, no offense intended, I'm sure that they're quite good for those less talented."

I just smiled.

She found one more question, "I hear that you're American?"

"That's right."

That seemed to have her stuck. She got up and walked toward the door in an abstracted way, focusing on the floor. I ran around her and opened the door for her. I sent her off with the injunction, "Have a better one."

She answered distantly, "You too."

That evening after supper, Minerva and I hung around the Great Hall talking. "I hear that you gave Skeeter quite an interview?"

"Oh, it seemed pretty boring to me."

"That's what I mean. I hope she doesn't decide to crucify you in print."

"I'm not too afraid. Do you want me to not see so much of you for a while? You don't want to get painted with the same brush as me. You might find our affair on the front page of the *Prophet*."

"Oh, I'm not worried. I just don't want to embarrass Hogwarts."

"It may be too late to avoid that."

In the meantime, I would keep my eyes open.

The Other Tournament

The next day, I was at lunch when an owl swooped down toward my table. That wasn't an unusual occurrence, and I didn't pay any attention to it until a manila envelope landed in my plate. I looked up and saw the tawny owl flying away toward an open window. Minerva came over and asked, "Well, you don't get mail very often. I wonder what it is."

"I wonder too."

"Well, I don't know."

I stared at it. I had a feeling that it was not the usual sort of mail I get—my magazine subscription, the occasional letter from my parents, the birthday cards from my relatives and the few friends that I still had State-side.

Minerva continued to look over my shoulder and eventually said, "You know the normal way to find out about who sent you a letter is to open it?"

I nodded but still was bothered. I had a bad feeling about it. I said, "Look Minerva, I think I'll open this letter at my desk."

"Do you think it's bad news?"

"I don't know. I just think that I'll head up there right now."

She seemed a bit concerned and asked, "May I come along. You've peaked my curiosity."

"Sure." We got up and walked briskly to my office. Minerva unlocked the door before I reached it. "I wish you wouldn't do that. It gives people the idea that anybody can do it. That Rita Skeeter did it. When I walked in yesterday I saw her seated in my seat and it gave me a fright."

"I understand that." But she didn't make any commitment about not unlocking my door in the future.

I took my seat and she sat on the edge of my desk next to me. I pulled out my Swiss Army Knife and slit the sealed flap. I pulled out the envelope inside. It was from a Muggle. I glanced at the return address. I didn't recognize the name. It only had initials where the name normally would be.

I slit the inner envelope and pulled two pages of typed text out. Minerva pretended not to be watching as I unfolded the pages and began to read. She asked, "What is it?"

I was speechless. Then I said, "This is the most amazing letter that I've ever received." Then I remembered my first letter from Minerva and corrected myself, "The second most amazing."

"The most amazing being?" She asked.

I simply looked up at her anSd smiled. She understood.

I quickly scanned the two pages and said, "This letter is from the F.I.D.E. They organize chess tournaments—the largest and most prestigious in the world. They are inviting Cedric to participate in a unique tournament. It is one of a kind. It will be an invitation-only winner take-all tournament of the greatest youth players in the world. The winner will get to play the current world champion, Gary Kasparov."

Minerva was impressed, "That's wonderful." She grabbed my arm and squeezed! "If he beats Kasparov, does that make him the world champion?"

"Not quite. The world champion is decided in a tournament organized by the FIDE, but not this tournament. I think this is mostly a publicity stunt, but it is a wonderful one. It's a great opportunity. It's a once-in-a-lifetime opportunity."

"When is the tournament?"

"Well the first round, the one that decides who will play Kasparov will be during the early spring. It's probably timed to let most kids compete during their spring break. And then the winner will play Kasparov in the late spring."

A frown hit her face. "Let me see the exact dates." I handed her the page and she read quickly. The frown turned to a scowl. "The first round interferes with the second task of the Tri-Wizard Tournament." Then her scowl turned to dismay, "The final round starts the same day as the third task of the Tri-Wizard Tournament."

"Oh, shit." I said. Talk about bad Karma!

"You know that he'll never accept the invitation."

I was in shock. Finally, I said, "They're both astounding opportunities, but I think he needs to think hard about what he wants to do. There's only one Tri-Wizard Tournament, but chess could be Cedric's career."

She shook her head slowly. Finally, she said, "You go ahead and ask him."

My heart sunk. I knew she was probably right.

○

I decided that I had to get it over with as soon as I could. The next morning at breakfast, I gave a note for Cedric to the first Huffelpuff that was at the end of their table. The note simply said, "Mr. Diggery, please drop by my office when you've got a free hour. I have some good news for you."

I didn't see him until the afternoon when we had our first overlapping free period. He came into my office, fairly bouncing. "Professor Wendt, what's the good news?"

I decided that this news was better delivered with both of us on our feet and walking, so I invited him to join me for a little walk out toward the Quidditch pitch. He shrugged and said, "Why not."

We walked out through the courtyard. When we were outside the castle, I began. "Yesterday, I got a very unusual letter in the owl post."

"Really? Who was it from?"

"The chairman of the F.I.D.E."

"Wow! What did he want?"

"Well, he paid you a very good complement. He invited you to play in an upcoming tournament that is, well, unique."

The first hint of a frown crossed Cedric lips briefly, but he is a basically optimistic person. It didn't last long, "Tell me about the tournament."

"Well, it's an invitation-only tournament. It's for the great youth players of the game."

"I like the sound of that."

"Yes, well, the winner of the tournament gets to play the world champion."

Cedric broke in excitedly, "Gary Kasparov?"

"Yes."

"Wow."

"Yes, it's a once-in-a-lifetime opportunity."

"When is it?"

I gave him the dates and he puzzled for a minute and asked hesitantly, "Isn't that during the second Tri-Wizard Tournament task?"

I just had noticed something that I should have remembered— the Quidditch Pitch had been disassembled to make room for the third task of the tournament. It was a field of growing shrubs. I had hesitated in answering and Cedric followed up quickly, "Isn't it!"

"Yes, yes, it is."

He slowly asked, "And when's the game with Kasparov?"

I just said impassively, "The same day as the final task of the Tournament."

He broke out laughing. I stared at him. When he calmed down, he said between gasps for air, "That's THE. . . best . . . practical . . . joke!

"Now, what was the letter about—really?"

"I'm afraid that was it."

"No, really. Come on, what are the chances that the dates would overlap exactly?"

"Really. I don't know, but it happened. Do you want to see the letter?"

Then he laughed a sort of forced chuckle. "Well, that works out perfectly, don't you think. It's even funny."

"I wish I could figure out what's funny about it."

"Come on, it's too perfect. I drop out of the Tri-Wizard Tournament so I can play in this tournament. Potter is the one champion for Hogwarts. Everyone's happy."

Somehow I had a feeling that nobody would be happy, but I asked, hoping against hope, "Would you do that?"

He simply said, "No."

"Why not. You said it, it's perfect. This chess tournament is the greatest opportunity that anyone could give you." I tried to summarize how wonderful it would be for him in a nice simple way that made sense.

"You probably wouldn't win it. There are at least a couple of youth players that are stronger than you. But think about the strength of competition you'd play against. You could pick up enough rating points to move up solidly into Grand Master. By the time you graduate from Hogwarts, you could be on the verge of being an International Grand Master. You could be ready to make an assault on the world championship by the time you were in your twenties." I laid it on plenty thick.

"If you were lucky enough to get to play Kasparov, you might even short-cut some of that. Very few people get to play against the likes of Kasparov. He rarely leaves the Soviet Union and he only does so to play in very big tournaments that happen almost anywhere in the world.

"Getting beaten by him would be a rare opportunity to learn. You just don't face that sort of competition outside the Soviet Union except once in a blue moon!"

Cedric stared at me a moment incredulously and then said, "Wow. This is big to you. But you know, the Tri-Wizard Tournament is pretty big too. If I won, I'd be the only person in hundreds of years to have won. I'd get 10,000 Galleons, just for a start. With that, I could pretty much write my ticket anywhere. I'd probably have my pick of Ministry jobs when I graduate."

"I admit that that's a big deal, but . . ."

"And then there's the point that I don't have a choice."

I was surprised for once. "What do you mean, you don't have a choice?"

"Simple, the way the head of the department of International Magical Cooperation or whatever puts it, the Goblet of Fire is a binding magical contract.

"I guess that means that when you sign your name to the parchment and throw it in the Goblet, you've signed a contract that binds you to compete in the tournament if you're chosen by the goblet.

"They tried to get Potter out on a technicality, but Crouch said that it wasn't possible. He didn't say what would happen if Potter didn't compete, but he implied it would be pretty awful."

I grumbled to myself that Minerva could have mentioned that detail to me.

We walked back to the castle. It was a slow and very quiet walk. We reached the entrance-way, and I headed back to my office.

Minerva and I hashed out the possibilities of Cedric getting excused from play. Minerva pointed out quite rightly that he really didn't want to get out AND if anyone was going to get out, it would be Potter. I eventually agreed.

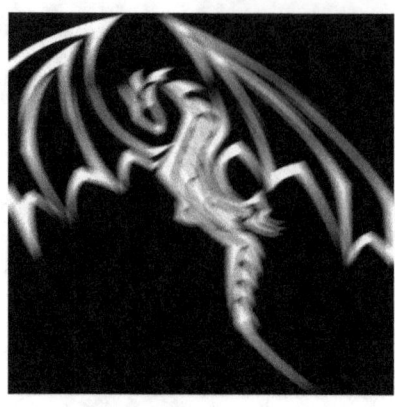

The Dragon

The next few days leading up to the first task of the tournament were slow. I wanted to get past it. Then, it would be real. I'd see Cedric on the field of play, and the truth that Cedric wasn't going to compete in the chess tournament would be final.

The first event was a surprise to most of us. It was only when a dragon was lead out into the field and secured to an iron ring sunk deep in bedrock that I realized the awful possibilities of the tournament. The color commentator was worse than useless. He didn't reveal anything useful to the crowd in his commentary. But, of course, no one was listening, riveted as we all were by the spectacle of a real dragon trying to fry or crush a young man or woman.

I turned to Minerva, "Who invented this task? Tell me it wasn't someone at Hogwarts."

Minerva seemed as disturbed as I was. She said, "Each school contributed a task. They had to be approved by the selection committee but each had one. I think this was from Durmstrang."

"Yeh, that makes sense."

"By the way, ours team's was selected as the task from Hogwarts."

"Good. I don't think ours is as barbarous as this one is. That means that the final one is from Beaux Batons. Do you know what it is?"

"No, it's a big secret. As a matter of fact, I wasn't supposed to reveal to anyone which was selected from Hogwarts."

"Well, the secret is safe with me."

Each champion had their own dragon. The task of stealing the golden egg from the dragon was cruel to everyone, including the dragon.

After everyone had finished the task, we were heading back to the castle when I noticed that Crouch was just ahead of us. I trotted up,

Minerva following and tugging at my sleeve, but I ignored her. When I caught up with him I asked, "You're Bartaemius Crouch aren't you, head of the International Magical Cooperation Department?"

He turned and said, "Yes. And you are?"

Minerva answered for me, "He's Professor James Wendt of Hogwarts. And I'm. . . "

Crouch interrupted, "Oh, I know who you are Professor McGonagall. What can I do for you?"

I answered, "I was wondering if you would care to have dinner with us at the Three Broomsticks?"

The question dumbfounded both Crouch and Minerva. He asked, "Why?"

That was the sticking point that I was afraid of, but I had an answer that I thought was not offensive. "I've heard of you from Percy Weasley. I know that he's very impressed with you. When I saw that you were on your own, I thought that it would be interesting to make your acquaintance."

Just then, Moody joined us. He said, "Good evening, Mr. Crouch. It was a wonderful start to the competition wasn't it." He turned to me and said, "Why don't we all have a drink at the Three Broomsticks."

Minerva said, "I doubt Mr.Crouch has time for us."

Crouch seemed to be confused trying to follow the various snippets of conversation, but he said, "Yes, I'd enjoy spending part of an evening in your company. What do you say?"

I mouthed a silent, "Thank You.".

Moody said, "Well, I suppose four's a crowd." and turned to leave.

I don't know if he really hoped to join us, but he seemed to be out for the moment. We turned our course from Hogwarts to Hoggsmeade. I kept the conversation going by asking about how the tournament was going, what he thought of Potter's performance today, and whether he was going to stay the night in Hoggsmeade.

Crouch mostly answered in short sentence fragments, seeming to have problems concentrating. When we reached the Three Broomsticks, I led the way in and got a table in a corner close to the fire place. It wasn't cold out and there wasn't a fire in the fireplace, so we were not close to any other people.

After placing our order, I waited to let Minerva and Crouch pursue conversational topics—if they had any. It was pretty quiet almost immediately. Minerva asked a few polite questions about the Ministry and how Percy was doing. Crouch had brief answers – Percy (or Pemberley, as he called him) was doing all right. The Ministry was very busy at the moment with the Tournament and the aftermath of the investigations of the disturbance at the World Cup.

When I thought that I couldn't wait any longer, our salads arrived and we started in on dinner. While we were waiting for the entrees, I started on the topic that I really wanted to discuss. "Mr. Crouch, it looked like Mr. Potter—and the other champions—might be seriously injured in the tournament today."

"Yes, it's sad. It would be very disturbing to lose any young person to . . uh . . the competition."

I nodded and said, "Can you tell me about the history of the Tournament."

He seemed to show some excitement for the first time and said, "Well, you see it started in the 13th Century—hardly more than a century from the founding of Hogwarts. At the time, there were four schools of Magic that sent champions. At that time the champions were chosen by the heads of their schools. This proved to be disastrous. Often, the best candidate wasn't sent, but rather the one whose parents could offer the best bribe to the school head.

"In the 15th Century, the Goblet of Fire was created to chose the most qualified student from each school. Throughout its history until this year, any student—even a 1st year could apply to be the school champion. There was even a year when a 1st year student actually won.

"But as time proceeded, the competition became more fierce and the tasks more dangerous. Each school wanted to make it difficult for competing schools to win, so they specialized and made especially difficult and dangerous tasks around their specialties.

"Then in the 18th Century, all contestants died during the tournament, and it was abandoned, and the Goblet of Fire went unused until this year."

Minerva let me do all the talking. I think that she must have wanted to see where I would take this. I then asked, "It seems like the first task was especially dangerous this year. Was there no way that a champion could withdraw from the competition?"

This brought the first real animation to Crouch's answers, "NO. NO. It's a sacred magical contract that the contestants have entered into. The consequences would be unspeakable if one tried to drop out."

"How do you know? It's been centuries since the time the tournament was run last."

He responded forcefully, "It's out of the question. No one can withdraw."

"Look, I understand about contracts, but surely this contract is invalid since Potter didn't actually sign anything."

"No. That doesn't matter. The name was thrown into the goblet. That's all that matters."

I appealed silently to Minerva, but all she did was to shrug.

I decided on a different tack. The entrees arrived and we started dinner. After we'd begun to have our fill, I went on, "Mr. Crouch, I've got to open the bag for you."

"Excuse me, 'open the bag?'"

Minerva said, "Oh, it's an American expression. It means reveal everything to you."

"Oh."

"Yes, anyway, I have a reason for wanting to find a way out for Potter. I mean besides the obvious humanitarian reason of not wanting to see him killed. I'm the faculty advisor for Mr. Diggery. He's an excellent Chess player, and he's even competed in some international tournaments.

"He's been invited to an extremely prestigious tournament that is by invitation only—a little like the Tri-Wizard Tournament. It would be very good for a career in Chess if he could compete in it.

"But, here's the rub. It happens at the same time as Tri-Wizard Tournament events. I'd like him to have the option to choose which he participates in. Is there any way to see if he can withdraw from the Tri-Wizard Tournament?

Crouch stared at me and asked, "Does he want to withdraw from the Tournament?"

"I don't know. Since he thinks that it's not possible, he hasn't given serious thought to it."

He seemed to be going through some sort of internal struggle. He stared off in the distance and began to say something and then shook his head. This happened at least twice. Eventually he just shook his head and said, "It's not possible. I wish. . . but no. Not possible."

Minerva stepped in at the last minute and asked, "You seemed unsure. Is there no way that we could test whether it is possible?"

He answered with what seemed like a real struggle to speak. "No, I would say not."

Minerva said, "Well, then, that leaves us only to enjoy dessert."

Madame Ross-Murta brought out the trolley with deserts. I chose a creme brulet, Minerva, a chocolate croissant, and Crouch just had coffee. He excused himself, saying that he had to get home.

I paid for our meal, realizing that he hadn't even offered to pay for his part. Well, that had been my intention, but still, it seemed strange that he hadn't at least offered. I mentioned that to Minerva and she said that he'd seemed distracted.

"Distracted! I've never seen a more deadpan, cold fish in my life!"

Minerva stopped walking and grasped my arm to turn me to face her. "The man is still mourning the death of not only his wife but his son as well. I'd think he'd be distracted!"

I admitted that she was probably right, but I pursued another point, "Don't you think he was overly sure of himself about the Goblet and magical contract and all that?"

"I don't know. I'm not a historian. I don't know how the stupid Goblet works." Then she turned a bit sharp, "What do you think? Do you suppose he has a reason to not want his Tournament apple cart overturned?"

"I suppose that you're right about that. He's not got any reason to be interested in deconstructing his carefully constructed competition.

Halloween

I was enjoying a nice croissant one Saturday morning after most of the school had moved on to other pursuits. I didn't think anyone else was in the Great Hall. I gazed out over the expanse of empty tables, the great vault of the heavens spread out above me in all its glory with broken clouds blowing swiftly across the scene and dropping shadows over the tables – king of all that I surveyed.

At that moment of my glory, I sensed someone nearby and a second later felt a blow on my left shoulder blade, "Hello, on this glorious morning!"

I sighed a sigh of resignation, "Well, it was."

Sinistra leaned over my shoulder to look into my left eye and said, "Doesn't it just make you want to dare anything, to break the surly bounds of earth and . . ."

I couldn't stand it any more, so I interrupted. "It makes me want to puke when you say those things before Halloween." I knew that I couldn't keep her from making her pitch, so I was ready to hear it out. "I'm sure that you have a sure fire idea for breaking the surly bounds of Earth. Just get on with it, so that I can say no and go back to my croissant."

She levitated a chair over the head table and set it in front of me on the opposite side of the table. She sat and gazed into my eyes—a gaze that I think psychologists call a copulative glance. "Well, since you insist, I do have a little idea for some light frivolity on Halloween."

I just nodded and said, "Go on."

"I was thinking, wouldn't it be droll to go to the party disguised as Mad-Eye Moody!"

81

I just stared at her a moment, "Well, you just go ahead and do that, but if you think that I'd find it droll to be blasted to smithereens when he got the first glance of me, you're as Mad as Mad Eye's Eye. He'd probably think that I was a dark wizard and I'd find myself on the way to Azkaban faster than a goblin after a galleon dropped on the floor."

She answered in a soothing voice, "No. No. He'd never think that any dark wizard would be so bold as to show up right under Dumbledore's nose regardless whom he was disguised as."

She might have a point there, but I couldn't help remembering the trash bin that was attacked outside Moody's flat in the summer. The real problem was who would Sinistra go disguised as. I raised this issue. "AND WHO would you be disguised as, hmmmm?"

She smiled broadly and said, "Oh, it's so delicious! I'll go disguised as Belatrix LeStrange. You could be taking me to Azkaban just after capturing me!"

I tried shaking the cobwebs out of my skull. I had to be hearing her wrong. "You want to go disguised as the most dangerous dark witch of our time! What are you thinking? And besides, how would you ever get a lock of hair or nail clipping from her. She's locked up in the high security end of Azkaban!"

That deflated her a bit. "Well, I have to admit that I don't have that little point covered yet, but I'm working it. I'll get it."

I thought that I had her. "Well, you go off and do your homework. If you ever get that little point covered, come back."

We both went away smiling – me because I was confident that she'd not come up with an idea to cover that and, I suppose, she was confident that she would come up with an idea.

I didn't think about it again and finished my croissant in peace and pleasure. That day was a Hogsmeade day, and I wrangled a tour of duty patrolling Hogsmeade with Minerva. She was in an exceptionally good mood. She was even willing to take a half hour off from our patrolling to have lunch with me at the Three Broomsticks where I got us a remote corner table and managed to play a little footsie with her.

She remarked on our good mood, "You seem to be really happy."

I nodded, "How could I not be happy being here with you, my Shipoopi?"

She gazed at me in amazement, "What in the world is a Shipoopi?"

"Oh, it's a word made-up by a song writer. It means roughly, 'a girl who's hard to get but is well worth the effort.'"

"Well, I'm not sure about either being hard to get or worth the effort, but I'll take it as a compliment."

"Oh, you should."

Minerva's eyes narrowed, and she asked, "Well, we both know a girl who's extremely easy to get. And, as it's getting close to Halloween, I'm surprised that you haven't heard from her."

All I could say was, "Uh, well." But we were both in such a good mood that she didn't press me for a denial that I'd heard from Sinistra."

When we were back in Hogwarts, she grilled me on another subject. "Any ideas about how to find the miscreant who put Potter's name in the Goblet?"

I had to admit that I was out of ideas.

⌒⌒

In the next week, I found that having our "visitors" around was becoming almost normal. They only had the main meal with us. They had been divided up by house so that there were some of each school together on each of the house tables. Apparently, they shared some classes with our students, but mostly they didn't. My classroom door was never darkened by a single one.

I occasionally got a question from one of them about what my subject was and blank stares when I explained what English Literature was. I would have thought that it wasn't that difficult a concept.

Then on Wednesday evening after dinner while I was in my office, there was a knock on the door. The person who wanted in was– Sinistra.

We were both smiling at the realization. I said, "I know why I'm smiling." I was confident that she'd come to admit defeat. "But I don't know why you're smiling."

In answer, she held up a small glass vial triumphantly.

I stared and being truly afraid to ask the obvious question, I said nothing, my mouth agape.

"Well, don't you want to know what this is?"

I mutely shook my head "no".

"Oh, you are such a party pooper! You know perfectly well what it is. Don't you want to know how I got it?"

My smile had first frozen and then sagged on my face into a sort of mask like the Greeks used to symbolize tragedy. "Not really."

"Well, I'm going to tell you anyway; because it is a long and virtuous search that I went through.

She sat unbidden in the red leather chair and asked, "Aren't you going to offer me something to drink."

Rather than say anything, I just opened the drawer of my desk, pulled out the strongest bottle of whiskey I had and poured two glasses. I handed one to her, and I dropped into my chair. I took a stiff swallow and was comforted by the astringent burn as it went down my throat. "You might as well get started."

Trixie

She smiled gaily and started her story:

"Well, my first thought was to get a lock of her hair from someone who works at Azkaban by bribing someone to get it.

"I went to the Auror office and just asked if I could have a list of people who work at Azkaban. They were polite but very firm. The employees of Azkaban held confidential posts and their names were not handed out to just anyone who happened along with a wand. You had to have a 'need to know', and I didn't have a need to know. I left the Auror office and went to the outdoor café to get a cup of coffee to think over my problem.

I ordered a cappuccino and sat at a table. The coffee shop copy of the *Prophet* was sitting on the table at an angle so that I couldn't read the headlines easily, but at the head of a column, I saw a photo of someone I recognized. I couldn't pull her name to mind immediately, but I knew that I'd seen her recently. I picked up the page, which was open to the home & leisure section. The photo was Rita Skeeter, and the column was her gossip column. She was doing a series on the love lives of the Tri-Wizard Tournament champions. This one was about Victor Krum's.

She didn't really have any detail – just speculation about whom he might fancy at Durmstrang and at the tournament. But seeing her gave me an idea. Journalists can usually get access to people and information that ordinary teachers can't. Maybe, I could talk her into finding the names and addresses of people who worked at Azkaban. I decided to try her.

I went to the hearths in the Atrium of the Ministry and went by floo to the offices of the *Prophet*. I landed in a small hearth in what was the reception room of the *Daily Prophet*. The walls were decorated with famous photos and front pages that they had featured over the years. There was a front page from the day that it was discovered that Harry Potter had defeated Valdemort. There was a photo of the Seeker holding up the Snitch in the toes of his left foot from the 1973 Quiditch Cup when Dragomir Stopchek had caught the Snitch between the big toe and middle toe of his left foot. A blodger had knocked off his boot earlier in the game just before he spotted the Snitch. The Snitch had dodged just before he would have caught it in his hands. With his foot unencumbered, he was able to nab it in his toes. There was a photo of one of the conferences during World War II in Yalta.

Anyway, I caught a break. Rita wasn't off getting an interview. She was in her office, writing her column for the next day. The receptionist sent a message owl to get her. She came out to the reception room and agreed to see me then. She took me down to the cafeteria rather than her office. We went through the printing press area. There were dozens of presses running parchment from huge rolls into the presses that sprayed ink from quills running back and forth over the parchment.

Rita stopped to show me one of the presses up close, "Isn't that amazing? Those quills fly back and forth over the parchment and shoot streams of little drops out the end. They make tiny little dots on the paper. If you look really closely at the next copy of the *Prophet*, you'll see that the runes and letters are made of millions of little dots."

I was impressed. When we got to the cafeteria, I bought her a coffee, and we sat at table. She started, "Funny you should show up just now. I've been trying to develop sources of inside info at Hogwarts for the Tournament. We call them stringers in the business. I was just trying to find someone who would be willing to do that for me. Quite a coincidence, eh?"

I leaned back and wondered if I dared make a deal with her. She looks innocent, in a kind of prurient, gossipy way. Well, I decided to see what kind of deal I could make, "Yes, it is. I've been trying to find a list of people who work at Azkaban. And, you know, it occurred to me that . . ."

Rita jumped in, "That a journalist might be able to get that kind of list?"

I shrugged and agreed. She nodded knowingly, "Yes, I think I could obtain that kind of information – IF I had a friendly agreement to trade information occasionally." She winked at me.

I felt like I did the one time when the captain of the Quidditch team back at Hogwarts took me to a dance and wanted some "action" after the dance. But I decided to swallow my pride and buy in, "That sounds possible. Just what sort of information would you be looking for?"

"Oh, just a little juicy gossip. You know, if one of the Tri-Wizard Champions had a girl friend, say like Harry Potter or especially that handsome Diggory. It would be nice to know about it. You know, nothing really personal. For example, if Krum were snogging with one of the young ladies from Beaux Batons, a photo would be just great. Of course, if you can't get a photo, an eye witness account would be almost as good."

I swallowed hard and said, "I think that would be possible, but I need contact information about employees of Azkaban."

Rita eyed me up and down, trying to size me up. "Every employee? That would be hard or would just certain ones, be OK."

I thought about what I really wanted. Should I ask for the prison barber right away or maybe someone else. After a few minutes of thought I decided on a strategy. "I'd like someone who would be willing to talk about what it's like in Azkaban, who does what and someone who might be willing to share information without too much uh . . . "

Rita nodded enthusiastically, "Without too many scruples, right?"

I found myself nodding. She pulled a scrap of parchment from her handbag and a quill and wrote something on it. She held it in her hand, half-way extended to me and said one word, "Deal?"

I said one word, "Deal"

Then she handed me the parchment, which I unfolded and found the name, Leo McGriff. I got up a little shakily. Rita noticed and said, "That wasn't so hard. It'll be easier later."

I disapparated to a post-office, hired an owl and sent a message to Leo. He sent an answer by the same owl. He'd meet me for dinner at the Leaky Cauldron. He arrived late – after 8 PM but I couldn't miss him. He was still wearing his guard uniform. He was at least six foot five and his hair was cut short. He looked like he could give Haggrid a run for his money if it came to a wrestling match.

He wanted a small table in a dark corner. He expected me to buy, and I suppose that I wasn't surprised by it, either. "So, what are you? Some kind of reporter?"

"No. I'm a teacher, but I want some information."

"About Azkaban?"

"Yes."

"What?"

Suddenly, it seemed that I was into someplace that I really didn't want to be, but I had committed myself to Rita and it was too late to back down. "I want to know who the barber is?"

I wasn't sure that he'd understood me. He just stared at me for a minute as if waiting for something more. Then he asked, "What barber?"

"Well, the barber of Azkaban."

Again he stared at me and slowly began to laugh. I didn't recognize what it was at first. It was a chuff of air and then another and they started coming faster, and I recognized them as laughing. "Azkaban doesn't have a barber."

"Well, surely it must. Who cuts the prisoners hair? If . you . . . don't. . ." He was just shaking his head negatively.

He rolled his eyes, "What do you think Azkaban is, a resort?"

I stuttered a moment looking for words, but he went on, "No, it ain't. They're lucky they get weekly showers, and the water is none too warm."

I finally found words, "And I suppose they can't trim their nails."

This time the laugh was immediate and boisterous, "No, no nail trimmers or files. Do you think that we'd let them have something that could become a weapon?" He must have seen the shock on my face because he answered my unasked question, "Yes, the nails get long, but they get brittle like and break off. No molly-codling criminals in Azkaban.

"Beside all that, I don't know who's on duty at Azkaban right now."

That puzzled me. "How could you not know who's got guard duty at Azkaban now?"

"Easy. We work three-month shifts. Everybody on one shift knows everybody else on that shift, but we generally don't know who's on the other three-month shifts"

I took that in and asked, "Then, you're not on duty now. When will you be?"

"Oh, a little over a month from now."

I tried one last question, "What about when their sentence comes to an end? Surely they get haircuts or something. . ." I trailed off and finally added weakly, "Don't they?"

He only smiled, "When they've finished paying their debt to wizarding society, they gets a new suit of robes, a pair of shoes and fifty galleons. If they decide to spend some of that on a haircut, that's their business."

That left me with a painful choice. I could ask him directly for what I wanted, hair or fingernail clippings from Belatrix LeStrange. Maybe he'd help, but I was afraid of giving a man like him a lever that he could use against me. The only other option that I saw was to just end it here. I decided to do that, "Well, thanks Mr. McGriff. I won't trouble you any more."

He stared at me again, "Wait, what is it that you wanted? What did you expect to get from the barber?"

I thought to myself, "What did I expect to get?" I guess I was expecting to find the barber – an unassuming little man who would say, "What izz it that I can do for you? What is ze favor you crave?" Somehow, I always think of barbers as being Italians or Spaniards. I suppose it's Mozart's fault—he and The Barber of Seville.

What I said was, "Nothing. I have everything I want." I rose and turned to go and felt him grip my arm and apply pressure to turn me back toward him.

"Now, wait one minute lady. You drag me away from my home, and I give you information, and what do I get out of it?" There was a determined grimace on his face that worried me.

But I turned full toward him, still standing and plunked my purse down on the table in front of me with a crash. "What did you get? You got a good supper and a lot of damn good liquor. More than your paltry information is worth." I reached into my purse and grasped the wand. He couldn't see it, but he seemed to sense what I'd done.

His grimace turned to more of a snarl and then relented into a genial smile, "Well, you can't blame a bloke for trying, can you? If you ever want some more information sometime, just look up old Leo."

I walked over to the bar, released my grip on the wand, searched for my purse, opened it, and pulled out a handful of galleons. I pounded

89

my fist on the bar and released my grip on the galleons. They spilled over the bar and some fell off on the floor on both sides of the bar. "I'm sorry Tom. I'm awfully clumsy tonight. Is this enough for our dinner?"

Tom didn't glance down but said, "Is that guy giving you trouble?"

"No. It's all right. But is this enough gold?"

Tom's face relaxed a little and said, "Way too much. I'll get your bill?"

"That's OK. Keep the rest as a tip."

His eyes widened, and he started to protest. I broke in, "I'm in a hurry. It's OK if I use the floo?"

He nodded, "Sure, but this is way too much."

I didn't stay to talk. I just walked directly to the hearth, took a handful of powder and spoke the words, "Hogwarts Great Hall."

You may think that was the end of it. I certainly thought it was. That night I went to bed and had a troubled sleep. Finally, in the middle of the night, I awakened in the middle of a dream. I was a student in my 7th year at Hogwarts. I had my yearbook in hand and was looking for someone in it. I got up and walked to my bookshelf to find my yearbook from my 7th year. I could almost remember the page that I was looking at in my dream but not quite.

I found the yearbook and thumbed through it. There were the usual portraits, class pictures, there were the various clubs: the astronomy club, the gobstone club, the dueling club, the various house photos, the Quidditch team photos. Then when I turned a page, I saw what I was looking for. It was the section devoted to the Yule ball photos. All the attendees were photographed whether going as couples or singly. I quickly turned the pages until I found the photo I was looking for. I put the yearbook back. Satisfied, I could go to bed. I knew what I'd been looking for and what I'd look for the next day when the library was open.

The next day, after dinner, I went to the library and started looking for school yearbooks. I couldn't find them quickly, so I went to Madame Pinz and asked her where they were. She showed them to me and asked me what I wanted. I just said, "I'll know it when I find it." She reluctantly went back to her desk and I put my hand on the yearbook that I hoped contained what I wanted.

It was the 1974 yearbook. I quickly thumbed through to the individual class photos and saw that I had the wrong yearbook. I returned it to the shelf and pulled the 1973 yearbook. My hands were now shaking. I knew this must be it. I flipped through and found the picture that I was looking for. I then flipped toward the end where the Yule Ball photos were. I found the page that I was looking for. It had a photo of Joseph Brackett and a Belatrix ("Trixie") LeStrange. I was looking at a younger, so much younger version of the Deatheater that was currently in Azkaban. Most of the time her head was turned away from the camera toward her escort. But occasionally, the face turned back toward the camera and leered for a moment.

I flipped the book shut and exchanged it for the 1972 yearbook. The Yule party pages were. . . My hand shook as I tried to turn the pages. Then I found it. A photo of Joseph Brackett and a Belatrix ("Trixie") LeStrange stared or maybe it was leered at me. I discovered that I could calmly put the yearbook back and pull out the '71 yearbook. A quick flip through the book, and I reached another photo of the young lovers. That did it. All I had to do was find Joseph Brackett.

I sat down at a table and took a minute to think. How could I find a random name from more than twenty years ago? I sat there for half an hour thinking. Did I dare go back to Rita? As I was pondering this, I suddenly realized that I was not alone. Madame Pinz was sitting across from me. She said, "What did you find. I've never seen someone go so deep after reading a book, especially . . . "

I had a crazy idea. "Listen, Madame Pinz. I need to find a former Hogwarts student. Do you have any idea how to do that?"

She looked up and smiled. "No problem."

I stared at her, "How can you be sure?"

"It's easy. What year did the person graduate?"

"What difference can that possibly make!"

She just got up, walked to her desk, /signaling me to follow. When I reached it, she opened a drawer and pulled out a sheet of parchment and repeated the question, "What year?"

I looked heavenward, exasperated but decided to humor her, "1973."

She scanned down the parchment and said, "Do you have parchment and quill?"

I opened my handbag and rummaged, finding them, "OK."

"Ruth Gross, 571 Civett Dr., Big Stoke, Shropshire."

My mouth was gaping wide, and I found the wits to ask, "Who is that?"

Pinz smiled, "She's the class secretary. Surely, you remember. Every graduating class has someone who's willing to keep track of the class members – names, addresses, how to contact them for things like class reunions, etc. It's always a girl and usually a wall. . ."

I'd interrupted, supplying the end of the formula, "Usually a wallflower. Didn't go to the Yule Ball with a date." Pinz didn't say anything. I remember the picture in my yearbook. It was me alone, looking straight at the camera the whole time, defiant.

I went to the Owlery and sent off an owl with a request to meet with her. She answered the next day. She could meet with me that night after dinner.

The house was a small cottage. The walk was lined with flowers and the door was painted pink. There was light flooding out the windows. I rang the bell, and she answered promptly. She was wearing an apron and had a dishtowel in hand. Apparently, she'd not quite finished cleaning up from dinner. I apologized and accepted the invitation to wait for her in the parlor. It was a neat house. Everything seemed to have an appropriate place. There was no dust on the furniture. There were shadow boxes with little knick-knacks on every wall. She entered the room, now without apron or dish towel. She invited me to sit.

"Well, young woman, what can I do for you?"

I had rehearsed my speech. It was simple, "I'd like to meet Joseph Brackett. Madame Pinz told me that you were the class secretary for their class and would know how to get in touch with him."

"Oh, yes. She was right. I've got the class list." She got up and walked to a desk in the corner. It had a roll top, but she opened a drawer and pulled out a file folder. In the folder was a sheaf of parchments. She talked to herself as she went through the pages. Then she pulled one out and said, 'Yes. Here we are. Joseph Brackett. His current address is. . ."She stopped and said, "I'll just write it down for you so you don't forget." She got a blank sheet of parchment and a quill out and wrote it.

After she finished, she said, "It's so sad. Do you know that our class, '73, lost so many to the battle with He-Who-Must-Not-Be-Named."

I nodded and said, "Yes, I know, my class lost many too."

"His case was so sad." She quickly said, "Oh, don't worry. He's still alive. It's just so sad. He and that LeStrange girl were so close. I think they were an item since 4th year. Then after graduation, they parted ways. I thought they would be the first in our class to marry, but they broke up because she became. . ." She hesitated and then said what she apparently didn't want to admit. "You know, dear, she became a Deatheater, and that was the end for the two of them. Poor Joseph couldn't stand the idea of her being a Deatheater. I hoped that he might find someone else, but . . . "

I was satisfied. I'd heard enough about the star-crossed lovers. I thanked her for the address and left. She had water heating for tea, but I told her that I had to get back to Hogwarts.

⌒◻

I sent another owl. It was two days before I heard back from Brackett but he invited me to visit him. That was just two days ago. Yesterday I arrived in the evening. He lives in an apartment in Soho. He invited me in and offered something to drink. I accepted and as he poured, I explained why I'd come.

At least I tried. I thought that it wouldn't be hard, but when it came to it, it was harder than I expected. I started off, "You were Belatrix Le..."

But he cut me off, "Yes, I was Trixie LeStrange's boy friend. You're some reporter or journalist who wants a story about the Bela back when." He quickly answered the question that he'd posed himself, "No."

"Really, that's not what I want." He'd gotten up and was heading for the door and had it open. "Please, Mr. Brackett, I'm a school teacher. I don't want to write a story or sell a story or anything like that."

The grim set of his jaw relaxed but he asked suspiciously, "What is it that you want?"

Now it would get really hard, "Well, I noticed that you two had gone to the Yule Ball together the last three years that you were at Hogwarts."

Still suspicious, he asked, "How do you know that?"

At last, an easy question, "I saw the yearbooks."

He nodded, "Of course, you saw Bela at her best. She looks nothing like that now. The last photo that I saw in the *Prophet* was

93

hideous. I guess she's just showing on the outside how she is on the inside."

I could hardly believe what I said next, "Well, it probably has a lot to do with the conditions at Azkaban."

He stared at me, "You aren't one of these Deatheater sympathizers?"

"Oh, no. no. I just know a little bit about the conditions in Azkaban."

I came to the hardest part, "I was wondering, since you were such close, uh .uh."

He interrupted me and spit out,"Just spit it out."

"Well, she didn't happen to give you a lock of hair, did she?"

He stared at me again. "No. I don't remember." Then he looked down at his left foot for a while, looking for an answer, 'You know, I think she did. Now, where would it be?"

While he was thinking, I asked something out of the blue, "You keep referring to her as Bela, but the yearbook says that her nickname was 'Trixie'?"

He laughed, "Well, the editor of the yearbook sort of cleaned that up. The real nickname she had was Tricksy, T. R. I. C. K. S. Y. She got that because she liked playing practical jokes – sometimes pretty cruel ones. But, of course, none of her real friends called her that. To them – and me – she was always Bela." Then he hit his forehead, "Of course, yearbook. I put the lock in one of the yearbooks."

He went to a bookshelf and pulled out the '73 yearbook. He riffled through it and didn't find what he was looking for. Then he pulled the '72 yearbook out and did the riffle again, but this time he stopped at the Yule Ball photos. He handed it to me. There pressed between the pages that had their photo was a lock of hair tied by a green ribbon. He was gazing off into the distance and said to himself more than me, "I took my worst wound the day that we broke up."

"May I have part of this lock?"

He shrugged and then asked, "Why do you want it?"

I didn't say anything but he didn't object when I separated some of the hair from the bow and put it in a glass vial.

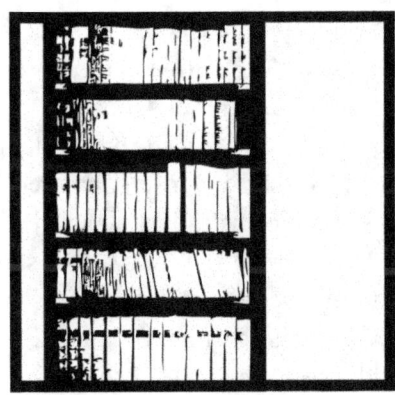

Halloween Redux

"So, now, I'm here with that lock of hair. I can dissolve it in Polyjuice potion and become Bela for a night."

I gazed wonderingly at her. I had to admit that she was a determined woman when she wanted to be. "So, you figure that this earns you the right to be Bela and I to be Moody for a night, eh?"

Her voice was almost pleading, "You couldn't turn me down now."

This was entirely too much. I would feel like a cad no matter what I did. If I turned her down, it would negate all the work that she'd done. On the other hand, I risked having another tiff with Minerva if I didn't turn her down.

She noticed my indecision and pounced on it, "Good, it's decided. I'll meet you at the Astronomy Tower tomorrow after the Banquet." She didn't leave me any time to object by running out the door and slamming it behind me. "Well," I thought to myself, "I can always just not show up."

That night was not an easy night for me. I dreamed of a dank dungeon with dirty, long-haired, long-nailed inmates, and they all had my face. Classes the next day were awful. I mostly just had them take turns reading aloud from whatever we were studying at that point. The banquet was awful. Well, actually, as usual it was wonderful. I just couldn't taste any of it. After the Banquet, everyone went off to change – either into costumes or just into good robes. I wandered up toward the Astronomy Tower. Of course, I ran into Sinistra who hurried me along with cheery suggestions about how wonderful it would be.

We arrived at the upper level of the Tower and she had a bundle for me. It was quite bulky. When I opened it, I discovered some things in addition to the outsize robes and shoes and so forth. There was an artificial leg. I puzzled over it a moment before I realized that the prosthesis matched the artificial limb of Moody.

Sinistra had a shorter robe and so forth. She handed me a flask. It had a liquid that seemed especially dense compared with previous times that I'd used it. I said so, and Sinistra just accused me of being a sissy. I carried all that stuff off to a corner that was out of sight, took off my own robes, held the flask up, opened the stopper, and stared at the god-awful stuff. I wondered what it would be like to have an artificial leg and only one natural eye. Would I really be able to see with the artificial eye? Or would it just look like the "mad eye"?

I took a deep breath, held my nose and swallowed. Of course, the stuff tasted hideous. I'd had it before and knew it would, but this time was different somehow. The first thing that I noticed beside the taste was that I was leaning toward the left and then falling. I caught myself with my left hand. At the same time both my left leg and my left eye went crazy with pain. The pain turned into a crazy headache as it lessened in my eye. But then something really strange happened. I could see all the dark corners. They were as bright as day, but superimposed on them was another darker image of the same thing. I wondered where Sinistra was and I suddenly found that my vision had split into two. One was the bright image, and it was whirling around in all directions, including up and down. The dark image was staying pretty stable. Shortly I saw Sinistra approaching from my side.

I realized that I'd better get some clothes on quickly, which I did. The only problem was the prosthesis. By the time she arrived, I was starting to figure out how to put it on. She saw my problem and took it, "Well, let me help you." She arranged the leg stretched out from the stump of my leg and started to strap them together.

Her cool hands ran up the stump of my leg, and I felt an electric thrill that ran, well, it ran someplace that I didn't want it to run to. She smiled. I said, "Just get it over with as quickly as possible, and leave your cotton-blooming hands away from my . . my . . "

She kept smiling and said, "Oh, don't be such a prude."

She finally finished and helped me stand unsteadily. I was forced to lean on her on the climb down from the Astronomy tower and I was less and less happy about the way things were working out.

We reached the main level. I started off without help in a sort of wobbly uncertain way but at least completely on my own. We rounded a corner and had a straight shot at the doors to the Great Hall when, coming from the other direction, the real Moody turned a corner, and we faced each other. For a split second, we just stared at each other. I don't know what he was thinking, but I was just trying to think of what to say. I started to take a confident step forward, as I saw him draw a wand from his robes.

I didn't see what he did next, because my left leg gave way under me, and I fell on my rump. But I heard a sizzle and crack as something small, hard and fast, hit me from behind. My "mad eye" swiveled around to the back and saw that a piece of stone had been blasted out of the wall behind me. The eye swiveled around to the front dizzyingly, and I saw Moody correcting his aim. Just then I heard Sinistra cry "No!" Minerva (now where had she come from?) had shot an Expelliamus spell that knocked the wand out of Moody's hand.

With her no nonsense manner Minerva addressed the room in general, "what has been going on here?"

I just then noticed the faux Belatrix. She was lovely in a very dark way with her long dark hair, her dark eyes and moody expression standing out on her extremely white face.. She didn't look much like the Belatrix of the *Prophet* photos. Belatrix said, "This is just a little Halloween disguise."

At the same time, Moody bellowed, "That's a very dark wizard impersonating me! Let me get my wand!" as he scrabbled across the floor in search of his wand that had disappeared for the moment.

At that moment, Dumbledore came out of the Great Hall, looked around and announced, "Well, I see that the three stooges are at it again." He looked over at Moody and asked, "You used a powerful freezing spell. What did you think you were doing?"

He stood up, still without wand, seeming somewhat contrite, "Well, I came around the corner and saw this, this doppelganger impersonating me. Of course, I had to shoot first and ask questions later."

Dumbledore seethed for a moment and said, "Well, the policy in this school is to ask question first and then not shoot at all. Professor Moody, let me re-introduce you to professor Wendt who seems to take pride in causing as much mayhem at Halloween as possible. His partner in crime is usually the fair Professor Sinistra, but at the moment, I see that she is Belatrix LeStrange as she was when she was a student here."

He stopped for breath, looked around and said, "Well, if we all have worked the fire out of ourselves for the night, I will let you join the rest of the school." He looked from one to another with a piercing gaze. We all agreed that we could play nicely, and the doors flung wide for us to enter.

As I entered, I found that I had not one person assisting me walk, but two – both Minerva and Belatrix. Snape approached us and laughed, "Well, I see that Prof. Moody is very popular tonight – probably more so than he has ever been in his life. I'm anxious to see Professor Moody dance with two partners at once."

We found a bench along one of the walls, and I sat. "I don't know how Moody manages to walk with this thing strapped to him."

Belatrix stood and Minerva said, "Good, you're going. Go find yourself another Deatheater and don't bother us."

She replied, "I was just getting two pumpkin juices for my date and me." And she walked off toward the refreshment table. Minerva just stayed and stroked my arm.

Cedric approached and asked me if I could give him some pointers on chess.

I said, "Everyone is a comic." Then, I just shooed him away and Sinistra returned and offered me a glass.

It would have been churlish to have refused it, so I took it and took a sip. It was good to have something cool go down my throat after all the excitement. But shortly after that sip, something strange happened. I shuddered all over and I felt my leg starting to grow back. "The transformation back has started."

Sinistra said, "That's impossible. It ought to be hours yet."

But Minerva countered, "Look, you can see him change for yourself. Quick, let's help get him up to his office."

Each took an arm and lifted. We staggered toward the door to the Great Hall. By the time we'd reached it, my eye had turned back to normal, and the straps that held the artificial leg to mine were tight as steel bands.

We got through the door, and I said, "It's going to be over by the time we reach the stairs." I was right. We weren't half-way there before I was completely transformed from Moody. But there was something wrong. Minerva noticed it first. She let go, stood back, and stared at me.

"Who are you?" She asked with a strained look on her face.

"Well, I'm Professor James Wendt."

But, Sinistra agreed, "No, you aren't."

I looked from one to the other and asked, "Where's the nearest mirror."

Sinistra opened her handbag and fished out a compact, opened it, and handed it to me. I looked at the person in the mirror, who was definitely NOT me. "What the hell. Who is this?"

Minerva said, "I don't know, but he looks vaguely familiar. I can't come up with a name, though. We'll all go up to your room and see what happens with you." At the same time, she pulled a wand out of her robes, and there was no doubt that it was pointed at me. Sinistra saw what Minerva did and followed suit. She said, "You lead the way."

We arrived at my office, I unlocked the door, and we all entered. They agreed that I should sit on the sofa, and they would sit on yellow chairs facing me. We sat for a while without anyone saying anything. Minerva broke the silence, "Suppose that we assume that the polyjuice potion is still working. How long until it wears off?"

Sinistra said, "Oh, maybe another two hours or so. You think that he's going to change again – back to himself?"

Minerva nodded without taking her eyes off of me. "I think so. Which raises the question, just where did you get the sample for the Polyjuice Potion. Could it have been a mixture?"

Sinistra shook her head, "I don't see how. I snipped a small sample from Moody's back hair one lunch when he was pre-occupied talking with Hagrid."

"Then who is this sitting here in front of us?"

I'd been thinking about that very question. I didn't have an answer either, but I had over two hours to think about it. The second transformation started, and the agonies that I went through were not so intense. When they were over, I was back to my normal self.

Sinistra said, "Hooray" when it was complete. "Let's go get some sleep."

Minerva said, "Not yet. We need to go find Dumbledore." Then she spoke to me, "Get up, walk slowly to the door, open it, and walk slowly to Dumbledore's Office. Sinistra and I will be following you, ready to stun you if you make any strange move."

Sinistra said, "We will? Is this really necessary?"

I spoke for the first time in a while, "You bet it is. If I were in your place, I'd sure be wondering who I was REALLY. Safety first."

We walked slowly and carefully to Dumbledore's Office. I was still wearing the robes that were sized for Moody and feeling pretty silly. At least I would have felt silly, if I didn't have Minerva at my back with her wand pointed at me. What I wouldn't have given for a "mad eye" just then to see what the expression on her face was.

We got to Dumbledore's Office and just got into the anteroom. He was apparently not back from the party yet. When he did arrive, he took about two seconds to survey the scene and come up with a conclusion, "Well, it looks like something funny happened on the way to the Forum."

Minerva asked, "What?"

"Oh, just a reference to a musical comedy. Well, let's go into my office and get a little more comfortable and start the explanations." He opened the door to his inner office and preceded us in. He took a seat behind his desk and invited us all to sit. Minerva was reluctant.

"Oh, Minerva, I'm in place now. You can relax your vigilance. I have things under control. By the way, would anyone like something to drink?"

Neither of the ladies did. I asked for a Johnny Walker Blue Label. Everyone stared at me and Dumbledore said, "I'm not familiar with that one. Would White Label be OK?"

"It would be just fine. Blue Label is really rare. It's been aged for sixty years. I just thought if I were facing the inquisition, I'd like to be sure to get a taste of Blue Label while I still could."

Dumbledore just said, "Sorry" and materialized a glass of what tasted close enough to White Label for me. He asked for an explanation of what had happened. The ladies provided a pretty cogent explanation, filling in and collaborating as needed to get a complete picture of the evening.

Dumbledore pulled his wand out and said, "I'm just going to do a little spell to verify who you really are. This shouldn't hurt."

It didn't. As a matter of fact, I didn't feel anything. Dumbledore said, "OK. There isn't any hidden personality that I can detect. I think you, Professor Wendt, are the 'Real McCoy' as your fellow Americans say.

"I've never heard of anything like this happening. I'll have to do a little research. But, first let me verify a couple of points.

"You, Sinistra didn't mix any material from anyone else besides Professor Moody?"

She agreed.

"None of you have any idea who this second person was?"

No one did, although Minerva admitted that I looked familiar to her in a vague way.

"And you, Wendt, don't know of anything unusual that has happened to you in the last several days. No, let's make that several weeks."

I thought for a number of minutes going over what had happened to me recently but for the life of me couldn't recall anything out of the ordinary. I added, "Of course, what's out of the ordinary around here is a lot different than what's out of the ordinary in Kansas."

Dumbledore smiled, "Understood." He steepled his hands and seemed to stare into space for quite a long time and finally said, "Well, I don't think there's anything further that any of us can do now. Just return to your quarters and proceed as though nothing out of the ordinary had happened."

Minerva asked, "And you'll let us know if something occurs to you?"

Dumbledore stared directly into her face and said, "Possibly." Then he looked around at the rest of us and said, "Off you go. Pip. Pip."

We'd all had as much excitement as we wanted for the night, and we all went off to our rooms silently.

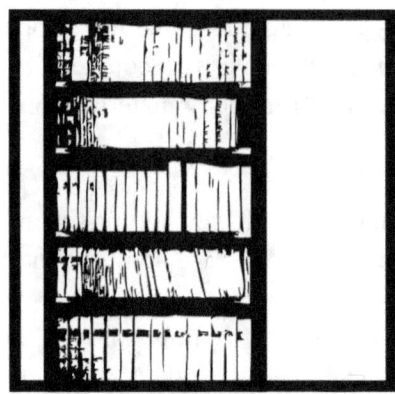

Cambridge

The next few days were the typical run of the mill days.

I had been grading my 6th year students' last papers. As I did that, I thought about my 6th year (Junior) year in high school and I thought about college application essays. Shouldn't all of these kids be thinking about post graduation?

That night when Minerva was in my office after dinner and we were talking about the day's events, I asked her about it, "Minerva. I've never really thought about it, but what do Hogwarts graduates do afterwards."

She shrugged and said, "Oh, you know, the usual."

I frowned, and she amplified, "They find a job someplace. Some go into the Ministry—you know—Aurors, bureaucrats. Others go to work for a manufacturer—brooms, clothes, and so forth. Others go into sales. Why?"

"What about post-graduate training?"

"Well, it depends on profession. Aurors have a training institute. I think the course takes something like 12 months or maybe 18. Manufacturers sometimes have training programs. You know, what you might call vocational ed."

"Does no one go to a four-year college?

"I've heard of a few who do. " Her face looked like she'd just remember something that she'd eaten that had tasted rotten. "Didn't Sinistra go to college in the States?"

I gave a brief, "Yes."

"Well, there you are." She looked as if she'd just demonstrated by example the lack of wisdom in that course of action. "But why do you ask?"

"OK. I think Cedric's a great candidate for higher education. He's really smart. He does well in my class. He's good at writing. He could probably get into almost any university in the country."

"Well, if you feel that way, why don't you talk with him about it? See what he wants to do."

I had to agree with her. At the next class, when I returned corrected parchments, I added a note to his that he should see me after class. He showed up at my desk and asked what I wanted. "Do you have another tournament for me?"

"No. No. I'd like to talk with you about your career after you're graduated from Hogwarts. Would you drop by at my office in the evening sometime when you're not busy with studies or preparation for your next task?"

He agreed. That evening, Minerva and I were talking idly about the day when there was a knock at the door. Minerva flicked her wand, and the door opened. She invited Cedric in and excused herself.

Cedric came in diffidently, and I invited him to the red leather chair that had been occupied by Minerva. He sat and asked, "Well?"

"I'd like you to think about what you'll do with yourself after Hogwarts."

"Yeh, I've been thinking about it a little. I have to anyway because I need to decide on Newt level courses for next year. I've been thinking that I'd like to make useful things. Maybe even invent them. What do you think?"

"I think that's a good goal." I hesitated as if I were mulling it over. "A lot of Muggles do some more learning before starting their life's career. They study things like other languages, writing, mathematics, philosophy. Do you think that might be interesting to you?"

Cedric was dumbstruck by the question. He'd apparently never heard of such a thing before. Finally he asked, "How does that work? How do you get started working on that kind of thing?"

"Well, you start by figuring out how good a student you are. I can tell you right now that I consider you to be an excellent student, but you shouldn't trust one person's opinion.

"There's a test that many students your age take that is good at figuring out how well a student will do at college. It's called the Scholastic Aptitude Test. It's so good at that that most colleges use it to decide who they will let study at their school."

Cedric seemed to take that in. Then he said, "I think I'd be interested to find out how good that test says that I am. How do I take it? Is there a way to study up for it?"

I was encouraged that he was interested that far. I told him, "Well, first, you have to register to take the test. The test is given once or twice a month, at most colleges and other schools. We'll have to send our application in. The earliest that you could take it would probably be in early January.

"Now, the idea of the SAT is that you can't study for it. And that's probably pretty true. But something that you can do is to practice taking it. Being used to the form of the test and knowing a procedure for grouping the questions into manageable lumps can give you a leg up.

"There's a whole cottage industry in helping people prepare to take the SAT."

"What's a cottage industry?"

"Oh, it just means that you don't have to have much to start a business like that. You just advertise your services and you really don't have to have much equipment or an office. You can do it from your home in a lot of cases.

"Anyway, I'd suggest that if you're interested, I get a book of practice tests and you take a few. You'll get an idea of what they look like, a few tricks for speeding up and doing better at answering the questions."

Cedric thought about it and asked, "When could we start?"

"I'll get down to London and buy a book. It'll probably have an application form in it,and we can fill out the application for you and start practicing. What do you say?"

"Sounds OK. How much will I owe you for the book?"

"Don't worry. It'll be my Christmas present to you, a little before Christmas."

"Wow. Thanks. Anything else that I have to do now?"

"Just keep doing your English Lit work and get ready for the next Tri-Wizard task."

Cedric got up and started to leave. At the door, he stopped and asked, "Do you know what the next task is?"

I smiled. "I don't know for sure, and you know that I couldn't tell you even if I did. As a matter of fact, I should make something up that's so scary that you'd want to drop out and do the Chess Tournament."

He snorted and closed the door behind him as he left.

The next day at breakfast I caught up with Minerva and asked if she'd like to go to London next weekend. She looked at me askance and asked, "You've got something not entirely kosher planned, don't you?"

I put my best surprised look on my face and said, "I don't know why you'd think that. I was just thinking that it would be nice to spend a night in some nice cozy bed and breakfast and do a little shopping while we were there."

She nodded and asked, "What is it you're looking to buy? Some Muggle contraption that only someone like Arthur Weasley would want?"

"No, no. The truth is that I only want to buy a book."

"That must be some book to drag you to London in the middle of term to get."

"It's not for me. It's a little early Christmas shopping, and you could stand to do some Christmas shopping and get ahead of the crowd."

She set her gimlet eye on me and seemed to be trying to find a way to figure out what nefarious scheme I had in mind. She said, "I suppose it sounds innocent enough. And maybe doing some Christmas shopping wouldn't be a bad idea, but you've got to have a list ready for me by then."

I groaned inside but said, "Sure. I'll cook up something that will give you lots of choice. So, you'll be ready Friday night?"

She sighed. I couldn't tell if it were a resigned sigh or a wistful sigh, but she said, "Good. It would be a pleasant change to have a little break from the term. Sure."

I was on my way.

◻

The next night at dinner, Dumbledore made one of his little announcements that everyone looks forward to. "I hope that everyone is settled into the routine of school and the Tri-Wizard tournament because I have a pleasant little surprise for everyone.

"We're going to have a Yule Ball this year as usual. It will be immediately after the end-of-term exams so that no one has to worry about the last-minute flurry of study that always seems to happen just before tests. They will all be over, and we can enjoy the evening before returning to our homes for the Christmas Holiday.

"Now, the Yule Ball is a dance where everyone is encouraged to invite a fellow student to the dance. No one is required to, but the Americans have a nice slogan for such occasions—'Last one to the Ball is a rotten egg!' The big change this year is that everyone will be able to invite guests from a different school. I hope that we will have some couples who cross school lines. Although again, nothing is required. The dress code will be formal robes.

"So enjoy your deserts and begin thinking about whom you would like to accompany to the Yule Ball this year!"

Well, that was a revelation. I decided that I ought to invite Minerva at my first opportunity. But I had some papers to grade for the next day, so I went straight to my office. I had hardly opened the door when I heard a familiar voice behind me.

"Hello-o. Professor Wendt, can I come in and talk with you for a few minutes of your precious time." I grimaced and decided that even if it didn't happen now, it would eventually happen. Better to get it out of the way right away.

So, I turned and said, "Of course, Sinistra, what can I do for you?"

I stepped in, holding the door for her and followed her after she had entered. She went directly to the red leather chair without hesitating to be asked to sit. I proceeded to my chair behind my desk and asked what I could do for her—as if I didn't have a darned good idea.

She smiled broadly and said, "How nice of you to ask, Professor. I'm sure that you heard the announcement this evening that Professor Dumbledore made."

"Yes."

"Well, I was thinking that you might enjoy attending the Yule Ball with me."

I had to hand it to her that she didn't try any fancy tricks. She just went directly to the point. That gave me the opportunity to go directly to the point as well. "No, ma'am. I've already got a date for the evening."

She stared and said, "You could hardly have asked anyone in the scant few minutes since the announcement."

"Well, you know that I have an arrangement with . . . "

But she anticipated me. "I know. I know. You and Minerva normally go out together to these little soirees."

Again, she came amazingly directly to the point. I did as well, "Yes, you're right. So, I suppose that concludes our business tonight."

She shook a dainty index finger at me, "Not so fast. Since you haven't actually asked Minerva to the Ball, you could decide to accompany some other woman, couldn't you?

"I suppose that I could, but would I? The answer is no."

"You are refreshingly honest, Professor."

"Thank you. Yes, I like to keep my affairs 'regular', despite your best efforts for it to be otherwise."

"Well, then I just want to ask you one thing."

"Go ahead."

"You're absolutely sure that you're going to the Ball with Minerva?"

This was beginning to get boring. I could see it coming—a long series of wheedles and whines to try to get me to change my mind. "Yes, I'm sure."

"And there's no chance you'll change your mind." A small smile had begun to play over her face, but she squashed it.

"Look, I've had enough experience with you to always want to be with Minerva."

"SOooo that's definitely decided." She was beginning to struggle with the smile again.

I was beginning to get a little wary. I cautiously said, "It's as definitely decided as it possibly could be."

With that she rose swiftly from the red leather chair and turned very quickly, striding to the door as though she were afraid that I would change my mind. She had to turn when she opened the door to leave. I caught a glimpse of an unsuppressed smile as she left. Through the door she said, "Au revoir."

That was truly spooky. As soon as I could I got together with Minerva and raised the topic. "Immediately after the announcement about the Yule Ball, guess who . . ."

She threw up her hands and said, "Sinistra."

"Right, again, your majesty. She dropped by to invite me to the Yule Ball, but then when I said that I was already committed to going with you, a strange thing happened."

She sneered and said, "She said, 'That's just fine with me.'"

"Not quite. But pretty close. It was even stranger than you suspect. She seemed to actually be happy about it and went to great lengths to make sure that I really meant it—that I was really going to go to the Ball with you."

Minerva chewed on that for a few minutes and asked, "And she didn't ask to be the back-up date?"

"No."

She leaned back and gazed at me, "I've got a bad feeling about this."

"So, do I. Do you have any ideas?"

"No, do you?"

I shook my head. "By the way, don't forget that I need a lift down to London on the weekend."

"Hardly. I expect to get paid handsomely for that favor."

I smiled happily, "You will be."

Friday arrived, and I showed up at Minerva's office with my traveling duffle bag. She walked to the fireplace and held out her hand. I commented, "You are in a hurry."

"Well, if I'm going to take a holiday on the weekend, I'm going to get going as quickly as I can."

She took my hand, and we walked into the fireplace and with a green flare as she threw some floo powder into the fireplace, we disappeared from Minerva's office at Hogwarts and appeared. . . Where? I looked around and recognized the Leaky Cauldron. Tom, the barman, took us to a table and we ordered dinner.

Minerva stretched and expressed how much she liked staying at the Cauldron. I had to beg that we stay at a Muggle hotel.

Minerva objected and wanted to know why. I provided the answer, "I need to go to a Muggle bookstore. That means that we need Muggle things—like phone directories and phones and so forth to find a good Muggle bookstore."

Minerva wasn't entirely happy but made the best of it. After dinner, we found a cab and went to a B&B that I knew near Paddington station. It wasn't fancy, but it was comfortable and close to Muggle transportation. Also, Minerva enjoyed it well enough for all that.

The next morning I looked up bookstores in the phone directory, found a couple that were near us, and called them to find out if they carried a recent SAT workbook. They all did. We selected one and found that it was within fairly easy walking distance of us. We took to our feet (somewhat to Minerva's chagrin) and set off for it.

As we went, we discussed what I was looking for. Minerva asked, "Just what is this 'sat' test? I presume that you sit it?"

"Very funny. It's an acronym for Scholastic Aptitude Test. It's a very good predictor of how students will perform in college. It's so successful that most schools require potential students to take it and largely base their admissions on it."

Minerva nodded wisely and said, "I see. This is for Cedric, isn't it?"

"Yes."

"Do you really believe that he should go to a Muggle college?"

I turned around and walked backwards so that I could look her directly in the eye as we talked about him. "I think he's extremely talented, and it would be a shame to lose that talent because he's a wizard who wouldn't ordinarily attend college."

"Have you talked with his parents about this yet?"

"No, but I want to wait to see how he does on the test before getting them involved. He might just be an average student and it would be a shame to fight any battles that I don't have to."

"I see. Who pays for the test?"\

"I will. It's not expensive, and if he doesn't test as exceptional, that'll be the end."

She nodded and said, "OK. But, he is an exceptional student and we both know it. You'll be talking to his parents sooner or later about college."

"Maybe."

We reached the bookstore and I found the college prep section. There were a variety of SAT study guides. Most had application forms to request a testing date. I chose one and went to the counter with it. We set it down on the counter, and the proprietress of the bookstore looked up at the two of us and asked, "Ah, this is for your son, I see."

Minerva's mouth twitched down, and I said, "Now, mum, don't take it too seriously." I turned to the innocent owner and said conspiratorially, "Mom's a little sensitive about her age. She's actually my step-mom and is not a whole lot older than I am."

The owner said, "Oh, I'm sorry if you were offended, but I meant no offense. It's just my way of making idle chatter."

Minerva was speechless until we exited the bookstore when she spoke a few expletives and said, "How she could think I was your mum I can't imagine. AND how she could think that you are young enough to need that book for yourself is a mystery too."

I took my life in my hands by pushing it a little further, "Oh, mom, you are always so sensitive!"

She grimaced and took my arm roughly and said, "Let's just go!"

After a safe interval, I declared, "Now, we have time for ourselves. What do you fancy?"

"It's a little early for Christmas shopping, but we're in London. Why don't we go to Diagon Alley and see what we can find?"

I was satisfied with the idea. She added, "And now that we've finished with your errand, can we disapparate there?"

"Oh, I suppose. It was too much to hope that I could go through an entire day without throwing up en route somewhere."

Minerva only "tsched".

We arrived outside the Cauldron, and I took her hand so that we could enter. Inside, it was just before the lunch trade. Tom waved but was too busy getting ready to waste any time with us. We went on through to Diagon Alley. There, we split up. I had to get some money from my vault at Gringotts if I were to do Christmas shopping. Minerva was apparently well-supplied.

In Gringotts, I presented my key, which I always keep in my purse, but, instead of taking me to my vault, I was conducted to the desk of a bank employee. He introduced himself and explained why I was at his desk rather than at my vault.

"Mr. Wendt, I have to apologize for this diversion from your vault, but something has come up."

"Really, go ahead." I was thinking, "Here the other shoe drops."

"Well, your vault, which is one of the smallest that we rent, is . . uh. . rather small."

"Yes, I'm pretty sure that I don't need a larger one." This was looking like a straight-forward sales pitch. I guess I was lucky that I hadn't been subjected to one earlier.

"Well, actually, it is large enough for the moment, but in a few months, it will become difficult to store all your gold in it."

That was a surprise, "How is that possible? My salary for the next five years, wouldn't fill it, even if I never spent a knut of it."

"Oh, but sir, you're forgetting that you have a second source of income."

"You're talking about the license deal that I signed with your bank."

"Yes, sir. You've already got more gold from the license deal than you have from all your earnings from Hogwarts over the last couple of years."

That was a surprise. "OK. How much will the next larger vault cost me."

"Well, only twice the nominal fee that we charge you now."

I nodded. But he went on, "But you really should get a larger vault than that. We'll be having this conversation again in less than a year otherwise."

I was beginning to feel put-upon, but maybe he wasn't kidding. I said, "Look, I'll be back before Christmas. I'll decide then about what larger vault I need. But for now, I'd just like to get to my vault."

The Goblin was very apologetic. "Well, sir. Before I let you go, my superiors want me to present an investment opportunity to you. It's really a waste not to invest at least some of your gold in a good safe investment that will increase your capital."

"We can do that at Christmas too. Just get me to my vault."

"Yes, sir."

After that, a junior goblin was summoned and took me to my vault. I had to admit that it was getting rather full. I took a good sum out and kept some in galleons and some in pounds sterling.

By the time that I left the bank, Minerva was outside waiting for me. I marveled that she had finished shopping while I was in the bank. She reminded me that I'd been in the bank for a long time and asked me what had kept me there.

"Well, you remember that I told you about a license deal that I have with the goblins?"

"I knew that would come to no good. So, what bad luck has befallen you?"

"Actually, none. They kept me there to convince me to get a larger vault to hold all the galleons that I was getting from the deal."

"And you believed them?"

"I saw my vault and its contents. Unless they're counterfeiting galleons, I'm making a lot of money out of the deal."

"They didn't give you an accounting?"

"No, they didn't. But come to think of it, I'm supposed to get quarterly reports and the first should be due at any time. Oh, yes, they wanted me to invest in a 'conservative' growth opportunity."

Minerva rolled her eyes. "Oh, great. Tell me you're not considering putting money in their hands."

"Don't worry. I've got the reputation of the goblins of Gringotts tattooed on my credit card."

Minerva was surprised and asked, "Your what?"

"Oh, it's a long story, and I'll tell you some time. But for now, don't worry. I'd find my own investments before I'd put money with the goblins. With their attitude toward the ownership of things, I couldn't be sure that they weren't figuring that it all belonged to them."

I went on, "Now, I do want to do a little Christmas shopping. So would you mind toddling along to the Cauldron and have a butter beer or go anywhere else that will allow me to do some shopping unobserved?"

She frowned, "How will you get out when you want to leave?"

"Oh, we can arrange a meeting time—here. Let's say two hours?"

"Well, I guess that's OK. Don't be late."

I watched her exit Diagon Alley by way of the wall at the back of the Cauldron. I gave her a couple of minutes to make sure that she wasn't going to return and spy on me. I then went directly to the wand shop of Olivander.

I entered the shop and started to look around the displays of wands and wand-cleaning tool kits and so forth. Shortly, Mr. Olivander entered the shop from a back room and said, "Ah, very interesting. What would a Muggle be doing in my shop? What would he be doing in Diagon Alley for that matter?"

I smiled, "You're sure that I'm a Muggle. I couldn't be a Squib?"

"Oh, yes. Even Squibbs cause wands to react—either favorably or unfavorably. You don't cause any tremor of reaction at all. You're a Muggle. What brings you into my shop?"

I nodded appreciatively. I had to admit that he was not the dullest knife in the drawer. I explained, "I'm Professor James Wendt of . . . "

He interrupted and said, "Yes, of Hogwarts. I know of you. You claim to be a Squibb but obviously you aren't. Why do you hide under an identity that isn't yours?"

"Well, you may know that some wizards are touchy about Muggles. Professor Dumbledore thought that it would be best if I didn't ruffle feathers that didn't have to be ruffled."

Olivander nodded and said, "In any case, what can I do for you?"

I continued my explanation, "I'm looking for a Christmas present for a witch, and I was hoping that you could help me. Is there anything wand-related that you could suggest?"

He came closer and rubbed the fabric of my shirt between his thumb and forefinger and whistled an odd tune. "Yes, she's disapparated you with her wand, fir with a core of dragon-heartstring. Probably 9 inches or so.." He thought for a moment and nodded, "Yes, that would be Minerva McGonagall, wouldn't it?"

I shook my head in disbelief, "You figured that out just by observing my shirt?"

"Magic always leaves an imprint that survives its immediate effect. She's disapparated you quite a number of times. Otherwise, I wouldn't have been able to recognize details about the wand. Once I knew the wand and had the hint of where she worked, it was fairly easy to deduce her identity.

"I'm afraid that I probably can't help you."

I was dumb-founded again, "How do you know? You sell wand accessories, don't you?"

"Oh, of course, I do. But I know that she got a fairly nice wand-cleaning kit from her sister for her last birthday. And, there's not much else that I sell that would be appropriate."

And I thought this was such a good idea. Now, I'd have to think more. In desperation I asked, "Isn't there some service or something else that you sell?"

Olivander bent his head toward his right shoulder and said, "Maybe there is. I do sell a wand tune-up service. Not a lot of wizards and witches use it. Their wands begin to be less precise in following spells but most don't pay attention. Only wizards who need very precise spells all the time use that service regularly, but I've always maintained that an occasional tune up would do every wand a world of good."

He added, "And, come to think of it, I don't think that Ms. McGonagall's wand has ever been tuned-up. That's a good idea. I can sell you a gift certificate for that service. How would that be?"

I said, "That's good. I'll take it." But I thought, "Great. Nobody really likes to get a gift certificate as a gift—especially a Christmas gift. I'll have to keep looking." However, I paid for the certificate, and Olivander filled out the gift certificate in a nice round hand on fine parchment and put it in a nice envelope.

"Is there anything else that I can do for you?"

I shook my head, thanked him for the idea, wished him a good day, and left. Then I had to think of another place to go. I thought about a book, some article of clothing like a scarf, and so forth and rejected them all. As I walked the street, I noticed a store that sold wine and spirits. I walked in and decided that I'd buy her a fifth of really good whiskey. I still wasn't totally satisfied, but that would have to do for this shopping trip.

Minerva and I met as planned and had a late lunch at the Cauldron. After it was over, she gave a sigh of relief and said, "You don't have any objection to going back to Hogwarts directly from here by floo, do you?"

I opened my mouth and her mouth turned down. I changed what I was going to say about finding out if the Hogwarts Express was available—a foolish thought. Instead, I said, "Sure, let's go." Her mouth relaxed, and she held out her hand. I took her hand, took a deep breath, and stepped into the hearth with her. We arrived in her office, and I doubled up with vertigo and nausea, but I managed to straighten up and return to my office.

A few days later, Cedric and I met. I showed him the SAT study guide. I explained how the tests work mechanically and told him that we'd do several practice tests and then decide where to go from there.

After I graded his first practice test, we got together again and we discussed the results. "Cedric, You got a score of 685 on the math part and 727 on the language part of the test.

"Those are good scores. They will get you into most colleges."

Cedric smiled ruefully, "But not into the best schools?"

I looked up at the ceiling to my right, trying to figure out how to explain it. "Well, there isn't any score that's going to guarantee you to get into the very best schools, but generally, to have a good shot at the very best schools, you have to be very close to a perfect score."

"So, I have to get two 800's?"

"No, it's not that bad, but with this score I'd say you'd have to have something else going for you to have a good shot at getting into the best."

"Something like?"

"Something like a relative who'd gone to that school or someone who donated a lot of money to the school."

"That kind of leaves me out. We're not rich, and nobody in my family went to a Muggle college."

"But," I added, "That score can probably be improved on."

Cedric smiled again, "How?"

"We'll have you take a couple of more practice exams. Just getting used to it will add points to your score. Most of the kids taking these tests have already taken a lot of tests that are pretty similar to the SAT, so they've got a leg up on you. We'll do some more practice and then see."

Over the next ten days, I met with him half a dozen times. He took two more math sample tests and two more language sample tests, and we reviewed the results. Then, I mostly let him tell me what the strategies that he'd developed were and how he thought they worked.

After the last session, I summarized things for him. "You've improved your scores to 723 math and 763 on the language. Getting above 750 is what your goal should be. You've already made it on the language side. The math side will take some work.

"You've got some good test-taking habits that you've developed. I like your idea of not limiting the time you spend working on any given question and the way that you make an educated guess on the questions that you aren't sure about."

Cedric nodded and said, "BUT?"

"But, there are some other techniques that would help you. For example, here's the way I'd handle time management. Set aside 80% of your time to do the questions that you're sure about. Take enough time to be sure that you understood the question. If you're sure about the answer, go with it. Make sure you don't exceed 80%. For you, that should be easy.

"Then, go back through to pick up questions that you weren't sure of, if there's more than one answer that seems right, guess and pick one quickly. Don't try to think it out, just mentally flip a coin or something and pick. Then, forget about the question and keep going."

"What if I don't have any idea? Do I come back through a third time to pick those up?"

"No, do it on the second round. If you don't have any idea about the answer, just pick one randomly."

Cedric puzzled over that and said, "Wouldn't it be good to just go sequentially through the letters? The first one that I don't know, pick A; the next one, B, the next one C; so forth?"

"No, pick them as randomly as you can. The truth is that somewhere deep in you, there may be an intuition that will only come out if you try to pick randomly."

Cedric smiled and said, "And then, if I have time left, go back and check them all one last time."

I shook my head, "No. If you finish and still have time left, just turn your test booklet upside down and put your pencil down on top of it."

"Really! But couldn't I improve by checking my answers to make sure that I didn't mark the wrong question with the right answer, or something?"

"No. It's more likely that you'll change a right answer to a wrong one that way."

I stood up and said, "And now, let's take a couple of days rest and next Thursday come back and we'll take the final practice test using everything you've got and that will be that."

Cedric said, "But, shouldn't I practice more. You know, the way we do in Quidditch? Our team captain wants us to practice more than anybody would have time for."

I smiled. "I think that's different. Quidditch has lots of complicated physical maneuvers that you have to ingrain in your very bones. This is different. What you've learned is a few simple rules of thumb. You have to be sure that you're following them, but you don't have to drill and drill and drill to ensure that you do."

Cedric left and I thought that we were close to perfection—for him. I was restless and decided to take a little walk by myself around the castle. I lost track of the time and discovered that it was dark and past all students curfews. I decided that I needed to get to bed myself. On the way back to my office, I heard a commotion in the distance. I decided that I should see what was going on. By the time I got close, it was all over, but I found Moody stomping along, apparently back to his office. He was muttering loudly to himself. I approached to say hello.

"Well, Professor Moody, what was all the hubbub?"

Moody didn't realize that someone was around and looked startled. He took a swig from his ever present flask. "Oh, it's you Wendt. You oughtn't to sneak up on a former Auror that way. You could get turned into a ferret."

I laughed, hoping he was joking, and asked, "You were doing quite a lot of muttering? What happened?"

"Oh, that stupid Potter nearly got caught. He's going to be the death of me yet. You'd think that if he were going to go around in that invisibility cloak of his after hours, he'd be more careful. He's going to get caught and expelled for a term and then where would we all be?"

I puzzled that over. It seemed unusual for Moody to take such concern for a student. Then something occurred to me, "How do you know he was in his invisibility cloak?"

Moody shook his head as though trying to clear it, "Did I say that?"

"You sure did."

"Well, uh," he hesitated and then seemed to make a decision, "You know my 'Mad Eye', and you don't have to worry about my feelings. I know what my nickname is—even if no one will use it to my face."

"Uh, yeh."

"Well, I can see through invisibility cloaks with it."

"Really! I can see how that would be useful for an Auror."

"You bet it would." Then he stopped walking and asked, "Didn't we pass the corridor that your office is in?"

I had to agree that we had, and I headed down that corridor and shortly was back to my office.

The Yule Ball

The next day, Minerva visited my office with a large box in hand. She entered, shut the door, and locked it. I asked, "I take it this is some sort of present?"

She smiled and said, "It's Christmas a little early. Open it. It won't wait for Christmas."

I smiled, opened the box, and found inside a new set of robes. I inspected them closer and realized they had a lot of subtle touches—the robes were Gryffindor red but had a black edge that shimmered opalescently. The cut was conservative, and I had to admit to myself that it looked good. "Well, I'm sorry that I don't have my Christmas gift for you together yet, but why the hurry and why robes as a gift?"

Minerva shook her head in disbelief. "You know there are times when I think that you're smart. Answer the questions yourself."

"Well, you were forced to give it to me before Christmas. OK. What's going on .before Christm . . " And it hit me. Of course, the Yule Ball. "All right. Yes, I get it. You want to be sure that I have dress robes that will be 'nice'."

She smiled and said, "Is there anything wrong with that?"

"No. The sad thing is that you have better taste in men's clothes than I do. Merry Christmas." I kissed her, and I was sincere in what I said. She lingered over the kiss, and she agreed that it was a Merry Christmas.

Then she asked how things were going with Cedric and the SAT.

"Oh, he's doing fine. We've done a couple of practice tests, and it looks like he'll get a very good score. I've gone ahead and filed an application for him to take the exam in January."

"Good enough to get him into the best schools?"

"Should be."

"Then you'd better get together with his parents. They'll need to know if he wants to go to college."

"Yes, you're right. And frankly, I'm not looking forward to it. Even with very good scores, if he wants to go to an excellent school, he may not get enough financial aid. He'll have to depend on his parents for help. It was hard enough talking them into letting him play chess, but this will be much worse."

She laughed and said, "Look on the bright side, Cedric might just win the 10,000 galleon prize."

"Yeh. But I wouldn't count on it." Then I thought of something even more glum, "And even if he does, 10,000 galleons won't go a really long way toward an excellent college education."

Rita Skeeter Victorious

The next day at breakfast I was reading the *Prophet*. As I was drinking some orange juice, a hand clapped me on the back. I choked a bit, and Snape's voice said, "Oh, sorry. I didn't realize you were drinking. You should look at Rita Skeeter's column in the *Prophet* today."

"You know, I think I'll just hold off on that for a while." Of course, I looked and saw an article by Rita Skeeter that made me stare in disbelief. I got up and went over to where Minerva was sitting. There was a seat free beside her, so I sat down and was about to ask her if she'd read the *Prophet* today.

She beat me to it. "You've seen the *Prophet* today, haven't you?"

It didn't name any names, but it asked the rhetorical question, "What Hogwarts Professor received a rather intimate gift from a Hogwarts assistant headmistress?" It went on to make wild suggestions as to what the gift might have been and wondered if there was some sort of reciprocation.

Just then Professor Dumbledore joined us and asked us to join him in his office immediately. When we got there, he asked, "I trust that there are good answers to these questions in the *Prophet* if I have to face the Board of Trustees of the school about these allegations."

I said, "Yes, there are. It was a suit of dress robes. It was an early Christmas present that I haven't reciprocated yet with either my own Christmas present to her or any other form of in-kind payment."

Dumbledore paced the floor, "Well, the horse is out the barn door, and there's nothing we can do about that. If I'm asked—officially or unofficially—I'll give your answer. The two of you had better: 1.) Answer such questions just as you have, regardless who asks. And answer politely. 2.) Be exceptionally circumspect in your behavior. You know." He paused as though wondering whether to say what he was about to say. He did, "It might be a good thing if you don't go to the Yule Ball together."

Both Minerva and I rose from our chairs, and Dumbledore put out a warning hand, "I'm not kidding. This will be hard enough to get through as it is, At least until the next term or maybe until summer holiday, it would be good for you to only see each other at official school events—and even then, only from a distance."

As we left Dumbledore's Office Minerva said, more to herself than me, "How did she arrange that?"

I snorted, "Nothing easier. Rita's more than happy to accept any gossip, supported or not. We should have seen something like this coming." I thought about the deal cut between Sinistra and Rita.

Minerva said, "But there was specific information in that article. I think it was very unlikely that Sinistra was watching me when I brought the package up here. I had the gift in my office from the moment that I arrived at Hogwarts until I left for your office. Had Sinistra been watching my office for weeks?" She thought a moment and then said, "Even if she had, how the heck could she have known that the present was clothes?"

I was happy to be walking. I do my best work thinking on my feet. "Could she somehow have some way of seeing inside my office?" I no more had said that than the implications of what I said hit me. It hit Minerva as well.

"So, everything we do could be public. Everything YOU do in private could go public!"

"Great. Is there some way that you can search my office for bugs?"

"Bugs, what do you mean? There are undoubtedly some insects here."

Despite the seriousness, I had to chuckle, "Bug is slang for a device that could let you secretly hear or even see what happens in a place."

"Strange. Why would anyone use that word for a spy?"

I thought a moment and then an idea hit me, "I don't know about the etymology, not to mention the entomology of that term. It occurs to me that Muggles have a saying,and I wonder if wizards have it too:

"'What I wouldn't give to be a fly on the wall in that room.'"

Minerva said, "No, I can't say that I've heard that expression." A little facial tick struck her and she said, "But now that you mention it, I think there might just be something to that." She pulled out her wand and swept around and muttered, "Revellio humano." Nothing happened.

She said, "Well, it's just possible that Sinistra is able to transform into a bug—just the way that I transform into a cat. It would be possible to check to see if she is a registered Animagus."

Now, I was surprised, "Animagus? What's that?"

"That's a person who has the ability to change at will to some animal. You have my example. I'm an animagus. But the ability is watched carefully by the ministry because of the potential for misuse. By law, all animagi are required to be registered. I can check to see if Sinistra is registered. If she isn't AND she actually is one, she could be penalized. It would give us some leverage on her."

"Well, it would be nice to be on the kicking end for once rather than constantly being kicked around."

Minerva nodded. "Let's go to your room and check it out. Maybe she's there now."

I rolled my eyes in disbelief, "We were just on the edge of being disciplined by Dumbledore about that very thing. I don't think this is the time to do that."

"Oh, you are such a wuss. How would you feel if Sinistra were in your rooms when you were changing into those cute boxer shorts that you wear to bed?"

"I'd think it would be nice to know. OK. OK. Come to my office and do your search, but make it quick. That's just about the last thing that I want showing up in the *Prophet*—you visiting my bedroom tonight."

She snorted, and we changed directions to head for my office. Minerva and I tried to keep our eyes open for signs that we were being observed, but neither of us could detect anyone watching us.

When we arrived, Minerva went in first and had me watch the hall for spies. She beckoned me in and said, "I've searched the room and can't find anything. Let's go into your bedroom."

"What a disgusting thought—being in the bedroom with you and not . . ." I was interrupted though by her incantation as she searched the room. No luck. I insisted on accompanying her to Gryffindor tower.

"Why in the world? It's not like two years ago when the monster was prowling the corridors."

"It seems like there's a monster prowling the corridors now." I said ruefully.

"Not one that I can't handle, though. But I would be careful if I were you."

I got back to my office safely and tried to get back to normal work. Fortunately, all the classes for the term were over, students should have been studying for finals, and professors should have been working on final grades.

It was a surprise when Cedric showed up that night just after dinner—as planned—to do the final dress-rehearsal practice SAT. He knocked on the door, and I asked him in. He just stood inside the door as I stared at him stupidly and then started to say, "Was this the wrong, night?"

I interrupted and said, "No, no. It's the right night. I've just been distracted lately."

He smiled and said, "Pretty much everyone has read the *Prophet* today."

"Well, it's not quite what it seems in the paper."

He turned a little red in the face and looked down at his shoes and asked, "I couldn't help being curious. . ." trailing off without completing the thought.

"I'll tell you what happened. It's not anything shocking or surprising," I said with some thankfulness in my heart if not my voice. "I don't mind telling you." I gestured to the red leather chair and invited him to sit.

"Here's a long story short. The gift was an early Christmas present. 'Why early', the inquiring mind asks? Simple, it was a set of dress robes that I could use at the Yule Ball, so it had to be an early present."

He turned even redder and stared more determinedly at his shoes, "And . . . "

"And nothing, really. It was a surprise and I didn't have my gift for her ready. I just gave her a simple, modest kiss as thanks.

"I'll be wearing it at the Yule Ball, so you'll get a look at it at the Ball. That assumes that you will be going, right?"

His flush subsided and he looked up with a big smile on his face. "Oh, yes. Cho Chang is going with me."

"Good. Anyway, there wasn't any further thanks for the present that night, despite the implications of Ms. Skeeter."

I got up and walked to my bookshelf where I'd prepared the test for tonight. "Are you ready for the test tonight?"

"Yes, sir."

I explained how we were going to work it. We would run it as much like the real test as we could. I'd time the tests. We'd do both tonight. He would sit at my desk, and I'd give all the normal prompts that the test proctor would and answer any questions the way the proctor would.

He said that he was ready. I handed him the math section of the test and two #2 lead pencils. "All right, I'll tell you when you may begin. You'll break the seal and begin the test. When you have five minutes left, I'll tell you. When time is up, I'll ask you to put your pencils down, and I'll gather the papers in.

"You may not leave the room or even get up until you hand in your test. Ready. You may begin."

He broke the makeshift seal that I'd made with spell-o-tape and began marking the answer sheet.

I sat down on the sofa and started reading an article in the latest *Scientific american*. I didn't make much progress on it.

I kept an eye on my watch and when five minutes were left gave the five minute warning. When time was up, Cedric was still working the test. But, he promptly put the test and his pencil down, and I collected it.

"Well, Cedric, let's take a little break. Why don't we both take a biology break, get something to drink, and then start up again in fifteen minutes?"

Cedric blinked his eyes and said, "Biology break?" And then the light seemed to dawn. "Oh, yes, sir."

"You can use my bathroom over there. There are doors into both my office and my bedroom, so don't use the wrong one, coming out."

He smiled. I then asked, "What would you like to drink? I could heat some tea or you could just have water.'

He had just entered the bathroom when he called back, "Water would be just fine."

After both he and I had used my bathroom, I poured us both tall glasses of water and commented, 'You won't be able to take water into

124

the test room with you, so finish having your drink and we'll do the Language test as soon as you're ready."

He took a last swallow, went back to my chair, sat and declared himself ready. I repeated the instructions, and he began the test. I paid a little more attention to him. He seemed to be more confident and faster marking the response paper. I could tell when he completed his first pass through the test and had started the second with about a half-hour left. He turned his paper over and laid his pencil down on top of it with about ten minutes left. I got up from the sofa and walked over to my desk and said, "Well, I'd advise you to stay seated until the end of the time and let the proctor collect your paper. You've still got ten minutes left. If you don't mind, I'll collect it right now."

"Not at all, professor."

I picked the paper and pencil up and started to walk to the door to let him out, when he leaned back in my chair and said, "Could you grade it now? I'd really like to know how I did."

My face dropped. It was late. It had been a long hard day, I just wanted to get to bed. The objection that I raised though was different, "Well, it's close to curfew already. If you wait until I grade it, I'll have to accompany you back to your dorm and make sure that Filch or Snape don't intercept you. Heck, even Professor Moody might get you. I hate to think what detention he might assign you."

Cedric laughed, "I don't need help to get back."

I sighed and sat down on the sofa. "OK. But I'm going back to your dorm with you." I rose and got the SAT book out of the bookshelf and opened to the answer key at the end. I'd ordinarily have taken the test myself and compared our answers with the answer key, but there really wasn't time for that, so, I just opened to the answer key and went through the tests as quickly as I could without making a mistake.

I finally finished and looked up at Cedric, who apparently had his eyes on me the whole time that I'd been grading. He said an expectant, "Well?"

I tried to hide my pleasure with the results but I couldn't help smiling, "Well, well. Your language score was 778. Really good job."

The anxious expression hadn't left his eyes, so I didn't delay longer and said, "And your math score was 761." He leaped up and whooped. I immediately said, "Congratulations!" and shook his hand. I went on, "With those scores, there isn't a school that wouldn't consider you very seriously."

125

Cedric turned thoughtful and asked, "Just what is the best college in England?"

"Well, you'd have your pick between two. There's Oxford and Cambridge. It would be hard to pick between them."

Cedric was definite without apparent thought. "Cambridge just sounds better. I'd like to see it."

"Then, the hard part starts." Then, I started to talk about next steps, but Cedric interrupted and said, "Professor, it's almost Christmas Holiday and the Yule Ball and everything. Let's just take a break until we return after the beginning of next term."

I nodded ruefully and said, "You are certainly right. Take it easy until next year."

He said, "I'll be seeing you at the Yule Ball with Professor McGonagall, I suppose?"

My mouth opened and then closed without saying anything. Finally, I said a weak, "We'll be there. I hope you and Ms. Chang enjoy it."

As he left the doorway, he waved and shouted over his shoulder, "You too."

Yeh, I thought, me too. He was so confident that I didn't escort him back to his dorm.

The next day was exam day for all English Lit classes. Each exam had two hours. The exams started at 8 AM and ended (after a break for lunch) at five. After the first exam ended, I started grading it while I proctored the next. I went on grading through the night, and after a 6 hour break for sleep, I continued the next day. I finished in the late afternoon. The day after was the Yule Ball and then we were done for the term. I submitted my grades and got a good night's sleep.

That next day, everyone was in a festive mood. The Brothers Weasleyov were playing little practical jokes on everyone. There was nothing serious. The worst was that Mr. Filch was short-sheeted at some point during the night. We knew because when Filch ran into the great hall during breakfast swearing blood and revenge against whoever had done it, the Weasleys stood and confessed. Dumbledore gave them a detention with Filch, postponed to the next term because, "The term officially ends after breakfast. The Hogwarts Express will take anyone who wishes back to Kings Cross. Therefore, there isn't time this term for serving detentions."

Then he added that if anything happened during the time from breakfast until the Hogwarts Express leaves tomorrow, "I'll personally disapparate you two directly to your Mum." That seemed to cool the ardor of the Brothers Weasleyov considerably. As far as I know, nothing else was traced to them before the next year. I think that as they both had dates for the Yule Ball, they were anxious not to leave before the next day.

After breakfast, I went back to my office and frankly took it easy. It had been a hard week so far, and I took a little nap. I did some reading and decided to skip lunch. I was beginning to think that I ought to skip the Yule Ball. What was there in it for me? I could go without Minerva, maybe get one dance in with her and maybe not. How revolting could you get?

But I finally decided that Minerva had bought the dress robes for me so that she could see me in them at the Yule Ball, and it would be a shame for her not to. So, I began wondering how I would while away the hours at the Ball. I decided that they'd have music—probably decent – and food—probably great. There would even be a chance to talk to people that I didn't much.

So, I skipped dinner too and showed up in the Great Hall at 8 PM when things were supposed to get started. I arrived and found that people were only beginning to filter in. The band was setting up. As a matter of fact, the only group that was on time was the house elves who had already set up a nice spread of food. I was beginning to feel the appetite that I'd not had earlier, so I went over and built myself a sandwich.

By the time that I'd finished it, the band had completed setting up and was almost ready to go. A number of students and teachers had arrived, including Minerva with Dumbledore. I waved, and she flapped one hand modestly. I smiled and then there was the introduction of the champions and their escorts. The first dance began. After the first dance, Minerva accompanied Dumbledore onto the dance floor,and many other couples joined them. I turned to look around for Moody. But before I could do that, a hand grasped me by the arm,and I swung around to find Sinistra!

She said, "Well, has Minerva abandoned you for Dumbledore?"

I actually sneered, "What do you think? You know perfectly well why we can't be seen together. As a matter of fact, didn't you arrange for Skeeter to find out about the present?"

127

She smiled, "And a very lovely Christmas present it is too. You look quite dashing in red and black."

"If you think that I'd spend two minutes with you after that sneaky, underhanded trick, then. . ."

She interrupted me, "I had nothing to do with it."

"What a joker you are. We knew that you'd try something, after you were so satisfied to know that I was certainly going with Minerva to the Ball. It was as easy as pie to keep an eye on us, waiting for something that might look, well, fishy and report it to Skeeter."

Her eyes flashed for a moment, "Oh, I admit that I had been trying to figure out a way to keep Minerva from going to the Ball, to leave you free. But I hadn't come up with something when the two of you contrived to do my work for me."

"Don't be ridiculous. How would Skeeter have found out about this, " I fingered the robe, "without you? Who else had a motive?"

"I don't know, but it wasn't me. Do you think that I spent all my time for the last two months following the both of you around looking for some little slip?

"I admit that I have no idea who did it, but it certainly wasn't me."

I had to admit that she had a point about not following us around for months on end. I didn't think anyone who had to teach at Hogwarts would ever have time for that. Then she asked, "Well, you can't dance with Minerva, and you're here at the Ball. It would be churlish and not very smart not to dance with someone. And who would be better than I?"

This was so stupid, but, I couldn't resist the temptation to ask, "What do you mean, 'not very smart'?"

"Well, think about it. If you don't dance with anyone, won't that just confirm Skeeter's contention that the two of you are in a, shall we say, compromising affair?"

I didn't like it, but I supposed that she was right. She went on, "Minerva didn't hesitate to dance with Dumbledore. Why shouldn't you dance with me?"

I grimaced and said, "I'd almost rather dance with Dumbledore than you."

"Oh, don't be a bad sport. Shouldn't you get some little pleasure out of this party?"

I was angry about it and challenged her, "Look, I'll dance with you on one condition."

She pursed her lips and said, "OK. What's the condition?"

"You have to prove to me that you weren't behind this."

She asked, "Would my solemn word be adequate."

I wasn't going to let her off easy. "No. It has to be something better than that."

"Oh, look, I've never lied to you. I've manipulated you a bit. I admit that, but I've never told you a flat out lie. And I never will."

I was seething, "Not good enough."

Her gaze seemed to turn inward. Then she said, "OK. You want serious proof. I'll give you serious proof. Suppose that I could let you ask one question of me that you could be absolutely sure that I answered truthfully. If I did that, would you be my escort tonight?"

I thought about it. I smelled a rotten fish somewhere, but I couldn't see it. I went back to her with an objection, "How could you possibly absolutely assure me that I could trust your answer."

She took a deep breath and asked, "Have you ever heard of the Unbreakable Vow?"

I sensed a trick here but had to answer honestly, "No, I haven't. What is it?"

"It's a kind of magical contract. If I take a vow, such as that I'll answer your question honestly, I have to do it."

I sniffed, "How does that contract get enforced? What if you don't answer honestly?"

She shrugged and answered in an airy fashion that belied the tension in her throat, "Then I die."

I gaped at her, "You're kidding. How can that be?"

"Oh, it's the truth. There are tons of wizards and witches around. Ask any of them."

"OK. I will." I looked around for a convenient, unoccupied wizard, and Moody came into my field of view. Yes, Moody. He was serious if anyone was, and I couldn't imagine his going along with any tom-foolery. I took her by the hand and led her over to where Moody was sitting.

He was looking the other direction as we approached but when we got within speaking range, he said, "Well, you two are an unusual pairing. What brings you over to talk to an old washed-up Auror?"

He turned as I explained, "I have a question about a particular kind of magical contract."

"Go ahead."

"Tell me about the Unbreakable Vow."

"Sure. Simple. You make a vow. Another wizard invokes the spell. You break the vow, you die."

"Right then and there?"

"Right then and there. I've never seen it myself, but I've heard that it's pretty gruesome. Why, are you thinking of making an Unbreakable Vow to Ms. Sinsistra?"

I said, "No, the other way around."

His eyes lifted in surprise, "Really. Just what are you thinking of vowing, Aurora?"

She looked him directly in the eye, "Simple and short. Just that I'll answer the first question that he asks in the next ten minutes completely and honestly."

A little smile broke across his face. "Well, interesting. I like it. Short time limit. Obligates you for one question. But a little too open-ended for my tastes. No limit on what the question can be? For example, tell me all about all the boyfriends you've ever had?"

"Oh, I trust Wendt, and he ought to trust me, but he has some lingering doubts."

He turned to me, "For obvious reasons, the vow is very dangerous. Are you sure that you want to put Professor Sinistra into that kind of danger?"

That was a good question. I thought for a minute and decided, "This is completely voluntary. If she takes the vow and answers my question, I'll spend the evening with her. There's no compulsion either physical or mental to take the vow. She suggested the idea. If she chooses to take the risk, I'll let her."

Moody smiled broadly. "More and more interesting. Well, Sinistra, if you still want to go ahead with it, I'll administer the oath for you."

She set her jaws determinedly and said firmly, "Yes, I do."

Moody said, "OK. These things are best done in quieter and less crowded surroundings. Let's go outside under the moonlight." He led the way. It was chilly—not quite cold enough for snow, but definitely sharp. He set us close together and said, "Sinistra, grasp Wendt's forearm near the wrist. Wendt, do the same."

He pulled his wand and administered the oath, "Aurora Sinistra, do you swear that you will answer completely and fully honestly . . ."

As he administered it, some sort of lines of blazing light left his wand and encircled our grasped arms. As he spoke, the lines first caressed our arms and then bound them tighter and tighter. Finally, I was afraid that we wouldn't be able to separate them, but when Sinistra spoke the "I do", they immediately disappeared as did the force. She gasped.

Moody turned and started hobbling away at a good pace, "Well, I'll leave you two to it. I don't want to see the gruesome results. Don't dawdle, it's cold out here."

I turned to her, still grasping her arm, as though I could use it as a lie detector. I asked my question, "Sinistra, did you have anything to do with Rita Skeeter learning about the present that Minerva gave me or the article that she wrote in the *Daily Prophet*."

Sinistra took a deep breathe and hesitated a minute, as if trying to be sure that what she said was complete and consistent. Beads of sweat began to appear on her forehead, despite the cold. Then she said, "James, I had absolutely nothing to do with the article—not suggesting it, or providing any information to Rita Skeeter for the article, or hinting to her that the two of you had any sort of relationship." She hadn't been breathing during the recitation, and then, as though she'd just remembered, she released her breath. I realized then that I'd been holding my breath as well. When it became clear that she wasn't going to die, I released my breath.

It was unbelievable. I swore to myself last year that this would never happen again, but here I was about to do it. I held out my hand, and she took it. We waltzed onto the dance floor, and she chatted away with an incessant stream of small talk, "Isn't it interesting that Harry Potter ended up with one of the Patel twins? I can never tell them apart. Do you know which he's escorting?"

I just shook my head and she went on, "I don't either. They aren't bad looking, but Potter could have had almost any date that he wanted. Why did he choose her?"

I shook the cobwebs out of my head and said, "I think they're both lovely young women. What I can't understand is how one of them got stuck with Ron Weasley."

"Oh, yes. Weasley. I give you that. She hesitated a few seconds and cocked her head as though remembering something. "Really. You think they're pretty?"

"Of course."

"Hmmm? What is the main aspect of their beauty?"

131

"Well, most men like women with long hair—the longer, the better."

"Is that so?" She fell silent for a moment as though she were thinking.

I saw an opening to waste time. She'd given me the perfect opening to do what I like next best – to lecture. Maybe I'd bore her to death. So, I gave it a go.

"Now, they actually have a lot of attributes that I, like most men, find attractive. Their hair is not just long. It's smooth and silky. It's a pure black. I think most men like that purity whether it's black or blonde or even gray."

She said, "You mean like Minerva's?"

"No comment. However, that's not all. They have a dark olive skin tone. Men find that fascinating. Their eyes are large, mysterious, dark – easy to gaze into for hours on end."

"Now, these are attributes that I find attractive along with almost all men. They have other characteristics that are not so popular among most men, but that I find fascinating."

She was interested in that. She encouraged, "Yes?"

"They're intelligent, self-motivated. They are good students."

"I think I heard a rumor that they asked the dynamic duo out."

She interrupted me, "Who? Oh, you mean Potter and Ron Weasley. Whom did you hear that rumor from?"

I smiled, "I think it was a Weasley or two."

She smirked, "Oh, you mean the real dynamic duo."

Then, the small talk machine started up again. "And what about that Viktor Krum taking Ms. Grainger. I will never understand what he sees in . . . " and on and on. Eventually after the first phase of traditional dances where it's actually possible to hold your partner in your arms and converse with her, the band switched to something more like punk rock. I didn't have to hold her or even talk to her. That was fortunate because it's hard to hold an attractive, intelligent woman in your arms and not begin to find it pleasant.

As a matter of fact, I insisted on "dancing the night away". She stopped once and insisted on getting something to drink. She begged that she wanted to catch her breath and cool off. So, after we got some punch she asked if I would take her outside to cool off. "It was so pleasant when we were out before."

132

I guess I was feeling the effects of having her in my arms for such a long time. I didn't object. It was a still, cool night, so you could walk and stay warm enough that it wasn't unpleasant. We found ourselves walking down to the lake. The ship was silhouetted against the moon as seen from the shore, and it was hard not to smile with her long lustrous dark hair cascading over the arm that had somehow gone around her shoulders.

She had been talking about how her classes were going. Somehow it didn't seem like the idle chatter while we were dancing. She talked about students learning the constellations and the planets. She pointed up to the two giants of the solar system, Jupiter and Saturn, which were both visible high in the sky away from the glare of the moon. "Jupiter may be the king of the planets, but then Saturn is the queen. She lies further out in the dark reaches of space. Her arms extend far from her subtly beautiful body, embracing her many lover moons." As she spoke of Saturn's arms embracing, her arm that had been pointing up into the sky came down on my shoulder while the other arm traveled around my waist. Her gaze flowed from the glorious heavens to my eyes. I found myself gently pulling her slowly to me, and my lips met hers in another embrace that was at once both soft and moist and hard and demanding. My left arm found its way to her waist and beyond her waist to the firm round hips below. Her mouth opened, and I found myself caressing her tongue with my lips. It lasted a second or an age. I'm still not sure. Our lips parted and hers went to my ear where she whispered, "Come to my bed." My head seemed to act on its own, both nodding and leading my lips to her warm vibrant neck. A warm chuckle escaped her lips, and she turned them back to mine.

At that moment, there was a crash as another couple tripped over a tree root on their way to the lake. She shouted, and he exclaimed, "Holy shit!"

Aurora took my hand firmly in hers and led me up the way to the castle. For me, the spell was broken. Of course, it was not a real magic spell. It was just the effect of a beautiful young woman on a man who had been holding her in his arms all night and leading her around the dance floor.

We reached the castle, and then we reached the point where one direction led to her office and another direction led to the Great Hall. My grasp on her hand tightened, and I led her toward the Great Hall. There was a sigh that escaped her lips, and she knew that she would end the night in her bed and I in mine.

When we arrived, many of the partiers had ended the night one way or the other. Moody was still sitting, listening to the music that had returned to slower beats and softer verses. He saw us and said, "Well, I see that the two young lovers are still alive, so the Vow must have come off all right."

Aurora just frowned, "Some people might say that."

I said, "You're right. We're BOTH still alive." And, I added to myself, "I've got a decent chance of surviving my next meeting with Minerva." We danced a final slow dance, and Aurora said that she was exhausted. I offered to take her to her office. She just smiled wanly, "That's OK. It's been an exciting night. To go only 90% is worse than not at all." and then hopefully, "Maybe again next year?"

I just smiled and thought to myself, "When Hell freezes over."

The Parents

The next day, we left for King's Cross by the Express. The younger kids had mostly left before the Yule Ball. It was pretty much only the 4th years and older on the train. It was only Minerva and I in the teacher's car. With only older students on the Express, there was less of the horse play that's inevitable with younger kids. The Ball had gone late, and a lot of the students were just trying to catch up on their sleep. The cars mostly had shades down, and in the subdued light, it was quiet.

Minerva and I took one pass through the train and decided that not much of anything was going to happen. Even if it did, there were older heads in all the cars that would look us up.

Minerva was subdued too. We talked mostly about Cedric and his test results and what came next. Minerva wanted me to get in touch with his parents immediately to talk about the possibilities for his future so that there would be no surprises. I objected that we hadn't really talked about next steps after I'd given him his final trial score. It would be premature to try to talk to his parents before even I knew what he was thinking.

"But that's the perfect time to talk to them when no one is set in their ideas." She insisted.

I was still opposed to it and I could see that we'd not had the end of this discussion. We arrived at Kings Cross. After we'd made sure all the kids were off with their parents, we left the magical part of the station and reached the street outside. It was then that I realized that we'd not really talked about what came next for us.

"Minerva would you like to have a cup'o to talk about what we do this Holiday?"

Her mouth froze into a hard line and then softened a bit, "Well, I suppose we should. Is there a Starbucks close?" I didn't say it, but I fervently agreed with meeting in neutral grounds—neither "mine" or "hers". We asked someone who looked like a commuter. He regarded us as morons for not knowing there was a Starbucks right there.

With a couple of cups of tea, the mood thawed some. I pointed out that we didn't have to be on "good behavior" in London.

Minerva sniffed, "You weren't exactly on 'good behavior' at the Ball. I'm sure I saw you leave it TWICE with Sinistra."

I took a deep breath and counted to five, resisting the temptation to note that she hadn't seen that Moody left with the two of us once. "Once, Moody came with us to administer the Unbreakable Vow." I would have gone on, but Minerva interrupted.

"What in the world for?"

"Well, Sinistra insisted that she hadn't ratted us out to Skeeter. When I wouldn't believe her, she suggested that she would swear to tell the truth about it, taking an Unbreakable Oath."

Minerva fell silent for a minute, "Then she didn't. That means that Skeeter found out some other way." More reflective silence followed and then she said, "I wonder if the bug theory is still good. I checked. Sinistra is not a registered animagus. I wonder if someone else at Hogwarts is?"

"Is there anyone at Hogwarts who could be her source?"

"You mean, are there any unregistered animagi at Hogwarts?"

"Why unregistered?"

"I'd know about it if they were registered. We do a back-ground check on all teachers with the Ministry before we hire them. Registered animagi would show up on that."

That raised a red flag for me, "Did you do a background check on me?"

She smiled at that. It wasn't a happy thought.

"You did, didn't you? How did you do it?"

She twisted her head so that it inclined on her left shoulder studying me, "Do you really want to know?"

"If it has anything to do with memory modification, no."

"Well, then . . . ' she let her voice trail off. I seethed for a few minutes in silence and then laughed.

"Well, I guess I must have passed. It's good to know."

Her knee brushed mine. Her voice turned silky, "You might wheedle it out of me, with the right inducement."

Our conversation turned to possible inducements.

⌐

The next day, I slept in and was awakened by a tapping on the window of my little on-again off-again garret apartment. It was an owl. I groggily opened the window, and the bird alighted on my bed's footboard. I was about to complain about the bird not landing closer—like my headboard and then thought better of it. The consequences might be pretty awful. I opened the note and read:

"Professor Wendt, would you please arrange to visit with my mum and dad about college. I've talked to them, and they're against my attending. Thanks. Cedric"

I noticed that the bird was waiting, as for a reply. I fumbled around on my dresser looking for a pen and used it to write a reply on the parchment. I wrote, "Yes. I suggest that we meet at the Starbucks in King's Cross station. Please write back with details. Regards, Prof. Wendt"

I crossed out my address and wrote Cedric Diggery below the old address and then realized that I didn't know how to complete the address. The bird was clearly getting impatient by this time. I just decided that I couldn't do better and did my best to re-tie it to the bird's leg. How did the wizards manage this? Then I realized the answer. It would be easy with magic. I got it attached pretty well, and the bird squawked and took off through the open window.

I didn't get an answer until the next day. But it was from Minerva. She showed up at the front door and rang the bell. I usually don't answer the doorbell, because it's never for me, but this time, I did. When I reached the door and glanced out the window in the door, I was glad that I had.

When I opened the door, she glanced up, "What are you going to do. We've got to get on the way if we're going to meet the Diggery's at the Cauldron for lunch."

My mouth dropped to my feet. "Uh, why, this is the first time that I've heard it."

"Well, you've heard it now, so get on your broom."

I ran up to my room and quickly put on the best clothes that I had, which weren't bad because I'd spent only a day or two in London wearing Muggle clothes. I ran down the stairs, caught her up quickly, kissed her, and we were off. She dragged me around the corner, and as we went out of plain view, we reappeared in an alley close to the Cauldron. My head was spinning as we staggered in.

Just as we did, the Diggery's were emerging from the fireplace. They noticed us almost immediately and came over. Amos was in front and held out his hand, almost aggressively, to shake. We shook hands around, Cedric smiling wanly. Tom came over and beckoned us to sit at a table in a corner away from either of the entrances.

He took drink orders immediately and then left. For a moment everyone was silent, and then the ladies began talking vigorously. I looked over at Amos and said, "I know we're here to talk about Cedric's career after Hogwarts. Do you want to start or do you want me to?"

Amos' face was slightly red and seemed to be getting redder. "Yes, I want to talk first, and then maybe you won't have anything to say.

"I want you to know that I've had about enough of your Muggle ideas. You started by encouraging my son to take more Muggle literature than he was required to. Then you got him interested in Muggle Chess. Oh, I know that he did well at it. And that's nice.

"But then you encouraged him to abandon his chances at winning the first Tri-Wizard Tournament in hundreds of years. Why in the world did you ever imagine that he would be better off not in the Tri-Wizard Tournament and, of all things, for a Muggle Tournament? And then. . ." He stopped and gathered his strength for one last tirade.

"And finally," he had reached the summit of all horrors, "you ask him to give up Wizard work and take up," he shuddered visibly, "Muggle work."

Everyone was staring at their empty places on the table except for Amos and me. I had been thinking and knew what I wanted to say. I stopped myself from rushing in. I needed to let Amos reflect on what he'd just said. I let the time stretch on as long as I could stand it. "Amos, Cedric is a wizard, and he'll never be anything else. He's a great young wizard. He wouldn't be in THE Tournament if he weren't.

"He's got so many talents that neither wizards nor Muggles have that it would be a shame to tell him, 'You have to forget about this talent and this talent and, oh, yes, especially that talent'. I want him to use all of his talents. I want him to be a man who can walk in both worlds—Muggle and Wizard—and hold his head high. I want him to have the chance to go to a college and find a Muggle talent.

"Wait, wait. What am I saying? The talents that colleges teach aren't Muggle talents and they aren't wizard talents. They are talents that all people use—that all people need. Everyone needs to be able to write, clearly and cogently. Everyone needs to be able to calculate how much they're worth. Everyone needs to be able to think clearly. Everyone needs to be able to figure out what's true and what's just self-exaggeration from politicians

"So, think about it. Think about what you want for your son and what he wants for himself. We have lots of time. This is about as young as anyone should start thinking about career and college anyway. If you decide differently, I'm always there." I stopped and there was silence again for a while. In the meantime, Tom returned with drinks and asked if we knew what we wanted to eat. Fortunately, we'd all eaten there enough that we could just reel off our favorite meals without any thought. Tom left with the order.

"Now, I suggest that we work our way through a good meal." That seemed to break the tension. The ladies resumed their conversation from before, and Amos asked what I thought of the Tournament.

"I couldn't believe my eyes when I saw that they had real, live dragons as one of the tasks. I can't imagine how you were able to sit there while your son was facing that creature."

His wife shuddered and said that she had her eyes closed the whole time. Minerva had had no trouble watching, I knew, but she expressed sympathy. "I know that in your place, I probably wouldn't even have come."

She nodded, "I almost didn't. It was really a close thing."

I chuckled, "In more than one way."

That got a laugh out of Amos. I insisted in paying for the meal, but Amos was not to be denied. I thanked him as graciously as I could and we went our separate ways.

On the way out, Minerva took my arm, "Well, that went better than I hoped for."

"Do you think he'll change his mind?"

"Well, it's two to one. Cedric and his mom have an awful lot of weight to throw around."

The phrase surprised me. "Interesting, I'd have said it slightly differently—they have a lot of throw weight."

Minerva stared but didn't ask.

But I did ask about our plans for Christmas. Minerva pursed her lips and said, "You can guess what Maggie had to say after reading that *Prophet* article."

"Yeh. I guess I can forget about visiting you this Christmas."

"Oh, don't be so sure. I doubt that she'll let you stay the night, but I think I can get you in for Christmas dinner. Also, if you give her a really nice gift, she might just let you come for New Year's eve as well." I made a note of that.

The Night Before New Year's

I spent the next several days doing a variety of shopping tasks, including shopping via phone with catalogs in the States, mainly the Penney catalog. It was strange. What had been my most difficult shopping task had suddenly turned into my easiest. I got catalogs more than a month in advance. I had plenty of time to decide. As soon as I got back to London, I made a couple of international calls and purchased for my States-side list including delivery before Christmas, gift-wrapping (better than I could do), and even custom brief notes for each recipient. It wasn't any more expensive than buying things in England, having them shipped air-freight, and still sometimes not arriving on time.

It was harder for my wizarding friends. But one or two lengthy shopping trips to Diagon Alley usually accomplished the same thing. When I got home after the last of those trips, I had a sack with several gifts for Maggie, Beryl (Maggie's sister), and one or two "spare" just-in-case gifts in case someone showed up that I wasn't expecting.

Christmas Eve would have been difficult if Minerva hadn't dropped by in the afternoon. We went to a movie. She still wasn't sure just how she felt about movies. There was nothing like it in the wizarding world, but she appreciated being able to sit alone in the dark with me. The distractions made up for what the film lacked. Unfortunately, she had to go back and have Christmas eve dinner with her sister, and so, we parted before 6 PM. However, she confirmed that I was invited for Christmas day itself and that I should come early. Very early.

Since my family tradition around Christmas was visiting a midnight church service, I found that the evening was tolerable. The next morning, I was up early, thinking about how I would greet Maggie. I was getting dressed when the doorbell rang. I quickly finished and ran down with my bag of presents over my shoulder—a little like old Saint Nick. Of course, it was the mom and dad of the renter of one of the other flats. There was a moment of embarrassment, which the mother worked past by simply saying, "I'm sure your mom will be anxious to see you too." I could only gape and try to smile.

An hour later Minerva did arrive and I wondered why she was so late after talking about being ready to go EARLY.

"Oh, you know, it's soooo hard to get up on Christmas morning," she said and stretched as though yawning, which lifted her breasts enough that they were visible through the robe that she wore."

"OK. OK. I get the idea. Let's go."

We ran up the stairs and past the Mom and Dad that I'd seen earlier. They were going down the stairs with someone who must be a daughter. As they passed, the Mom said, "Merry Christmas. I hope you and your son have a wonderful day together."

Minerva just smiled and said, "I'm sure we will."

The morning was wonderful. Minerva got up from the bed first and quickly dressed. She nudged me with her foot and urged me to get ready to go. I reluctantly did.

Then she kissed me, and a few minutes later we were at her sister's house.

We were greeted at the door (if greeted is the right word) frostily, but with no cross words. Maggie had prepared a brunch, and we were all hungry. Minerva and I were ready to exchange gifts right away. But Maggie kept stalling. First, we had to do the dishes and then we had to finish decorating the tree. Then she wanted to get the old photo albums. When it seemed like every possible excuse for waiting had been exhausted, Minerva lost her good nature. "What in the world are we waiting for? Any other Christmas, we'd have all the packages opened long ago. Are you holding off for Boxing Day?"

Maggie admitted that we were waiting for someone. Minerva clapped her hands together and said, "Aunt Beryl!"

Maggie wanted it to be a surprise, but she admitted it and we all were happy to wait for her. We pretended to be surprised when Beryl arrived. I didn't even have to dig into my supply of "what-if" presents for her. I had found a fancy set of playing cards that had all the Headmasters of Hogwarts on the cards, including the four founders. Believe it or not, I'd found it in the Weasley's Wizard Weazes Catalog.

When Beryl saw them at first, she commented on the fact that they were all marked cards. You could tell which cards someone had from the face on the back. But then she discovered the saving grace. "Why, the backs change every time a card is revealed. How clever!"

I had not found any better gifts for Minerva,and I was rather ashamed when she opened the simple envelope with the gift certificate in it. But something that I'd never seen before happened. She started crying. She dried her tears and hugged me. I could see over her shoulder that her sister didn't approve. As a matter of fact, Maggie started to say something but Beryl put her hand on her shoulder,and she didn't say what she was thinking of.

Minerva was still on the point of tears after we broke from the hug, but she clearly wanted to say something. After a moment was able to, "Oh, dearest. This is such a wonderful present. I've always wanted to have my wand tuned up but I've always thought it was such an extravagance that I've never dared do it for myself." Her eyes filled with tears again but they didn't overflow. Then she just patted my knee. Eventually, she whispered in my ear, "How did you ever know?"

A dozen snappy responses came to mind, but I just said what I wished were true, "I think that people who are really close begin to communicate without realizing that it's happening." She nodded and was unable to speak again.

Maggie had wanted to say something but this silenced her. She was much more relaxed for the rest of the evening, and Beryl insisted that we play some card games with her new cards. Maggie wanted her to keep them un-opened. I suggested that she hold them for New Year's Eve (hoping against hope that we would all be together again then).

She refused and insisted that we play with them right now. So, we played Gin and the Black-Hearted Queen (the wizard version of what we call Spades in the States).

Beryl did promise to come back for New Years—provided that ALL of us would be there. Maggie tried to object, but Beryl was adamant. It was ALL of us, or she would spend the Eve with her nephew and niece on the other side of the family – the Sackvilles – despite the fact that they were boors and stuck-up, not at all like this side of the family.

With that Maggie could not say anything other than, "Well, we certainly aren't boors. There's no telling what's going to happen or what will show up in the *Prophet* about our side." And she nodded in my direction.

Beryl was exultant, "You're absolutely right. There's more fun over here than you can find in a dozen Sackvilles."

I couldn't help smiling that I'd found a party for New Year's.

Minerva and I got together most days between Boxing Day and New Year's. They were blissfully boring days filled with wasted time and long rambling walks.

New Year's Eve arrived, and we had a little party much like the old ones of previous years. Even Maggie thoroughly enjoyed herself. Finally at the end of the evening, she pulled me aside about an hour after midnight, "I would like for you to be able to stay the night. I know how much Minerva cares for you."

I tried to object (honestly) that I didn't think she really was that attached to me, but she cut me off, "I just can't see my name or Beryl's ending up in that awful Skeeter woman's article."

I assured her that I understood and I hoped for better times next year. She nodded. Then suddenly, Beryl, Minerva, and I had gone our separate ways. Minerva would return after dropping me off, though.

A couple of days later, she and I and a train-load of kids were back on the Express headed for Hogwarts. This run was the worst of the year. It was full of kids who had received all sorts of presents—safe and unsafe. Their heads were full of a desire to have one last blow-out before the beginning of the term and they were all stuck together in close quarters.

Half the teachers of Hogwarts were coerced to go along to ride shotgun on this mad adventure. I was tempted at times to bring a shotgun, but, of course, I would never even get the Glock out (except in true emergency). I walked the cars with Minerva at my side and tried to look intimidating—a hopeless task. We eventually did reach Hogwarts station without major mishap.

Of course, the Weasley twins always had some sort of high-jinx planned, and usually their plans succeeded. This time, they snuck a concoction of their own, Tongue Ton Toffee, on and had managed to get Malfoy's friends, Crab and Goyle, to try some. It was disgusting, and I won't draw you into the morass with the details.

We arrived and a new term had begun.

The Exam

The term started fairly easily. Waiting for me in my office among the boring mail was a letter from SAT-England. I'd ripped off the outer layer of the envelope and saw that it was addressed to Cedric % me. I decided that he should have the honor of opening the inside envelope, so I asked him to come to my office after dinner that night.

He arrived, and I handed him the envelope. The return address was the SAT organization. He glanced at it and opened it. Inside, he found a letter telling him where to go to take the SAT on the 15th of January at 9 AM – University College, Room 211 and how to prepare for the test. It had a ticket that he'd use to take the exam. He wondered about the location, "Is this Oxford, THE Oxford where the university is?"

"The one and same."

"Wow. Can we do a tour of it before we come back?

"That's a good idea."

We weren't sure how we'd get there, but I consulted with Minerva. She had to do a little consulting as well. After a couple of days, she came back to me with an idea. "There's a pub in Oxford off George Street, called the 'Green Dragon'. It has a nice fireplace and is on the floo network. So, you could go directly from my office to there, and we could all have lunch there afterwards."

"Sounds good. I'll make arrangements with Cedric."

We didn't have a lot of time, so when I happened to notice him between classes, I nabbed him. We went up to my office to make arrangements. "Cedric. Minerva had a great idea. There's a wizarding pub in Oxford, just off campus called the Green Dragon. It's on the floo network, so we can just go there by floo powder."

Cedric interrupted me before I could say anything else, "Great, Professor. You and I can take the Great Hall floo network connection directly there and get back the same way. It'll be a piece of cake. We just have to make sure that the pub will be open that early. You can send them an owl and ask them to leave the floo connection open. We can promise to lock the door behind us."

I just stared at him for a moment, and then I started to look for objections, "Well, is that possible?"

"That's OK, Professor."

I didn't have anything to say. What could I say? I was an adult. I would accompany him into the bad world of Muggles, and he could get us there and back. Why was there any need for Minerva? I had only to send an owl to request the pub let us use their floo connection early Saturday morning.

That didn't turn out to be so easy. I wrote a nice respectful note to the pub owner, and Cedric saw that it got sent by owl. The response said that we should just wait until the pub opened like everyone else would at 10 AM. Of course, I'd explained why we had to be there before 8AM. So, I wrote another respectful but assertive letter explaining why it would do us no good to arrive there at 10 AM. Then, the reply came asking "why the bleeding hell does a wizard have to take a test at a Muggle school. Isn't Hogwarts good enough for him?"

In my next letter, I offered to pay the pub for the cost of having someone on duty from 8 AM to 10 AM. They were even more abusive and said that they'd refuse to let us use the floo connection at all if they could do it legally.

I showed the last letter to Minerva in desperation. "Well, you've certainly painted yourself into a corner, haven't you? But, I'd be very happy to take you both there by apparition. Why didn't you ask earlier?"

I didn't really want to have to explain the embarrassing truth that I'd not offered her services to Cedric earlier, but I made the best that I could of it. I suggested that she could just drop us off and then return immediately and not have to hang around while Cedric took his test. Minerva thought about it a bit and then agreed, "You two aren't sure how long things are going to take. I'll come back here and when you're finished you can get back here by floo from that pub and you two can take me out to dinner at the Three Broomsticks."

I agreed to that.

So, when the day came, it all came off pretty well. Minerva dropped us off in George Street. We walked to the University College where the exam was being given. The exam room was pretty easy to find and I dropped Cedric off with a wish of good luck. It was a cold day, but I decided that I'd like to walk the campus.

I arrived back at University College with about a half-hour to go. I'd brought along a book to read if I had to wait long, but I'd only read a couple of pages when the kids sitting the exam started filing out. Cedric was among the last. He had a big smile on his face and he just nodded at me.

When we were outside, I suggested that we get something to eat. We wandered a bit and settled on the Three Goats Head. It was good and reasonably priced. We were sitting in a quiet corner, enjoying lunch, when a couple of fellows, who had been sitting by themselves, drinking, seemed to notice us. The older one got up and walked over. He was thin but not gaunt, with white hair, but looked like it was prematurely white. There was something familiar about him, but I couldn't quite place him.

He reached our table. "Excuse me, but I couldn't help thinking that I've met you before. It's been a few years, but I rarely forget a face. The names sometimes escape me, but never a face. Your name is . . " He scratched his head and he tried, "Winton. No, but something like that."

By now, I'd begun to remember his face as well. I agreed, "Yes. You're familiar. You're an inspector."

But then he had it, "You're Wendt. A Professor, but not at Oxford. Some finishing school in the far north, right?"

"Yes. I guess I should introduce my star student, Cedric Diggery." I turned to him and said, "Mr. Diggery, allow me to introduce a police inspector here on the . . ."

I was stuck, but the Inspector supplied the missing information, "I'm Chief Inspector Morse of the Thames Valley CID.

"Your professor was once involved with a suspicious death here a few years ago. He's perfectly innocent, but we did have an interesting case, which is one of the few that I've never solved.

"What brings you two here? Does Mr. Diggery hope to go to Oxford?"

Diggery supplied his reason for being here, "I just sat the SAT exam. I'm only a 6th year, but I hope to attend a good college."

"Oxford is my school, and I've never entirely left it—as you can see. I don't think that you could find a finer one. Would you care to join my sergeant and me?"

Cedric asked, "What about Cambridge?"

Morse grimaced and said, "That is a fine school too."

I suggested that we didn't want to burden him, and his sergeant with making conversation with us and he accepted the excuse.

But, just then, Minerva stepped into the room, saw us, and came over. She glanced at Morse and asked him, "Well, Inspector Morse, are you planning on arresting our Professor."

He seemed to recall her name more easily than mine, "Ms. McGonagall. It's indeed a pleasure to see you again. As a matter of fact, it's a pleasure that I never dared hope to have again. After the case was over that you were involved in, I tried to find how to get hold of you, but you had seemingly fallen off the grid."

She was apparently pleased with the complement and took his arm briefly. "Well, you are gallant. I'm sorry you had such a hard time. I must leave you my address."

Morse smiled and bowed, "I would truly appreciate that."

I needed to break this up, so I asked, "Minerva, I thought we were going to meet you for dinner back at the school?"

"Oh, Wendt, don't worry, we'll still do that. I just couldn't wait to find out how Cedric had done."

I pulled up a chair for her, cementing the fact that we were staying at our table and giving Cedric a moment to think. He was happy to answer, though, "I thought I did well. It was very much like my practice exams."

Morse remained a minute, deciding what to do. Unfortunately it occurred to him, "Well, Minerva. Here's my card. Please get in touch sometime, and we can perhaps get together for dinner or a concert?"

"Thank you, Inspector. Perhaps."

I asked Minerva if she wanted anything to eat. She just wanted to hear more from Cedric. So, we talked a bit while we finished lunch, and I ordered her a glass of white wine. Cedric was still determined to go back to Hogwarts by floo. So after lunch, we split up. Minerva to disapparate directly to Hogwarts (I hoped) and we to find the Green Dragon.

We did. But Cedric wanted to take a walking tour before returning. We did. He was surprised at Oxford. "Professor, it reminds me a lot of of "

I supplied for him, "Hogwarts?"

"Why, yes, sir. They both are designed similarly and have the same old stone masonry. I was hoping to find something like Hogwarts when I was looking for a college. Maybe Oxford is it."

"Oh, I wouldn't judge too quickly. We still need to see Cambridge."

He agreed and asked if I'd take him there for a visit if we could find a place with a floo connection nearby.

"Of course. But even if it doesn't have a floo connection, I'm sure that Minerva would be glad to take us."

He completely changed subject then, "Do you think Professor McGonagall likes him?"

I stared for a minute trying to understand the new direction the conversation was taking. "Do you mean, Inspector Morse?"

"Yes."

I muttered to myself, "I hope not." Cedric didn't catch that but he heard something and asked what I'd said. I answered, "I rarely understand women's motivations. It's entirely possible. He is intelligent and handsome."

"What about you?"

I chose to interpret the question as being about my feelings for Minerva. "It would be bad ethics for me to discuss a fellow Professor."

"So, you do?"

I maintained a dignified silence.

The Second Task

A little over a week before the next task of the Tournament, Cedric showed up at my door, uninvited. I invited him in. He had a strange question, "May I ask you something privately?"

"Well, it depends. If it involves some kind of harm to someone else or is a criticism, I can't promise that I'll keep what you say confidential. With that limitation, I'll promise to keep our conversation confidential."

He stood and walked around the room looking at my bookshelves, as though one of the books might hold the resolution of what appeared to be a dilemma. After a few minutes he said, "This involves the Tri-Wizard Tournament."

"Go ahead. But I'm keeping my limitations."

"OK. Here's the thing. It's sort of a question of ethics.

"I want to do something, and I'm not sure it's the right thing to do."

"Tell me about the situation. Take your time. Then tell me what you want to do and why you want to do it. Then tell me how you see it ethically."

Cedric nodded, "OK. We have to go back a bit in time."

"Not before this school year, I hope."

"No. No. Just back to the beginning of the year, before the first task of the Tournament.

"I was trying to prepare for the first task, and I didn't have any idea what it was. So I was pretty much floundering around—just practicing the spells that I already knew and reading up on spells that I'd never done but thought might be useful. For example, the ability to cast the light from wand tip far away and have it continue to light an area seemed like it might be useful.

"Anyway, one day, just a short time before the first task, another contestant came to me and just said, 'It's dragons. The first task is dragons.' He didn't ask me if I wanted to know what the first task was. He just told me.

"Well, then I had two problems."

I tried to see if I could guess what they were, "You wondered first whether to believe him and second, if you believed him, whether it was ethical to prepare specifically for dragons."

"Right. I decided that I should believe him,and then I decided— without really thinking about it—to work on dragons. You see, I didn't have time. I only had a short amount of time. If I didn't start immediately and put all my effort in it, it wouldn't make a difference whether I knew about them or not."

"So, you've had time to think about it. Do you think that was ethical?"

"That's been worrying me. I just can't see my way clear to an answer. Sometimes, I think that I wasn't sure about whether it was true or not. That it wasn't much different than if I'd just guessed that it was dragons. What do you think?"

I wasn't much surer than he was. I decided to keep him talking and maybe it would be clear from what he had to say next. "Cedric. Tell me the rest of your story, and then I'll tell you what I think about that."

He frowned at that, but kept on, "Well, you know what happened, I did pretty well at the task. I might not have finished it, if I hadn't had a hint to start with.

"So, now, I figure that I owe this guy pretty big."

"Do you have an idea about doing something about it?"

Cedric looked down at his feet and didn't bring his eyes up as he spoke, 'Well, that's it. I do have an idea, but I don't feel really feel good about it. It takes a little explaining.

"At the end of the last task, we ended up with an egg with a message inside. Only, the message wasn't in a human language. It didn't sound like it was in any language, actually. So part of getting ready for the next task was figuring out what the message was and then using the message to help prepare for the next task.

"So, it was really hard. I just got the key to it by accident. So, I figure that the guy who helped me on the first task might use some help with the next task."

"And you want to know if it's ethical to give him some help to clear your debt to him?"

"That's pretty much it. What do you think?"

"You've not finished yet. You still haven't told me how you see it ethically."

He turned a bit red, "I was hoping you might have forgotten about that. Well, the way I see it ethically is that I owe this guy something, and I need to repay him and repay him in the same way, sort of. You know, it wouldn't be right to pay him in money. That wouldn't help him with the tournament, the way he helped me."

"But."

"But, it just seems wrong to give him something that he was supposed to figure out for himself."

"OK. So, you've got two competing moral impulses—to repay for help and not to give unfair advantage. Do you have a way to resolve that conflict?"

Cedric seemed to really be struggling with the dilemma. But he came to a decision, "I think it would be fair to everyone if I just gave my friend the clue in the egg. He still has to solve the puzzle in the egg. I'd not give him the solution."

I nodded and didn't say anything. Then he said, "Well? What do you think?"

I had been dreading this moment. If he came up with a really good solution on his own or even just an entirely acceptable solution like saying that he would not do anything, I'd have felt comfortable in giving my approval., Like him, I was really uncertain about this proposal, "Well, Cedric, I promised you my opinion, and I'll give it to you, but not till tomorrow. I believe in sleeping on important decisions, and this is really an important decision. So I will sleep on it. Come back in a few days and I'll give you an answer."

Cedric, of course, was not happy with that, but he could hardly complain about it, so he was gone.

The next day, I ran into Minerva in the Great Hall after lunch. "Minerva, this prohibition on meeting is driving me gonzo."

"Yes, I know what you mean even if I've not the slightest idea what that word is."

"Look I've got a problem that I'd dearly like to consult you on."

"Right. But we really can't do that sort of thing except, well, maybe offsite."

I brightened. Sure. If we went off to someplace—probably not Hoggsmeade but somewhere, maybe even just someplace that we could reach by floo network, it might work. "That's good. Couldn't we just go someplace, like the Cauldron to spend a night? Maybe this weekend."

A smile that had been forming disappeared. "Well, this weekend, I've got a commitment. Actually, I was wondering if you would substitute for me in Gryffindor tower on Saturday night?"

"Oh," I wondered what she was doing, but I simply said, "Sure." rather uncertainly.

She reached out as if to touch my arm but thought better of it and I left for my next class.

A couple of days went by uneventfully and then, during breakfast, an owl drew a bead-eye on my bowl of oatmeal and landed a letter square in the middle. I dug it out, cleaned it of the now-inedible oatmeal and ripped it open. Inside was a letter from the SAT. I jumped up to see if Cedric was still in the hall. He was. I walked up to him and handed him the letter. He stared at it for a minute and then ripped it open as fast as he could.

I couldn't see the letter but the big smile on his face was enough. All that he said—and I'm not sure that he even said it aloud but just mouthed it—was two numbers, 753 and 791. I gasped, and he nodded. Nothing more need be said then.

Later in the day, he dropped by my office and took the red leather chair. I expressed the only thing that I could think of, "Well, you probably want to know what's next."

"No, er, I mean I do want to know that, but what I really want right now is your verdict on what I should do about the next task."

Oh, my God, I'd forgotten that completely and I owed him that days before. He must have been giving me the benefit of the doubt. So, I just nodded and wished that I had a habit like smoking a pipe so that I could temporize by cleaning, filling and lighting my pipe. Instead, I had to give him my thoughts right now. So, I did what I should have done from the start—give him my first impulse, which is usually the right one, both in test-taking and ethics.

"OK Cedric. I don't claim to be an ethical genius, so don't take my idea as *vox dei*. But I think you're giving too much away. You should do the minimum to help your friend that you can."

Cedric was puzzled, "How can I do that? I'm not going to tell him how to solve the problem that the next task is, just what that problem is."

"OK. You said that you only got the key by accident. Think about it. How did that accident happen?" Cedric started to explain, but I cut him off, "I don't want to know details. That would probably be unethical on my part. Just think about how you 'accidentally' discovered the trick or the key or whatever and give him a hint to help him have the same 'accident'. Do you think that you can do that?"

He thought a moment, "Yes. I think that I can do that. And, really, that's a neat solution. I think that he's kind of a proud guy, but he might just accept that much help."

Of course, long ago, I'd decided who the mystery person was, but this really confirmed it. Too proud to accept help. I couldn't see either of the guests as filling that bill. So, I turned to the topic that I thought was on Cedric's mind when he came in the door, "I hope you want to know what comes next after the SAT."

"Sure."

"OK. Here's the deal. Your dad probably hasn't changed how he feels, I suppose."

"No. I'm afraid not."

"Well, we don't have to do too much right away. As a matter of fact, we don't have to do anything. The directors of admissions will be getting this score just as soon as we did. They look really carefully at people who get scores above 700. I think that you can count on getting lots of mail in the next month or two.

"Absolutely all of them will suggest that you come and visit their campus and get a guided tour. Some will want to come here and visit you."

Cedric face lit up with a smile, "Really?" Then he added, "But we can't let Muggles come here to meet me."

"Right. But we can offer to meet them on their campus. They probably won't be bothered by that."

"Do you think that I'll get a letter from Cambridge?"

"Oh, I think it's pretty likely."

After that he left my office.

That was a Thursday. The next day, I checked with Minerva to see if she still needed me to baby-sit on Saturday night. She did.

Saturday morning, she invited me to a little meeting that was compulsory for all the Gryffindors. It was in a crowded common room. She reminded everyone who I was. She announced that she had some personal business in town, and that I would be in charge overnight. I was to be treated exactly as though I were she. If there were anything that went badly for me, everyone in Gryffindor would regret it. There would be no attempt to find the guilty party. Absolutely everyone would be treated as equally guilty.

She had a special word for the Weasleys. "There are a couple of Gryffindors who will go nameless but if these twins should be involved in any way, in addition to the discipline that everyone else will have, I will personally visit their mother to inform her of what happened."

There was a cry of "you wouldn't" from the back of the room, but it was strictly *pro forma*. They knew perfectly well that she had every intention of doing it.

I wished Minerva a good trip, and that was about all that I could wish her. She had her single small bag packed and was off to the gates of Hogwarts beyond which she could disapparate. She walked like the wind, and I was barely able to keep up, let alone having enough "wind" to say more than, "Have a safe trip." She didn't look back but simply disappeared.

I went back to the castle and briefly visited my office to pick up some homework and headed for Gryffindor tower. The fat lady was very talkative when I gave her the password to get into Gryffindor, "Well, Wendt, do you know what Minerva's up to?"

"I haven't the slightest."

She gave a little mock gasp and expressed disbelief.

"Oh, come on. Give me a break. You two are usually joined at the hips. Surely you know what she's doing."

An idea occurred to me, "And you don't."

She blushed a bit. That was something that I'd seen but found harder to understand than moving and talking figures in a painting. Somehow something as simple as that seemed harder to understand in a painting. "You do know something." I declared.

"Not really. I just heard from another painting that she was packing something very nice to wear."

All I could say was "Hmmm."

I'd find out later, I was sure.

The evening went better than I expected. It didn't quiet down until after midnight, but that was pretty much par for Gryffindor when I was living there. I actually got a good night's sleep. That probably has more to do with the fact that it was Sunday morning than anything else. I didn't go down to breakfast. I usually didn't sleep in that much, but usually I could expect to see Minerva there. This time, I couldn't. I didn't have any motivation.

So by lunch time, I was fairly hungry and was quite happy to go down early. I found Minerva there. I sat beside her and asked how her trip was. She had been speaking gaily with Snape. That was unusual in itself. I had to "harumph" to get her attention. She looked around and turned a shade of pink quickly and then it dissipated. She was still smiling, but it wasn't the broad smile that I'd caught a glimpse of as she turned.

I spoke first, "How was your trip?"

Her smile deflated further, "Good. It was," she hesitated as she seemed to be searching for an adjective. "Yes, good."

"Could you be more specific?"

Her smile broadened a bit, "No."

My eyebrows shot up involuntarily, but she would say no more.

Shortly thereafter, she left. I turned to Snape, and he asked, "Do you know what's gotten into her?"

I was amazed by the question, "I haven't the slightest. The way she was talking to you, I'd have thought you would know."

Snape seemed bemused, "I really don't. The last time I saw her like this was years ago."

"Yes."

He avoided my eyes and said, "It's been a long time."

"Really?"

"Yes." But he wouldn't elaborate.

That was a really bizarre week.

On Tuesday, another couple of owls took a bombing run on my breakfast plate. There were three letters on my plate. I delivered them to Cedric. They were letters from Universities. They invited him to visit their campus and had contact information for their recruiter.

On Wednesday, there were five. Thursday there were none, but Minerva approached me again to sub for Gryffindor again. I agreed of course, but she wouldn't say anything more about her mysterious trip.

There wasn't a problem, of course, because she was even more explicit about what would happen if there were any problem than she had been the last time. On Sunday, she didn't show up until dinner.

When she finally did arrive, she was bubbling over with happiness. Frankly, I was a little worried. This couldn't be good for me.

On Monday, there were a dozen letters that bombarded me from four different owls at breakfast. Of course, they were all for Cedric. I didn't even open them. I just dumped them on his plate.

That evening, he stopped in and had only one letter in hand. He hadn't opened it. He just handed it to me, "I don't have the courage to open it. Would you please?"

I looked down to it. It was from Oxford. I opened it as calmly as I could. There was only one thing it could say, but I was shaking a little as I opened it and read aloud, "Dear Mr. Diggery, your performance on your recent SAT exam is exemplary, and we at Oxford would like you to consider applying to our school. We feel that no candidate should make a decision on a school—even one so prestigious as Oxford."

At this point, Diggery chortled and said, "Full of themselves, aren't they?"

"Well, they are Oxford." And I went on with the letter, "without visiting and speaking with professors and current students. Please feel free to contact me at any time to make an appointment so that I can give you a tour and provide contacts for professors who may be in fields that you are interested in, Yours sincerely, etc. etc."

"What do you think, Professor?"

I chortled myself, "Are you interested in seeing them?"

"Are you kidding?"

"Well, then, let's compose a reply and send it off tomorrow. I doubt that they can get you in this weekend, but maybe the weekend after next."

So, we wrote a letter, and Cedric got it posted that night by night owl.

We got a reply the following Tuesday. They offered us a morning meeting on Saturday. Cedric wanted us to be able to go there by floo, so he proposed an afternoon meeting. They replied offering a 1PM meeting, which we accepted.

When we were together drafting our acceptance of their proposal, I asked Cedric what had happened with the "hint" he was going to give "someone".

"Oh, I did it. It wasn't easy." He chuckled. "To be honest, I had a hard time convincing him that it was a real hint. But, I think that I succeeded. We'll see how he does in the second task."

"Are you preparing?"

"You bet."

I didn't see Cedric outside class again until Saturday morning.

I was starting a class when one of the second years came up to me and handed me a note. I opened it and discovered a request from Dumbledore to meet him at his office after my class was over.

That was scary. I didn't think that he'd summoned me to a meeting more than twice this year. I fumbled through the class on automatic and headed directly to Dumbledore's Office. I almost got there when I realized that I didn't remember the current password. I quickly ran back to my office and dug around in my desk, looking for it.

As quickly as I could I ran back to Dumbledore's Office, almost running over Filch on the way. He called something after me about getting together sometime. I shouted a vague agreement over my shoulder as I ran headlong down the corridor. I reached the gargoyle that guards Dumbledore's Office and responded to his silent challenge, "Lemon Bars." It rotated out of the way, and I took the revolving steps two at a time up to Dumbledore's Office.

"Well, you didn't have to run all the way."

I was a bit winded and didn't answer immediately. "Yes." I huffed and puffed, 'but I thought it must be urgent."

Dumbledore steepled his fingers on his beard, "Well, first, let me assure you that it's not anything to do with school or your performance."

That was a puzzler. I couldn't remember many times that we'd talked about anything else. "What do you want to talk about then?"

"Have you paid attention to Ms. McGonagall lately?"

That was a strange question, but I answered as straight as I could, "I always pay attention to Minerva. Is there something wrong?"

He stared at me a minute, "I was hoping you might tell me the answer to that question. You've surely noticed that she is . . Well, how can I describe it? Bouncier? Carefree? Intoxicated? I don't know. But surely you do?"

I agreed. "You're right. I have noticed that."

"I don't think that I've seen her that way, well, since she met you. And you know that she's spent a couple of Saturday evenings away from the castle. That isn't good. Would you agree?"

I had to admit that he was right. He went on, "You know, when she met you, I thought, 'there's the makings of an odd couple', but, you know, they're both intelligent, caring people. They just might be good for each other. I don't know if you remember, but I actually encouraged the two of you a little." He sighed and added, "Not that either of you noticed."

"Oh, I agree. I didn't realize it for a long time, but I eventually did. It's been the happiest development in my life, I think."

His mouth tightened into a frown, "Then why in the world aren't you doing something about it? It seems to me that she's met someone new and I can't see that you even realize it's happened."

I had to agree, "You're right. But what can I do? I promised to be circumspect—we both did. Now, you want me to break it?"

"Well, of course, I do. You made that promise when you were close, and you didn't have any rivals. This is different. Do you think that I went to that effort and don't expect you to put in some effort of your own? Man, you're positively enabling her. The thought of you chaperoning Gryffindor while . . ."

"No, sir."

"Well, get along with you. I've done what I can. I hope you do too."

I assured him that I would.

I left and thought about what I could do. As I was walking down the staircase, I wondered if the danger might be over. She'd not left the castle last weekend. Maybe it was a brief infatuation that had run its course.

But the next day, I found out that it hadn't. She asked me to sub for her the next Saturday. I was surprised and could only blurt, "I don't think I can. I'm taking Cedric on a college tour and I don't know when we'll be back."

She didn't seem to take it badly. I thought I might see some of her temper, but she just said that she'd find someone else, and we parted.

The next day was Saturday. Cedric and I had arranged to meet at 11AM. It was our plan to take the floo network to the Green Dragon and then probably go back to the pub that we'd had lunch in the last time. Finally, we would meet the dean of students at one.

Things went well. We arrived just after the Dragon opened. We saw the proprietor who approached us and asked if we were in for an early lunch.

"No. We've got an appointment and want to be sure that we're not late for it." I certainly wasn't going to give him my custom. Cedric asked me about it. I agreed that we'd stop for one after our meetings, "I'm rather disgusted with him and really don't want to do anything more for him than have a drink on our way out of town."

Cedric was satisfied with the answer, and we headed directly for the Three Goats Head. We arrived and were happy to find that it was nearly empty. We took a table and ordered drinks. I was facing away from the main entrance; Cedric was facing it. As we were waiting, Cedric glanced over toward the door, and his eyes got really wide, "Guess who just came in."

"I don't know, Minister Fudge?" I had started the day in a foul mood, and it was getting no better.

"No. It's Professor McGonagall."

I swung around quickly and saw not just Minerva but that she was accompanied. It was Inspector Morse. I forgot to shut my mouth. As I watched with horror, she noticed us and then looked away. But her companion noticed and didn't look away. He took her hand. He was way too familiar with her hand. He led her, seemingly not entirely willingly over to our table.

I got up shakily and took his proffered hand weakly. "Well, what a coincidence. It's Mr. Wendt, isn't it? And Mr. Diggery, I believe."

Diggery agreed. Meanwhile I couldn't catch Minerva's eyes. Morse was going on, "Well, what brings you to Oxford town?"

Diggery talked about a tour of the Oxford campus, "Oh, good. I hope you eventually come here to study. Minerv . uh.. Ms. McGonagall tells me you really are quite the student."

I finally found my voice and said, "Well, Minerva, is this what I've been subbing for you for?"

Morse said, "Oh, you've been helping her get time off service dur in order to spend some time with me. Well, I really must thank you. We're going to an opera performance tonight, Rigoletto, in town, but Ms. McGonagall has agreed to let me show her some of Oxford today. Perhaps we might run into each other again."

I was trying to bore into Minerva's eyes with mine, as I said, "Well, I wish you'd let me know what you were up to. I'd have been happy to send my regards to Inspector Morse."

She did look up, and I could see some of her fire in her eyes, "Well, not that it's any of your business. But, yes. Inspector Morse has been very kind to give me some of his time. I I, . " she seemed to be searching for something cutting to say, but couldn't quite find it. So, we parted and I sat back down.

Cedric was studying his menu intently, apparently getting the idea that Minerva and I weren't currently on the best of terms. The waiter returned with our drinks and took our order. Minerva and Morse were still enjoying each other's company. I had tried not to stare at them, but I couldn't help noticing that she had a sparkle in her eyes as she talked with Morse. His knee apparently accidentally brushed hers every minute or two and her reaction was as though that were perfectly normal and to be expected or even wished for. Every now and then she would grasp his forearm, apparently idly while making a point.

I paid for our meal and went mechanically through the rest of the day with Cedric. We met the dean of students, who introduced us to a lecturer in mathematics who took us for a tour of the grounds. Cedric noted that Oxford reminded him of his current school, and the lecturer commented that he was lucky indeed to have a school that reminded him of Oxford.

He took us to meet a couple of students, and they talked about the transition from prep school to college. I barely heard what they said and just could hardly make minimal grunts as responses when required.

At the end of the day, we returned to the Dragon. Despite my unhappiness with them, I agreed with Cedric to have dinner there. It was really pretty decent, the crowd was relatively quiet, and left you to yourself if you wanted. That was a definite plus for me that day.

We returned to the castle by floo, I left Diggery, and went to my office.

Of course, Minerva wasn't there for breakfast the next day or lunch or dinner. I hardly ate anything at any of the meals. I sat through them from the earliest to the latest points, hoping to catch a glimpse of Minerva. What I'd do if I spied her, I hadn't the slightest. I was sure that I would think of something. I never found out what.

I sleep-walked through the rest of the week, but something happened on the weekend. I received an owl on Friday at breakfast. Why did they always find my bowl of oatmeal so inviting? I opened it and discovered it was from Amos Diggery. He and his wife wanted to meet me on Saturday. He suggested lunch at the Three Broomsticks. I found Cedric and showed him the letter. He said that he knew his parents wanted to talk to me, and he offered to send a reply immediately. I said that I was happy to meet his parents at the suggested time and place.

"Cedric, do you know what they want to talk about?"

"I do, but they don't want me to mention it to you before you meet them. And, anyway, you'll find out tomorrow."

Cedric ran off to send my letter by owl post, and I went on to class.

Saturday, I ambled over to Hoggsmeade so as to be there before noon. It was a cool, even a cold day but there wasn't any snow on the ground, and I made good time. The bare, lifeless trees gave no promise of spring approaching.

I arrived and took a table well away from the entrance and the bar so that we could have some privacy for our discussion. I ordered a hot tea (it was before noon, after all). The tea had just arrived when the door opened, and Amos and Reina entered. They saw me and immediately walked to my table. I stood and greeted them, offered chairs and hot tea. Reina agreed to tea and Amos briefly considered something stronger, but settled on hot tea as well.

We talked briefly about the weather and the upcoming 2nd task of the Tournament while waiting for the waiter to take our order. He did and brought a pot of hot tea. Amos immediately settled down to his topic.

"Professor Wendt, we've decided—my wife and I—to let Cedric decide what he wants to do after graduating from Hogwarts. We think it's the right thing to do. So, what do we have to do?"

"Well, eventually, quite a lot. But for the time being, you don't have to do much. Cedric has been getting lots of reading materials from the various schools that are interested in him based on his SAT scores. He has to decide which schools he's interested in.

"Usually after deciding on schools, most students want to visit at least the ones that are their top picks to make sure that they look as good in person as they do on parchment."

Reina asked, "Can parents go along?"

"I would definitely suggest parents go along where feasible. From the school's perspective, they want non-adult students to have a responsible adult along. It frequently is the parent, but could be an older sibling or guidance counselor."

Amos inserted, "Like you?"

"Yes, I would be an OK choice."

"After college visits and frequently while they're still going on, a student chooses three or four colleges to apply for. Usually, the theory is to select one aspirational college—that is one that would be very good to get into, but would be something of a long shot. Then, the student would select the one that he really thinks that he can get into and would be a good school for him. Then, you pick one or two 'sure bets'—schools that you're virtually sure to get into, just in case."

Reina wanted to know about any decisions that Cedric might have made, 'Has he chosen any of those?"

"Not as far as I know, but I have to say that he seems to be very impressed by Cambridge."

Amos wanted to know, "Is that a good school."

I laughed, "There are a lot of people who think it's the finest school in England – maybe the world."

"What do you think?"

"It's hard to choose between Cambridge and Oxford. I think you could flip a galleon between them and not go wrong."

"What is next after applying to schools?"

"Well, that's the nervous part—waiting for decisions and then comes the fun part—choosing among the ones that have accepted you.

"But finally, comes the hardest part. First, paying for school. Cedric's really excellent scores almost insure that most schools would find ways to pay for his tuition without cost to him. But, schools like Oxford and Cambridge only very rarely pay all the expenses for a student. They'd provide most of the cost but between you and Cedric, the difference would have to be made up. Cedric could work and borrow money and, of course, you could contribute as well."

Amos almost leaped up, "No son of mine is going to have to borrow money to go to Oxford. We'll find a way to afford it."

I was amazed at how far the Diggories had turned around their opinions about Muggle schools. "I admire your determination, but a lot of people—parents, teachers, even students—think that students should have 'skin in the game', so to speak. That is, have a stake in their education so that they do their very best."

Amos declared, "That's not necessary with Ced. He's a great kid and doesn't need any shins in the game."

I had to agree. By this time our orders had arrived and we had started the meal. They asked a few additional questions during the meal, but they were satisfied.

Later I was talking with Cedric, and he told me that I needn't have worried about getting permission from his parents, "All you have to do is sell Mom on an idea, and Dad might as well forget it."

He also had made some decisions about schools. "I want to apply to Cambridge, Harvard, Princeton."

"But you haven't seen any of those schools. Are you sure that you want to go ahead without getting an idea about what they're like?"

"Well, Cambridge is the best in England, right?"

"There are a lot of people who feel that way."

"Ok. Harvard and Princeton are the best in the States, right?"

"Well, I know some people from the University of Chicago who might disagree and if you were interested in engineering. , ."

Cedric cut in, "I'm not interested in engineering, and Chicago is the windy City, isn't it?"

"That's what it's called, but that doesn't mean that it's actually very windy."

Cedric had made up his mind on those, so I took a different tack, "Almost everyone thinks that you should apply to one or two schools that are 'safe', that is, that you could be virtually certain of getting into."

He thought about that a minute and then said, "OK. What school would you recommend?"

"I'd recommend that you read the brochures and decide for yourself—maybe even go there."

"OK. I'll take a look."

Morse Ascendant

In the late afternoon, I was walking around the castle for exercise and ran into Minerva. "Minerva, I'm" I hesitated. I didn't want to say something stupid that I might regret, so I started again, "Minerva, I'm glad I ran into you. I thought you might like to do something tonight—like going to." Again, I halted so that I could work through the possibilities before speaking. There probably would be a concert somewhere that we could get tickets for, but could we find it at the last minute? So, I decided on something easier, "Oh, say, a movie?"

She seemed stuck for an answer. It was apparently not what she expected to hear, "Are you sure?"

"Perfectly."

"But, you know that I've been seeing Morse the last couple of weeks."

I had to tread easy here, "Yes, but that doesn't change how I feel about you."

Here there be dragons. She still seemed lost for words. Just keep calm. Let her think it through. "Wendt, I was going to go out tonight with Morse, but he had to work on a case."

"Well, then, why not go out with me tonight?"

"I don't know." She turned introspective and said slowly, "He's just about my age, maybe a little older. He's handsome. He's smart and funny. I enjoy being with him."

I held onto my temper and kept looking her in the eye, "I just want to be with you. I'll be second string if I can't be first."

She turned away quickly, but I saw the beginning of a tear in her eye. I heard a suppressed sob, and I tried to figure out a way to press my advantage. I guess not saying anything was the way, because she said in a voice so soft that I almost didn't hear it, "OK. Are there any good movies showing?"

I said almost too quickly, "There are always good movies showing."

She laughed, "You can't know that."

"Sure I can, I used to go to a different movie every week when I was in the States."

She laughed again, "Your'e just making fun of me."

"Am not."

"OK. Where do we go?"

"I'd suggest that we go to London. We'll pick up a *Times* and see what's playing where. Maybe we'll go to the movie and then have dinner." It was just then that I noticed that she was wearing an eye popping red dress and whistled. "Well, dressed as you are, we could go anywhere to eat."

"Thank you."

She offered me her hand, and I didn't complain about disapparation in the slightest. We appeared outside a bookstore. We went in. I bought a *Times* and started looking at the listings. I found a movie that I thought ought to be good. I said, "Here's a good one. It just won an academy award."

"What's that?"

"Oh, it's actually the Motion Picture Academy of the Performing Arts. It's the most famous of the organizations that gives prizes to films. The movies that they give awards to aren't always the best, but they're nearly always pretty entertaining."

"But you've not seen this movie?"

"I've not seen any of the movies that are in the theatres now. I just have to trust other people's opinions. I don't even know what this movie is about, but it was chosen as the #1 movie in the world in 1994."

"Good enough for me then."

We found a theatre that had an address that Minerva knew how to get to. Again, I didn't complain for a second about disapparation for getting there. We arrived at the theatre about a half an hour before show time. I bought tickets, and we went in. The theatre was nearly empty, and I asked Minerva where she wanted to sit. She had no idea at first, but then thought about it. She really didn't want to sit as close as she had the only other time that we'd been to a movie.

"OK. I'm good with that. Let's sit near the back."

She looked at me suspiciously, "Why is it that I'm suspicious about that?"

"I don't know. I'm happy to sit wherever you want to."

She just smiled and said, "The back of the theatre is good. I kind of want to find out why you're happy about that choice."

We had to wait through interminable commercials. At one point, Minerva was ready to leave the theatre and return closer to show time to avoid the obnoxious fare. None-the-less, I convinced her that the theatre would fill up, and she'd be better off staying put and trying to ignore the tripe on the screen.

"Tripe. Tripe can be good. This is far worse. It's squid or sushi or something." I had to laugh. It was the first time that I'd laughed all night, and it felt good.

She reached over, took my left hand and put it on her purse that she had on her knee and held it there with her hand. Eventually, the movie started, and I moved my hand off the purse and she didn't object. My heart was in my mouth until that maneuver was completed successfully.

After the movie, she suggested that we go to the first restaurant that we ran across walking the streets. I certainly wasn't going to object. We found a little Italian restaurant and were seated pretty quickly.

As we were waiting for dinner, she asked, "Was that story true? Is there really a Schindler?"

"I don't know. I'd never heard of the movie before tonight. I only picked it because the advert said that it had won the Academy Award for best picture."

"But you know about World War II. Surely, you'd know if it were a true story?"

"Oh, I hate to disappoint you. I don't really follow news that closely."

She thought a moment and said, "That was such a sad story." Inadvertently (yes, I really think it was inadvertent), her hand fell on mine on the table and she squeezed, "Did Muggles really kill millions of people just because they were Jewish?"

"I'm afraid they did. They thought they were doing a service to mankind."

"I thought it was hideous the way that soldier was playing the piano while they were rounding up and killing people. The music was so beautiful. How could it co-exist with that evil? How could anyone who made that kind of music do such terrible things?"

I had to think long about that. "I think Socrates was right. You just don't know whether a life is happy or not until the end. And you don't know whether a life has been lived well until the end. I suppose to Socrates there wasn't any difference been living well and happily."

Her hand squeezed tighter. "But, surely, we wizards can do things that make it better than this story."

I laughed internally at the way she'd said, "We wizards" as though I were one. But, I tried to answer as honestly as I could, "I don't know. Wizards have plenty of problems as well. No wizard's done anything so terrible—yet. On the other hand, Cedric seems to have all the world at his feet, but who knows?"

Minerva suddenly realized that she'd been holding my hand the whole time. She let go rather self-consciously. Just then the first course of our meal arrived. We don't always talk a lot during a meal out together, but this time, we said practically nothing. I dared hope for nothing more than that.

After it was over, we had a real dilemma. She had a substitute, so she didn't have to go home tonight. On the other hand, where would we go? A hotel? Her sister's? Minerva answered that thought, "You know, Maggie is kind of happy that I'm seeing someone else."

"Even if he's a Muggle?"

"Well, yes. Rather than a Squibb."

"We could tell her the truth about me."

Minerva didn't say anything for a long time as we stood outside the Italian restaurant. "I don't know. It was really a nice evening. Maybe I shouldn't have let you take me out. Now, I don't know what to do."

Well, I wasn't going to make it any easier for her. She spoke in clear frustration, "Oh, why do you have to make it so hard for me? I feel like I'm an old lady kicking a boy scout trying to help her cross the street."

I still maintained my silence.

She said, "Don't you have SOME funny remark?"

I shrugged and said, "Well, first of all, you're not an old lady. And second, I'm sure not a boy scout."

The stupid joke seemed to break the tension. She got a good laugh out of it, 'You certainly aren't." But then she returned to her old mood. "Why can't one of you, at least, have the decency to be a cad? It would be so much easier to break up with one of you."

That sounded good to me. I hadn't been "broken-up with" yet. She decided to go back to Hogwarts, and I again was happy to be disapparating with her. Forget the churning stomach and spinning head.

When we got back, I accompanied her up to the portrait of the Fat Lady and asked her if we could do something like that next weekend. She wouldn't have to get a substitute. We could go out. I'd find something else to do than a movie and return before "lights out". She relaxed, smiled, "Maybe. But it could be a movie again, if you find one like Schindler."

"If you liked Schindler, I know another, what we call a Western with one of my favorite actors, Clint Eastwood." She just smiled.

She gave the password, the picture opened and then closed. I stared after her and then realized that I was staring at the Fat Lady. She winked at me and said, "Good Going. That's the way to go." She added in almost a whisper, "I'm rooting for you."

"Thanks."

◿

During the next week, I met a couple of times with Cedric, working on applications. He was surprised that he had to write essays for them. but I pointed out, that you could use one essay for several applications. It would be necessary to write two, maybe three, but not six or eight.

When he'd finish an essay, I'd grade it, being as critical as I reasonably could. That really wasn't very critical because, after all, he was a really good student. He'd rewrite it and then come back and we'd go through the cycle again. By the end of the first week, we'd got one essay to the point that I thought it was really good.

Minerva had decided not to go out with me that weekend, but she didn't go out with Morse either. I looked on that as a minor victory. By the second weekend, she was ready to go out again. But this time, it was with Morse. I hadn't given up.

I was looking for a way to gain some points on Morse. Then it occurred to me. I could get her fresh flowers. Well, I could if I could get to London. So, how could I get to London? I couldn't have Minerva take me, could I?

I decided to consult a different wizard. I buttonholed Snape after dinner one evening. I asked him to come to my office. He agreed reluctantly. When we got there, I gave him a seat in the red leather chair and asked if he would like something to drink.

"What do you have?" I got out my best bottle (almost my only bottle) of whiskey and showed it to him. "Well, I think that might just work."

I pulled us both good stiff shots and let him take a sip and enjoy it for a minute before going on. "I have a favor to ask of you."

"Why is that not a surprise? What is it?"

"I'd like you to take me to London."

He stared incredulously, "Is this a date?"

I guffawed, "No. It's a favor like I said. I want to get something that I can only get in a large place like London."

He was still suspicious, "And what would that be?"

I was a little embarrassed, but I looked him in the eye and said, "Some flowers."

At that he smiled and said, "Well, do I understand that you've got some competition for the lady fair? I thought you two were like this." He twined his forefinger and middle finger together.

"Well, maybe not quite that close, but, will you do it or not?"

"I think I will. This should be interesting. When do you want to go?"

"I'd prefer to go before the weekend. If you have a couple of hours free on an afternoon or morning, it'd be good." We took a little time finding a couple of hours when we both had free.

Thursday afternoon came and Snape came to my office. "Well, Snape, where do we go?"

"Nowhere. You've got a fireplace, don't you?"

I looked over at the fireplace. Well, certainly I have a fireplace, I thought. He said, "Well, it's connected to the floo network. Just because you've never used it, doesn't mean it doesn't work."

There was even a small urn of floo powder on the mantle. We appeared in the Cauldron's main dining room. Tom greeted us and then noticed that Minerva wasn't there. "Well, Wendt, strange seeing you without Minerva. How are things going?"

I just nodded, mumbled something, and we left. Once we'd left the Cauldron, I found a shop. I don't even remember what they sold. I asked to use the phone directory and found a florist that was close. It

171

took a while doing that. When we left the shop, Snape was derisive, "Well, is this the way Muggles get around? I'm surprised you ever get anything done." I had no comment.

We left for the florist's. We arrived and went in. Snape started browsing, looking at everything. I went to the proprietress and asked about potted plants. She showed me several. They weren't quite what I was looking for. I asked, "Do you have any plants that also have flowers in them? I want something that will last, but also be beautiful, if you know what I mean."

She started to explain that she could make something up to order. Meanwhile Snape came over and listened as I talked and interrupted me. "I think that you'd be better off with flowers rather than a boring plant."

I looked at him and said, "Who's buying the flowers here? Why do you say that? I want something that will last."

"Well, women want something extravagant. It doesn't matter if it doesn't last very long. As a matter of fact, it's better if it doesn't. It gives you a chance to repeat the gift soon." The shopkeeper nodded with every point.

"OK. I'll just go with flowers. How about some yellow roses." Snape shook his head and pulled me aside. "Red will go better with her hair and are more romantic anyway." He unaccountably seemed to know what he was talking about, so I went with the suggestion.

As we walked back to the Cauldron, I asked him, "How do you know so much about romance anyway?"

"You think you're the only one who has had a girl friend?"

"Well, you never seem to show any interest that way. I've never seen you with a lady. I've never heard you talk about anyone special."

He looked down, 'Well, I did once."

I wondered about Snape, "Did that one get away?"

"Oh, I suppose you could say so, she died a long time ago."

"I am sorry. And you never were interested again? There was never anyone else that you cared for?"

He turned suddenly so as to directly look at me, "No. I never cared for anyone else. She was my. . . " He hesitated on the word and then said it, "Love from the earliest time that I loved."

"I really am sorry." We walked on in silence. Eventually we got to the Cauldron and went in. Tom had something to say. I guess it was about the flowers, but I didn't pay attention. We walked into the fireplace and came out in my office. I thanked Snape, and he looked at me still holding the flower vase, smiling.

"I hope yours doesn't."

I looked at him quizzically and he finished. "'get away'."

That evening after dinner, I cornered the Weasley twins and offered them a bribe. "I'll give you 20 galleons if you'll sneak something into Minerva's office without anyone knowing."

Fred eyed me suspiciously, "Just what would that be? A stink bomb?"

George added, "Yeh, it depends just how big a stink it makes, how much we charge for that kind of trick."

They said in unison, "The bigger the stink, the less we charge."

"Come with me gentlemen. I guess that in a way you could say that it will cause a stink." They followed me up to my office. I let them in and locked the door behind me.

Fred wondered, "Why do you do that? A lock like that wouldn't keep anyone out."

"Never mind. Just wait here a minute." I went back to my room and brought the flowers out.

George oohed, "Neat. Brilliant, even. You could really catch her by surprise. She bends over to sniff the flowers and blam! I love it. We'll do it for free."

"No. No. It's not a practical joke. They're real flowers. No trick."

They both sighed and George asked, "Why aren't you playing a practical joke. I hear that she played a real joke on you. Dumping you for that pleasemaam."

I corrected them, "It's not pleasemaam, it's policeman and she hasn't dumped me. Yet. That's what this is about. Trying to keep her from dumping me. I swear that you two will regret it as you've never regretted anything if you do anything to mess this up."

"OK."

"OK." They said in unison. "But with no practical joke, this will cost you. If it ever got out that we did something nice to someone, we'd never live down the ignominy."

"Yeh. We'd need at least fifty."

George correct, "sixty galleons."

"You two would pick a pensioner's pocket."

"Every time."

"Well, take it and make sure it happens before tomorrow morning."

Fred called back over his shoulder as he and George left with the flowers, "Service with."

"A laugh," Completed George

The next morning at breakfast, I was watching the skies carefully lest another flock of owls were delivering Cedric some mail via me. As my eyes were averted someone walked behind me and patted me on the back while the voice that I know best said, "Well, done." with its scotch brogue.

It wasn't a lot, but it made my day.

The Lake

The next week was the second part of the Tournament. I saw it as an opportunity to sit by Minerva innocently for a couple of hours. The day of the tournament, we discovered that there were stands magically erected in the lake itself.

On the way there, I ran into the Weasley twins. They were making book on the competition. One of them stopped me, "We're giving two to one odds against Potter. How much of the action do you want?"

"You're betting against your fellow Gryffindor?"

The other twin said, "We're honest business men. We can only offer odds that we believe in."

"I'll put a tenner on Potter. I should put more on him and make you pay for your lack of loyalty."

They laughed and approached the next person, who was a second year.

We were ferried out to the stands, and I managed to get next to Minerva. She didn't seem to object.

I wondered about what we'd see, "I don't get it. If this is our task, it's all going to happen underwater. I don't think anyone will be able to see anything until the whole thing's over."

"Oh, don't be so particular. The point is being there when it happens and knowing as soon as possible who won. Who do you think will win?"

I thought about how much I could or should reveal of what I knew. I decided, "Well, I do know that Cedric has a good idea of what the task is. He told me that he'd cracked the secret of listening to the message in the clear. He's smart, so he'll have been working on how to operate underwater without problems.

"Now, how many of the others have cracked it? If he's the only one, he'll have a big leg up. If he isn't—and my bet is that he isn't—it's anybody's game. My bet is that at least Karkaroff and Madame Maxime will have helped their champions crack it if they haven't done it on their own."

"Are you charging them with cheating?"

"Not yet. I said, 'If'. They're all smart people. They are perfectly capable of working it out on their own."

"But what about Potter. I know that no teacher at Hogwarts would help him. Can he get it on his own?"

There was the challenge. I decided that I couldn't ethically assure her that Potter should have the key. "I don't know. He seems to have a way of bumbling through these things and coming out smelling, well, smelling like a rose."

She smiled and pointed out the rose on her hat, "That rose came from you."

I smiled too.

The champions arrived, and the task was announced. My immediate reaction to Minerva was, 'What the heck! We didn't sign up for innocent 3rd parties dying if their champion fails. I don't remember that at all in our proposal."

She shook her head and whispered, "Softer, please. You're' right, it wasn't part of the proposal. That was added afterwards by the committee. BUT nobody is going to die. That's just a little window dressing to encourage the champions. But it won't happen."

I was relieved to hear that. We watched the entry of the champions to the dark waters of the Loch. Potter's seemed to be a bit reluctant. For a long time there was nothing to do but watch the occasional ripples that crossed the lake and wonder what was going on below. The first thing that happened was that Ms. Delacourt returned without her sister, whom we learned was her objective. I commented, "Well, we're going to test that principle that innocent 3rd parties don't get hurt."

Minerva just sniffed.

The time limit was an hour and it was soon to be reached. I looked over at Minerva and wondered, "Will anyone come back? Will Ms. Delacourt be declared winner by default."

She didn't seem quite so sure of herself and didn't give her patented sniff. As a matter of fact, a few worry lines appeared on her brow.

The clock ran up to the one hour limit, kissed it, and rolled along. Still no one had returned. Now Minerva had pronounced worry lines on her forehead. Her hands closed convulsively and pounded her knees. "Why isn't anyone back?" She asked plaintively. The minutes continued to tick. At the judges table, there didn't appear to be concern.

Then some very stange things began to happen. First, Ms. Delacourt's sister's head bobbed out of the water close to the platform where the judges were. Several teachers quickly retrieved her from the cold water.

"Did you notice who released the sister?"

Minerva looked around, "No. You didn't?"

"Nope."

"It's got to be Krum, Cedric or Potter. Who do you think?"

"Cedric for me. He's nice and as the more experienced, he's likely to have had the time to spare." I said.

"Then Potter for me."

"You're just saying that because he's in your house."

"Well, you're just saying Cedric because you're his mentor."

I had an inspiration. "Let's see you put something of value where your mouth is."

"How many galleons do you want to lose?" Minerva smirked.

"I was thinking of something more interesting. I'll bet you dinner out. Winner picks the restaurant. Loser pays."

"You are devious."

"I'm a good businessman. It's a win-win proposition."

She smiled at that, "Yes, it's win-win for YOU, whether you win or lose, you get to take me out to dinner."

"I am absolutely guilty as charged. It is a win-win-win-win getting to go out with you."

Her face colored a bit, and that was easily worth it all. While we were talking, Cedric and his hostage, Cho Chang appeared in the water. The Hufflepuffs shouted for joy. Shortly after that Hermione Granger appeared with Victor Krum.

The clock crept on its relentless course. It was beginning to look bad for Potter. Then, Ron Weasley appeared and we all breathed sighs of relief. Prematurely. The clock continued to tick, and Potter hadn't appeared. Dumbledore strode to the edge of the platform, and I had the bizarre feeling that he was about to leap into the water. Then, I noticed that Moody was right beside him, whether to prevent Dumbledore from entering the water or join him, I couldn't tell.

But, before anything else could happen, Potter shot into the air and then was quickly retrieved from the cold. I looked over at Minerva triumphantly. "Well, it looks like you're going to be paying." She didn't seem troubled.

People began to queue up to get on the boats to return to shore. I took Minerva by the arm and turned her gently, "There's no hurry, is there?"

She smiled, "I'm getting cold."

I was about to point out the remedy for that when Dumbledore's voice boomed out. It appeared that our surmise that Cedric had saved the DelaCourt girl was premature. It had actually been Potter who had done that. And that had been done within the time limit, although his rescue of Wesley had been the last. The judges had decided that Cedric and Potter deserved top marks for that.

Minerva smirked, "Well, it looks like you didn't win."

"Well, if I didn't win then you didn't either."

"That means that nobody goes to dinner."

"Wait, wait, wait. This is crazy. Both our champions won and nobody wins the bet. That's perverse. However, being the gentleman that I am, I'll grant that you win the bet. You pick the restaurant and I pay."

A playful glimmer entered her eye. "That's generous of you. But I can be a gentlewoman if you can be a gentleman. You win. You choose the restaurant and I'll pay."

She seemed to have an inspiration, "No. Better. We go to dinner twice. One you choose and I pay. The other, I choose, you pay."

"More than fair," I declared, "but I insist that you choose first."

She thought a moment and said, "Fine. The Three Broomsticks, tonight."

"But isn't it a little close to home for comfort?"

"Oh, I think there's enough excitement about the 2nd task that we don't have to worry about being observed. I'll tell you what. We walk there separately."

"Agreed."

It was only time for lunch, so we returned to the castle. On the way I happened to run into the twins. I demanded my winnings from them. Their line was that since Potter hadn't won outright, they shouldn't have to pay.

"In that case, there was no result, and you should refund everyone's bets that involved Cedric or Potter."

That was an idea that was foreign to their constitutions and they protested vigorously. I finally brought out my final weapon, "You know, I think that there's a school regulation against student gambling. I'd hate to invoke that against you two fine entrepreneurs but. . . "

Fred grumbled, "Unfair." but he pulled out his purse and counted out ten galleons into my hand.

That evening we arrived and found the Broomsticks rather crowded. We had to wait for a table. There were the regulars but, in addition, there were several people who had come to Hogwarts for the competition—journalists and officials from the various ministries involved. As we waited, Minerva pointed out Ludo Bagman, "He seems to be having a little dispute with those goblins. I wonder what's going on?" I paid closer attention. It was what I would call, "heated". "I wonder what it could be. I can't believe that it's about the Tri-Wizard Tournament. Goblins don't have a dog in that fight, surely."

Minerva hmmmed, 'Maybe they do. They do gamble. I wonder if they are having a dispute like you had with the Weasley's about who won this round of the competition?"

The Final Round

Sunday was a real anti-climax after the 2nd round of the tournament. A few days later, I was having lunch and had gotten so engrossed in an article in the *Scientific american* that I hadn't realized that almost everyone had finished. What brought me to this realization was that a boy who must have been about 3rd year was tugging on my sleeve. When he finally got my attention, he handed me a note. I thanked him perfunctorily and opened it. It was from Dumbledore. He'd called an emergency faculty meeting in his office for right now.

I jumped up and walked at my best pace to the office. I had to think hard to remember the current password for the Gargoyle. When it occurred to me, I had to smack my head in frustration. How could I have forgotten it? An even more interesting question is how Dumbledore ever learned about it. His penchant for using passwords that were candy or candy-related had led him to use some very obscure passwords, but how had he ever learned about "buckeyes?" I said the password and was admitted.

I had expected the office to be filled to the brim with all the teachers in the school there, but instead I found only Snape, Flitwick, Grubbily-Plank, Minerva and me. All the heads of houses and me. Why me? I had arrived late so I wasn't about to cause more disturbance by bringing up my question. I just found a chair as quickly as I could, pulled it up close as I could to Minerva and sat.

Dumbledore had been saying something that I hadn't really caught. He continued as though I'd not arrived late, "The body of Mr. Crouch was found an hour ago. The Aurors have been summoned and are examining it now. One of the main purposes of this meeting is to decide what we should say publicly to our students and the public about

180

this death on our grounds. I want this message to be consistent throughout our discussions with the media and to our students. Now, I open the floor to discussion."

Snape stood and said, "I think it's simple. We just say that the body of Mr. Crouch was discovered in the Dark Forest. We have no idea about how he died. The Aurors are investigating and any further comment should come from them."

I raised my hand. Dumbledore recognized me.

"I think that we need to know more before we decide on that. What else do we know?"

You could hear the mild sneer in Snape's voice, "If you'd been here on time, you'd know more."

Dumbledore gave Snape a frown, "Professor Wendt is right. Here's what we know. I'm telling you what I discovered from examining the body. First of all, this death happened the day of the 2nd challenge. It was not an accidental death or a death by disease. The most likely thing is that he was killed by the avra kedavra curse."

"Could it have been suicide?"

Snape broke in, "Obviously not. If it had been suicide, an examination of the wand would have shown the killing curse immediately. His wand was examined and the last spell was the disapparation here." Under his breath, "Just what you'd expect of a Squibb."

"Then, I don't think we can be satisfied with a simple statement about the death." I went on.

Dumbledore smiled and said, "Why not?"

I stood and found a path to pace in that would allow me to be seen by everyone and vice versa. "Before I tell you why I think that, we need to do a little ground work.

"Who is likely to be the killer?" I asked the question and everyone was silent.

Dumbledore leaned back in his chair, as if he were enjoying this, "Well, I've heard it said that almost all people who are murdered are killed by people they know well."

"I think that's true. So, who did Crouch know well?"

Flitwig gave an answer, "Well, his close relatives are all dead. He only had one child, a son, who died and his wife. . . "Flitwig's voice trailed off.

181

I tried to be sympathetic, "Yes. I know. She died as well, recently. Does he have any other close relatives?" Everyone looked around at each other; even Dumbledore seemed not to know. That might have been the end of that discussion, but an unexpected visitor walked into the office.

Dumbledore greeted him, "Mr. Weasley. What brings you here?"

Percy Weasley looked around the room and apologized, "I'm sorry. I didn't know you were having a meeting. I can wait outside."

Dumbledore looked at me, "You have the floor professor. Do you want to yield it?"

I thought that a visit from Percy Weasley was unusual enough that it was worth finding out what he had to say. So, I just smiled, "Yes, of course. I've not seen you in a year or so, Mr. Weasley. I'm curious what brings you out of the Ministry?"

Percy had his hat in his hand and fumbled with it, not quite sure what to do as he began. "Thank you. I was asked by the Aurors to officially identify the . . uh . . body. It seems that they couldn't find a relative to officially identify the body."

I interrupted, "You mean to say that Mr. Crouch has no living relatives at all? Not even a distant one?"

"No, sir. As a matter of fact, that poses another problem. You see, his house elf, Winkie, is." He seemed to be stuck for a way to proceed but he did eventually continue. "Well, apparently no one owns her. The will, which hadn't been updated, gives everything to his wife. She is dead,and she, as well, has no surviving relatives." He added, "Not that that matters because the will was invalid as soon as she died.

"So, the real reason that I'm here is to take temporary custody of the elf until somewhere can be found to place her. It's almost a unique case. House elves can be freed only when presented with clothes by their master. In this case there is no apparent surviving master. I think there was a case like this in the last century, and it turned out that the house elf was freed by the death of his last master.

"What makes it more difficult is that she seems not to want to leave Hogwarts. We really have a dilemma."

Dumbledore had been contemplating something on the ceiling, apparently not paying attention, but quickly spoke. "May I suggest that we would take Winkie in? She could stay with our house elves until her final disposition is decided. If she is a free elf, we'd be happy to pay her a fair salary, backdated to today."

Weasley relaxed when he heard that, "Would you really do that for me?"

"Certainly."

"That would make things so much easier for me. Thank you."

He turned as if to go, but I stopped him, "Mr. Weasley."

He turned back, and his appearance returned to the nervous supplicant. "Yes, sir?"

If we could have a few more minutes of your time, I have a question or two that I'd like to ask you about your former boss."

Weasley relaxed a little but seemed to still be wary, "Of course."

"First, why did they send you to officially identify the body and help with Winkie? I know that there was no next-of-kin, but were you the closest at work to him?"

Weasley positively brightened, "As a matter of fact, yes. The department of international magical co-operation is fairly small. We don't have many people in the department, and I was as close as anyone."

Snape broke in, "And you were perhaps the most junior – one who could object least?"

Weasley cleared his throat and said a subdued, "Maybe. Probably."

I went on, "So, there was no one at work that he was closer to than you?"

He nodded. I thought for a moment before continuing, "Was there anyone at work who didn't like Crouch or maybe had a grievance with him?"

Weasley seemed surprised by the question and answered slowly, "Not that I know of. He really wasn't very easy to get close to." He paused and said, "To be honest with you, I got the impression that he was only marking time until his retirement."

"Was there anyone who was hoping that the retirement would come quickly? Perhaps for career advancement?"

Weasley seemed surprised to hear the question, "You mean 'was there anyone who would like to have seen him dead?'"

"Yes."

"I can't imagine anyone who would have done such a thing."

"What about enemies outside the department?"

Weasley seemed shocked, "The Department of International Magical Cooperation is an important department. Almost anyone would

183

have liked to become its head, but I can't imagine anyone would kill for it."

"Mr. Weasley, what will happen to you when there is a new department head? Do you think that in the re-alignment there will be a promotion for you?"

Weasley was the closest to indignant that I'd seen, "I object to your implication. There will probably be an under-Minister from some other department appointed permanent head of our department, and I will not have any sort of advancement."

I tried to be placating, "I'm sorry to have offended you, but I just want to thoroughly understand Mr. Crouch's position and who would have benefited from his death."

"What about lady friends? Did he have any? Is it possible that there was a husband who objected to Mr. Crouch?"

Weasley was genuinely surprised, "I know that you may not trust everything I say, but believe me, there was no man who was more devoted to his family. His wife died only recently; he was still in shock, and I can't believe that he became interested in any woman more recently."

I tried to come up with other useful questions, but couldn't. He asked, "Can I go now and drop off Winkie in the kitchens?"

I nodded and Dumbledore thanked him for his time.

Dumbledore asked, "Well, it sounds like there are none of the usual suspects for murder. So, let's go on Mr. Wendt with your idea."

"Well, this is clearer than I thought. I think that the killer had to be someone who was associated with this tournament. That's really all that we have left. It means that the killer is still here now."

That brought a stunned silence. Minerva was the first to break it. "What about Ludo Bagman? He has a lot riding on this tournament."

Yes, I thought, he does. And based on that fiery conversation that he had with the goblins, he may have acted unethically and have a lot of his personal galleons riding on it. I thought about mentioning it, but decided not to, "Yes, I'll admit that he may well have motivation, but the rest of the people who have motivation are staying here right now— the other heads of schools, even, I suppose, heads of houses." I knew that I would not win points with the woman I was trying to win back, but I had to say it.

Dumbledore asked, "What do you propose that we do then?"

"First of all, I think that in our statement to the press, we should admit the likelihood that the death is related to the tournament and that it implies the possibility of danger for the champions."

Dumbledore grimaced and asked, "Just how sure do you think we are of that?"

"Pretty sure. We've not got any tenable alternatives to motives related to the tournament."

Snape shrugged, "How can it make any difference. The champions are bound to the tournament by a magical contract that can't be broken. What could anyone do differently by knowing about this danger – IF it really exists?"

I replied, "Even if they can't do anything differently, don't you think that we're honor bound to reveal the danger?"

Dumbledore had risen and was striding back and forth. He finally stopped and said, "I agree with Professor Snape. We are really unsure of this danger, and since no one can do anything to avoid it, I think we shouldn't raise the possibility." Then he turned to Minerva, "What do you think?"

Minerva glanced back and forth between Dumbledore and me. She squeezed my arm and said, "It may turn out to be nothing. Let's wait a bit and see how things develop."

I was really torn between wanting to do the right thing and supporting Minerva. I decided to go on to my next point.

"I think that we should keep our eyes on all the obvious people who have motivation to affect the outcome of the tournament."

Amazingly, Snape didn't make a comment about how I would be watching one particular head of house especially well. I gave him a moment to do it and was ready to go on when Minerva said, "I think there might be other people who have motivations. Anyone who has a large bet on the outcome of the tournament would be suspect. They might be outside Hogwarts."

I knew whom she was thinking of.

Then I went on, "Next, for the reason that there might be others both outside and inside Hogwarts who have motives, we've got to be generally vigilant for anything out of the ordinary."

Snape rustled in his chair, "Uh. Along those lines, I've been having some unusual thefts from my store of ingredients for potions.

"I've noticed that boom-slang wings have been disappearing. I'd initially thought it must be Potter or his gang. A couple of years ago they stole ingredients for PolyJuice Potion."

Under my breathe I whispered, "Just what we'd expect from Snape."

"But, now, I'm not so sure. It could be someone else who's using Polyjuice potion to disguise him or herself as someone else to commit this crime and maybe future ones."

Dumbledore almost jumped at that comment. "Really, you should have told me Severus." He turned to me and asked, "Any other precautions you suggest?"

"I think this raises the real possibility that someone will attempt to rig the final task. We need to be especially wary of any unauthorized activity there – wherever that is."

Dumbledore agreed and said that he'd assign people (read us) to guard the QuIdditch field that was being converted for the final competition ground. There would be assignment sheets.

As we left, I looked over to Minerva and said, "It's deja vu all over again—two years ago."

"Don't remind me. But this time, we're not going to be paired up —for obvious reasons, and you'd better never be paired up with Sinistra."

"Amen."

She added, "By the way, it's kind of sexy the way you stood up to both Dumbledore and Snape."

I couldn't help smiling at that and said, "You think?"

◁

The next day there was a roster in the Teacher's Lounge for the rest of the time to the finale. It was just over ten weeks and I wasn't anywhere on it. And as a matter of fact, the only people who were, were the heads of houses, Moody, Haggrid and Dumbledore himself. They were running two four hour shifts a day—one daytime and one night-time. With seven people on the list, there was continuous turnaround so that no one had the same shifts more frequently than once a week. It seemed good. But somehow I just had a bad feeling about it.

As a matter of fact, one day, after about a week, I went in to talk with Dumbledore about it. He'd just missed some sleep the previous night, and was in a little bit of a foul mood.

"Oh, Wendt, what is it now? I was hoping to get some sleep."

"I'm sorry. I just have got a bad feeling about it. I really wish that you would put two people on each shift."

"What? Are you wanting to work some shifts, yourself?"

I grimaced. "I would be willing to if you wanted to assign me to someone."

"Oh, why would I burden a wizard with you?"

"OK" I kept my eyes on him and eventually he relented a bit.

"I don't blame you. Whoever put Potter's name in the goblet of fire, might well have killed Crouch. Anyone who can do those things is pretty darn formidable, and I don't think that the rest of the staff—who are good wizards, but not great wizards—would make a difference. I have my O-team out there, and if that's not good enough, we're lost."

I shook my head and said, "Then, I think we're lost."

Dumbledore said, "There are times that I agree with you. Help me make that wrong."

Snape

During this period, we started to get responses from colleges that Cedric had applied to. The safety colleges that he'd applied to had sent back qualified letters of acceptance. Cedric had come to my office with the first of these.

"Professor, what does this mean?" He handed one of these letters of acceptance to me, and I scanned it quickly.

"OK. Here's what's going on here. Most colleges won't issue a letter of acceptance until they get the transcript from the first term of 7th year. It's just good sense. Even very talented students have a maturity failure from time to time and don't perform up to their potential in the final year.

"So, they want to see further proof of your maturity. Now, for students that they really want to come to their school, they make a sort of exception to that. What they do is to offer students 'qualified' acceptances. Not all schools call them that or even offer them.

"Basically, they offer the student guaranteed acceptance,"

Cedric interrupted, "If it's guaranteed, how can it be qualified?" He seemed rather excited about that possibility.

"OK. Bear with me. The acceptance has conditions. First, you have to actually have acceptable grades at the end of the first term. Second you have to graduate. Third, you have to actually guarantee that you won't accept some other school. That's usually the hard one.

"So, if you're willing to guarantee that you will go to the school, by the way, which one is it?"

I looked at the letter, "Oh, yes, The University of Bristol. If you want to guarantee them that you'll attend there, you can get early acceptance."

Cedric chewed on that for a bit. "Well, I would like to go to something like Cambridge or even Oxford."

"Good. I agree. I think that you should wait to decide. Probably even beyond next term. In the mean time, I'd suggest that you sit back and enjoy all the colleges and universities writing to you trying to convince you to attend their school."

Cedric chuckled at that. "Maybe, I will."

It was only a couple of days later that I got a letter in my oatmeal. "One of these days", I swore to myself, "I'm going to get a sniper rifle and take out one of those owls when he drops a letter in my oatmeal."

This time, I pulled the letter out of the oatmeal and wiped it off. And then I froze as I wiped off the return address. It was the University of Cambridge. I dropped my napkin, got up and ran up to my office. I reached it, got a towel out of the bathroom to wipe the outer envelope off. My hands were shaking as I did.

I took a deep breath, got my Swiss Army knife out of my pocket and carefully slit the envelope at the flap. I pulled out the inner envelope and discovered that it was addressed to me and no one else. I looked longingly at the drawer that I kept a bottle of whiskey in. I just shook my head and slit the inner envelope open.

There was no mistake. The letter was addressed to me. I read it slowly and carefully. I had to reread some paragraphs. I'd never seen a letter quite like it. In essence, the letter said:

a. We really like what we've seen of Mr. Diggery. His SAT, and even more important, his essays are really impressive.

b. We've never heard of Hoggwarts school. We need to know more about it.

c. The recommendation that you wrote was impassioned, but the only thing that we know about you is that you have a degree from Stanford, but we can't find any trace of you since. We need to know more about you.

d. Mr. Diggery's performance in international chess tournaments is astounding. We'd like him to be on our chess team.

e. We'd like you to visit us and give us more details about you and your school. If you can satisfy us as we're sure you can, we would love to have Mr. Diggery as a student

189

and we'd be happy to offer him acceptance and substantial scholarship assistance.

That was a fascinating document. It was everything that Cedric wanted, but it depended on my convincing them that Hogwarts and I were on the level.

I put the letter down and leaned back in my chair. How was I to ever to do that? Hoggwarts was only recognized by wizarding bodies. I set the answerless question aside and went back to the pedestrian task of grading papers and lesson planning.

I stuck with those tasks for a couple of days and finally decided that I had to approach Dumbledore. I couldn't remember ever having had to ask him for help—oh, yes, except where the Weasley twins were concerned. I wrote a little note and left it in Dumbledore's pigeonhole in the Teacher's Lounge. I'd never heard of anyone doing it, but I did. I described the request that Cambridge had made to me and asked for help in convincing Cambridge that we were for real.

I didn't hear anything for three days. Then, there was a small note in my box. It was in the somewhat crabbed hand of Professor Dumbledore. It said that if I visited his office sometime later in the day, he would have something that I could use when I visited Cambridge.

A small smile worked over my face. I knew he had something. I looked at my schedule and then found an opening—the first one that I had and decided to go then.

I arrived at the gargoyle and tried "buckeyes." I couldn't remember if it had changed. It hadn't. I trotted up the spiral staircase. At the top, I opened the door and entered the office. I'd never seen Dumbledore in such a pleased mood—as though he were the cat who'd swallowed the canary. He swept his hand, inviting me wordlessly to sit.

I did. He asked me if I would like something to drink. My first inclination was to rush him to get down to details, but then I had a second thought. Dumbledore clearly wanted us to enjoy the moment. I decided that was OK with me, 'Yes, I think I will. You don't happen to have some good whiskey?"

Dumbledore smiled and almost seemed to be surprised pleasantly at what I asked for, "Yes, I think I can find something from Tennessee." A couple of glasses appeared and one settled on Dumbledore's desk just in front of me. I picked it up and had a sip. It burned its way down my throat, and I appreciated the feel. I nodded appreciatively.

Dumbledore took a stiff sip and set down his glass. "Considering that Mr. Diggery is the first Hoggwarts student to be interested in attending a Muggle University in a very long time, he seems to have done very well."

"I think so."

Dumbledore opened a drawer in his desk and pulled out an envelope. It seemed to be very stiff, and I thought I saw an embossed seal on it. He handed it over to me, "I think this may be useful to you and Cedric."

I took it and found that it hadn't been sealed. I opened it and pulled out a heavy bond letter. It was folded twice and I couldn't see through it. I carefully unfolded it and even more carefully read it. It was addressed to the Provost of Cambridge. The letterhead was of the Prime Minister of the United Kingdom.

It stated that the Hogwarts School was one of the oldest residential finishing schools in the United Kingdom. Further, the privacy of the exclusive youth who attend it was so strict that the secret of the very existence of Hogwarts is guaranteed by the government. It lists Dumbledore as the Headmaster and Minerva McGonagall as assistant head-mistress.

I was overwhelmed, "How in the world did you ever get the Prime Minister involved in this?"

"Oh, the Ministry of Magic has good relations with the government of the UK. We do occasional favors for them and they reciprocate likewise. Fudge likewise owes me a favor and he doesn't mind throwing around his weight occasionally." He then pulled another envelope out and handed it over to me.

It contained a single page letter on the letterhead of Hogwarts. It explained that I was hired by Hogwarts five years ago and that I'm the head of the English department. I stopped there, "You could have gone on to say that I founded the English department."

Dumbledore smiled, "I don't like to lay it on too much. Read on."

I kept reading and found that he had said that I was the best English Literature instructor that he'd ever had work for him. I commented, "Are you going to give me a real complement at any time— really, best instructor you've ever had."

"Read on."

He went on to say that I'd been not only an excellent head of the English Department but had given a great deal of good advice on the running of the school. Finally, he signed the letter with his full name. "I thought you didn't believe in laying it on. This signature is laying it on if ever there were one."

Dumbledore chuckled and then said, "Do you think that will help?"

"Yes. That should do very well. I really appreciate your help."

"Well, then, get along." I got up and turned to go when he added, "Oh, one more thing. I had to promise that you would return that letter. They don't want it to get out to the public—either the British government or the Ministry."

My heart fell. I could just imagine what they would say about that at Cambridge. I started to object but Dumbledore added, "If they doubt the genuineness of the letter, they can contact the office of the Prime Minister. They should just say that it is an inquiry about the 'mirror' government." He apparently noticed the question forming on my lips, 'Yes. 'Mirror' government, not 'Shadow' government."

I left Dumbledore's Office and immediately walked down to Snape's office, hoping to find him there. I was in luck.

"Well, Wendt, what can I do for you?"

"Actually, I have a rather substantial favor to ask you. I need to travel to Cambridge sometime during the next week or so and I need a 'lift'."

"And you'd like me to give you the 'lift'?"

"Yes, please."

"And you can't ask your 'sweetie' because you're not supposed to be seen with her for a while. Hmmmm." He thought about it and then said, "Yes, I'll help you, but you have to find a time that I've not got classes." He handed me a sheet of parchment, "Here's my schedule of classes. Try to stay away from them."

I thanked him profusely, and he sent me off.

I returned the letter to Cambridge, saying that I would be happy to present myself for a meeting and giving them a list of times that would work for a meeting. By good fortune, both Snape and I had Friday afternoons off. So that was one time, along with Saturdays that I could suggest.

A couple of days later I got a response from Cambridge, requesting that we meet for lunch on the following Friday, We would then have a one hour meeting, where we could discuss Cedric and admissions.

I immediately sent a letter back accepting the proposed meeting after going down to verify the time with Snape.

That Friday arrived. Snape and I met at the Entrance to Hogwarts at 11:30. We were going at Fitzbillies for lunch. We walked off the Hogwarts grounds to where we could disapparate and appeared near the restaurant. We went in and secured a table.

A very dignified, man wearing a conservative grey suit with a little grey in his dark brown hair entered the restaurant at 2 minutes before noon. It seemed as though he must be our man. I approached him and introduced myself. It turned out that he was the provost, Robert Peeler. I explained that we'd gotten a table, I brought him over, and I introduced Snape.

He was a bit surprised, "I wasn't expecting a delegation from Hogwarts."

Snape smiled and said, "Well, Mr. Wendt doesn't have a license to disapparate, so he asked me to come along to help him get here."

"I see. Well, since you're here, you should join us for lunch, but the appointment is only between Mr. Wendt and me. I'll have to ask you to stay in the waiting room while we meet."

Snape was his oiliest in insisting that he had business of his own to transact, and he would just accompany us to the office so that he would know where to meet him in an hour.

I asked if there were anything that he recommended for lunch here.

"Oh, I can recommend the pate—especially the lobster pate. In my position, I shouldn't be seen drinking at lunch, so I'll have tea. However, do order as you wish. And, by the way, I'm hosting you, so I'll pick up the tab."

I began to object, but he insisted, "No, really, you should get something out of this trip." He emphasized "something" as though there were nothing else that we could gain from the trip.

I saw Snape bristle at that a bit.

Peeler asked what Snape taught.

"I am the Master of," he hesitated a moment coming up with the proper Muggle subject, "Chemistry."

But Peeler didn't follow up on that. He turned to me, "Well, Mr. Wendt, I understand that you're an American. You grew up in Ohio."

"Yes. Are you familiar with Ohio at all?"

"Oh, I gather that it is one of the mid-western states. Beyond that I really don't know much."

"Well, it's actually closer to the East than the Midwest. It's bordered by two great bodies of water—Lake Erie and the Ohio river." I smiled at that and Peeler wondered if there were something funny about the Ohio river.

"Just that no foot of the Ohio River is actually in Ohio even though it borders Ohio.

"Ohio is one of the most populous states of the United States but most of its population lives in small towns and farms. Oddly, the western states, known for their great wide open spaces are the most urban states in the country.

"I grew up in a small town. I attended The Ohio State University where I majored in English. Then I went to Stanford."

"Where you took a master's degree in English Literature." Peeler interjected, "I know that and I know that you came to England afterward. Why didn't you stay at Stanford for a Doctorate, and why did you come to England instead?"

Our orders arrived and the interruption gave me a chance to think about my answer, "I left Stanford because I had gotten tired of studying. I'd heard that one's twenties were the freest time of one's life, and I decided that I should come to the seat of English Literature then. I perhaps never would be able later to spend time in the source of my field of study."

"Sounds admirable. How did that work for you?"

"Not as well as I hoped. I was not independently wealthy. I had to find a job almost immediately to support my visits to the locales of the great English authors."

Peeler added for me, "Jobs at Starbucks."

"Yes, you're very well informed. The advantage of that job is having a fair amount of freedom to take several days off at a time and visit places—such as the neighborhood of East Bourne."

Peeler eyes lit up, "The home of Elizabeth Bennet. So, Jane Austen is one of your favorite authors?"

194

"Certainly."

"Some would claim that she was the best novelist of the English language. What do you think?"

I smiled, "Well, I admire her very much. But the field is far too broad to admit of one greatest author. I also admire Samuel Clemens and Steinbeck and even Hemmingway."

"Hedge your bets, eh?"

"Just simple honesty."

"What about you, Professor Snape? Do you have a favorite author?"

Snape stared at him and said, "I'm not a fanatic of literature— English or otherwise."

Peeler turned back to me, "Did you have other endeavors while you were working at Starbucks?"

"Oh, yes. I want to write. I had hoped to do more writing, but I found that the only time that I had free to write was what a friend of mine at Stanford who really was a published writer had—after 10PM."

"Yes, day jobs do tend to get in the way of our avocations. Well, how did you come to be a professor at Hogwarts?"

Snape entered the conversation, "Our Headmaster found himself in need of someone to teach English Literature. He also wanted to increase the diversity of our teaching staff, so he put adverts in the major papers around England—very discreet adverts. Mr. Wendt answered one of them."

Peeler looked surprised, "You were hired to promote diversity? You seem to be a prime 'white male protestant.' Is protestant right?"

"Yes, I am."

Snape's eyes bored into his, "Oh, but Mr. Wendt is very much a minority at Hogwarts—an American, a commoner—not in a pejorative sense, and fresh out of school."

Peeler seemed a bit stunned by Snape's intensity. I resumed, "That's right. I saw the advert and answered it. My first interview was with Professor Dumbledore, and I had a followup interview with the assistant headmistress.

"They both impressed me with their desire to. . ." I hesitated, somewhat lost for words and found what I wanted, "to make education at Hogwarts more than a preparation for vocation.

"I once read a speech delivered by the president of the University of Chicago to a class of incoming freshmen. He debunked the idea that a college education was good as a preparation for a career. Instead he insisted that the proper purpose of education was preparation to live a good life.

"I said something of the sort myself in my interview with Ms. McGonagall, the assistant headmistress. That apparently impressed her. In any case, they hired me, and I've taught there ever since."

Snape was somewhat testy, "Yes, I have to agree that Mr. Wendt has succeeded in that goal of changing the nature of education at Hogwarts."

Peeler picked up on the disapproval in his voice, "Then you don't approve of the change, Professor Snape?"

"Let's say that I think that there is little enough time for students to learn my subject and other necessary subjects to add further burdens to them."

Peeler nodded but didn't appear to agree, "Oh, the philosophy that Mr. Wendt has expressed would be a fair representation of Cambridge's philosophy of education."

Snape shrugged, and Peeler glanced down at his watch, "Oh, I didn't realize how late it had gotten on. We really need to go to my office for the official interview. Let me work with the waiter and you two can go outside. I'll join you shortly."

We did. He came out and we walked briskly to a University building and up to his office. As we went, Snape whispered to me, "Do you want me to confund him. It would be easy."

"No." I hissed through barred teeth.

Peeler who was a couple of paces ahead turned, "Is there a problem I can help with?"

Snape glared at him, "We're just talking about what happens when we get together after your meeting."

We swept into his outer office. He shook Snape's hand and said, "Professor Snape, it's been a pleasure meeting you. I suppose we probably won't cross paths again. I wish you a good school term and future fortune."

He turned to his secretary and told her to hold calls until we'd finished. He then opened the door to his office and invited me to sit. The office had a wall of bookshelves, a fine oak desk that had appeared to have seen many provosts. There were a few reproductions of paintings on the walls. I thought they were mainly Turners. As I sat, I asked him about that, "Are you a fan of Turner?"

196

He smiled and said, "Yes. I like his subject matter. Even though I'm not a great fan of impressionism, Turner appeals to me."

He sat and opened a file that was sitting on his desk, "This is Cedric Diggery's file." He pulled out a parchment sheet, "This is his transcript. It's interesting. I don't think that I've ever seen a transcript on parchment in calligraphy."

"Yeh, me too. But you know, you go to the Hogwarts secretary and ask for a transcript and that's what you get. I'm sure you've faced something like that."

He smiled. And he went on to what I thought was safe ground, "Mr. Diggery is a great chess player—even now, as a youth. How do you think he acquired that ability?"

I smiled as well, "He has an amazing talent, and it doesn't hurt that he's quite intelligent. And you know, there are lots of great chess players who have nothing else in their lives, So a loss or a setback in chess threatens their self-image in a very challenging way. He is a well-rounded player. He is a great athlete, and he is an accomplished scholar. Setbacks on the chessboard don't trouble him."

Peeler shook his head, 'Well, I'll tell you what I think. I think that you're the secretary and the Headmaster as well. I think that you are a private tutor who has been teaching Mr. Diggery reading, writing and 'rithmetic. But most important, and why you were probably hired—to teach him chess. Now that he wants to attend University, you have lost your way and tried to imitate a legitimate school.

"Don't misunderstand. I think you've done a marvelous job—especially the chess. A home-schooled—isn't that what you call it in the States—student can be very good. We have admitted a number of them and find them generally to be quite accomplished. So, please drop this silly pretense that you work for a real school."

I sighed, and my shoulders drooped at the magnitude of the sales job that I'd have to do. In the interim, Peeler offered me something to drink. I thought about what to do. I decided that I should accept something. "Would you happen to have claret?"

"Oh, don't ask for that just because you think that's what we all drink in academia. I have something harder from the state of Kentucky." He put emphasis on the first syllable, and I did my best not to smirk at the pronunciation.

"That sounds good. My tastes tend toward the products of Tennessee, but Kentucky bourbon is good too."

He got out glasses and poured. That gave me time to think. I suppose that was his intention—to give me every chance to trip myself up by over-thinking. He sat, and I waited for my first sip. It was good.

I began, "I hardly know where to go with all of these points. First, I am NOT the secretary of Hogwarts.

"I'm terribly flattered that you think I might be the chess tutor of Mr. Diggery. But, to tutor him, you'd have to be at least a chess master—which I definitely am not. As a matter of fact there is probably only one game that Mr. Diggery has ever played that I would have had a chance at beating him—his first. And by the way, Mr. Diggery only started playing chess less than three years ago.

"Now, my Headmaster anticipated that you might have some doubts that needed to be addressed. He sent two letters along with me that I'd like to show you." I handed him the Prime Minister's letter.

He opened it by tearing it along one end and blew to open it wider. Then he pulled out the folded sheet. "Very nice bond. A good choice." He unfolded it, and for a moment, his eyes popped. He quickly scanned the contents.

"Well, I have to admit that you have courage. It certainly shows the power of desktop publishing. You can create documents that really look legitimate." His voice was thick with sarcasm.

I sighed again. "My Headmaster thought that you might be skeptical of the document's authenticity, so he suggests that you contact the office of the Prime Minister. "I grimaced at what I had to say next, "I'm afraid that I have to ask for the document back."

Peeler laughed uproariously.

"Please, bear with me, just contact them."

With that, he frowned and picked up the phone at his desk. He punched a button, "Ms. Harkins, please get the office of the Prime Minister on the line.

"Yes, I said the Prime Minister, Downing Street, yes."

"Well, tell them that we're inquiring about."

I interrupted him and said, "Tell them that you want to inquire about the 'Mirror' government."

Peeler's face dropped, "You mean the 'Shadow' government."

"No, sir. I mean the 'Mirror' government."

He turned back to the phone handset and said, "Tell them that we're calling about the 'Mirror' government."

"Yes, NOT 'Shadow' government. 'Mirror' government. Be sure to be careful that you actually get the Prime Minister's office. Put me through if anyone answers."

He turned back to me, "Well, do we spend the rest of the time waiting for the call, or do you have anything else to say?"

"I do, but I'd like to wait a couple of minutes to see if you get through, before proceeding."

He shook his head and said, apparently to himself, "He isn't even trying to dodge it."

I sat calmly, praying that some undersecretary actually knew about the 'Mirror' government, whatever that was. I was just about to pull out my other letter when the phone rang.

Peeler picked it up with a smirk on his face and started speaking immediately, "I know, nobody's ever heard of the 'Mirror' government. That's OK, Ms. Harkins." Then he paused.

"Oh, really. They have."

"Are you sure that it's the Prime Minister's office?"

"Yes. Yes. I want to talk to him."

"Hello. . . You're?"

"Yes. I understand—the second undersecretary for foreign affairs."

He paused, "Yes, I know that you're busy. I'll be brief."

There was another brief pause, "I received a letter from the Prime Minister concerning a school called Hogwarts."

"Yes. I do want to know if it's authentic.

"Yes sir. I understand. I'll send it back with him."

"Thank you for your time." Then he hung up.

He looked around the office, avoiding my gaze. He glanced down at his desk and noticed his glass of bourbon as though he'd not seen it before. He picked it up and emptied it at a swallow. "That was the secretary for foreign affairs. He was very clear. There is a Hogwarts as described in the letter. The Headmaster is a professor Dumbledore. You can take the letter back."

He seemed to be reacting to a shock. He straightened in his chair and looked at me for the first time in a while. "OK. You said something about another letter."

I nodded, pulled it out, and held out my hand to receive the original letter. He took a moment to realize what I wanted, and he

199

handed over the letter. He opened the second letter and glanced at it. And then he read more carefully.

"OK. Professor Wendt. This is a glowing recommendation. I don't really suppose that there's much more to say.

He seemed to recover himself a bit more. "We would be pleased to admit Mr. Diggery when he's finished another couple of terms and has updated his," he looked down at the transcript, still lying on the table, "transcript."

I rose and said, "It looks like I don't have any more business here. I'll be in touch at the end of the current term and the next one."

Peeler frowned in concentration, "Oh, one more thing before you go. We really would like to have Mr. Diggery on the chess team when he's here. Would you please have a word?"

I smiled, "Certainly. After the official acceptance arrives." I couldn't resist adding that dig. But then I had one other thing to add on that topic.

"By the way, I'd think twice about having him practice with the ordinary team members. We used to have a chess club that I was the adviser of. When he joined, the rest of the club just gave up and went on to other interests. Having such an overwhelming power on the club was pretty devastating to the rest of the players—strong and weak."

He blinked, "I'll try to remember to suggest that to the chess adviser."

I glanced at my watch and found that it was a quarter past two PM. In the outer office, Snape was waiting. He immediately commented, "Having a chummy time, were you?"

Peeler came out, nodded at Snape, and shook my hand. "Don't forget the chess. Please."

Snape and I left. I told him how things had gone. His comment was, "You can always count on Dumbledore in a tight spot. But only in tight spots." With that I took his hand, and I re-appeared outside Hogwarts ground. My head was spinning as was my stomach. So much so, that I knew I was going to throw up. I went behind a tree and was sick. I came back from behind it and said, "I think it must have been that rich lobster pate."

Snape mercifully said nothing, and we returned to the castle.

The weekend was quiet.

Winkie

I had an idea about investigating Crouch's murder further. So, one evening, I left a note in Dumbledore's pigeon-hole in the Teacher's Lounge. I wanted to meet with him as soon as was convenient. The next morning during class, I was interrupted by a knock on my door. I thought to myself, "Blast, who is it now?" But I invited the intruder in. He happened to be Professor Dumbledore.

"Professor Dumbledore, what can I do for you?"

"Oh, I just thought that I'd observe your class." He hesitated and added, "If you don't mind."

"Of course not, please take a seat." He did and was absolutely quiet. We were reading a passage from the "Rhyme of the Ancient Mariner." The discussion centered around the albatrosses that people carry around their neck.

At one point, I thought that I heard a cleared throat in the back, 'Professor Dumbledore, would you like to ask a question or make a comment?"

He cleared his throat again and just said, 'No. Just a sore throat." But I could have sworn that I saw a glisten in his eye.

After the class, I was clearing my desk to go to lunch. Dumbledore said casually, "Would you like to have that discussion you want in my office now?"

'Of course." We went directly there.

On the way, he asked what I would like to talk about.

"I'd like for us to interview Winkie."

"Really. All right," He saw a fifth year approaching us. He materialized a scrap of parchment and a quill and scribbled a short note.

He interrupted him and said, "Excuse me, would you please take this note down to the kitchens and give it to an elf named Winkie?"

We arrived at the gargoyle. Rather than give the password, he said that we would wait. He didn't reveal who or what we were waiting for. After a few minutes, I saw a house elf approaching down the corridor. I've never been very good at identifying house elves, so I was happy when she got close enough that I could recognize Winkie. As she approached, I could see that she had little perturbations as she walked. She shook slightly as she walked—not enough to make walking hazardous but enough to be noticeable.

She reached us and said, "Professor Dumbledore, it is Winkie. I is coming like you wanted." There was a very noticeable quaver in her voice.

Dumbledore said the password almost inaudibly and the gargoyle moved out of the way. He then encouraged her, "Come along now, Winkie, we just want to talk with you a bit. You've not done anything wrong, and you shouldn't worry." However, that didn't seem to allay her fears much. She seemed no less nervous as she made her unsteady way up the stairs.

Dumbledore asked her to sit and offered her something to drink. He suggested pumpkin juice or water, but she wasn't interested in either.

When we were all seated, Dumbledore looked to me, and I began. "Winkie, I want to talk to you about something that may be disturbing to you. But I want you to know that we don't think that you've done anything wrong and we're just hoping that you may know something that hasn't occurred to you to tell anyone. That something may seem tiny and even worthless to you, but it might turn out to be very valuable to us. Do you understand?"

"Winkie understands, sir."

I was trying to make her as comfortable and easy as I could. "Good. Now, I want you to think about the time that your old master, Mr. Crouch, died."

Winkie's shaking doubled, 'I is afraid, sir."

I tried to reassure her. "We know that you couldn't have killed Mr. Crouch, right Professor?"

"Yes, Winkie. A house elf couldn't kill her master."

I went on, "Winkie, you have to obey orders given to you by wizards, right."

"You is right, sir. A house elf has to obey orders given by any wizard in her master's family."

"But, even if a member of the family gave you an order, you couldn't kill or even harm your master. You couldn't even stand by and let anyone else kill him. Isn't that true?"

"Yes, sir. You is right."

"So, then, you couldn't have killed your master or even helped someone kill him, right?"

"Yes, sir."

"And if you don't have an order from your master or his family to obey, what do you do?"

Winkie seemed to be puzzling over that question. She seemed to think about it but did not have an answer.

I prodded her gently, "If you don't have an order to do, can you do what you want?"

Winkie seemed puzzled by the concept. I went on, "When you're having dinner and no one tells you what to eat, can you choose what you want to eat?"

Winkie immediately answered, "Winkie eats what she wants at dinner."

"Then sometimes, you can do what you want?"

"Winkie does what she wants at meals."

I had another idea that I tried to pursue. "Winkie, do you want to go to live somewhere else?"

She answered enigmatically, "Winkie has to stay here, sir."

Dumbledore quickly assured her that no one wanted to make her leave.

I was stymied by that answer, so I went on to what I really wanted to talk with her about. "Well, then you don't have anything to worry about, do you, Winkie?"

"Winkie is worried."

I thought about that a minute. I decided that I just had to keep going even though she seemed to be frightened about something. Something occurred to me at this point. Her master was dead, and there was no heir to his estate. Wasn't Winkie free?

"Winkie, who is your master?"

She didn't hesitate at all, but said, "Master Crouch."

"I know he was your last master, but who is your master now?"

"Master Crouch."

That set me back on my heels. I looked over at Dumbledore with the question in my eyes. He looked at Winkie with his penetrating gaze. "Winkie, Bartholomew Crouch is dead. He can't be your master. Who is?"

Winkie wouldn't budge, "Master Crouch."

"OK. I think that's one that we're going to have to set aside for a bit. So, you were nearby when your master died. Is there anything that you can tell us about that? Anything at all?"

She was stubborn about that, "Winkie is knowing nothing about master Crouch when he died."

"Were you with him when he died?"

Winkie's shaking became more pronounced, and her already squeaky voice became even squeakier. "Winkie is knowing nothing."

I looked an appeal at Dumbledore. He soundlessly shrugged, and we seemed to have reached an impasse. Dumbledore dismissed her. Then he turned to me when she'd started down the stairs, "Well, that was unproductive."

I had to admit that it was, and I apologized for wasting his time.

"No. No. You've at least got ideas. I'm afraid that I'm as far out of ideas as the Aurors are on this case."

We walked down to lunch together. On the way, I asked him, "What do you suppose Winkie meant when she said that Crouch was her master? Just that he had been her last master?"

"I don't know. That could be, but house elves are very literal. Unfortunately, none of them has a very good command of English. I wonder if there is a way that Crouch could still be her master."

An idea occurred to me about language, "I know that you know a lot of obscure languages. I've even heard that you know the language of the Merpeople."

Dumbledore supplied, "Merish. That's right, I do."

"Do you know the native language of the house elves?"

"No. I don't think anyone does. No doubt you're thinking that you'd like a translator to help you question Winkie?"

"Well, yes. That would be nice."

"The only person that I ever knew who might just have known the language of house elves was Barty Crouch. He knew more languages than I've even heard of. But no help there. Sorry."

"Thanks," I said ruefully.

Spies

A couple of weeks later, I was checking my pigeon-hole in the Teacher's Lounge more frequently. This time, it had a letter in it—from Dumbledore. It requested that I visit him that evening after dinner. As I walked to the gargoyle who liked sweets, I thought about the number of times that I'd made that trip with Minerva. It had been months since I'd made that trip with her. I was just getting tired.

I arrived and gave the password of the day—pralines. The Gargoyle moved out of the way, and I worked my way up the stairs. Dumbledore was standing at the top of the stairs and greeted me with a handshake when I reached him. He led me into his office and we sat across his desk from each other.

I smiled wanly and asked what he wanted to talk about. He got up and began to pace. "We're in trouble. We've followed your idea about patrolling the maze for the final task. It's not working. Something bad is going to happen if we don't get to the bottom of the question of who put Potter's name in the Goblet of Fire."

He looked at me expectantly. "We need a better idea. Let's try to get one."

It looked like it would be a long night. I took a deep breath and took a moment to clear my head. I looked at my feet and then returned my gaze to Dumbledore. "Well, let's look at this from another perspective. Snape says that someone has been stealing the materials for Polyjuice Potion. Let's start with the supposition that it is related to Potter being sent into the tournament."

Dumbledore pulled on his beard absently and said, "It sounds reasonable. Where does that take us?"

"Well, let's look at who could be responsible. It's got to be someone here all the time, who's disguising himself as someone else. Let's think about who are possible candidates.

"There're the students."

Dumbledore stared at me and then his eyes narrowed, "Yes. That would be a clever idea. It's hard to take a student seriously as a threat— even the Weasley twins. Yes, why not?"

I nodded and said, "I think that's a real possibility, but isn't that group the least likely? They have the least potential for doing things. They can't move around the castle freely at any time. Anyone can send them to class at any time.

"They all have lots of people who know them intimately. A few missteps and their classmates in their house notice."

Dumbledore nodded and added, "To use Polyjuice potion for months at a time, you have to have the person that you're impersonating around to take samples of hair to keep making polyjuice potion. It's possible, but if you've got to share your room with four other students, how do you do it, month after month."

"I didn't realize that. Anyway, that takes us to the next group, the teachers of Hogwarts that have been around for years. They're better posed to hide than students. They can move freely at\ any time of the day or night. They have easy access to everything in Hogwarts. They have private rooms where they can hide the real person they're impersonating.

"But there are lots of teachers and even a few students who know them well. They have to fool them continuously for months. They're more likely to be targets, but not the most likely group.

"Then there are the Headmasters of the other schools."

Dumbledore sniffed, "What about me?"

"Oh, if you are an impersonator and have the real Dumbledore squirreled away somewhere, we're lost. Game over. Full Stop.

"These have nearly all the freedom of teachers in Hogwarts. They have far fewer friends present. Maybe only one each."

Dumbledore grimaced. "You seem to have covered everyone." He got up and walked about the room. "But that is not quite everyone, is it?"

I nodded, as I twirled around trying to keep him in focus. "There's one person that I haven't mentioned. There's Moody."

I grimaced as I said it, "Yes, I know that you and he go back a long way. He was an Auror when Valdemort was active."

Dumbledore said, "More than that. He tracked down and brought many Deatheaters to justice. We lost many friends in that war. It would be sad if he were being impersonated and forced to participate in this against his will."

"But he would be the ideal person to attack. He is well known to only a teacher or two here. He has access to everything." I had an additional thought, "Do you really know him—well enough to detect a clever imposter?"

"I thought I did. But maybe not. I don't recall that he drank as much as he does now. People change." He sighed and went on, "So, where do we go from here?"

"Well, I think that there are a few people whom we can trust. I already told you that I trust you. I think that we can trust Filch and me." A thought occurred to me, "Can you tell if I'm magical? You should test me."

Dumbledore shook his head, "I did that when I greeted you at the door. You're OK. Yes, anyone who doesn't have magical powers is not someone we have to worry about. But, who else? Surely not Severus. He's the one who pointed out the missing ingredients for Polyjuice potion. We'd never have known about it otherwise."

"Yes, I agree. Minerva's OK too." Dumbledore looked at me doubtfully, 'Oh, I know that I haven't seen much of her lately, but before that stupid article appeared in the *Prophet*, I saw enough of her to convince me that she is herself."

Dumbledore smiled at that, "Did you? Well, you're the ultimate expert on her. I'll trust you – for now. How about the heads of other houses?"

I shook my head, 'I don't know. I don't know them well enough to judge."

"Anyone else?" Dumbledore had a twinkle in his eye at that.

I colored slightly as it occurred to me of one other person, "Yes." I said ruefully, "Yes, I have to admit that Sinistra is someone that I can validate. She is definitely her old self and no doubt about it. As a matter of fact, my evidence for her is more recent than for Minerva, but they've both got to be good."

Dumbledore said, "What about Haggrid?"

"I can't say. I sure want to say that he's good. You know, there are so many things that go against the idea of Haggrid being impersonated. In the first place, I think that an impersonator would want to lie low—not do anything unusual or unexpected. Here Haggrid goes romancing Madame Maxime. What the heck is that for someone who's trying to lie low?

"There's another point. It's technical, and I want your opinion about it. Something that's come out now is that Haggrid is part giant. Does Polyjuice potion work with giants? Part giant? If not, or not dependably, that would seem to let both Haggrid and Maxime out. Would you take chances with polyjuice potion on giant/part giant?"

Dumbledore turned to me and then sat. "Like you, I just don't know for sure. You're right in that nobody has tried Polyjuice potion, at least that I know, on a giant or a part giant. Polyjuice doesn't work with non-humans, so I'm pretty sure it wouldn't work with a giant, but a part giant? I don't know. I just don't know. Would someone try it with Haggrid?" He shook his head, "I don't like the idea that someone's impersonating Haggrid, but that's all it is—liking and not liking.

"So, what do you suggest for the next steps?

"Let's get the people that we're sure of together and try to get us all working at narrowing down the list of possibles."

We agreed that Dumbledore would call a meeting of all the people that we'd cleared and have a brainstorming session. It would happen in the next couple of days.

◻

A few days later, the six of us—Dumbledore, Snape, Minerva, Filch (yes Filch), Sinistra and me—met in Dumbledore's Office. I don't think that I'd ever seen so many people in that office for a party at one time. He summarized what we'd discussed a few days before and then raised the question, "How can we eliminate people from suspicion? I don't think that we can eliminate everyone, but I think we can get down to a list of a few people whom we need to watch closely. Ideas?" There were a lot of one-on-one conversations. There were a couple of people who resisted the idea of an impersonator keeping up an impersonation for months and months. Finally, Dumbledore got tired of it or decided that you have to allow people some time to get used to a new idea. In any case, he raised his voice slightly, "Ladies and gentlemen. I'd like you to listen for a minute."

Everyone fell silent, and he began. "Now, how can we work through all the teachers and guests and decide who the impersonator is."

Snape raised his hand, "Headmaster, I have a suggestion. Each of us should get a piece of parchment and a quill and write down on it the names of all the people whom you know that you share some exclusive piece of knowledge with. This should be something that you're sure that no one else knows about. Then, each of us will, over the next week or so, bring that up casually in conversation to see if their memory matches ours. We get back together and check off the names that pass and see if anyone fails the test.

Sinistra asked, "What if the other person has legitimately forgotten. That happens."

Snape sneered, "Well, of course, you pick something that you're sure that they would never forget."

I spoke up, "But, I'd suggest that you have at least two private memories, just in case."

Dumbledore conjured a half-dozen pieces of parchment and quills from thin air and invited us to begin thinking, "Now, take fifteen minutes for this exercise. Then we'll review the results."

We all found a corner and began writing. I decided that I'd write both the name and the private pieces of information, but as hard as I tried, I couldn't think of anyone that I hadn't already contributed in the earlier meeting.

Dumbledore called us back, but a couple of people begged for a little more time. Sinistra laughed, "This isn't a final exam, after all."

I couldn't help thinking that it might be a final exam for someone.

When we did re-convene, Dumbledore invited someone to volunteer. No one did. But then Filch sprung up, 'Oh, oh. I've got one. Ms. Prince, the Librarian. One day . . "

But Snape interrupted. "I don't want to know the details."

I said, "No. None of us should share details. That makes the results of interviewing them suspect. We should just talk with them when we're alone with them, work the memory or fact into the conversation, and judge whether they know about it or not."

A broad smile came over Filch's face.

Snape volunteered for Karkaroff, "We were," he paused and his face was downcast, "Deatheaters together. I have an idea that I think would be foolproof with him. I'm afraid I don't know anyone else that well." No one was surprised at that.

Minerva volunteered to check Pomona Sprout. Sinistra volunteered for Professor Vector.

Dumbledore turned to me, "Well?"

"I'm afraid that I can't add anyone."

He frowned and asked, "What about Charity Burbage. Surely, someone who has spent so much time with Muggles should have something that only Muggles and Muggles Study teachers would know?"

If looks could kill, Dumbledore would have been carried away in a handbasket, "I don't think that kind of knowledge meets the criteria of being known only to the two of us."

He sighed, "Too bad."

He went on, "I'll take Sibyll. I hired her and we go back a long way. I'll also take Madame Maxime.

"That still leaves us with Babbling, Flitwik, Hooch, Pomfrey, and Hagrid, although, I think we can exclude Hagrid. Does no one else know any of these well enough to investigate them?" He looked around at the seated teachers slowly and finally returned his gaze to me.

I apologized, "Sorry, I can't help you with any of them."

Minerva cleared her throat, "I think that I can handle Pomfrey." She said this with downcast eyes."

Dumbledore spread his hands, "Flitwik, anyone? No?" Everyone had their eyes averted as though they'd just noticed a particularly interesting portrait of a former Headmaster. "Very well."

There was some discussion of details about how to bring something up innocently and how we'd report results. It was decided to return exactly a week in the future.

As I was leaving, Dumbledore drew me aside, "You know that there is one person who we very much need checked who hasn't been?"

"Of course, Mad-Eye. God, I wish we could check him."

After the meeting, Filch grabbed my elbow and dragged me out of the way. "Come down to my office and let's have a drink."

I was a bit surprised because we hadn't really done anything together this term—not that I had objections, so we went down into the lower level to his office.

He was in a good mood. All the way down he talked about how he had an idea about how to catch Potter at one of his nocturnal prowls. "And if I'm lucky, I'll get that Weasley kid and maybe even Grainger."

I had my doubts about that. I just replied that I wished him luck.

We arrived at the office, and he didn't wait to ask me what I'd like. He just got out his usual bottle of the stuff that he called fire whiskey. It seemed more like turpentine to me, but I wouldn't say that aloud—either to his face or behind his back.

Once we were seated with tumblers of stuff in our hands, he explained, "I can't thank you enough for including me in this. It's just the kind of thing that I love. Sneaking around, spying on evil doers.

"AND, Dumbledore himself assigned it to me." He smirked as widely as I'd ever seen him do. "He hired me, but sometimes I think that he doesn't really get the importance of being ever vigilant to catch students misbehaving. And now, I have the chance of catching a teacher!"

I really didn't know what to say, but I decided that it was better to not say anything. So I just took a sip of the stuff in my glass and pretended not to gag on it.

When Filch got onto a topic, very little in the way of dialogue was required, and this was no exception. I did think that it was necessary for me to be honest and admit that I really hadn't been the one responsible for his attendance at the meeting.

"Really, who then?"

I shrugged, "Who else? Dumbledore."

I saw a little glistening in his eye, "REALLY? Dumbledore."

"Absolutely. You are a necessary part of this . . uh . . adventure."

He seemed to be swallowing down a sob and for a moment was silent. Then a troubled look came over his face, "There's just one thing. I've got to talk to Ms. Prinz."

I agreed.

"But, you know. uh. that is, I'm not exactly uh. "

He seemed to have gotten stuck. So, I supplied a word or two to him. "You mean that you're not sure quite how to approach the Librarian?"

"Not really. That is, I mean that I think it would be easier if I had someone along to help a little."

I saw it coming and tried to head it off, "Now, you heard what Dumbledore said. It's important that this be a one-on-one thing so that no one gets hints from third parties."

He suddenly discovered that his shoe was untied and attended to it for a minute and then returned his gaze to me. "You would be such a help. You wouldn't have to stay—just help me get started talking to her."

I sighed internally and considered for a moment suggesting that he take a good swig or two from his fire whiskey. I decided that that might defeat the grand purpose, so I bit my tongue and said, "Well, I don't think that it would be bad if I just sort of got you started and then backed away and let your charming self come forward on its own."

"Oh, that would be just great."

"OK. When do we do it?"

He looked at me with a bit of panic in his eyes, "Oh, what about next week?"

"It's better to finish up quickly, so that you can rest assured that you'll have something to report next week. How about tomorrow? We could go to the library after dinner, and I could get you started and you could finish up."

He gulped and admitted that that would be OK.

The next day at dinner, we sat together. I didn't want him sneaking off before I could get over to him. His appetite was off, but I made up for him, which wasn't hard at table in the Great Hall. The house elves do amazing things with dinner.

After he finished what little he was going to eat, he got up and said, "I'll be back in a minute."

I knew better than that. I got up too and suggested that we ought to make our way up to the library since Ms. Prinz had already left. We arrived and found her at the Librarian's desk. There were a couple of students in the stacks studying something other than herbology. I told Filch, "Perfect. It's time to go."

"Wait. Wait. There are students in the library."

"There always are."

"But, "

"But nothing. They're too engrossed in something else. Even if they get in the way, I'm sure that we can threaten them with revealing their extra-curricular studies."

"Wait!" Filch was almost panicked. "What are we going to say?"

"Don't worry. I'll think of something. Just follow along and take my lead."

"That's crazy."

But, I took him by the collar and dragged him along as we entered the library. Prinz looked up quickly with a severe look on her face, which changed to one of bemused wonder.

"Well, Mr. Filch, what brings you here? Can I help you find a book?"

With such a greeting, you'd think that he'd jump on it like a hound on a steak bone. However, all that happened was that his mouth dropped open and he stood before her, stunned. I said, "Ms. Pinz. Filch and I were having a little dispute about your memory. I said that you couldn't possibly remember what books each student had checked out. He said you could. So would you oblige us?"

She smiled at Filch, "Did you really say that?"

He nodded voicelessly.

"Well, I want to see a demonstration. What does Harry Potter have checked out right now?"

She laughed, and I'm not so sure that I wouldn't have called it a cackle. "That's easy. Potter never checks any books out. He doesn't have any. How about something hard?"

I thought a moment and said, "OK. Then here's a challenge. How about Hermione Grainger?"

She brightened. "Yes, that is more difficult. Well, she's nearly always got the latest edition of Hogwarts a History, checked out. In addition," she hesitated as she consulted her memory.

I interrupted, "Knowing Hermione, this may take a bit. Let me suggest that you, Argus, check Pinz's memory out and then report which one of us won the bet."

"A good idea," Pinz said, "because it will take a little time. Since you're going to lose anyway, you might as well trot along and check back with Mr. Filch later."

I agreed and backed slowly out of the library.

The next day, I ran into Filch at breakfast. He was beaming. I inquired, "Who won the bet?"

His smile didn't falter, "Oh, I won all right."

"Good, I hope that it didn't interfere with your rounds of the Castle."

He colored a bit and admitted that he might not have been as thorough as was his wont.

"Oh, I bet that you were mighty thorough at some things." and bumped him in the ribs.

When we did reconvene, there was a rapid roll call. It was unlike any other roll call in that each person spoke the name of the person whom they'd been investigating and the result. Everyone's result was negative. Everyone was sure that their assignment was not being impersonated.

Dumbledore summarized, "Well, then. We have four unknowns."

Snape interrupted, "But, Headmaster, I count three: Babbling, Flitwik, Hooch. Did I miss someone?"

"I'm afraid you did, Severus. It's Moody."

Snape was startled, "But, sir, you yourself hired him just months ago. Surely, he can't be the guilty party?"

"Why do you think that he wasn't invited to the last meeting?"

Snape simply gaped. Apparently the idea of a wizard who could fool Dumbledore was beyond him.

Dumbledore continued, "Well, we're down to the Four. Each of us must take one of these as their personal assignment. You must watch them carefully—without being detected. You listen to their conversations, watch their actions. If you see something that doesn't seem . . uh . . 'kosher', you must report to me immediately. Don't attempt to investigate further yourself."

"We can only hope that one of them makes a slip that someone observes. Now, we need volunteers.

No one spoke. We all found that there was something fascinating happening with our shoes or maybe the carpet or her robe. Dumbledore looked around in disgust, "All right, then we'll take it one at a time. I'll

214

name a name and someone WILL volunteer for that name. If someone doesn't volunteer, I'll volunteer someone.

"First, Babbling."

Sinistra modestly raised her hand, "I can do Babbling."

"Good. Next, Flitwick."

This time, Snape volunteered, not happily, but without complaint.

"Next, Hooch."

Minerva actually popped up to a standing position. "That would be me, sir."

"Thank you. And now, finally, Moody."

No one said anything for a moment, but then Snape asked a question, "Can't any of the 'cleared' teachers take on assignments?"

Dumbledore gave one rapid shake of the head as though to emphasize the finality of the decision, "No, Mr. Snape. This wizard who's doing the impersonating is World Class. I want only top wizards and witches to take on this assignment." With that, Sinistra straightened a little in her chair.

I started to raise my hand, but Dumbledore headed me off, "What is it about the phrase First Class Wizard that you didn't understand Mr. Wendt. I meant those words. You are not capable of taking on this assignment."

Snape smiled. Dumbledore went on. "I knew that we likely wouldn't have anyone volunteer for Moody. So, I will. I brought him onboard. It's only appropriate that I follow up with him.

"Now, everyone has an assignment except Filch and Wendt. I want the both of you to keep an eye generally on the remaining four. Don't go out of your way to talk to them. Just be aware."

Filch gave a funny little salute and said, "Yes, sir."

I just nodded.

Dumbledore finished by assigning us to return a week later for a follow up meeting.

This time, it was a glum group that met. Dumbledore called the meeting to order with a word, "parturient". Then we got down to business. "Report, please—alphabetically by first name."

That took us a few minutes to figure out the correct order, but we eventually figured it out. The first was Filch (who had to be urged to go ahead), "I don't have anything to report."

Then there was Sinistra, who almost went before FIlch, "I'm sorry Headmaster. I haven't made any progress."

I was next and just shook my head. Then came Minerva who simply said, "Nothing." and finally Severus, "Nothing Headmaster."

Strangely, Dumbledore didn't seem particularly disappointed, "I didn't really expect anything different. The first day none of you could think of anything particular and private to talk with them about. I didn't really expect that you'd do that later, but we had to try."

"Are we stuck then?" Sinistra had her chin buried in her hands.

I had to ask although the answer seemed obvious, 'What about you, Dumbledore. What about Moody."

He just shook his head.

"There's only one thing to do."

"OK, Wendt. How do we go from here?"

I stood up and paced to think it through. "OK. We've got to get Moody off of guard duty at the maze. We've got to try to keep eyes on him. How the hell we do it, I have no idea. And we've got to keep any spare eyes that we might happen to have on our other three candidates."

Minerva ran a finger through her hair, "What about Karkaroff? Can he help us? It would be good to have another hand or two."

Snape shook his head, "He's on a razor edge. He's scared to death that something is happening with Deatheaters. As a former Deatheater, he knows that there's nothing that Deatheaters who've been in Azkaban hate more than a Deatheater who bought himself out. It always happened at the expense of other Deatheaters going to Azkaban. He's out of it. I even wonder if he'll be there for the final task of the Tri-Wizard tournament."

"Great," Minerva said glumly.

Dumbledore looked around and cleared his throat, 'Oh, one more thing. We need to start planning security during the tournament. Remember that Crouch died AFTER the second task. I don't want something like that happening again. I want each of you to come up with at least one proposal for a security measure."

Minerva threw up her hands. I'd never seen her do something like that before, "First, we watch the Maze, and then we watch our suspects, AND we do our normal teaching AND, if we're head of house, we run our house, AND ONE MORE THING, we have to plan security. This is crazy."

Dumbledore shrugged and sent us on our way. I was the last one out the door. I got on the stair and suddenly found that I wasn't alone. A very familiar voice said in my left ear. "I'm going to go crazy if we don't get to the end of this tournament soon so we can be off our good behavior." I turned to comment to her face but wasn't able to comment because I found her mouth smothering mine. As quickly as it had started, it ended, and she was speed-walking down the corridor toward the Gryffindor tower. I smiled because I figured that Morse must have lost out!

Ten days after that, I was doing my regular check of my teacher mailbox in the Teacher's Lounge. Hardly except announcements, like the next Hoggsmeade weekend was coming up, showed up there. However, this time there was an invitation to Dumbledore's Office. I thought, "It must be the security meeting."

Well, I had been thinking about it, but, it was very hard to think about really hard problems without her to talk to. I'd once heard an extrovert defined as someone who can only think his best by talking to other people. I'd always believed that I was an introvert because I found it hard to introduce myself, and ask girls out and so forth.

I'd never really thought about that definition, but I now realized that it was true. I'd not been able to talk with Minerva for more than a few minutes at a time for four or was it five months. It had been "good morning", "good afternoon", or "good evening" every day for nearly all that time. It was driving me crazy.

When I'd had the epiphany about being an extrovert, I'd briefly considered picking another thinking buddy. Then the problem appeared. Who? The one person that I could count on to listen to what I had to say was Filch, but he was worthless for critiquing my ideas. I'd briefly thought about using Snape, but I just couldn't imagine him having the patience to listen as I thought through out loud my crazy ideas till I finally hit a decent one.

Oh, yes. There was Sinistra. She'd be oooh soooo happy to listen to my ideas and would probably even provide good critique. I really,

really, really didn't want her getting the idea that she could be a permanent stand-in for Minerva.

I'd also briefly thought about Dumbledore. I'd actually used him as a sort of stand in for Minerva, but I found that I just didn't quite trust him completely. He was very aloof. Good, I suppose in a Headmaster, but I wasn't so sure that it was good for someone you wanted to brain-storm with.

So, I'd been struggling with ideas for security while I was grading. I'd spend an hour grading. I'd take fifteen or twenty minutes and work on security ideas and then back to grading or on to lesson plans or walking the halls. That was another way that I sometimes managed to think creatively. As I walked, I meditated. I was still taking the Glock out into the hills for target practice occasionally and during those long walks I'd think.

Anyway, I had a couple of ideas to take to the meeting. I arrived and there were the usual dreary reports. No one had seen anything that made them think that any of the frantic four were more likely to be the imposter or clear them of it. The only person who was actually kind of happy was Filch because he kept being invited to these meetings, and he could report like everyone else. As a matter of fact, he was happy to report his strenuous efforts to keep the four under observation. He had almost entirely forgotten students, and the students were actually having a pretty easy time for doing minor infractions. No one bothered to mention to Filch that despite this epidemic of minor infractions, Hogwarts was going along in its educational business quite nicely, thank you.

Dumbledore had to actually cut Filch off when he wanted to come to the real topic of the meeting. "Thank you, Mr. Filch. I think I can honestly say that I've never heard such a thorough report in my entire career.'

Filch beamed, bowed to Dumbledore, actually turned and bowed to the rest of us, and sat down. I had the hardest time trying to keep myself from laughing. I really didn't want to laugh. Filch was not such a bad fellow. He just lived in perpetual fear that someone would replace him. Not an unreasonable fear, given that he was a Squibb and wasn't especially clever. That fear drove him to become the ultimate martinet. By making himself the scourge of students, he thought he was proving himself to be indispensable.

I had tried for years to first understand him and then to convince him that all he had to do was look around to realize that Dumbledore would never fire him. There were Hagrid, Sibyll, and even me. We were all people that the vast majority of Headmasters of a school of wizardry would fire in a minute for one reason or another. Amazingly, he never had.

There were times that I thought that Filch was the funniest character that I knew, but then I realized that it was the other way around. The world had played a joke on him, and he was the only one who didn't get it.

But Dumbledore was starting to talk, so I paid attention. He called for ideas.

Snape got up, "You've got to start out with the rules for the final competition. I know that some of you are well familiar with them but not all of you are. So, I'll very quickly summarize them. Professor Hagrid has planted the maze and it's quite close to mature.

"The object is to be the first to reach the Tri-Wizard cup at the heart of the maze. The various champions will be released to enter the maze at varying times based on how they've scored on the previous competitions. There are various sorts of hazards along the way. Some require magic to get around them. Some require intelligence. Potter will go first. Questions on the rules?"

I stood immediately, "Is it a left-handed maze?"

Snape stared at me and asked, "A left-handed maze?"

"Yes, there's a lot of mathematical theory on solving mazes. One ancient rule for solving mazes was to place your left hand on a wall and walk forward, not retracing your steps at any time and never removing your hand from the left-hand wall. Now, there are mazes that the left-hand rule won't solve. Is this one of them?"

Snape continued to stare and then looked around the room. Finally his eyes rested on Dumbledore, who answered, "I have no idea. I will tell you that Hagrid and I collaborated on the design of the maze."

Minerva asked, "What if someone wishes to withdraw from the competition?"

Snape replied, "This brings me to my suggestions. I propose that they fire sparks from their wand high into the air. We will have wizards placed on the edges. In that case they will enter the maze and go directly to the aid of the champion who requested help."

Dumbledore went to the blackboard that I'd seen in his office occasionally. He drew a square near the top and beneath it a semi-circle that didn't connect with the square. Next to the square on one side was a squiggly line and at the very bottom was an oval. "Not elegant art, but I'll label it. You'll get the idea."

The square was the maze. The squiggle was the forest. The semi-circle was the stands at the maze. The oval was Hogwarts castle. He pointed at one edge of the square. "I want someone to volunteer to cover each edge of the maze. I've already asked Professor Hagrid to watch the back edge. Professor Snape, would you take the left edge?"

Snape nodded soundlessly. Dumbledore went on, "The right edge will be taken by Professor Sinistra?" The rising lilt of his voice turned it into a question.

Sinistra nodded, "Of course."

He went on, "I'll take the side with the stands, but never fear. If you weren't assigned something, there are plenty of things to do.

"Now, will the rest of you proceed with your security ideas."

Minerva stood, "I think that we've got to have control of outsiders coming in to view the event. There should only be a very limited number. Certain legitimate, reasonable," here I thought about one person who wouldn't pass that test, "press correspondents should be allowed to come. We have to allow a few representatives from the Ministry of International Cooperation to come and, of course, the immediate families of champions."

Dumbledore agreed, "Yes. We are allowing only two from the Ministry—Mr. Percy Weasley and another, whom they've not named. Probably, the acting Minister.

"Then there are the families. No one from Potter's family. The Delacourt family including her sister will be attending. Cedric's mom and dad. Victor's father will attend.

"I've received several requests for press passes and have granted them all. Altogether, it's currently 16. I wanted them all accompanied from the moment they arrive.

Filch stood up at that, "There aren't enough of us to put one person on each guest."

Dumbledore nodded, "You're right, but we can require groups to stay together. Each family has to stay together. The people from the Ministry have to stay together. The press corps has to stay together."

Filch was as pleased as punch that he had something to say that made sense and required Dumbledore to come up with an answer.

I saw a problem but I didn't stand I just said, "Oh, you know that you can't force any group of people to stay together."

Dumbledore was getting exasperated, "Yes, I know that, but how do we manage them?"

"Here's what we do." Then the beauty of my idea hit me. I smiled.

Snape said sarcastically, "Another brainstorm."

"No, this is really good. It solves two problems at once.

"First, everyone who is invited has to check in with security. When they do, we give them a color-coded ID badge with their name and photo. People who aren't invited, but just show up don't have a badge.

"OK. If anyone sees anyone who isn't a student, teacher, or who is not wearing a color-coded badge, we stop them on the spot.

"We assign one person to each family and other groups. If anyone breaks off from their group, a spare follows them and tries to get them back to the main group. That misfires and anyone notices someone with a badge alone, they join them immediately and get them back to their group."

No one had a reaction. Everyone seemed to be mulling over the implications of that idea. Dumbledore had a question, "What will you and Mr. Filch be doing?"

"Oh, Filch and I and anyone else who has a spare eye will keep it on our students to make sure that they don't do anything stupid." Filch enthusiastically seconded that idea.

Dumbledore asked for any other ideas. Nobody had any. He set up a final meeting for the night before the final task of the tournament, and we split up.

Moody's Revelation

A couple of days later, I was walking in the courtyard in the early evening. I had the feeling that someone was watching me. I slowly made a circuit of the moon-lit courtyard. The alcoves were in deep shadows of the moon and the rest of it was bathed in an eerie black and white light that made you feel like you were in an ancient TV program.

I was spooked enough to make me decide to cut my walk short and return to my office. As I reached the door back inside the castle, someone materialized out of the shadows behind me and said, "Laddie, do you have a minute?"

It was Moody. I had a bad feeling about it, but I seemed to be stuck, "How about coming in to my office and we can have a drink." That, of course, was a mistake because he never drank anything except whatever he kept in that hip flask of his

"Naw. This won't take long. Just wanted to know what's going on."

The sweat started breaking out on my forehead one bead at a time. "Yeah, I wish I knew myself."

"What do you mean?"

That made me feel a little better. "Well, there's something funny going on. Crouch getting killed, Potter in the tournament, all the weird reporting of things happening here in the *Prophet*. Don't you think that's a lot to not understand?"

There was some tension in his voice that seemed to relax. But he went on. "Yeh. But what I was thinking was why am I suddenly not on guard duty rotation for the Maze? Why am I suddenly guarding my office?"

"Oh. Yeah. That is odd. You know, that's Dumbledore for you. He does things and never tells anyone why. He's always keeping his own counsel."

"But you seem to have the inside track on everything that goes on here."

I took a breath and tried to lick my lips without seeming to. This was the moment when the real lie was about to be told. "You know, I used to have the inside track when Minerva and I were like this." I held up my forefinger and my middle finger crossed, "But now, I can't see her except to say 'Hi' and we never talk. She has the ear of Dumbledore if anyone does."

He seemed to consider that a moment and then said, "Yeh. She's a hard case. Did you know that she used to be married?"

"Really. She never told me that." That was the truth. Thank goodness. I've never had an easy time lying.

"Oh, yes. He was a Muggle." My heart fell. Oh, shit. That's why she's never going to take me seriously. She had a Muggle husband who let her down and she can't trust any of us that way again.

Moody seemed to be enjoying this. "Yes. He died. It was during the first rise of the Dark Lord. He was killed by a Deatheater. I caught up with him and sent him to Azkaban. I was furious with him, but he just laughed in my face about killing her husband. Do you know what he said when I caught up with him?"

I shook my head.

"He said, 'Do you think he gets a pass just because she's a witch!"

I was astounded that she'd never let some hint drop. "So she's a widow!"

"Yes, didn't she tell you?"

Nervelessly, I said, "No. No, she didn't." It didn't matter. I wasn't afraid of Moody. It didn't matter if he were the imposter.

"You seem discouraged."

"Yeh." It was a real effort to talk, but I went on because I had to. "Widows rarely re-marry."

"How do you know?" He seemed almost solicitous.

"Oh, I have an aunt. She was my favorite aunt. In a way she was my favorite person when I was growing up."

She was a widow. She didn't have any kids, so she sort of adopted my siblings and me as her kids. We visited her on most weekends. She was always baking cookies or something for us. She was an attractive woman in middle age. I was just a kid and didn't know much about beauty, but she always seemed nice-looking to me.

She was smart and had a funny sense of humor. She was always making jokes using word play. Much later, I discovered that she was a writer and was published in national magazines. I probably had a crush on her toward the end.

Anyway, one day when my brother and I were with her on a weekend, the door-bell rang. We all raced to see who could get to the door first and answer it. Of course, she always let one of us kids do it.

I won this race and flung the door open. Standing on the small stucco porch was a man wearing a suit and holding a bouquet of flowers. He looked at me and my brother and behind us both, my aunt. He blushed and spoke directly to her. I don't remember what he said or she said, but I remember the emotions that were obvious on each face.

First, he offered her the flowers. He was excited and happy. She took them and invited him in for a minute. She took us all out to the kitchen where she found a glass vase and put them in it. She added water, thanking him. She seemed a little embarrassed, but mostly she seemed to be sad and kind at the same time.

He asked her if she would see him again. She said, "No."

He was very sad.

I didn't understand what had happened at the time except in the simplest way.

Anyway, she had a suitor who loved her, I think. She couldn't bring herself to consider anyone—either while her husband was alive or afterwards.

"And you think that's the way Ms. McGonagall is?"

"Yes."

Moody just frowned and slapped me on the back. "Sorry, laddie. You have a tough one." I went on in to my office, and I don't know where Moody went.

The Final Preparation

I was in my office trying to find something to do. Oh, there were plenty of things to do. There were final exams to prepare and a stack of term parchments lying on my desk threateningly. Frustratingly, it would have been futile to attempt any of those tasks. Just as futile as trying to work the *London Times* crossword would have been.

There is that time before an important event. Maybe it's an important final. Maybe it's a job interview. Maybe it's a battle. You know that you've done everything that you can to prepare. The only thing left is waiting. The only thing possible is waiting. Every focus of your mind and muscle and heart is on that coming struggle, and to attempt anything else is to fail at it. At times like these, I used to be able to find refuge in music. But, there were no Walkmen, no stereos, no radios that played music that I wanted to hear.

It was the day before the final task of the Tri-Wizard Tournament, and I couldn't do anything except stare at the fireplace—as though someone would walk out of it to break this mood of nervous expectation that I was in.

But something did happen. There was a knock on the door. I invited the welcome diversion in.

The door opened, and Cedric stuck his head through, "Professor, may I come in?"

"Certainly. What can I do for you?"

"Do you know what happened in the Chess tournament?"

I chuckled. Of all the questions to ask, why that one? "No, I haven't been following it."

He nodded slowly, "Well, I guess that I just wanted to come in and apologize for choosing the Tri-Wizard over it."

"No apology necessary. You chose what was closest to your heart. You should always do that in the most important things in your life. Always trust your heart. I hope you're not having second thoughts."

"No, sir. I just wanted to let you know before the tournament that I want to thank you for all the help you've given me. You know, when people win the big game, they become generous and say things that you may not always trust. I just thought it was better to say it now before. . . well, before we know what will happen."

"Cedric, you're welcome to the help. You know that I'd do that for any of my students whether they wanted to go to Cambridge or if they would be lucky to get into Southern States Community College."

"Sir? I've never heard of that."

"And you probably never will again. It's a college in Ohio in the States that will accept almost anyone. I grew up in an area that was served by it.

"You'll always be able to play chess tournaments. You've got talent and ability and can work hard. You'll be able to go as far as you want in chess. I don't want to give you a swelled head, but that includes the world championship—if you want it."

I was torn with indecision over what to do next. I could tell him about what they'd told me at Cambridge. I decided not to. For one thing, Cambridge should send that information first. Besides, it seemed like it was wrong to talk about something that was still very contingent and chancy. Instead, I wished him good luck, "Cedric, I want to wish you good luck tomorrow. It won't be easy for anyone. I want you to know that I'm rooting for you."

Cedric laughed.

I gave him a quizzical stare, and he said, "Oh, I know whom you're really rooting for. Potter is in Gryffindor, and we all know who the Head of Gryffindor is."

In that moment, I so much wanted to tell him that I'd always been rooting for him; that I'd bet on him in the second task. It seemed to me like it would be bad Karma to do that. I didn't want to jinx him before this final task.

So, instead, I said, "Let me pay you a compliment. There are a lot of people around who think 'Potter stinks' because he seems to have broken the rules and got into the tournament. You've never felt that way, and it's really to your credit.

"But let's just get through this. I'll be really happy next Monday when we're back in class and everyone's not looking over everyone else's shoulders."

Cedric smiled and agreed, "Yes, sir." He stood and we shook hands. That was the last time that I saw him before the final task.

That brief respite left me wishing all the more that it was just all over.

Later that evening, I had to go to the final pre-tournament security meeting with Dumbledore. The usual group was there but this time it had an urgency that I'd never felt before. Dumbledore simply raised a piece of parchment to his moon-shaped glasses lens and read off a checklist.

"Every family has a wizard assigned?"

Minerva said, "Potter—no one. Delacourt—Pomona Sprout. Diggery—Filius Flitwick. Krum – Septima Vector."

"Press Corp?"

"Me." Minerva confirmed.

"Ministry?"

"Sibyll Trelawny."

"Really?"

"Yes." Tiredly.

"Backup—Moody." Dumbledore frowned at that.

Dumbledore went to a new item. "Guest badges?"

Snape, "Made: Green for family, Blue for Ministry, Red for Press."

Filch was on his feet with his hands raised, "Me. Me. I'll check guests in and give them the right color."

Dumbledore just mumbled, "Yes, Filch."

Snape went on. "There's a spell on these badges. Once, they're applied to clothes, they can't be removed for 24 hours."

Dumbledore looked up from his parchment. "Really? Good idea. I wish I'd thought of it. It would be a real nuisance if there were legitimate guests getting dragged in because they didn't have their badges."

He went on, "Other ideas? This is your last chance. It will simply be too late tomorrow to add anything to the program." He hesitated and added, "Maybe it's too late all ready. We all have very full plates."

Everyone looked around at each other. I just made a pointless observation, "I wish we had walkie-talkies. If we could only communicate live with each other, we would be so much more effective."

Snape asked, "That's a Muggle thing, right?"

"Yes. It works on electricity. They wouldn't work if we brought them here."

Snape sniffed and said, "Typical Muggle contraption."

Dumbledore who was showing signs of tiring just said, "Snape. Give it a rest. If there's nothing else?" He hesitated to see if anyone else wanted to speak. No one did. "Then we'll see you tomorrow at breakfast."

I got up, and decided to take a walk around the grounds of the school. It was now beginning to get really dark on a moonless night. The stars burned brightly in the cool, dry air, and I had almost reached the former Quidditch pitch before I realized it.

There was a sharp voice that demanded, "Who goes there?"

"Oh, it's me Snape. You can drop the wand. I'm not going to attack you."

"It would be bad for you if you did. Why are you out here?"

"Oh, I just was too nervous about tomorrow's tournament task to stay still. I thought I'd walk until I got tired enough to sleep."

"Yes, I know. I'm actually kind of happy to have a reason to be out here on guard. I'm surprised that you aren't with your drinking buddy, Filch." I could tell by the tone of his voice that he wasn't being nasty, just emphasizing how everyone was ready for this competition to be over.

"Do you just stay in one place?"

I couldn't make out Snape's face but I could hear his voice, "No, I walk circuits of the maze."

"I'll join you."

"Sure."

We slowly walked off toward the counterclockwise direction around the maze. It was important to keep your eyes and the nerves in your feet aware and focused or you'd land on your back or your nose. It was actually something that did divert my attention from the ever-so-slowly ticking clock.

We were silent for a while, and then I broke it, "What do you think will happen tomorrow?"

"I?" Snape asked, "I think that somehow Potter will win by good luck and the help and sacrifice of others."

"Do you really think so? I don't think that anyone is going to give any quarter tomorrow."

"Oh, I've seen him in so many tight scrapes and somehow be able to weasel his way out that I have no doubt that it'll happen again tomorrow."

"But he's so much less experienced than everyone else."

"That hasn't bothered him in the past." He stopped walking and turned to me, "You watch. Somehow tomorrow, he'll get into a scrape and someone will take mercy on him. Maybe it will be that girl from Beaux Batons whose sister he saved. Maybe it will be your buddy Cedric. And by the way, you should be wearing a Potter Stinks button shouldn't you. He's been beating Cedric, hasn't he?"

Despite the fact that Snape could probably hardly see it, I shrugged, "Well, Potter has had some pretty big disadvantages and is still in the hunt. I can't begrudge him hard work and courage."

"I don't either. It's that infernal luck that always seems to follow him around and get between him and trouble." He paused and added, "No, not trouble. Justice. He's constantly being protected from justice."

I laughed, "Where I come from, we'd call that Karma—destiny. It's both a blessing and a curse. You just see the blessing side. And, I'd be careful about calling for justice. I'm not sure that any of us would stand long when justice comes to town."

Snape snorted, and we continued his rounds.

"Any sign of an attempt to meddle with the maze?"

Snape snorted again, "No. I think Dumbledore's on the wrong trail. Sure, the Headmasters have motivation to meddle, but I don't think they will."

Those were the last words that we exchanged that night.

I worked my way back to the Castle and bed. But I mostly was just thinking horizontally rather than vertically. I did have several bouts of sleep that lasted an hour or two each. The sun wakened me. I looked at my watch and saw 5:05 AM. Great. I tried to get back to sleep again, but there was no chance of it.

It was way too early for breakfast. I decided that it was overdue for me to clean my Glock. So, I got up, put on a pair of jeans and a sweatshirt and started to very carefully clean and oil it. I was about to put it back in my purse when I decided that I should have it more easily available. I slowly and carefully loaded both magazines. I slipped one into the Glock and the other into the left front pocket of my jeans. I made sure the safety was on and started to put it into the right front jeans pocket. I had second thoughts about that and decided it should go in one of the pockets of the robes that I was going to wear. I put my robes on. I checked that there wasn't a cartridge in the cylinder and put the Glock in the right inner pocket of my robes. I put my purse in the left inner pocket of my robes and decided that even though breakfast wasn't ready, I'd just go down anyway.

Apparently, there were a number of other people who were having trouble sleeping too. There were a scattering of people at the house tables and the head table. I walked down the central corridor and noticed that Malfoy was sitting by himself at the Slytherin table. On a whim, I stopped and said good morning to him.

He was looking glum. So, I asked him how things were going. He raised his head and looked at me, "Oh, you don't care."

"I wouldn't have asked you if I didn't."

He looked at me doubtfully and then looked around to see if anyone were within earshot. "Well, this is a terrible day. Slytherin doesn't have anyone in the Tri-Wizard. Potter broke all the rules and seems to be winning it. Nobody except Slytherins are wearing 'Potter stinks' badges." His attitude became defiant, 'So tell me that the world is looking up."

I thought for a minute. I could tell him about all the ways that the world was unfair to everyone. I so much wanted to unload on him all the worry that the teachers had gone through, all the danger that there was still to everyone, about how there might be one or more innocent people dead by the end of the day. Instead I said, "Yep, you're right. The world is pretty miserable for you. If you ever want to talk about it again, my office is always open."

He looked up at me with an incredulous face, "Go stuff it."

I shrugged and headed on up toward the head table, but I heard behind me a voice say, "Maybe."

I took my normal seat near the end of the table. I had started thinking of what I should do before the afternoon when everything started moving too fast for thought. As I was sunk deep in thought, I heard a voice near me, "I've been good, haven't I?"

I recognized the voice, but I was too surprised not to look up to see Sinistra sitting down next to me. I couldn't help the look of tired resignation that came over my face, but she wasn't looking. The table had just filled with breakfast items. I looked around for something, anything that would excite some appetite. I saw nothing.

She seemed excited as she pulled a tureen of scrambled eggs toward her and then reached for a muffin, "Don't you think that I've been very restrained in your time of exile from Minerva?"

I was forced to admire her. She not only had an appetite, but she could joke. I admitted as much, "Well, Sinistra, I've got to say that you've got a good appetite. I can hardly stand to look at all this food. And, I have to admit that you've been very considerate. Have you turned over a new leaf? Are you going to finally let me decide for myself whom I date?"

She turned thoughtful, "Well, maybe I'm just trying to prove to you that I'd be a considerate and helpful . . " She seemed to be stuck for just the right word. She didn't say anything else. Maybe she hoped that I hadn't heard the "a".

"Well, I do appreciate it." I smiled and added, "If you kept it up for sixty or seventy years, you might convince me."

Her smile didn't flicker as I said it. Either she was a great actor or she was absolutely genuine. I decided that it didn't matter which really. I was saved from having to continue the conversation by the arrival of Dumbledore. He stood up, cleared his voice, and did something that I couldn't remember his ever doing at breakfast, he spoke.

"I hope you all are enjoying the unequaled cuisine of the Hogwarts house elves this morning. I just want to remind you that we are going to have some guests joining us today for the final task in the Tri-Wizard Tournament.

"I expect three things of all Hogwarts students and staff:

"Courtesy at all times shown to guests, fellow students and the staff. I hope that it is a needless exercise to remind you that things like the 'Potter Stinks' buttons are not courteous.

"Safe behavior. I want to urge you as strongly as I can to be alert to the possibility of dangerous situations arising. I request that you inform a teacher or staff member immediately if you see something that makes you suspect a dangerous situation is developing. And, of course, do your best to not make any dangerous situation worse.

"Finally, within these limits, have a SPECTACULAR good time." With that, there was a whoop of joy. I thought I heard the Weasley twins, who were seated near the front of the Gryffindor table say, "Bad luck."

By this time, I'd had enough of breakfast and walked out of the Great Hall and the Castle. I decided that I'd walk down to the Maze and look around. What I was looking for, I couldn't have told anyone—least of all myself. The morning was cool, and the sky had some scudding clouds. I walked through the stands and went to the top. As I looked out at the Maze, I realized there was no chance of telling what was going on in the maze from there or, really, anywhere on the grounds.

I walked down to the maze and resisted the temptation to enter. I'd have gotten in a lot of trouble from the guard, if I had. I started to circumnavigate the maze when a booming voice sounded behind me.

"Professor! Wait up."

I turned and saw and felt Hagrid jog toward me. "Sure. What's up?"

Hagrid reached me, beaming and happy. "It's a glorious day isn't it? I was so happy that I got guard duty this morning. I could not have waited another day."

I smiled, thinking about how that was the very thought on a whole lot of minds this morning. "I don't think you could find a single person in the castle who doesn't completely agree with you."

He nodded, and his bubbling good humor just seemed to overflow. I was starting to see the fun of it. I actually laughed. Hagrid thumped me on the back, and it occurred to me that he would be the greatest at the Heimlich maneuver ever. "I want to go up and check on the sign-in desk. See you later, Hagrid."

And I really did. I wasn't in a big hurry because no one expected any guests before lunch, but I had a feeling that Filch would be there just in case. I eventually arrived at the main gate and indeed, Filch was there sitting at a fold-up table. As I got close, I could see that he had the list of expected guests and neat stacks of color-coded badges with name and photos.

Filch heard me approach and turned, "Hi, professor. Beautiful day, isn't it?"

I nodded. "If you get tired of watching out here, I'd be glad to sub for you. I'll drop by every hour or so."

"No sir." He seemed to be a bit nervous. Perhaps he was afraid someone would steal his post.

"OK. I'll relieve you for lunch." He was about to say something, so I quickly added, "Just for lunch."

His face relaxed, "Thanks."

I whiled away the hours walking the grounds. I wished I could think of something better to do, but it was better—much better—than doing nothing.

Supper came, and I went in, not much hungrier than I had been for breakfast or lunch. This time, though, the tables were crowded. An extra table had been set up for all the guests. It had the potential to be a little chaotic with all the families and the press corps together. But maybe that was good. It brought together the people whom the press wanted to interview all at one table and gave them all something to talk about over dinner.

Dumbledore was at his best. All sense of worry and nervousness were gone. He smoothly and quickly introduced and welcomed the guests—all bedecked in their colorful name badges. He told one quick and funny joke. Then he lifted up a word of grace – "benignant" and then closed with his standard instruction, "Tuck in."

Long before the meal was over, I walked out to check on Filch. He had checked in his last guest over an hour before, but he stood to his post. I instructed him to lock the gate and get some supper. "It's all over. Get something to eat and head down to the Pitch and set up to keep your eye on everything."

I then walked down to the Pitch, where I found Minerva walking guard duty. No one had come down yet, so when she rounded a corner, I went down and greeted her with a good kiss. She enjoyed it, "The first of many."

"Right. Look Minerva. I've got a bad feeling about this." I took her forearm in my hand and just said, "Be careful." She just nodded and went on with her watch.

I walked up into the stands and took a seat in the top row. I wouldn't stay there after the festivities started, but I wanted one last look over the scene. How I longed that they'd left one of the elevated stands from the Quidditch pitch still standing. It would have made a great birds nest for spotting problems—especially inside the maze.

The crowd started to arrive, and I left my aerie to do my own guard duty. When I was out of the stands and out of sight, I reached into my pocket, pulled out the Glock, checked the chamber, the safety, and just stared at it for a minute. I wondered how many times I'd done that this day.

From that point on, I kept my eyes on the crowd. I tried to examine every face as it entered the stands to be sure that it was a student or had one of the colored badges on—and the right color at that.

Everyone got seated, and Dumbledore began explaining the rules. Of course, I knew them, and I knew who would be entering the maze in what order. Every now and then, I spared an eye for the other watchers. One of them was a traitor. One of them was an imposter. One of them must have kidnapped someone, probably a friend of mine. One of them was probably a murderer. I had my number one suspect, but I wasn't going to assume that I was right. Everyone in the stands and a few of the teachers were suspect.

I don't think I heard the signal when Filch fired the cannon to start the final task. I didn't know when the other champions entered the maze, but I heard the sparks fly up. I swung around and saw them arc through the dark sky. I hoped that nothing really bad had happened.

Then I went back to scanning the crowd. The sparks flew again. Two left.

Then nothing happened for a very long time. I glanced down at my watch. It had already been more than an hour since the last sparks had flown. I drifted away from my vantage on the left side of the entrance to the maze and, without taking my eyes from the crowd, I approached Dumbledore's position. Bagman was already there talking expressively.

I arrived and still wouldn't take my eyes from the crowd as I spoke, "Mr. Bagman, Professor, don't you think that Potter and Cedric have been in there for an awfully long time?"

The discussion that I'd interrupted had apparently been concerning that very topic. His face showed exasperation, 'You just can't abandon the game. It's hardly been two hours." Apparently, Bagman had reached a point beyond speech. He flung his hands up. Then he went on, "You know that Quidditch matches have gone on for days. This is just a warm-up for any REAL game."

Dumbledore was perhaps beginning to be a bit warm himself. "This IS NOT a professional competition, and this is not Quidditch. There's no reason that the competition oughtn't to finish in less than two hours." He turned to me, "Look, Wendt, you know something about mazes. How long should it take to solve that maze?"

I had to take a deep breath. The last thing in the world that I expected was to be appealed to concerning a magical game. So, I did my best, "Well, bear in mind that I haven't seen the maze. Also, I asked the question, 'Is it a left-hand maze.'" To Bagman's mystified expression I explained, "That just means that it's pretty easy to solve. No one knew. So, this is really just a guess. Based on the apparent size of the maze and the size of the corridors, I'd say that an hour, surely not more than two should be enough."

Bagman would not be dissuaded, "But there are puzzles and hazards to be gotten past. Surely they're worth another hour or two on top of the time to solve it."

By this time, a representative of the Ministry of International Cooperation arrived—Percy Weasley, "What's going on here?"

Dumbledore quickly explained the situation—that Dumbledore wanted to declare the contest over and get inside to make sure that the remaining champions were safe.

Weasley objected, "Then who'd be the winner?"

Dumbledore sighed as he saw the other two Headmasters arrive. This was beginning to look like it would disintegrate into a shouting match. When they arrived, I decided that I would try to inject a little sanity into the proceedings, and I spoke before anyone else could muddy the waters further.

"Look, let's cut through to the chase. Both Krum and Delacourt are disqualified, so there's no way that they could win. That leaves only the Hogwarts champions. If we can get Diggery's family to agree to declare the contest a tie, then there's no reason to prolong what may be a dangerous situation."

Everyone was opening their mouths, apparently to object, but no sound came out. Instead their eyes widened and then there was a general scream of, well, of joy? I was facing away from the maze, so I turned around to see what had happened.

It was apparent that there were two victorious champions as I had proposed. Diggery and Potter were staggering through the entrance to the maze, the Tri-Wizard Cup clutched jointly by them. They had hardly left the maze when the two of them had tripped and fallen.

But there was something wrong. Potter was staggering up but Diggery was unmoving. I had misjudged what happened.

The Maze

The field next to the maze was bedlam. When Potter dragged Diggery out of the maze with the Cup, Minerva had immediately jumped up from her seat. I was almost as quick in leaving the conference with Bagman, Percy Weasley, and the other officials. Potter was saying something about Valdemort, and I couldn't make it all out. Dumbledore was with Diggery's parents, and Minerva was trying to get the crowd in some sort of order. I was looking around for some way to be useful. It was then that I saw Moody practically carrying Potter up toward the castle. I thought that seemed unusual. Maybe he was taking him to the hospital wing, but then I noticed that Madame Pomfrey was bent over Diggery's body, perhaps trying to be sure whether he really was alive.

I turned to Minerva, who had succeeded in getting everyone's attention and directing the students to go back to their dorms, led by each houses' prefects. As soon as she seemed to be interruptible, I interrupted her, "Minerva, come on. There's something strange going on." I grabbed her hand and started to drag her off.

She resisted me, so I had to drag her close and whispered in her ear, "Moody's dragged Potter off somewhere. I've got a bad feeling about it. Come on, let's go. I don't think Moody should be alone with him." I didn't even think Moody was Moody.

She stared at me and seemed about to put up an objection, but I think she saw the determination in my eye. We'd been through enough together that she must have decided to reserve judgment and let me go with my intuition until events proved me wrong.

Not having any better idea, I led her up toward the castle at as good a pace as we could make. Minerva wasn't much on the run, but she could walk up a real storm. The distance to the castle was not a short sprint, so it probably was best to do a very brisk walk rather than a jog up hill that neither of us could sustain. As bad a shape as Potter seemed to be in, I doubted that Moody could have dragged him any faster than we were going anyway.

It was dark, and even with Minerva's wand lit, we could only make out far enough ahead to keep from tripping over anything that might have been in the way. I thought that I could see Moody's wand lit up ahead, so we stood a decent chance of finding where he was going. He or the light seemed to be heading straight for the castle.

By the time that we arrived at the castle, it was clear that he'd entered it. We were both puffing hard, but I managed to say, "Minerva, see if you can get Dumbledore. I'm going to get my . . '

But she anticipated me, "I know, you're damn Glock. And how do you expect me to conjure up Dumbledore. We've done our best to outdistance him up to the castle."

"Well, give it five minutes, and if you can't find him, then meet me outside Moody's office."

She simply nodded, and we separated. I sprinted down the one flight to the floor where Filch's office was. I was in, rummaged through the disorderly pile of tools that he had, grabbed a sledge hammer just in case I needed to break into Moody's office, and sprinted up the stairs toward his office. When I rounded a corner and his office came into view, I saw Dumbledore, Snape and Minerva huddled around the door as Dumbledore blasted it open. They entered, and I broke into a full run to get there as quickly as I could. When I entered the door, Moody looked like he'd been on the losing end of a fight with a grizzly. Snape was bent over him administering some vile looking concoction that turns out to have been Veritas Serum. I had my Glock out, and I decided to stand in the doorway – just in case there were a consipirator following us.

Under questioning, it was discovered that he was not "Mad-Eye" Moody, but the supposedly dead Deatheater, Bartholomew Crouch Jr. Dumbledore went to summon some Aurors to accompany him back to Azkaban prison. Snape left to find the Minister of Magic. They left Minerva and me to guard the prisoner.

As we waited for people to return, I asked Minerva, "So, you figure that Moody was the mastermind behind getting Potter into the tournament and engineering it so that he'd win it. All that just to get him to be the first to touch the Cup which Crouch Jr. made into a port key to transport Potter to Valdemort."

"Sure, that's what he said under Veritas serum"

"Then, I figure that he's an accessory to Diggery's death as much as anyone is."

Minerva looked at me with almost as much surprise as she regarded the faux Moody. She said, "What are you thinking of?" She paid close attention to the gun that I held in my hand, pointed directly at his head. 'You weren't thinking of taking justice into your own hands."

I eyed Moody for another uneasy minute and said to her, "I have to admit that I'm tempted, but I'm not going to. He knows a lot about the Deatheaters that are still active, the whereabouts of Valdemort, all sorts of things that we need to get out of him before we're done with him. I'm satisfied to let justice work, just so long as we learn all those details."

Minerva seemed to breathe a sigh, perhaps of relief. Just then, the Minister of Magic entered the room – alone. She turned to him while I had my full attention on Crouch, and said, "Minister. Good. Crouch has been doing a lot of talking. There's some really interesting things that he's let slip – about Valdemort, his own involvement in the death of Diggery. You should hear."

Fudge seemed to be a bit wild-eyed as he looked around the room. "Barty Crouch Jr., eh? He must be mad. Valdemort is gone – forever. He's been driven crazy by his time in Azkaban."

Minerva said, "But sir, what he says agrees with what Potter has been saying. I think Valdemort's back and . . . "

But Fudge interrupted her. "No, NO. He's just a crazy Deatheater wishing for the return of his old master. This was all just a tragic mistake on his part." He hesitated and then seemed to make a decision because what he said next seemed to have determination in it, "No. We've got to put an end to this pernicious rumor that Valdemort's back before it goes any further. Yes, nip it in the bud."

He seemed to be arguing with himself, "He was serving a life sentence. If we knew he had escaped, we'd have posted a reward, dead or alive. The Dementors could do it. Yes, I've got to go send for them." I had begun to wonder if Fudge weren't at least as crazy as Crouch.

I stepped forward and put my gun in an inside pocket of my robes. "Minister, even if he's not entirely sane, he may have valuable information – about Deatheaters who are still active, how he escaped from Azkaban – all very valuable. We can't kill him before he reveals those things."

He was not paying attention to me and was striding out the door.

239

I was disgusted, "This beats all. We've got to keep him," I looked over at that miserable wretch, Crouch, "alive – at least until he does some talking.

"Minerva, I'm going to go try to find Dumbledore or Snape or anybody who can keep Fudge from this insanity."

She thought a second and said, "OK. I'll get Dumbledore, you guard Crouch."

I agreed and she headed for the door. I pulled out my Glock and sat down. I advanced a bullet into the cylinder and leant forward with my gun at the ready.

"Good. Let's have a little talk." I said to Crouch.

She looked at me for a minute and said, "On second thought maybe I'd better guard Crouch, you get Dumbledore."

I said, "OK. You guard him." I handed her my Glock and said, "Here, take this."

"But I've got my wand. That'll be fine."

"No, take it. Point it at him like this." I took the gun in both hands to provide a steady aim and pointed it about a foot to the right of his right knee. "If he so much as twitches a muscle, put a bullet in one of his knees. That's really painful but won't kill him.'

Minerva reluctantly took the gun and grasped it as I'd shown her. She seemed to have the feel of it. I turned to Crouch and said, "I hope you do try something. I want you to survive to do a lot of talking, but if it weren't for that, I'd be right in there with the Minister about what he wants to do to you."

I went to the door and was about to leave when I turned to Minerva and said, "Be careful. I want to see a whole lot more of you."

She smiled and said, 'I'll guarantee that."

I ran out the open door and headed for Dumbledore's Office. I arrived and found he wasn't there. My next place to try was the Owlery. I ran into him just coming down. I was nearly breathless but managed to gasp, "Fudge has gone to send for Dementors. I'm sure he means them to perform the 'kiss' on Crouch."

Dumbledore came the closest to losing his temper that I'd ever seen him go. He took off the cap he was wearing and threw it to the stone floor of the hall that we were walking on. His face turned white, but he didn't say anything. Then he took off at a run, and he asked, "I suppose he's still in his office where we left him. Who's guarding him? Snape?"

"No, Minerva."

"Well, at least the most sensible woman is there with him. Let's get going, maybe we can cut Fudge off and still save the day."

"Yes, sir." We headed off as quickly as we could manage. I was walking at the briskest pace that I could manage. Dumbledore was practically flying. He could have qualified as an Olympic walker. Fortunately, I could keep up by occasionally breaking into a brief sprint in which I caught up with Dumbledore, Then, I'd drop back into my fastest walk, during which I lost ground to Dumbledore.

We reached Crouch's office and burst in to find Minerva holding the Glock on Crouch. Dumbledore walked over to her and grasped the Glock and removed it from her hand while he commented, "And I thought you were the most responsible person standing. Ah, well. You've been spending too much time with Wendt, I think."

Minerva smiled coyly but had her wand out. Just then Fudge entered the room, and it went deathly cold. Dumbledore turned to me and said, "Professor Wendt, I think that you can be excused at this point. We have plenty of warm bodies to guard Mr. Crouch – not to mention the cold-blooded ones."

He was referring to the Dementors that no doubt had arrived and were even now invisibly in the room—that is invisible to me and visible to everyone else. I could tell by the look on Dumbledore's face that protest was futile. He meant me to be out of the room in the dispute to come. I never got an account of what was said or done in that next hour. All I know was that Minerva had come to my office after it was over. She just motioned me to come to the old sofa that was along one wall of my office. When I sat, she came into my arms and lap and sobbed a few times into my right shoulder. Then she got up and walked out of the office without having said a word. I never asked her about it again, but both of us felt empty and hopeless.

◁

The hopelessness for me gradually switched from the death of Moody back to the death of Cedric. Minerva immediately corrected me that Moody hadn't died, but just had be "demented."

I responded, "Sure, having your soul sucked out of you is way better than being dead."

All classes were canceled. At breakfast, I was staring at my plate trying to decide what tasteless item of food I would put on it and force myself to eat, when someone sat beside me.

Minerva put her hand on my shoulder, "Wendt, We're going to have a memorial service for Cedric tomorrow at 2PM."

I looked up, puzzled, and she went on, "Dumbledore wants you to attend and say something."

"Really." I was feeling pretty depressed and the full import hadn't hit me yet.

"Yes. It'll be tomorrow afternoon. Will you come?"

I was slow reacting. Finally, I realized that Minerva had asked me something. I reconstructed what it was, "Yes, but I don't know what they would. . . " And then I realized that they wanted me to speak. "I suppose you're coming to speak."

Her face flushed a bit, and she cleared her throat, "No. That is, I've not been invited."

"That's ridiculous."

Minerva flushed again, "Dumbledore wants you."

I frowned and admitted that. "When is it?"

"Tomorrow at 2PM. Let's meet here at 1:30."

"OK." What could I say? I spent the morning trying to jot down notes but I didn't get very far. The next day, I was so depressed that I didn't show up for breakfast. About 11 AM, I got up, showered, dressed and dragged myself down to lunch. Minerva was there and joined me. It was a quiet meal.

Once she started to ask me what I would say, but only got half-way through the question and dropped it.

After lunch we just sat in the Great Hall. When, 1:30 finally came, I was already there.

Eventually, after a butter beer had been put in my hand, Dumbledore rose and said, "We've invited one of Cedric's professors to say a few words about Ced. Anyone else who wants to say something should know they are welcome to as well."

I walked over to the fireplace because I just didn't feel it was right to speak from the podium. I thanked him, "To start, I have to tell you that I am honored to be invited to Cedric's memorial to speak.

"I hope you will remember two things as I talk about him. One, I knew him for a much shorter time than many of you and also, please, remember my background. I'll only take one minute to tell you about it.

"That background is far different from any of yours. I was born and raised in America. As many of you know, I am a Squibb." There was a gasp or two from the back of the room, which I ignored. "And I was raised by Muggles and educated in the Muggle education system in the States.

"I tell you that so that if I may say something that seems strange, you will take into account my unfamiliarity with English wizarding customs. You see, when I came to Hogwarts some five years ago, I knew no more about wizarding than," I grasped for a comparison, 'than Harry Potter in his first year at Hogwarts.

"Anyway, I want to speak for Cedric. I want to tell you what he might have achieved had he lived and grown into the perfect version of himself.

"You all know that Cedric was a gifted athlete. He was the Seeker for the Hufflepuff house Quidditch team. I'm not an expert at Quidditch, but I'm told that he almost single-handedly kept Hufflepuff competitive in a league where Gryffindor and Slitherin were much more likely to be considered the Quidditch powers of Hogwarts.

"I don't know if he would have been a candidate to become a professional Quidditch player, but I do know that he would have been competitive had he chosen athletics as he life's work.

"You may not realize that he has. . " I stopped there and choked on swallowed tears as I realized that I was speaking of him in the present tense. I started again, "You may not realize that he had amazing academic abilities. He recently competed in an academic contest called the Scholastic Aptitude Test. He was a Merit Scholarship Finalist. His scores placed him easily in the top one thousandth of all competitors. Since many youths don't compete, it is not a great exaggeration to say that he was one in a million academically.

"I am in that field and I say that I've never met any one in seven years of teaching both here and in the States, where I taught for two years in a great Muggle institution of learning, who matched him in ability or achievement.

"He might well have had a brilliant future in higher learning.

"However, that was NOT his strongest suit. He excelled at another field of competition. Three years ago, he played his first game of wizard chess. In the three years since, he developed himself into a chess player who competed in international tournaments at the adult level and won the last one that he played in.

"In this last year, he was invited to an international youth tournament, the winner of which would play against the world champion. He was unable to accept that invitation. Had he accepted, I'm convinced that he would have had a very good chance of playing against the world champion.

"If he chose to pursue chess professionally, I have no doubt that in his twenties he would have been a competitor for the world championship. Chess is a field that is full of prodigies, but Cedric stood out among them as a prodigy among prodigies.

"I don't know what field Cedric would have entered, but I know a few things about Cedric that tell me something about the kind of career he would have had:

"He was a fierce competitor. He studied hard. He practiced hard. He played hard with no quarter asked or given.

"He was a good loser and a good winner. He was gracious to his competitors both before the match and after. He was not one to try to gain a small advantage by intimidation of his opponent before the match, and he yielded no advantage to those who tried that with him. On and off the pitch he was a credit to his family.

"He was generous to a fault.

"He brought humor to everything he did.

"Whatever kind of career he entered, I'm sure that he would have excelled and been admired and liked by his associates – a rare combination of attributes.

"I know that I will miss him, and when I look back to the students that I've taught, I'll remember him as the best."

I stepped away from the fireplace and lost myself. Dumbledore stood and said something that I don't remember. I managed to find a chair in a corner and sat there. I really didn't want to talk to anyone, and most people respected that wish. Minerva came by later and thanked me for speaking. I stayed in the great hall until dinner.

Minerva commented, "I was afraid that you would say something about Muggles and Cedric that would embarrass us, but Dumbledore really was glad that you'd spoken."

I nodded thanks and said goodnight.

The Riddle Homestead

The next morning, I had time to think about everything that had happened with Cedric. The Tri-Wizard Tournament, the tournament that he missed. The Head of International Cooperation. His son. The real Moody. Why didn't I get him out of the Tri-Wizard? Magical contracts. Did Crouch, Sr. lie about it? That night, I slept on and off.

The next morning, I stumbled down to the Great Hall for breakfast. Minerva came over and sat next to me and talked to me. Just at me. I didn't have anything to say. I just stared down at the oatmeal that I was stirring with my spoon.

I eventually looked up at her and said, "It's my fault."

"What?"

"Cedric."

"How do you figure?"

"I should have kept him out of the Tri-Wizard."

"Oh, come on. How could you? Crouch said the magical contract was binding."

"It doesn't matter what he said. It was obvious."

She had incredulity in her voice, "How was that obvious! I'm not sure that I believe it even now."

"No, it was obvious. He couldn't have known for sure, but he was so sure. He was either crazy or had an ulterior motive. I guess it was a little of both."

"OK. Let's assume that your dubious reasoning were correct. How does that convert to getting him out of the tournament? He wanted to play."

"I could have challenged him more. I could have convinced him that the chess was the bigger opportunity."

"Oh, Jim. You just want someone to punish because he's dead, and you're the only candidate. Crouch, Sr. is dead. Crouch, Jr. is dead. Valdemort is really the guilty party, and he's out of your reach."

I hardly heard what she was saying after that. But after a minute, I realized that something that she said was significant. "What did you just say?"

"That you just want someone to punish."

"No, at the end?"

"That Crouch's, Jr. and Sr. are dead?"

"No. You said that Valdemort is out of my reach."

"Yeh. So what?"

I muttered to myself, "I wonder."

"What did you say?"

"Nothing. I'll see you." I got up and headed back to my office.

The next day I was sitting by myself in the Great Hall. The stunning events had left me without conscious purpose. I'd walked into the Great Hall without quite realizing that I'd been there. I sat at one of the house tables. I stared blankly into space for a timeless period. Finally, someone put a hand on my shoulder and speaking softly said, "Jim, why don't you go to bed. It won't do anyone any good for you to just sit here."

I looked up as one dazed and said, "Minerva. Why was it Diggery? What purpose did his death serve? Why?"

She just sat down, took my hand in hers, and kneaded it gently between her hands. She said nothing.

I stood up and gently disengaged my hand from hers. I started to pace slowly and said, first slowly and then picking up pace as I thought, "He was my best student. Not just this year – any year that I've taught. Even at Stanford.

"When I came here, I knew that I would never be a popular teacher. I knew that my subject would never inspire the vast majority of students. Do you know that while I've been here, not a single student has graduated and gone on to college? They all go into the ministry or work as an apprentice for somebody."

"Oh, Jim, don't torture yourself this way!" Minerva said as she wrung her hands.

"No, it's true. I don't blame myself for that. That's the way that it's been – probably forever. But Diggery was different from all the other students. He was not just smart; he was brilliant. He didn't just enjoy

246

tough subjects, he devoured them for breakfast. And he enjoyed English Literature!" For a moment I forgot that he was dead, and then the terrible truth returned. I went on, "He was going to go to college. Did you know that I was supposed to teach 2nd and 4th years this year?"

Minerva silently nodded.

I went on, "I talked Dumbledore into letting me take 6th years again so that I could teach Diggery his last year – next year. I took him off campus to take the College Board exams. I got him to apply to Cambridge, Princeton, and Harvard.

"A don at Cambridge told me privately that he'd been accepted there. I got a letter from the Provost of Princeton who said that he was going to be accepted with the first batch of acceptances. I'd not heard anything from Harvard yet.

"And he was a modest, happy kid. He loved sports.

"And now that bastard, Riddle, has put an end to him." I picked up a coffee cup that had somehow been left behind by the house elves and stared at it, not quite realizing what it was. Then I threw it at the wall as hard as I could. It hit and smashed with a sound that failed to satisfy.

Minerva put her arms around me, and I sobbed. She rubbed my back and said, "OK. Let's go to bed." We walked up toward the Gryffindor tower, and I tried to turn from it to my office. She gently pulled me back and pulled me up a few stairs. I gave in. Who the hell cared what anyone thought tonight?

◻

The next day, there was a cold, black rage in my chest. And I thought and thought about my next steps. I thought about the Crouch house elf, Winkie. During breakfast, I went down to the kitchen to find her.

A house-elf noticed me immediately and asked with some alarm in his voice, 'Is there being a problem with breakfast?"

"No, I just want to talk with Winkie."

"Of course, sir. But we is very busy right now. Could you come back in a couple of hours?"

"No." The anger was slowly growing in my chest, 'I'll wait. Is there a room that I could wait in?"

The house elf looked around and had an idea, 'Yes, sir. There is. You could wait in the house elf quiet room."

"Quiet room?"

"Yes, when the castle is quiet, and our work is finished, we go there to be quiet and talk."

"Yes, OK. Where is it?"

He led me down a short passage to a room that had several long tables with simple chairs. They were scaled to house elf size, but I couldn't have sat even if they were people-sized. I paced and paced my impatience growing with each minute.

Finally, the door opened and Winkie entered. I stared, suddenly unsure how to start. Then it just burst out, "Why didn't you tell anyone?"

She was clearly surprised, "Tell anyone what?"

I paced, my anger keeping me from making a sensible question, "Tell anyone that Moody was a fake! Tell anyone that Moody was a Deatheater. TELL ANYONE THAT MOODY WAS A KILLER!"

She began sobbing, "But Barty Crouch was my master."

I screamed at her, "You killed your master! You let his son get away with MURDER!"

Tears streamed down her face. "Tell me why you didn't tell what you knew."

"Winkie was doing her duty to the family."

I suddenly realized that I still had my Glock in the pocket of my robes. I pulled it out and screamed at her, "TELL ME.' The sobbing just continued.

I pointed it at her head, "You'd better just tell me right now, if you want to walk out of here." Still nothing.

I advanced a bullet into the chamber, "TELL me why you killed Cedric."

She was still sobbing. I thumbed the safety off and screamed, "WHY DID YOU KILL CEDRIC?"

Something in my voice broke through the torrents of tears that she was crying. She looked at me for the first time, "What is you saying?" came out between sobs.

The question shook me, "I said 'Why did you kill Cedric Diggery?"

"Winkie isn't killing Master Diggery."

"Cedric is dead. He wouldn't be dead if you'd told what you knew about your master's son." I was still pointing the Glock between her glistening eyes, and I noticed that they were glistening.

She said, "I's not knowing what you mean."

I slumped down to sit on one of the undersized tables and my hand dropped so that the Glock was pointed at the floor. "Cedric was killed in a trap that your master's son, Barty Crouch Junior set. He meant to kill Harry Potter but it didn't work out that way."

"Winkie was just following her master's orders." The sobs resumed but were not overwhelming her as they had before.

I realized that she was only doing what she had little or no choice about and probably didn't begin to guess about the possible consequences. "OK. Go. But I never want to see you again, understand."

Through her sobs, she nodded and left the room. Then I broke into sobs myself. After a while, I got up and went up to my office. On the way, for just a moment, I thought about lifting the Glock to my own head.

∩⊳

I got up from bed shortly after dawn. Minerva's hair flowed over her pillow and down her shoulder and back. I had the image of a witch flying through the sky on a broomstick with her long hair trailing behind her in the wind. She was still asleep. I wouldn't wake her. She deserved the release of sleep from the tragedy.

I walked toward her office door, which would lead out of her bedroom and then out of her office and then out of Gryffindor tower and then out of Hogwarts and toward revenge. But before I reached the first door, Minerva said, "Where are you going so early? I've never known you to get up before me."

I didn't turn but just said, "It's not a day that I can sleep in late." I was afraid to look her in the eye. I was afraid that my resolve might weaken, that the dark hole in my heart would melt and leave me without determination.

I could hear her rising from the bed. There was the beginning of alarm in her voice, "Jim, what are you going to do?"

I started walking and said, "I've got to get to work."

She sounded more alarmed than ever, "Don't leave." There was a hesitation and then, "Please." It had real pleading tension in it.

"I'm going."

I hurried out the doors, really worried now that I wouldn't be able to keep going if I ever looked back. I reached my office, entered and changed clothes as quickly as I could. I had to wait for breakfast for my next move, so I went down to the kitchens. I'd never been up this early on a Saturday, so I didn't know how early breakfast started. When I arrived, the house elves were scurrying around. One of the elves stopped to ask me what I needed.

"Oh, I was just wondering when breakfast starts."

The elf said, "We can get you something? What would you like?"

I could only say, "I just want to eat with everyone else. How long will that be?"

"You is very early. There's at least forty-five minutes before breakfast in the great hall."

"That's OK. I'll just go up and wait."

I did. Apparently, a lot of other people couldn't sleep very well either. There were a fair number of people – both student and teacher – waiting in the great hall for breakfast. I sat down by myself at the Huffelpuff table. I waited in silence and finally breakfast appeared at the tables. I started eating mechanically. I kept a watch on the doors and finally the person that I was waiting for appeared. She walked up to the dais. I immediately went up and joined her at the table.

"Sinistra, how are you this morning?"

She was surprised to see me, but she recovered quickly and asked, "I'm surprised to see you here by yourself. And, weren't you sitting at the Hufflepuff table?"

"Today I am a Hufflepuff. And, I was hoping to find you. I need help from you."

"From me? Whatever in the world would you need from me?"

"I'd like to send an owl to someone."

"What about your sweetie? I'm sure that she'd be overjoyed to help you."

"That's not possible."

Her eyes widened in apparent surprise. "Really? Have you got your letter ready?"

I had brought parchment and quill. "I'll have it finished in a few minutes."

"You are in one big hurry!"

"I'm afraid so. Could we go up to the Owlery right after breakfast?"

She looked at me searchingly. "You're not doing something illegal or immoral?"

"I wouldn't say so."

"What would you say?"

I was loosing my patience, "Just tell me whether you'll do it or not."

She shrugged, "Sure. I guess I owe you."

"Damn right you do."

I quickly composed my letter, stuffed it in an envelope and addressed it. Sinistra held out her hand, "Do you mind?"

"How could I, you're going to have to see it shortly anyway."

She scanned the address and handed it back, "Mr. Weasley. I don't think you can get in trouble with him."

I mentally gave a sigh of relief. She obviously didn't know the Weasleys – any of them.

After a quick breakfast, we walked up to the Owlery and Sinistra sent the letter off with a tawny owl. I went back to my office and refused all attempts on Sinistra's part to learn what was in the letter. Shortly before lunch the owl flew in through an open window in my office and dropped a note on my desk and took off. I wondered what that meant.

I opened the letter and read, "I agree to help you. Meet me at the Three Broomsticks for lunch." I hadn't much time, so I jumped up and left Hogwarts as quickly as I could for the Broomsticks. I arrived about ten minutes after noon but Mr. Weasley wasn't there. I doubted that he'd already given up waiting for me, so I found a table and sat to wait. Weasley showed up about ten minutes later. He approached my table and I leaped up and offered to buy him a drink. He asked for a butter beer, which I immediately ordered and we sat.

"OK. What's this all about then?"

"Well, I need your help. It's rather like the Glock that you helped me get. Only, it will take more time, and it will be a good bit more dangerous. If you don't want to get involved, just say so. I won't be offended."

Weasley looked at me as if he'd never seen me before. "Why don't you fill me in on details, and then we'll see."

"Fine. I want help getting something that is not exactly legal for me to have. Sort of like the Glock only much more dangerous. I'd want you to take me to the British Museum in London so that I can do some research. After I've found the information that I want, I'd need you to

251

disapparate me to the place where I can get this thing. Then, I'd want you to disapparate me back here."

"Hmmm. Just how dangerous are we talking?"

"I don't know. I think that it's remotely possible that you might get severely injured."

Then he surprised me. Instead of simply turning me down flat, he simply asked, "What's the purpose of this."

I looked at him intently. I didn't know how he would take the truth. Frankly, I wasn't sure how I'd take the truth – if I said it out loud. I finally decided that I had to do just that – for me if no one else.

"I'm planning on killing Valdemort."

His smile dropped to the floor and he didn't think to pick it up. "What are you planning to do?"

"I'm planning to kill Valdemort." Saying it the second time seemed to make it somehow real in a way that it hadn't been so far today.

"And did you just get up this morning with the thought, 'this would be a good day to die?'"

"No, I didn't. Did you read the *Prophet* lately?"

"Yes. The Diggery boy. But the *Prophet* said that it was a tragic accident in the Tri-Wizard tournament."

"You know, you should never believe anything you read in the *Prophet*."

"Yea. I suppose you're right about that. So what's your story?"

"It's Potter's story, but I believe him. Valdemort's returned. Somehow the tri-Wizard tournament was sort of a cover for getting Potter to where Valdemort was, and he killed Diggery who inadvertently was along for the ride. I think I know where Valdemort is. I want to collect some Muggle weapons and go kill him."

"Just like that?"

"Pretty much."

"Do you need help getting to the place where Valdemort is?" He asked it matter-of-factly – as if we were talking about taking the Express to London. He might just volunteer to come along.

"No. This is pretty much a one man show. I can get myself there."

"And you just want help collecting Glocs?"

"Not Glocks this time. I've got something else in mind."

He sighed and said, as if it were his greatest regret, "Molly would kill me."

"Better her than Valdemort."

Weasley laughed at that."Yes, I suppose you're right. I'll help you. But, understand, it's not that I'm helping you get yourself killed. I don't think you can get within a hundred miles of Valdemort – if he's really around somewhere. But I'm all for trying."

"Thanks. First, can you drop me off at the British Museum?"

"Sure. But let's have lunch first. There's nothing worse than getting killed on an empty stomach."

"Now I see where the twins get it?"

"You mean their rugged good looks and steely determination?"

"I was thinking of their sense of humor."

We had lunch and another butter beer each. Then, we walked out to the street, I took Weasley's hand, and we disappeared. We arrived in an alley across the street from the Museum. We both went in, and I started working my way through the reference materials. As the afternoon wore away, Weasley marveled at the electronic card catalog. He succeeded in breaking one CRT before we were finished, but I eventually found what I wanted.

"Well, what's our next destination?"

I wondered just how far we could disapparate at one jump. "Can we disapparate as far as Darmstadt, Germany?"

"Sure, I think so. Let's try."

"Wait, I have a specific spot that I want to go to."

"Where's that?"

"There's an American Air base there that is shared with the 6th US Armored division."

Mr. Weasley closed his eyes and seemed to be imagining something. Then he said, "Yes, we can do it in one jump. Take my hand."

The world dissolved around me and then re-formed. I walked confidently forward without the slightest hint of nausea and found that we were outside a high chain link fence topped by razor wire. I looked up and down the street that we were on. No vehicles or people were visible. I opened my purse and pulled out a compact pair of binoculars. I lifted them to my eyes and scanned the buildings on the other side of the razor wire and saw the one that I was looking for. They looked a good bit different from the ground level than they do from space photos.

"Mr. Weasley, take the binoculars. I want you to look at the building that is just to the right of that large airplane." He took the binoculars and found the building that I was pointing out.

"OK. Is that our building?"

"Yes. It's a warehouse. What I want you to do is get me inside. After I'm in, come back here and then return for me in half an hour."

"What if you're not finished with whatever you're stealing by then?"

"I guess we'll cross that bridge when we arrive there."

'What if you're not there when I come back for you?"

"Leave immediately. I'll take care of myself."

He looked at me for a while, I guess trying to figure out if I were serious. Finally, he agreed. I took his hand and we were outside the building. He had his wand out, passing it over the wall of the building. Finally, he said, "OK. Are you ready?"

"Yes." He held out his hand, I took it, and we were inside a dark warehouse. It was poorly lit, but I could see Weasley fine. I nodded at him and waved goodbye. He disappeared. I got out the purse, opened it and pulled out a flash light. I began searching the warehouse. I read every crate's title and had not found anything I was looking for in the first 15 minutes. I began to imagine that I heard sounds at the other end of the building. I kept searching.

Then I found it. I opened the purse again and pulled out a small pry bar. I began working on the packing case. In a moment, I had pulled up two slats. I flashed the light inside and found what I was looking for. I reached in and started pulling them out. While I was doing that I heard real noises heading my way. I hurried up and had about 20 tossed into my purse. I pulled the strings tight and tossed it into my pocket. The noise was quite close, and I saw two men round a corner. One flashed a light toward me. He shouted, "You, there. Put your hands up and don't move."

I dropped and rounded into a corridor and ran back to the original spot that Weasley and I had disapparated. I ran as fast as I could hunched over. By my count, I had at least three or four minutes before Weasley would show up. I had almost reached the wall where we had disapparated and my pursuers had rounded the last corner and were in sight again. "Stop. Stop."

I had reached the spot where we'd disapparated and the two guards couldn't be a minute behind me and in full view. They were 20

254

yards away and had their guns out. They slowly approached. One motioned upward with his hand gun. I took the hint and raised my hands.

Then, there was a green flash, and Weasley was beside me. Then we were standing outside the chain link fence again. Weasley said, "Those two didn't look very friendly."

"You're right. I'm glad you happened along when you did."

"Did you get what you were looking for?"

"Yes. But those two gentlemen didn't want me to finish my thievery."

"Can we leave?"

"Yes. Let's go back to Hogsmeade."

So, we did. After arriving, I thanked Weasley profusely and tried to get him to join me for a pint at the Broomsticks, but he said that he needed to get back home. We parted. I found my way back to Hogwarts and decided that there would be no better time than the present to try out one or two of my toys.

After getting to my room, I changed clothes and headed out on the walk that was so nearly second nature to me, that I could have walked with my eyes closed at night. I arrived at my favorite cave. This time, I didn't walk in. It wasn't necessary for me to use my flash to light it. I leaned against the rough rock wall next to the cave mouth. I opened my purse, reached inside and pulled out one of the objects that I'd pilfered. I stared at it for minute after minute. Now that it was in my hand, I wasn't that anxious to try using it. But I finally set myself, took a deep breath and counted to three.

I pulled the pin out of it and tossed it far back into the cave. There was a muffled roar and dust blew out of the cave mouth. I walked inside and tried to see where the hand grenade had fallen, but it was impossible to tell. I walked slowly back to the castle. I was in time to have some supper before the elves cleaned up. Minerva was there.

"Where have you been?"

Between mouthfuls I said, "I've been away."

"You aren't doing something that you'll regret, are you?"

"No."

She reached out and put her hand over mine. She didn't say anything but squeezed. I went to my rooms and thought long and hard.

The next day, I worked on final exams. On Tuesday my classes sat their final exam, and I graded on Wednesday. I was nearly done with the term, so Thursday I walked out to the cave again.

This time, I wanted to test an idea. I had taken a towel and sewed three hand grenades to it by looping thread through the ring. I placed the towel on the floor of the cave. I weighed it down with a couple of large stones. I tied a string around a pin of one of the grenades. I walked out of the cave, trailing the string. When I was satisfied that I was in a safe position, I took a deep breath and pulled on the string until it was taught and then gave a sudden jerk. The string released and I counted off an eternity before the resounding explosion, obviously far more powerful than the last time I'd been there. I went into the cave and searched assiduously for any sign that any of the other two grenades had survived. I finally concluded that they hadn't and that a chain reaction was inevitable.

The next day I finished grading and turned in my final grades to the administration. The next day was interminable. Finally, the day ended, I spent a fitful night tossing and turning in my sleep. Minerva accompanied me on the train back to London. She said nothing. We sat in silence, alone in the teacher's car. She took me through the barrier, and we parted in silence until we kissed.

She said, "I don't know what you're going to do, but whatever it is, talk to me as soon as it's over."

"I will."

I purchased a ticket for a station about ten miles from the Riddle homestead at Little Hangleton. I was sure that no one was following me. They all had bigger fish to fry. As did I. When I arrived at the station, I found a cab. I tossed my bags in and gave the cabbie rather unusual instructions. I had him stop about two miles away from my target. I paid him to wait for two hours and then, if I'd not returned, he was to take my bags to the local hotel where he would leave the bags until I arrived. I thought about the possibility that I would never go to retrieve them.

I trotted through the waning light of the lowering sun toward the Riddle home. I arrived at the family graveyard and stood at my Rubicon. I stood for a while before I shrugged and walked across the graveyard toward the mansion. I reached the front door. There was a trace of light coming through one of the upper level windows. I opened the door as silently as I could and entered the rapidly darkening entryway. I opened my purse and pulled out the vest that I'd fashioned. It had eight hand grenades loosely sewn to it. I put it on.

I pulled one of the hand grenades off the vest and pulled out the Glock and held it in my right hand. I walked up the stairs to the 2nd floor. From the landing, I saw light coming from the partially open door to one room. I approached it and as I did, I heard a hissing inside the room. With that the door flung open, and on the other side, I saw a tall cadaverous man in black robes. Beside him was a man whom I later remembered was Wormtail.

Riddle said, "Wormtail, we have a guest. Allow me to welcome you. And a Muggle too!" He started to lazily raise his wand and I heard him begin to say, "Avra". I pulled the pin out of the grenade with my teeth and strode toward him. With my motion he dropped to the floor, grabbed the snake that was at his feet and disapparated. I continued striding toward Wormtail. He too disappeared almost as quickly as his master.

The Malfois Homestead

The man disapparated before the massive ornate gate of the mansion. He had a huge snake wrapped around his neck. He pulled his sleeve up and touched his bare arm with his wand and a moment later, the other man appeared next to him.

"My Lord, why did you disapparate. It was only a Muggle."

"Don't be a fool Wormtail, I could see Death in his eyes – my death. And I could tell that it wouldn't matter if I killed him or not. The final thing I heard in his mind was 'I am Shiva.'"

"What shall we do?"

"There's no reason to return there. Our dear friends, the Malfoys, will be happy to put us up for a few nights."

I was aware that I was alone in the Riddle mansion. I had had my opportunity and it had slipped from my hands. The two people responsible for Diggery's death had been in the same room with me and I'd killed neither of them. In that instant I realized that I'd never get another opportunity. With that realization, I knew that there was no point in allowing them to send reinforcements back. I ran down the stairs and reached the entrance that I'd come in through. I noticed that I was still holding the hand grenade with the safety lever depressed. I decided to let the occupants know, if they ever returned, that they really were in danger. I released the safety lever and threw the grenades as far back into the house as I could and went flat on the porch. The explosion was satisfyingly loud and with it, I leaped up and ran for my life. After tripping over a grave, I pulled out my flashlight and lit my way, although every step that I took I was convinced that I was attracting Deatheaters to me with the light. Every delay going around a grave marker was another second that I was giving them.

I reached the street. Its regular surface tempted me to turn off the flash, but I kept it on. After going over a hill I could no longer see the Riddle house. I slowed to a trot and my breath began to come hard. I still had a good mile to reach the cab, which I seemed to have left years before. I was certain that it had left already, and I was beginning to plan what to do on foot. I rounded a curving hill, and there was the cab where I'd left it.

The cabbie greeted me and said, "I thought you were going to be a couple of hours?"

I looked at my watch and saw that I'd hardly been gone more than an hour. "Get going. Look, just how far would you be willing to take me if I paid you." I paused to calculate what I had in my purse in pounds sterling, "Oh, say, two hundred pounds?"

His eyes bugged out, "I'd take you to London."

"Really?"

"Sure."

"Do, it. And don't pay attention to the speed limit."

"Are you kidding? For two hundred pounds, we'll get there before we left." He gunned the engine to prove that he was serious and we hared off.

On the road back I began to think over the adventures of the last week. I realized that I'd just gone from flying below the radar to flying very much straight into it. Wormtail surely would recognize me. Well, I guessed, it's definitely my war now. I probably just became HeWhoMustNotBeNamed's number two enemy. On second thought, I was probably more like the #3 or #4 enemy. Besides Potter, there was still Dumbledore and maybe other people.

We arrived in London before midnight. I had the cabbie stop at a likely looking hotel on the outskirts of London. I checked in and went to my room. I decided to see if Minerva still had the cell phone, and if she remembered how to use it. I rang her number. It rang and rang and eventually I got the default voicemail message. I'd never taught her how to use voicemail, so I just hung up. Then about five minutes later my phone rang.

I picked up and heard the sweetest sound that I'd ever heard, "Why the Bloody Hell didn't you call sooner and why doesn't this bloody phone keep ringing until you pick up?"

I laughed for about three minutes. Minerva's swearing became so profuse that I finally caught my breath and said, "I called as soon as I thought that I was safe. I'm at a hotel in London. I was wondering if I could stay with you and your sis for a few days."

"What's the hotel? I'll be there in 15 seconds."

"I'm at the Islington Hilton hotel."

With that the phone went dead. I almost had decided to ring her up again when the phone rang. It was Minerva. "I'm in the lobby. You come down here right now and check out. . . Or . . ."

"Or what?"

"Or I'll disapparate up and disapparate you straight to sis'!"

That was good enough for me. I grabbed my bags that I hadn't even had time to unpack, and left the key on the dresser and trotted down to the elevator. Minerva was waiting at the main entrance to the Hilton. She threw her arms around me and kissed me as though we'd been apart for the whole summer. She "whispered" in my ear so loud that it was ringing long after she'd finished asking me, "What the hell were you doing?"

"I'll tell you after we leave here."

She seemed to remember where she was. She loosened her grip on me and said, "Oh, yes. Let's go." I checked out of the hotel, paying with my Gringott's credit card. The desk clerk asked the obligatory question, "Did you enjoy your stay?"

I couldn't quite figure out if he saw the humor in the situation, but I thought that I'd assume that he did. "Oh, yes. It's the best stay that I've ever had at a Hilton."

"Wonderful, sir."

I thought to myself, "Yes, it's the best stay on so many levels. It's the only stay. It only lasted about 5 minutes, so that made it a good stay for sure."

Minerva finally dragged me out of the hotel. She insisted on knowing what I'd done before we went anywhere.

"Look, Minerva. It's late. I'm tired. Let's go to your sis' and talk there."

"I don't want her alarmed. You tell me now."

"OK. I think there's probably a restaurant or two around here still open. Let's find one and talk seated. Heck, we could go into the coffee shop of this Hilton." She agreed to that. We found a table, were there with tea cups in front of us, and I began to tell her what happened.

"I set out to kill Valdemort."

"You what? No, no, don't repeat it. You actually did, didn't you? What in the world would possess you to do such a STUPID thing?"

"Well, I just couldn't let Diggery's death go, well, unavenged."

"Don't be melodramatic."

"No, I'm serious."

Her tone softened as she came to grips with the fact that it was over and done. There was nothing that could undo it and we would just have to live with it for the rest of our lives – however short they might be. "I don't suppose it's worthwhile crying over spilt milk. Well, you've got to leave the country and hope that Valdemort doesn't decide that he needs to avenge himself of this attack to maintain discipline in his ranks."

"No, I'm not."

"Now, I know that you are crazy. You've got to go. Even if Valdemort doesn't come after you personally, every Deatheater around will be trying to win favor by killing you. Why in the world wouldn't you go back?"

"Why don't you leave England? You're probably as much hated as I am. Everyone who stood against Valdemort is."

"But this is different. Nobody ever got close to Valdemort. Even Potter didn't go after Valdemort and actually find him and try to kill him." She hesitated a minute as if thinking about what she'd just said, and then she went on in a more thoughtful tone of voice, "What did happen when you found him anyway? Why are you still alive?"

'I don't know." I considered a minute. Did I dare bring out a hand grenade and show it to her? I looked around to see if there were anyone within earshot or who could see. Our waitress was over at the cash register talking with a cook. So, I got out my purse and undid the drawstrings. "OK. I'm thinking about showing you something. You've got to promise me not to tell anyone about what I show you or, I don't know, scream."

"Why would I be tempted to scream?"

261

"Well, probably not. I just want you to be prepared." I opened the purse fully and reached in and pulled out a hand grenade. I held it in my open palm and Minerva laughed.

"What is this—some new kind of snitch?" With that she picked it off my palm and tossed it back and forth between her hands. I started to say, "Don't play with those." Then she put a finger through the ring of the pin and had started to twirl it on her index finger.

I shouted, "No." She dropped it and looked at me as if I'd done something stupid. The waitress and cook turned toward us. Minerva asked, "I thought you said that I shouldn't scream."

"Well, I wasn't expecting you to try to kill us."

She looked at the hand grenade that I was quickly stuffing into my purse and said, "That? That could kill us?"

"Yes. It could. It's called a hand grenade. If you'd pulled that ring out, we'd have had about 10 seconds to do something with it."

"And if we didn't do something with it in those ten seconds?"

"Well, the thing would have exploded, and we'd both have been peppered with shrapnel."

"I wouldn't. I'd have disapparated." And then it dawned on her. "That's what Valdemort did, right?"

"Yes."

She looked at me and her eyes widened as she said, "You were going to kill yourself, weren't you?"

"I wasn't planning on it, but given everything, I thought it was pretty likely."

"OK. I guess I can't keep you out of this. Although, God, I wish that I could." She mused to herself, "I suppose I really could keep you out of it. A memory charm and the Imperius curse and you'd leave England and forget that you ever knew me."

I felt cold furry welling up in me. "You wouldn't. I would never love you again."

She looked wistful as she said, "I suppose you wouldn't."

I was not going to be waylaid, "You've got to promise that you'll never do anything like that to me as long as you live."

She turned business-like, "Oh, dear boy. Don't be so melodramatic again. If I were going to do it, you'd already be on your way to America now."

In my heart, I guess that I knew that she'd never do something to violate my personality so thoroughly. She reached out to take my hand in hers and said, "Now, let's get going. And tell me how you got Valdemort's address."

I paid our bill, and we walked outside with my bags and Minerva held out her hand. I took it and nothing happened. I asked, "Aren't we going?"

She was just staring at me and finally said, "Aren't you going to complain about having to disapparate?"

"No. We've got to get going. I'm tired. Let's get this over with, and I'll tell you what happened." She stared at me for another few seconds, and then, we appeared outside her sister's house.

We went in and I found that I had the real guest room. It was quite late for Maggie, and she'd gone to bed. I also discovered to my great joy that I was sharing the room with Minerva. I didn't always have that privilege. That was good because it allowed us to talk until any hour without disturbing Maggie or anyone else who might have been in the house.

Minerva was so anxious to hear what had happened that she insisted that we sit up and talk about it rather than other occupations before sleep. We sat on the bed fully clothed and talked. I told her about hand grenades and how I got them. She was amazed at Weasley's part in the affair. I told her about traveling to Valdemort's lair.

"I can't believe that you actually charged at Valdemort when he discovered you. What if he'd stayed and killed you."

"Then I think that we'd all be dead by now – me, Valdemort, Wormtail. He wouldn't have understood the significance of the grenades. They'd have."

Minerva interrupted me and asked "Grenades. You had more than one?"

"Sure. I had a special vest with eight of them. When Valdemort saw me, I pulled one off and pulled the pin, but kept my finger on the safety and charged him. At the time, it seemed like the safest thing to do. Just for a fraction of a second, I thought that some presence was in my head. Then it and Valdemort disappeared. A second later Wormtail was gone too. I got out almost as quickly. But I left the grenades as a sort of calling card.

"I ran as fast as I could and escaped."

Minerva and I were holding hands, and I could feel the relief of tension when I related my escape. But she tensed quickly again and asked, "How in the world did you find Valdemort? Aurors tried to find him the last time for years and never succeeded."

"Oh, it really wasn't so hard. If you think about it a minute, you'll realize that you know where he was."

She dropped my hands for a second and then took them again. "I don't think that I do."

I squinted at her. "Sure you do. Here's a little hint. Dumbledore once told us where he was."

She stared back and said, "It's funny, I really don't recall Dumbledore telling us that he knew where Valdemort was, let alone where that was."

"Think. He told us about a very unusual death early in the last term."

This time Minerva dropped my hands, and didn't pick them up immediately. Her eyes widened and their focus moved to the distance. "Yes. Yes, he did tell us about a strange death. Like the Avra Cadavra curse. Where was that?" I was starting to open my mouth to speak but she shushed me, "Oh, be quiet, I know what the name is, I just have to think for a moment."

She concentrated and then her face cleared of worry lines, "Yes. It was Hangleton."

"Close.'

"Oh, yes. LITTLE Hangleton. That's where you went?"

"Yes. I found the mansion where the death had occurred without any problem, and I found Valdemort with lots of problems."

Minerva slumped and said, "This is as much excitement as I can take in one day. You've got to promise me that you'll never go off on your own to take on Valdemort again."

"Sure. You know, I have this spooky feeling that I'll never have a chance like that again. Maybe, never see him in the flesh again."

Minerva pulled me to her and wrapped her arms around my shoulders and shook softly. Finally she said, "God, I hope not." She extinguished the lights with her wand, we got under the covers, and both fell asleep so quickly that I don't think that we kissed good-night.

The next morning we both slept in. She woke before I did, as usual. When I did, she was sitting on the edge of the bed looking at me with a hand resting lightly on my right knee. She had changed from yesterday's clothes to a night gown sometime during the night. I was still in street clothes from yesterday. "Are you ready for breakfast?"

I frowned because an idea had occurred to me, and I didn't like it, "I really have to leave right away."

"Why, are you afraid of offending sis' sensibilities?"

"No, I'm a danger to anyone that I'm with. I can't endanger your sister."

"Why don't you let Maggie decide that for herself? Let's go down and have breakfast and you can talk about it."

It wasn't an idea I was completely comfortable with – admitting to Maggie the kind of danger that I'd put her in, but it was the right thing to do. So I gritted my teeth and quickly dressed to get it all over with as soon as possible. When we got down to the kitchen, we found that Maggie had made French toast and left them in a warm oven along with bacon. We got out plates, silver, and glasses for orange juice. Maggie must have noticed the commotion because she came to the kitchen, sat at the kitchen table, and poured herself a cup of coffee. She watched us and commented about how late we'd slept in.

We started on our breakfast while she drank coffee and I broached The Topic. "Maggie, I've got to be honest about something that I did yesterday. Let me tell it and then if you want to kick me out, I'll go. As a matter of fact, I might just go anyway." She nodded and I went on, "Well. . . ," and I stopped because I wasn't sure just how to put it. Did I say, "You'll never guess whom I just tried to kill?" or "Every Deatheater in England is trying to find me at this minute?"

I finally settled on a simple, "Last night I tried to kill Valdemort. I figure that anyone who helps me will be in grave danger."

Maggie stared at me for a minute and then burst out laughing. She had a hard time breathing for a minute and when she regained control she said, "Minnie, you never told me that Wendt had such a sense of humor. He's a riot."

"Sis, I don't think that he's kidding."

Her face turned to one of solicitude and said, "I'm sorry. I didn't realize that, well, that you were." She turned to Minerva and said, "Of course he can stay until he's better."

She thought I was deranged.

"Look, I can't stay here. I'm a danger to whoever harbors me."

She just shook her head and said, "You're going to stay here until you're feeling better."

I looked over to Minerva in appeal, but she just shook her head too. I decided that they couldn't keep me from going, but I wanted to talk

265

with Minerva in private before I did. I said, "OK. OK. I'm not going right away, but I do want to do some writing if I'm going to be here for a while." I volunteered to clean up after breakfast. When that was finished I went back to our room to get paper and pen. I dug it out of my bag and sat at the small bureau and picked up where I'd left off.

Before a few minutes had passed I heard the door open and smelled Minerva's perfume. "Well, this is a fine mess I've got myself into."

She came over and sat on the edge of the bed as I turned to face her. "Why do you think that anyone would think that you'd be here?"

"Come on, the only people at Hogwarts who doesn't know that we're in love is Filch and the first years. Where else would someone look for me than with you?"

She reached out and rubbed my knee, which was the only part of me in easy reach of her, "You really think that the Deatheaters will be out for you?"

"Yes. And the only way that I or you or your sister will be safe is for me to be buried in some Muggle hole someplace." She absently stroked my knee more aggressively. It was all that I could do to go on and say, "I'm going to find a nice quiet rooming house where I can hole up for a couple of months. But that doesn't mean that we can't see each other. I'll call you every now and then. We will agree on a place to meet, and we'll have dinner or lunch or brunch or breakfast or anything you want."

She smiled wickedly and asked, "Can we have a midnight snack?"

"I think we might just arrange that sometimes."

The next couple of days I searched *The Times* for likely spots. Minerva was a good sport and disapparated me to them to check them out.

Minerva suggested that we travel to the States to visit with my family. After all, they'd come here.

I was against it, "Look, I want to go hide someplace. I don't want to bring problems to even more people—especially people that I love."

She took her schoolmarmly stance with her hands on her hips, "You would not be endangering anyone. Do you really think that they have taken the trouble to find out anything about where you come from?

I don't even know where you come from, really. How would those morons?"

I could see where this was going. She really wanted to visit where I'd grown up again, and she'd never give up. Maybe she was right. Maybe we could sneak off, and no one could trace us.

Eventually, I had to agree. She made arrangements for us to go by Port Key. We arrived at a wizarding customs station in New York City underneath Grand Central Station. We had to endure the indignity of Probity Probes, but we were soon in Grand Central Station itself. We found a quiet little restaurant where we had dinner.

I ordered for us and said, "Do you know a wizarding inn somewhere in the States?"

She thought a minute and said, "Yes, I suppose so. The Scarlet Rose. It's in Boston."

"OK. Then let's stay there, because we need to do some talking and I've been putting it off. I just can't put it off further."

Minerva was bemused, "Really? You want to talk. This I want to see . . er . . . hear."

I suddenly realized that I'd not really thought out what I wanted to say, so I thought for a moment. I really had only two points. How hard could it be? "To start off, I've got a question."

"Shoot."

"Well, the source of this question isn't exactly impeccable. It came from the faux Moody. Bear that in mind. He told me that you are a widow. Is that true?"

She apparently had no idea that that would be the question. Her eyes widened, and she seemed to temporize with another question, "Did you check that with Dumbledore or Snape or anyone?'"

I didn't want her to weasel out of talking about this, "No. It was not a subject that I was comfortable talking about."

"Well, it's true." She stopped talking, and I gave her a good long time to amplify.

Afet a good while, I tried to phrase my next question as innocently as I could. "Would you mind expanding on that a bit?"

She brought her hand to her mouth and bit a knuckle—seemingly unconsciously. Then she proceeded, "Yes. A widow. Me. No woman likes to think about the idea. The possibility of being alone after being together is painful.

She took a deep breath, "I married a long time ago. He was a Muggle. He was wonderful. He didn't hesitate for a second when I told him that I was a witch. It was as though I'd said that I was a Liberal. I loved him very, very much.

"We got married about twenty years ago. Valdemort was around but no one appreciated how dangerous he was. Hardly anyone knew him.

"My husband was a teacher." She stopped. Her throat seemed to be full.

I couldn't stop myself from saying the truth that leapt into my head, "He taught English Literature."

The throat was full of suppressed tears. She forced it through the throat, "Close enough. English Composition."

I went on, "How did he die?"

That seemed to dry her tears a bit. "I don't know." I was tempted to be incredulous, but I held back. She went on, "It was just as Valdemort was rising. He left home one day to go to his school, and he didn't return. He was never seen again—by anyone."

"Do you think. ."

She had apparently made a decision, because she went on directly and calmly, "I think he was killed by a Deatheater. It happened all the time. Someone disappeared and was never seen again. Their body was transfigured to something else – unidentifiable."

She broke down again for a moment. The next words that she said were almost inaudible, "I didn't even have a body to bury, a grave to visit."

We were silent for a while.

"For what it's worth – personally I think it might be worth a lot – the faux Moody told me that he'd caught a Deatheater who had killed your husband."

Minerva broke down completely and cried and cried. Then she said, "I knew it. I knew it in my heart. Do you suppose it was Crouch?"

I nodded, unable to speak for a while myself. I then said weakly, "I'm pretty sure it was Crouch. I think he was having a little joke on me."

She nodded. Then she asked, "What was your other question?"

I thought hard. Beside this revelation, it seemed trivial. It was so full of the importuning present, of the trivial daily necessity that I was ashamed to voice it. But it was something that we had to face, and it would be cowardly not to bring it up.

I kicked the can, "Let's discuss it over coffee after dinner."

We ate in peaceful silence. There is a silence that is full of unsaid truths and bitter recriminations that can make silence scream. This was the opposite. The silence of comfortable presence made us, if not happy, at least satisfied.

Coffee came, and I spoke without preamble, "When we reach Ohio, my parents are not going to be easy until they've asked us where we're going with our relationship. And I suppose they'll keep asking that question until the answer is either marriage or separation. I want to be able to give them an answer that we are both comfortable with. I don't particularly care if they're comfortable with it."

Our eyes met and she said, "I don't have an answer for that. There are times that I think that I could do anything and everything with you and times when you're too much like," her voice caught and she couldn't speak.

And then she did, "I don't know."

I still had her eye, which made me happy, "Then that's our answer—Simple, direct, inarguable."

That night we went to the Scarlet Rose and found an inn that made us both think of the Cauldron. Our room had a four-poster bed, a wooden armoire, a dressing table, a couple of armchairs that were a real contrast to the typical American hotel room that had the obligatory desk and single chair.

When we went to bed, Minerva asked to be held, which quickly converted to spooning her. We both fell asleep happy to be holding/held.

The next day we had breakfast at the Rose. I wasn't good for conversation, because I was preparing myself for the ordeal that I knew was coming. We checked out, found an alley, rounded the corner and disapparated to my parents' street.

The Punishment

We arrived and were greeted by the family, including an aunt and a couple of uncles. I faced one of the toughest grillings that I'd ever had from the uncles about Minerva. They thought there was something definitely unusual about her BESIDES being way too old for me.

But one of my uncles, in many ways my favorite, Noye, was always ready for the unusual. He greeted Minerva with, "Well, when are the two of you getting married?" That was Uncle Noye all over. He always was honest and open, sometimes embarrassingly open with his opinions. To him, if we had been seeing each other for more than six months (and we'd been seeing each other for over four years), it must be time to be engaged at least.

Minerva took it well. She answered, "Uncle Noye, tell me, would you marry this guy if you had the chance?"

That had him. He was busy puzzling over all the implications of that most of the rest of the night. I loved him, but anyone who could derail his train of thought for a while was worth her weight in gold in my book.

◁

After that ordeal, we settled in and were down for breakfast the next morning. My family liked reading the paper over a leisurely breakfast. My dad had the front page. Apparently he'd wrestled mom for it before we got down from our bedroom. My mom had the home section. Minerva wanted to see what American sports were like, so she took the sports section, and that left the business section for me.

There was an article about the CEO of a film company. Apparently, he'd gotten back to be some sort of advisory CEO for the company that he'd originally founded. His life was fascinating. One paragraph struck me particularly. I quoted it almost verbatim:

"He has always felt that he was special and that the normal rules don't apply to him. For example, his Mercedes doesn't have license plates. When he was stopped shortly after buying it by a patrol car, he faced down the officer and got off without even a warning."

My mom interrupted. "What a conceited ass. That officer should have arrested him."

My dad agreed, "I'm not sure I'd call him an ass. He is brilliant, but with gifts come responsibilities."

Minerva said, "I wish I'd had him in a transfiguration class. I almost agree with that fake Moody that some people ought to be turned into ferrets. They'd probably be happier too."

I went on, "He routinely parks in handicapped parking spots, sometimes taking up two spaces with his silver Mercedes."

Minerva and my mom stood up in unison as though they had rehearsed the move. They both said variations on, "Somebody should teach that asshole a lesson."

I looked from one to the other and said to Minerva, "What do you think? Are you up for a little mischief?"

"I certainly am. When do we start?"

"How about this afternoon? I have an idea that I think makes the punishment fit the crime."

⌒⌒

Steve had had a good day. His team had finally begun to get some ideas that were not completely shit about the new product lines, and he was practically walking on air when he reached the parking lot. Spoiling the moment, there seemed to be a problem with the tires on one side of his car. Both of them were as flat as pancakes. He walked around the car to see if there was any other damage. When he got to the other side he instantly realized that the other two tires were also flat. He walked back to the reception desk and called a towing service to take the Mercedes to the dealership and called a cab to take him home.

When he got home he told Lureen about the way all four tires were flat. He had gone to the security office and the people watching the security cameras hadn't seen anything out of the ordinary.

"Well, Steve, maybe it's just an incredible coincidence and all four tires just failed at about the same time."

"No, I don't believe in coincidences—at least not at that level. Somebody must want to play a practical joke on me. "

The next day, Lureen dropped him off at work because the dealership was going to return his car off at home, and he didn't want to have to arrange to get the second car home. Reception called him about 10AM to tell him that the dealership had brought the car. He told her to have them park it in his usual parking spot—the first handicap space. At noon he went down to go to lunch with the new industrial designer he'd just hired.

When the two of them arrived at the car, they found that two of the tires were flat. As a matter of fact all four were. He stormed back to the security office and demanded to see the head of security.

Steve's moods were famous—even after a decade. The security chief prepared for a tirade. He wasn't disappointed. After it was over, he took Steve to the monitor room, and they found the security camera that was showing the part of the lot that included the handicap spots. They backed up the security tape and reviewed it at fast forward. Nothing showed up, but Steve noticed when the tires had gone flat. They backed up the tape and went through it at slow motion. The tires went suddenly flat—one at a time, and there was nobody within fifty feet of the car.

When he saw that, Steve called the dealership and asked to talk to the service manager. He told him that somebody had been playing a joke on him that had caused the tires to go flat. He insisted that they find out how it was done. Was it some kind of bullet fired from a distance or was there a device that could be triggered remotely to puncture the tires.

Steve had a hard time concentrating on work. Finally at 4 PM he got a call from the Service Manager. "I'm sorry sir. We looked for every cause that we could find. There wasn't anything like a bullet hole and no bullets. There were no devices in the wheel wells or anywhere on or in the car.

"The tires failed along long lines where the steel sidewalls are thickest. I'm not sure you could have made those cuts with a machete. That almost requires a surgical quality band saw. I presume that no one noticed someone with a band saw working on your tires in the parking lot before they failed?"

"No, of course not. That's all a pile of shit. It had to be done before the car reached the parking lot."

"That would require very precise cuts that went through all but the last couple of millimeters of the tire, AND it's very likely that one or more tires would fail while being driven."

"Well that's crap. The only other hands that touched MY Mercedes beside mine have been in your shop."

"Surely you don't mean to accuse us . . ."

"Well, if the shoe or the tire fits, wear it."

The voice on the other end of the wire lost its urbane English accent and reverted to the original German intonations. "The sort of sabotage that you're talking about could not be done in a shop without everyone in the shop knowing about it. That implies that you are accusing the shop."

"That's what it sounds like."

"You are accusing this shop not just of criminal neglect but of attempted murder. That sort of accusation is actionable. If you care to make that accusation before witnesses, it will be our pleasure to sue you for criminal slander." The next sound Steve heard was the phone at the other end being slammed down.

"The asshole." He looked around, half-hoping that he had an audience, but he didn't. Shortly after that he was informed that the shop had delivered the car. He practically sprinted to the parking lot and drove off to home.

At home, he told the story to Lureen. She thought about the astounding story and asked, "Let's do a little analysis. Where has your car been when these tires burst?"

"Where else? At work."

"Yes, but where at work?"

"You know that I always park next to the main entrance."

"In the handicap slots?"

"Well, of course."

"And it's never happened when you were parked here or anywhere else?"

"No, but it hasn't been parked many places since this started happening."

"Would you humor me and tomorrow park in an ordinary parking slot?"

Steve was on the verge of shouting at Lureen, but he decided that he'd just do that and prove to everyone that it was someone at work. One of those brilliant engineers that had come up with some oh-so clever way to play a practical joke on him—like the time they'd painted a Mercedes on one of the handicap signs at work.

"OK. Let's try the experiment tomorrow. I'll park in a normal parking spot, and we'll see what happens."

The next day, when he went in to work, he arrived earlier than normal and found a parking spot pretty close to the main entrance. He couldn't keep himself from looking back multiple times at his car as he entered the building. He went directly to the security office and spoke to the head of security again.

"I want that car under continuous close surveillance by security camera, and I want a guard close by watching it."

The head of security walked Steve into the monitor room and asked Steve to tell him which camera was showing his car. He took a couple of minutes looking and found the one. The head of Security said, "OK. Jim, would you zoom camera four onto the silver Mercedes on the first row?"

"Yes, sir." The camera panned a little and then zoomed in. When it just contained the car, the zoom stopped.

Steve looked for a few seconds and said, "Back out a little. I want to be able to see anyone who approaches it closely," They backed the view out, he nodded and headed for the door but stopped. He turned and said, "Zoom in a little bit." The guard running the camera shrugged and zoomed in a bit. He stood a moment and then said, "No, back out a little."

After they'd done this a couple of times, the security head said, "Are you going to spend all day here." Steve's gaze flashed away from the screen to him and just stared at him. The security head had heard about the famous man's gaze but had never seen it before. He said nothing.

After a while, Steve said, "Put another camera on my car. One will do a wide view, the other a close up."

The security head asked the guard, "Can you put another eye-in-the-sky on it?"

He nodded and said, "I think so." Another monitor started changing focus. It panned and panned and eventually caught the Mercedes in the edge of the field of view. "That's the best I can do. This would be the wide view, and the other will be the close up."

The security head turned to Steve and asked, "OK?"

"Yes." And he left without another word.

At noon, Steve went out to the parking lot with the CEO, Gil. They were headed for lunch. Steve was going to drive. They arrived at the Mercedes, and Steve circled the car examining it carefully. Gil asked, "Steve, I've heard about your problems with your car. What's been going on?"

Steve frowned and said, "Oh, I think some wise-guy engineer has been playing a practical joke on me."

Gil asked, "Would you like me to drive."

Steve went on, "The last couple of days, my car has had flats. The Mercedes dealership says that the way it was done, the flats could happen while driving and it could be fatal."

Gil gulped involuntarily and said, "Really, I'd be happy to drive."

Steve continued to stand away from the Mercedes, speechless. Then he said, "No, Gil. Come on. I'll drive."

"Really, Steve, I don't think it's a good idea for two of the top officers of the company to be driving together, especially if there is some danger . . ." His voice trailed off.

"Come on Gil. This is just a practical joke. Get in." But Steve had not yet gotten into the Mercedes.

Gil walked off briskly saying over his shoulder, "I'll meet you at the restaurant. It's no problem at all. Really."

Steve drove to the restaurant, had lunch with Gil and returned for the afternoon. About 5:30 PM, he called security and asked if anything had happened with the Mercedes. There was a change of shift, but the guard immediately said, "No, sir. Your Mercedes is safe and sound."

Steve then called home and told Lureen, "I'm on my way home. We'll have dinner a little early so that we can go see Apollo 13."

Lureen was surprised, "Is this Wednesday? Who are you and what have you done to my husband?"

"Come on Lureen, it's me. I just read a great review of *Apollo 13*, and I want to see it. It'll be impossible to get into on the weekends."

"OK. We'll have something thrown together by the time that you arrive."

He got home, and there was true vegetarian pizza on the table. After dinner started, Lureen asked, "Well, I see that your Mercedes is healthy. How'd it go?"

Steve said, "OK. Nothing happened, but that doesn't prove anything."

"Is this little outing to prove something?"

"Yes. We'll go to the Century theater and park at the Stanford mall—in a handicapped spot and see what happens."

"OK. You're being more of an ass about this than usual, but we'll get an evening out anyway."

Everyone was anxious to get to the theatre before the movie started. Steve let Lureen out at the theatre with instructions to get a ticket and save him a seat. He then drove the couple of blocks to the Stanford mall and parked in a handicap slot. He went in and found the mall office and attracted the attention of a guard. He convinced him to take him to the security manager.

He got directly to the point, "You know who I am. I've been having a problem with vandalism of my car. I've parked in a handicap spot and want you to keep a security camera pointed at it at all times."

"Look, sir, we don't do that for anyone but visiting officials of foreign countries."

"But, I'm the CEO of of of." He seemed on the verge of apoplexy. "You're going to do it." He turned to go and then added, " Oh, yes. One more thing. I want to hire one of your guards to watch the car until I get back from the movie."

There was some discussion, but finally, the manager agreed about the security camera. The best he would do was to say, "Look. I've got to get a replacement in for my man if you hire him for the night. If I can't do that, he's back on normal duty. Now, the deal you make with him is between you and him."

Steve accepted that, and he asked the guard who had let him in if he was interested in making a thousand dollars.

"It depends on what I have to do."

"Simple. Just watch my car until I get back from the Century movie theater, and keep anybody from damaging it."

He nodded and said, "Let's see the thou."

"You don't get it until I'm back, and my car is OK."

"No deal. I've heard a little about you and your whims. I need at least half up front, and I keep it regardless what happens to your car."

Steve got out his wallet and peeled off five hundred dollar bills. The guard held them up to the light and declared them good. Steve left for the theater.

Phil (Phyllis) Huggins was at the Il Fornaio restaurant in the Garden Court Hotel with her boyfriend. It looked like he was pretty serious. This was a pretty serious restaurant. He was smart and was a full professor of Physics at Stanford. But most of all, he wasn't put off by her profession. She was a Lieutenant Detective with the Palo Alto police. He was just making a comment about the Oakland A's when her pager went off. She had to excuse herself.

"Sorry, Ted, I've got to call in on this."

"Don't worry. I knew the job was dangerous when I took it." He squeezed her hand, which was resting on the tablecloth, briefly. Oh, yes. This one was a keeper if she could only be with him for more than an hour at a time.

She entered the lobby and went to the front desk. She pulled out her shield and said, "I need to use a phone. This is official police business."

She called the number on the pager. It was the dispatcher. "This is Phil. What's up?"

The voice on the other end said, "There's a problem at the Stanford Mall. The commissioner wants a detective to investigate."

"A problem? What kind of problem."

"The commissioner just wants you to go there and investigate." There was a pause and then, "I hear that some corporate big-wig got his ride boosted."

That made her burn. Why did they need a detective for a simple grand theft auto. A patrolman could do as much as she could tonight. "OK. I'm on my way. Luckily I'm within walking distance. I don't have my car but I'll get a ride home from the beat cop. There is one there isn't there?"

"Sure. Sent him there fifteen minutes ago myself."

"OK. I'm on my way." "As soon as I say goodbye to my date," she added mentally.

She went back to their table. Ted got up (he was always a gentleman about that) and said, 'I'll save you the trouble of disappointing me. You have to go investigate something. I'll give you a ride."

Gosh, he was a keeper. "Yeh. But you don't have to give me a ride. It's just over at the Stanford Mall."

"Oh, no problem. Where else would I want to go on a beautiful night like tonight?"

"Well, thanks. Let's go."

He left a wad of bills at the table and found the Maitre D'. He told him, "I've got to leave in a hurry, but I'm pretty sure I left enough on the table to cover the tab and a fair tip. If it's not enough, you can get hold of me here." With that, he pulled a business card out of a little card holder and handed it to the Maitre D'.

Luckily they'd parked on the street. He opened her door for her (always a gentleman!) and pulled out. They reached the mall and could immediately see where the commotion was. It was close to a mall entrance. The squad was parked in the handicap area. Ted pulled close and stopped. He started to get out but she refused, saying, "No, it won't look good for me if you let me out. Thanks for an evening that was beginning to be wonderful."

He nodded and said, "Look, if you need a ride home, give me a call. I'll be home the rest of the night."

"Thanks, but this may be one that goes really late." He reached out and squeezed her arm. She wanted so much to kiss him good night, but that wouldn't be good for the rep either. So, she smiled as warmly as she could, opened the door, and let herself out.

She walked over to the squad that was parked next to a silver late-model Mercedes. She immediately saw that two, no!, all four tires were flat. She walked up to the beat cop and asked, "Christ Almighty! Is this what you called me out for? Doesn't this high roller have triple-A?"

"Ma'am, the high roller,' he lowered his voice and went on, "is Steve .."

"Jack-off." She interrupted him with the expletive. That news didn't make her feel any happier. The beat cop was leading her over to Steve. He started to introduce her, but she interrupted, "Sir, I'm Lieutenant Detective Phyllis Huggins, Palo Alto PD. Is four flats why you called me away from my date tonight."

Steve stared at her unblinking for a minute. She turned to the beat cop and asked, "Was he injured, maybe a concussion?"

Steve said, "Why do you say that?"

"Well, normally people who call the police have something to say when they arrive."

Steve's frown turned to a scowl. "This is a pile of crap."

Phil said, "Oh, I kind of like your Merc."

"NO! I mean that the police can't protect citizens from vandals in a public parking lot."

"Well, perhaps you'd like to file a complaint. I don't usually carry the forms with me, but if you drop in to city hall tomorrow, I'm sure that they'll oblige you."

"What are you going to do about this!"

Phil shook her head and tried counting to five. Then she said, "We'll help you get it to a place where you can have it repaired, and we'll investigate the crime. You'll have to fill out a report and. . . "

"But there's a security camera that's been pointed at this car all night."

"Good. We'll get the tapes tomorrow and see if we can identify any of the criminals."

"Look, this is." Steve had turned to the car and abruptly stopped talking.

Phil asked him, "Are you sure you don't have epilepsy?"

"No, I don't, but look at that." He pointed at the windshield. There was something written on the windshield, backwards, with something that seemed like it must have been a red marker. She translated it frontward, "You'd better get license plates before it's too late." As she finished, she couldn't help laughing.

"What's so funny about that?"

She took a step back and noticed something that should have stood out immediately when she approached the car. It didn't have license plates. Then she answered him, "You should have read that before you called us. Now, it is too late.

"Sir, would you please unlock the car door. You can do that without touching the car, right?"

"Yes." He got out a ring of keys, and punched a button on one of them and the driver's door unlocked.

Phil rummaged around in her purse where she always had a couple of latex gloves and a few evidence bags. She put the latex gloves on and gingerly opened the car door. She stuck her head in and nodded, mumbling, "I thought so.". Then she pulled her head out and gingerly closed the car door. She turned to Steve and asked, "Who has keys to your car?"

"The only other person is my wife. Why?"

"Well, that message is on the inside of the windshield, so whoever did it, must have been on the inside. And, funny, it seems like it's written in lipstick. The forensic scientists will tell us about that, but would you recognize your wife's color?"

Steve screamed, "That's obviously a threat. They're trying to kill me. Are you accusing my wife of doing that? You've got to do something about this."

She nodded, "Yes, I guess you're threatened with justice. We will do something about it."

Steve went back to his original point, "But you've got to look at the security tape now. Someone might destroy it."

This was going to be even worse than she feared. She glanced around and saw a mall cop. She asked him, "Is what he says true?"

"Sure. He hired me to watch his car for him and got the shift manager to point a security camera at his car all night."

"Really. So, what happened?"

"I was here the whole time. All of a sudden at about 8:45PM, all four tires popped—one at a time."

"And?"

"And nothing. Nobody was near. I didn't hear any gun shots."

Maybe there was a little more than met the eye here. "OK. Let's go have a look at those security tapes right now. Lead the way."

The mall cop walked ahead of them. They went to the mall offices, and he let them in. The shift manager met them and said, "I didn't expect you tonight. But when I saw the tires pop, I pulled the security tape and cued it up to just before it happened. I guess you want to see it."

"Sure. This should be interesting."

The manager led them into the monitor room and said to the guard there, "Play the tape."

He nodded and touched a button. A blank monitor lit up and a view of the silver Mercedes with the mall cop in the background showed up. The clock counter on the bottom of the screen said, 07/05/95 08:40:04PM. There was no change on the screen except the ticking clock and an occasional stutter step by the mall cop. Then at 8:44:05PM, a tire popped, followed in quick succession by the other on that side and then the far fender of the car dropped a bit, followed by the last fender. The whole thing was over by 8:44:20PM.

"Well, I'll be damned. I've never seen anything like this." Phil was obviously intrigued. She turned to the mall cop, "And you didn't see or hear anything unusual?"

"Other than the loud pop and hiss of the tires, no. I don't think there were gun shots. I'd have heard an echo if there were."

Steve leaped upright. "You see! There's the proof! Somebody's out to get me."

Phil stared at him for a minute. "I've got to admit that it's damn unusual. We'll track this down if it can be."

"What do you mean, 'if it can be?' That's a pile of shit. You've got to do something right now."

"Well, do you want to come down to city hall and see what I can do right now?" People who knew Phil knew that when she stared at you with that unblinking hard look, you'd better be prepared for trouble.

'You bet I do."

"You've got it." She spit it out.

'How, can I get there? My car. . . "

"Oh, don't worry, we'll get you there. Come with me."

They went back out, and she opened the rear door of the cruiser for him. Then she got in the front with the beat cop and said simply, "Let's go."

On the ride, Steve called his wife on his cell phone and explained that he was going to police headquarters.

In a few minutes they'd reached the police station where they went up to an interrogation room. She opened the door for him, and he entered. As she went in, she picked up the phone and dialed an extension. "Send up somebody to witness an interrogation." They objected that at this hour, there wasn't another detective in. "Just send anybody that's on the force and can sign his name."

She invited Steve to take a seat. He asked, "Have you got somebody to interrogate already?"

"Oh, yes."

In a minute a beat cop came up and said, "They sent me up to witness an interrogation."

She said, "Good." She turned on the tape recorder and said, "This interrogation started at 11:21PM, Wednesday, July 5, 1995. I'm officer Phyllis Huggins and the other interrogator is," She hesitated as she looked for his name on his ID badge, "Officer Pete Scully. We're about to read the suspect his rights."

She then looked directly at Steve and said, "You have the right to remain silent. Anything that you say may be used in evidence against you. You have the right to an attorney. If you can't afford one, an attorney will be appointed by the court."

His mouth fell open. "You're reading me, my rights! What am I a suspect of doing, asking for help from the police?"

"On the evening of the Fifth of July, the suspect was in possession of a silver Mercedes, license plate number. Oh, yes. There wasn't a license plate, was there? That's an offense. The vehicle was parked in a parking space clearly marked for handicapped drivers. There was no handicap placard displayed.

"Do you want a lawyer?"

"You're fucking crazy! You'd think that I'd done something wrong. Somebody's trying to kill me, and you want to talk about license plates."

"The suspect declines to request counsel."

Steve buried his face in his hands and started to cry. "What are you doing? This is a nightmare. It's shitting crazy."

"How long has it been since your car had license plates?"

Then he seemed to gather himself together. "You'd better hope that you've got a good lawyer yourselves. When my lawyer gets through with you, you'll be lucky to get a job as a meter girl in Nome, Alaska."

"Oh, do you think so." Just then the phone in the room rang. The beat cop picked it up and listened for a minute. Then he came over to Phil and whispered in her ear. She turned to him and whispered, "Yes. Hold her for a couple of minutes. I'll call back down." The cop relayed the message quietly.

Then she turned back to Steve. "That was your wife arriving below. Should I send for her to come up?"

Steve jumped up and simultaneously shouted, "NO."

"Oh, I think she might just be interested to see you just now."

Steve, seeing the aggressive stance of the beat cop, calmed down, and sat, "No. It's been a while since I had a plate on my car. Is there some sort of bargain we can work?"

282

Phil seemed to consider the question for a moment and said slowly, "Oh, I think there might be. What do you say about this? You make sure that plates—current plates—get on your car and stay on it from now on. And from now on, you stay away from handicap parking."

"That's a pile of . . . " But the beat cop had picked up the phone. "OK. OK. That's reasonable. I'll agree to it. But you've got to agree to not tell my wife about what really went on here. You were just interviewing me about the vandalism, right?"

"That sounds OK. Now, get out of here, while I can still keep my stomach under control." He got up and started to leave. Then she said, "Oh, one more thing. Whenever you talk to your wife or anyone about this. . ." She stopped for a minute and stared at him.

Steve said, "Yes, yes. What is it?"

"It was just a polite discussion on both sides concerning the vandalism. If I ever get a hint otherwise, then . . ." She let her voice trail off.

"Right, right. Polite discussions all around."

Minerva and I were standing next to a fire hydrant in the Stanford Mall parking lot. We'd had enough practice going disillusioned that we could get along quite well without being able to see one another.

We had been following him for several days in a rent car and when he parked somewhere, Minerva had used the disillusionment charm. Then, we disapparated close to where he'd parked in the Stanford Mall parking lot. We followed him to the security office and went in with him. Minerva used the Imperturbable charm so that we could talk unheard.

Minerva squeezed my arm, a signal that we had for indicating that she was going to say something, "Well, this sounds like a challenge to us, don't you think?"

"It sure does. We'll have to come up with something more than just slashing his tires, although that's sure to elicit a fun response from Steverino."

So, we followed Steve out and watched him recruiting a body guard for his car. I squeezed Minerva's arm and said, "Wow, I think I might volunteer for that job – a thousand dollars for a couple of hours boredom."

She harrumphed, "Oh, this will be far from boring for him."

We all got out to where the Mercedes was parked and made sure that the guard was in place. "OK. Minerva, how long do you think we should wait?"

"Oh, let's be sure that he doesn't have second thoughts before we start. In the mean time we can be thinking of something special to do to the car."

"Sure. Did you have anything in mind?"

"Well, it should be obvious that it's impossible with someone watching."

"Sure. But it should be impossible to miss when he comes back to get the car."

Minerva absently squeezed my arm twice, which was our equivalent of a nod. I was trying thinking and made a couple of suggestions, "How about taking everything out of the glove compartment and piling it on the driver's seat?"

Minerva squeezed my arm one long squeeze – the equivalent of a negative nod. "That's just trivially annoying. We want something that will really sting."

She suggested, "If it were only rainy, we could roll the windows down."

"Well, it's not rainy, and the guard would catch on. Then, he'd do something. However, if his car were a convertible, and it were rainy, that would be neat."

She just gave my arm a long squeeze. An idea occurred to me, "What about leaving a note on the driver's seat. You know, a little mildly threatening note – like 'Get a license plate before it's too late!'"

She laughed, "That's good, but I've got a better idea. What about writing a note on the inside of the front window – what do you call it?"

"Oh, yeah. It's called a windshield. But what could you write it with? I don't have a marker with me, and I doubt that you do."

She gave my arm a long squeeze, released and then said, "Oh, yes, I do."

We hadn't developed a signal for a wide-eyed stare, but I made do with a verbal explanation of surprise followed by the question, "What are you talking about?"

I would have loved to have seen her face at that moment because her voice sounded crafty and devious, "How about a lipstick?"

I released her hand, slapped my leg and said, "Beautiful – both you and the idea!"

"What are we waiting for?"

She led me toward the car and something occurred to me, "Can you disapparate to the inside safely?"

There were two quick squeezes on my arm, "At this range? You bet."

"Well, do the thing with the lipstick before you deflate the tires."

She agreed and disapparated. Then, I saw one of the spookier things that I've seen since coming to Hogwarts. Red letters began writing themselves in script in reverse on the windshield of the Mercedes. A moment later, I felt her hand on my arm and I noted, "Good job. It was really spooky watching those letters form on the windshield. The guard doesn't seem to have noticed, but the sodium vapor lamps out here are not good for seeing that sort of thing."

We walked around the car and I heard Minerva deflate the tires in quick succession with the "Diffindo" charm.

I commented, "First inning, five hits, five runs and none left on base."

"What the heck are you talking about?"

"Oh, it's baseball terminology. A game is divided into innings, and tonight, you're batting a thousand with five RBI's."

She commented, "Whatever. Well, another job well done. But what are we going to do while we wait for him to show up?"

"Oh, not much, I suppose. It is kind of boring, waiting."

But as it turned out, we didn't have to wait very long. After a short while, the security shift manager showed up and asked the off-duty guard, "What the hell happened out here. I've been watching the car on one of the security cameras and I noticed that you've got flat tires out here."

The guard assured him that all that he saw was the tires deflate suddenly. The shift manager paced a minute or two and made a decision, "I'm going to call the police. Steve will be hopping mad when he gets out here. We've got to be ready when he arrives. You stay here, and don't let anything else happen."

After the manager left, the guard sneered, "As if I could."

I commented, "Second inning, one hit, one run, none left on base."

Minerva squeezed long and said, "I wish I could appreciate the humor, but things are going well anyway."

The police arrived in a squad car with the sirens screaming. One of the uniformed officers jumped out and ran to the uniformed, but off duty security guard and asked what happened. "Look at the Merc. All four tires are ripped. I was standing here the whole time and didn't see anyone do anything."

"Come on. You don't get tires as flat as a fritter on a car that's sitting still in a parking place if there wasn't somebody doing something!"

"Well, you can check the video in the security office. Nobody came closer to the Merc than I am right now."

The patrolman was skeptical, "How can you possibly know that? Haven't you been on duty all evening inside?"

"Nope. The owner hired me to watch the car. Paid half in advance – five C notes."

The patrolman's eyes bugged a little and he looked at the car again. "And nobody was closer than ten feet to it. Whose is it?"

"Steve uh. You know, the CEO of that cartoon company."

The patrolman shook his head as if trying to clear it, "Who?"

A little exasperated, the guard clarified, "You know," And here he made a fair imitation, "Buz Lightyear – to Infinity and Beyond!"

The patrolman answered, "Oh, that Steve. It must be toy actors playing pranks on him."

"Laugh now. It's the last chance you'll have tonight. He is no fun to deal with."

The patrolman was looking over the car more carefully now. "I suppose that the pranksters got the license plates too."

The guard came over and took a closer look, "Well, I'll be. I didn't notice if he had license plates when he came in, but I suppose he did."

I commented, "Third inning: two hits, two runs, none left on base."

Shortly after that, Steve himself appeared. He strode decisively over to the car, looked at the two officers and said, "Well, if it isn't the Keystone Kops. Do either of you have any idea how this happened?"

The policeman straightened up and asked, "Are you the owner of this vehicle?"

Steve sneered, "Of course, I am. I insist on this vandalism being investigated immediately!"

"Very well. I'll take an informal statement right now and you can come down to the police station in the morning to file a formal report."

Steve rolled his eyes, "What is this crap? I want to file a report right now, and I want to see a detective – not some flunky cop car jockey!"

"Sir," the patrolman said calmly, "We don't normally call out a detective for minor vandalism."

"What do you mean, MINOR vandalism? All four tires are slashed!"

"Yes, sir. That's minor vandalism. If, in addition, the car's windows had been smashed in and the lights broken or someone had used a Molotov cocktail on your car – that would have been serious vandalism."

"I don't care. If you don't get a detective down here right now, the city will be dealing with my lawyers!"

The patrolman sighed and glanced over at the guard who just shrugged. He picked up his walkie-talkie and called the police station, "Dispatcher, this is Jensen, car 054. We need a detective out here to help investigate this case of vandalism. The victim is Steve . . . .." There was a moment when I couldn't make out the conversation, but then the patrolman replied, "Yes, THAT Steve." There was another squawked response that I couldn't make out and then the patrolman turned to him and said, "Someone will be here as soon as they can page them."

He responded with not a word of thanks but got out his cell phone and called a number that turned out to be his wife. "Yeh, honey, I'm sorry. Someone vandalized the car again, and I'm waiting for a detective to arrive. You should take a cab home." There was a moment's silence and then he said, "Yeh, I don't understand it at all. See you at home."

I commented, "Fourth inning: solo home run."

Minerva asked, "What do you think will happen next?"

"Well, the police detective is going to arrive–maybe in half an hour or so, and then things should get interesting again. It's the seventh inning stretch. Do you want to go into the mall and get something to drink? There must be a Starbucks or something there."

Minerva agreed, and we walked into the mall. She reversed the disillusionment charm. We found a "Seattle's Best Coffee" and got tea. I said, "You know we don't need to be disillusioned now. We can just go out and be curious bystanders."

Minerva shrugged, "Suits me. It's hard keeping track of you all the time."

We got out and found that the detective hadn't arrived yet. But it wasn't long before a late model Toyota Camry pulled up close to the Mercedes. After a couple of minutes a young woman got out looking dressed for a date. The Camry pulled away and the woman walked over to the where the patrolman, the guard and Steve were standing.

Minerva commented as we watched her walk resolutely over to the crime scene in high heels, "This should be fun. She looks like she could eat him alive."

I said under my breath, "It takes one to know one."

We moved a little closer because we didn't want to miss any of it. It did live up to our expectations. But when he insisted on going in to see the security tape, I nudged Minerva and hissed, "Quick, disillusion us, so we can go in with them."

She did and we followed them in. The group was large but it was so late that there weren't many people entering or leaving the mall entrances, so it was difficult finding a good opportunity to get in. We got fairly far behind them and had to run to catch up before the door closed into the secured part of the building.

Minerva was disgusted, "Why are we hurrying? We can just use Alohamora to get into the security room if we miss the door closing."

"Sure, but I don't want to attract attention."

In any case, we didn't have to use a spell to get in. Everyone was crowded around the monitor where they were showing the tape. It was a real pleasure to see our work. Minerva was particularly excited, "Oooo! Oooo! Look at the moving finger writing on the windscreen!"

"You mean the moving lipstick writing. Yes, it's pretty impressive, but no one noticed it on the tape. Should we dis-disillusion to point out your handiwork?"

"Oh, don't be a spoilsport. It's too bad that we can't take credit."

After the excitement was over, everyone left the security offices and we watched the end of the drama. When the female detective drove off, I commented, "Game over! Home run in the ninth!"

Minerva smiled, "I think our work here is done, Kemo Sabe." She squeezed my arm twice. When we got out of the mall, we found a nook where she could reverse the disillusion spell. We then returned to our rent car, and I drove us back to our motel. It was our last night, and it was the first time that I'd been able to sleep well. Minerva wanted to have sex, but I was forced to admit that I wasn't ready. She kissed me chastely, and we fell asleep holding hands.

The next day, we returned the car to the airport rental agency. The rental folks wanted to give us a lift to the airport. After fumbling a bit, I agreed. The inevitable question came – what flight? I had some time to think and my response was quick, "Southwest." That was satisfactory. They dropped us off at the Southwest part of the terminal. We carried our bags into the terminal and found the restrooms. We sat by our suitcases, apparently each of us waiting for a partner to come out of the restrooms. When there was no one watching we clasp hands and disappeared.

We landed in the backyard of my parents' house. We went up to the back door and I knocked. It seemed weird, but I didn't want to scare anybody by just opening the door with my key and barging in. Mom got there first and complained that we didn't have to knock. I just smiled.

There was a debate about what to do for dinner. My mom wanted to have it at home, but she would cook all afternoon. I suggested that we eat at a restaurant after dad got home from work. That way we could eat and talk at leisure.

Minerva chimed in, "You bet! We've got lots to talk about."

Mom wasn't super excited about it, "Oh, Jim, I hate having you spend so much money on this trip. It's so expensive flying internationally."

Minerva, exasperated, broke in, "Now, in the first place, you know that we didn't fly here."

Mom was a bit flustered but held up her point, "I don't know how you got here, but it couldn't have been cheap."

Minerva, unperturbed, went on, "And secondly, your son is rich– well, maybe rich is putting it too strongly, but he's got a good source of income besides teaching. Believe you me, he can afford it."

Mom looked at me suspiciously, "Why haven't you told us anything about that?"

"Well, to be honest with you, it's just a little licensing deal, and I didn't expect to be getting much income from it. But I just discovered that it's turned out to be pretty profitable. I guess it just slipped my mind with all the other things that have been going on."

She was still not entirely satisfied, "This isn't something illegal, is it?"

"No. No. I just invented a process that wizard financiers use. They've been very ethical in licensing it from me and paying a fair price for it."

She finally reluctantly agreed to eat out and called our dad, arranging for us to meet him there after work. That gave me an idea, "Listen mom, would you like to travel wizard-style to the restaurant?"

She frowned but was curious enough to ask how that was done. Minerva exclaimed that that would be fun. I clarified what she meant by fun, "Well, you have to understand how it works. You disappear from where you are and almost instantly arrive where you're going. Now, it does have a down side. The first few times, it's pretty disconcerting – not just suddenly being someplace completely different – but also, there are some equilibrium issues."

Mom looked at me a bit puzzled, "You mean, I could be dizzy and maybe throw up?"

I grimaced a bit and agreed. "No thank you. That may be your 'thing', but I'll sit in the back of the car while you drive there, thank you."

Minerva hadn't quite given up. She tried to convince mom that the minor inconvenience of being dizzy was small potatoes compared with the safety of not having to drive on the dangerous highways. Mom wasn't having any of it.

So, we arrived at the Ponderosa Steakhouse at 5:30 PM just before my dad arrived. After we had walked the line, filled our plates, and gotten seated, Minerva asked about the name of the restaurant.

I explained that there was a television show back before I was born called "Ponderosa".

Minerva wanted to know what it was about.

I explained, "Oh, it was a western, set in Nevada territory in the second half of the 19th century. Ponderosa was the name of a large ranch. The main characters were the owner, a widower, and his three sons."

She wanted to know where the name came from. "It makes me think of the word ponderous."

Dad immediately jumped in. "They are related. I think the ranch was named after the kind of pine trees that grew on parts of the ranch – Ponderosa pines. But the name of the pine trees comes from the Latin word that means large or heavy – because the pine cones are so large. At a deeper level, the name describes the size of the ranch – ponderous, large, extensive. At an even deeper level, the name describes the spirit and nature of the family. One of the sons was quite large, tall, strong—so much so, that they nicknamed him "Hoss", that is, as big as a horse. But at an even deeper level, Ponderosa is meant to describe the spirit and the hopes of the early settlers of the West. That spirit is one that we Americans take pride in."

Minerva had been listening raptly. She commented, "I've never heard such a scholarly discussion of the name of a T.B. show."

I kicked her under the table and whispered, "That's TV."

Meanwhile my mom was a bit miffed at the open admiration she showed dad and commented, "There's lots of good qualities that he has that YOU'll never know."

Fortunately, our steaks showed up just then, and we had an excuse not to speak for a few minutes. When we had taken the edge off our appetites, Minerva and I described our adventures on the West Coast. Dad laughed so hard at one point that I was afraid that he might need someone to administer the Heimlich maneuver. It was near the end when we described Steve being driven off in the back of a police cruiser.

"Oh, you can't imagine how much I'd like to have been there to see that!"

I couldn't help replying, "I wish you had too."

"But, son, I don't get how you had the daring to go ahead and do such a thing? I'd have been scared witless of getting caught.

"And, well, it seems like you've got a little of the vigilante in you."

That was a really serious accusation for my dad. He was serious about law and order – and not just from the "order" side like many Americans seem to be. He genuinely believed in justice UNDER law. So, I had to think pretty carefully before I answered.

"Well, dad, it's this way. I have to go back and explain some things that have happened at school that I've not talked about yet." At that word, Minerva reached over and squeezed my hand and shook her head negatively.

"I'm afraid I do, Minerva. I know that you don't want my parents thinking badly of our school, but I really do have to explain this.

"You see, dad, mom, something happened at the end of the last term that was very disturbing. A student died in a school competition. He was my best student." I had to stop because my throat had filled with tears held back from spilling from my eyes. It took me a couple of minutes to regain my composure. Both mom and dad were disturbed too.

Mom said, "You don't have to talk about this now."

I shook my head and struggled on, "Oh, I do. You see, it wasn't a tragic accident. It was simply murder – and pointless murder at that. One of the other teachers had conspired to make it possible.

"Cedric, was not just the best student that I'd ever taught, he was the best student that I'd ever met – at OSU, at Stanford, anywhere. He had SAT's well above 750. He could have gone anywhere to college.

"But he was also a brilliant chess player. He'd played in international tournaments and had won one and finished very well in others. He could have had a career as an International Chess Master.

"But he was a skilled athlete as well."

I was choking up and couldn't speak again. Minerva's hand had been holding mine and I hadn't even realized it. I went on, "It was just such a tragedy that I tried to be a real vigilante. I tried to kill the man responsible – Valdemort. I think that we've talked about him a little before."

Mom gasped and Dad's frown was growing ever deeper.

"Oh, don't worry. It didn't work. He is too powerful for any sort of ordinary attack to work with him. After that, I was shocked back into a more rational state of mind. I needed a vacation and we came here.

"Then when that article came up about that other sadistic martinet, I just saw a chance to have revenge on somebody who deserved to be put in his place!"

My dad had a look on his face that I recognized from long ago. It was the look of restraint that had reached almost the breaking point. He began, "Look, son. I don't understand. No, I do understand that you are hurting because of the death of this lad, and you want to strike back at someone–anyone. But, picking this CEO as a stand-in for this Valdemort. . ."

I jumped back at him as I'd rarely done. "No, wait, dad. Listen. Do you remember the movie, Mr. Roberts?"

"Sure. The title character is the executive officer on a supply boat in World War II. He's far away from the front, and is dying to get in on the action against the forces of despotism. His problem is that he's a talented officer and his captain wants to keep him so that he can win awards for transporting supplies."

"Right. He has a room-mate, Ensign Pulver, who is just marginally capable and wants to stay as far from the war as he can."

Dad nodded, knowingly, "And you see yourself as Roberts, striking a blow for freedom against the cowardly, Captain Morton?"

"No, sir. I see myself as Pulver, who has one brave moment when he builds a bomb to use to do some petty damage and frustrate Morton. He is something of a klutz, and true to form, he fails. It goes off in the laundry room, and he fails even at that. If I can't succeed with a bomb, I'll throw the Captain's Mercedes overboard."

My dad looked at me long and hard and said, "I do understand that. I wish that you weren't in a position where you have to make choices like you have." He stopped, and everyone was silent for a long moment. Then he said it, "Would you please, please, consider coming back and resigning from Hogwarts?"

Mom had tears in her eyes and was nodding. Minerva was grasping my hand convulsively. I shook my head, "You know that I can't do that. AND you know why."

The rest of the meal was very quiet. We came home, and we all went to bed early. The next day, we returned to the "norm" for the visit. It was Saturday. We took an outing to the Cincinnati Zoo with a picnic lunch and enjoyed ourselves.

Two days later was the end of our visit. Minerva had arranged for a port key to be available on the campus of OSU. Mom and Dad drove us up there. As we got close, he asked where we should be dropped off.

Minerva said, "It's supposed to be near something called, Fawcett Hollow Pond, whatever that is."

Dad laughed, "I know it!"

I did too. It was a couple of dozen yards off a street. We arrived. Dad illegally parked, and I helped Minerva out with her bag. After hugging and kissing goodbye, Minerva and I walked over toward the pond. "OK, Minerva, what is the port key that we're looking for?"

She was scanning the water and squealed when she saw what she was looking for. "There it is, on the pond."

I looked carefully and saw a small boat. When we got closer, I saw that it looked like a paper origami sailboat. We got closer still. She picked up the boat and held it out to me with her right hand. I took it in my left hand. She said, "We have about five minutes."

I nodded, and we waited silently. And then the world began to spin around us and it took all my concentration to hold on. It was strange, it didn't require physical strength to hold on, just determination. It seemed like our limbs were flung out from us by centrifugal force. Then suddenly, I had to release the port key, and I dropped to the ground. Minerva was nearby. We were in a stand of trees.

"Minerva, where are we?"

She smiled broadly. "If a wheel hasn't fallen off, we're at home —to be specific, Hyde Park."

About the Author

William Wilkin lived in a small Southern Ohio town until he began his college career. He has a Bachelor's degree in Physics from The Ohio State University and a Master's degree in Physics from The University of Chicago.

He had a career in corporate Information Technology.and currently lives in Nashville, TN.

He enjoys music, both "serious" and "classic Rock". He reads classic Detective fiction and Science Fiction & Fantasy as well as trying to stay current in Physics.

He began writing seriously about 2005. He has a blog, in-mid-world, where he writes about Science Fiction & Fantasy and remotely related topics.